Kyoko M.

The Black Parade

For my loved ones, those related by blood and spirit

BOOK ONE: THE BLACK PARADE

I have no home on earth and none below, not with the living, not with the breathless dead. –*Antigone*, Sophocles

CHAPTER ONE

The alarm clock went off like a duck being strangled with a telephone cord. I always tried and failed to remember to buy a new one. Groaning, I lurched onto my side and slapped at the device until it went silent. Sunlight streamed in, golden and annoying, through a gap in the dingy grey curtains of the window across from the bed. I threw the comforter over my head and lay there with my face pressed into the mattress, breathing in the faint smell of fabric softener and fried chicken. I really did need to wash these sheets.

After about a minute, I reluctantly climbed out from underneath the blanket and stumbled towards the closet to find my white button up shirt and short black skirt. My shift at the restaurant would start in half an hour. Colton would kick my ass if I was late again.

After wriggling into my work clothes, I wandered into the kitchen and began the nearly involuntary process of making coffee. Once it was brewing, I retreated to the bathroom. As I brushed my teeth, I read the list of the names and addresses I'd taped to the vanity mirror: Linda, Ming-Na, and Ron. I only worked a five-hour shift today so I should have been able to take care of all three of them. After I finished brushing my teeth, I swept my hair up into something that vaguely resembled a bun and took a deep breath before staring into my reflection for a brief analysis.

To be frank, I looked like shit. The skin beneath my eyes was dark with circles since I hadn't gotten a decent amount of sleep in about two years, my complexion that had once been a rich brown was now a sickly brown-paper-bag color, and my weight had dropped significantly from lack of decent meals. Lord knows how I managed to keep my job looking like this. Cue the makeup — some foundation to cover up the spots and black eyeliner to further divert attention from my unhealthy pallor. A dash of lip gloss and *voila*, I was once again presentable for public consumption.

My gaze fell across the list again. I sighed. "Ninety-six down, four to go."

I snatched the Post-It off the mirror and grabbed my flats on the way to the kitchen where my coffee was ready. When I got to the kitchen, I shrieked in surprise.

My favorite forest-green coffee mug was already out and filled with coffee.

I glanced to my right and my left, letting my eyes sweep across the small room carefully. Nothing. Not a soul.

It took a moment for me to calm down enough to tiptoe around the apartment and check the closet, the bathroom, and even underneath my bed, for any signs of an intruder. Nothing had been moved and there were no signs of entry. I took a deep breath and walked back into the kitchen, sniffing the coffee for any signs of irregularity but I could smell nothing except for the enticing aroma.

I put enough sugar and cream in to turn the dark brown a rich caramel color and sipped away my exhaustion. Maybe I'd poured the coffee without thinking and forgot. It was early and my brain hadn't kick-started yet. I grabbed a Nutra-Grain bar from the cabinet, my keys, and headed out the door, giving one last salute to the worn, leather-bound book sitting on top of my refrigerator. After all, I needed all the luck I could get today.

The first things I noticed about Linda were that she was small, blonde, and probably about seven years old. Her cheeks were still round and pink with baby fat that she hadn't grown out of yet and her dress was bright orange with yellow flowers dotted down the length of it. The look would have been complete with a pair of white or black Mary Janes but since she didn't have any feet, it was impossible. Linda was, after all, a ghost.

"What's your name?"

I paused, having been lost in my thoughts after analyzing her appearance. "Jordan."

She smiled, seeming interested. "Isn't that a boy's name?"

I resisted the urge to wince. She was just a kid, and a dead one at that, so she didn't know any better. "Yeah, I get that a lot. Mind if I ask you a couple questions?"

"Sure."

"What's the last thing you remember before you ended up here?" I asked the little spirit in my sweetest voice. Linda glanced up from the dandelion she had been attempting to pick up, surprised that her small hand phased right through it.

"Um, I don't know. Mom, she told me to sit next to my brother on the log by the lake. My brother kept poking me so I got up. The water was really pretty that day," she added with another bright smile.

I nodded, scribbling her comments down on my ragged notepad. "What did you do after that?"

"I saw a frog and I wanted to catch it to bring it back to Mommy. My mean old brother told me to come back. I bet he thought I couldn't catch it. So I tried my best to catch 'im, but he was really fast. Then I woke up over there." She pointed to the tall oak tree a few feet from where we stood by the lake, where police tape had been stretched across the bank.

"Is there anything you want to tell your mother or your brother?"

The little girl nodded. I suppressed a sigh. This meant I'd have to get the address of the family, and the police were pretty stingy with those sorts of details. Maybe I could find another way to get her to see them. The funeral, perhaps. Much easier to access and far less suspicious to look for.

"Can you remember your last name?"

Linda's face scrunched in thought. "Nu-uh."

Great. No last name. This case was going to take even longer than I thought and I was already short on time. Three days left to deadline.

I took a deep breath, dispelling the disturbing thought. "Okay, I'll tell you what — why don't you go play on the playground until I come back and then we can go see Mommy. Does that sound good?"

She beamed. "Mom'll be so proud that I caught that frog. Bye, Jordan!"

The ghost scampered off for the abandoned playground, which was off-limits until the investigation was over. I stuffed my notepad in my grey duster and shoved my hands in my pockets, walking in the opposite direction. The park was only a block or two away from the nearest newsstand, where I might be able to find the child's last name. What a loss, though. The kid was so cute she could put little orphan Annie to shame.

I paid a few dollars to a man at a newsstand and collected a handful of papers, searching through the obituaries one by one for her name. It wasn't until the very last one that I found a matching picture: *Linda Margaret Hamilton, age 7, died August 5th, 2010. Loving daughter, wonderful sister, and family jewel that will never be forgotten. Funeral services held Sunday, August 8th at Wm. J. Rockefeller Funeral Home, Inc., 165 Columbia Turnpike, Rensselaer, N.Y at 6:00PM.*

Good news for me. I could get her there and be home before any of my shows came on. The wind picked up around me so I buttoned up my duster, heading back in the direction of the park where I had left her. Surely no one in Albany, New York would think it odd to see a black girl in shades talking to a jungle gym. Normal people couldn't see ghosts. They were lucky that way. Ghosts are terrible nuisances once you notice them because they are always on the look out for someone to help them. As far as I knew, there weren't others like me. To put it mildly, my situation was decidedly unique.

"Linda?"

When I turned, I discovered the new ghost had achieved a limited amount of solidity. She was hanging from the monkey bars. When I called her, she hopped off of them without hesitation. My hands shot out to catch her out of reflex, but she slipped right through them, sending a cold shock up my spine. I hated the tingly feeling of dead souls against my skin.

"Yep?"

"I'm going to come back on Sunday afternoon and take you to Mommy. Is that okay?"

She nodded. "Are ya gonna come visit before then?"

I winced. "Well, I am a little busy, but I'll come see you if I can. Be good, alright?"

"Okay!" She giggled and started back on her climbing, blissfully unaware of anything else. At least the dead had that going for them. She was just a ghost child so she retained her early behavior. Other ghosts I'd met weren't nearly this cheerful.

I waved and headed back in the direction of the city to catch the bus. I noticed a brown-haired guy smiling at me as I walked past the bench he sat on. He was my age at least with strikingly attractive features, so much so that I found it odd he was paying any attention to me. Did he know me or was he just friendly? Either way, I flashed him a brief smile and kept going. Shame, though. A couple years ago, I might have stopped for a chat, maybe asked him to grab a cup of coffee with me. If only I had a life that didn't involve taking care of dead people.

Night had folded in around the edges of the city by the time I trudged back to my crappy apartment after solving Ming-Na and Ron's cases. The rent was cheap because it was in a lousy neighborhood, wedged between a liquor store and a barbershop. Lucky for me, it was on the bus line so I didn't need a car. Work was only a fifteen-minute ride so it all balanced out pretty well. It would probably be more depressing if I weren't so used to it.

I opened the door to the apartment to find an obscenely tall blond man standing in front of my kitchen counter, stooped over the red leather book that had been on top of the fridge. A year ago, this would have been a strange sight. I didn't even bat an eyelash—just tossed my keys next to the book and shrugged out of my duster.

"Evening, Gabriel."

The archangel Gabriel smiled down at me with sky blue eyes. "Good evening, Jordan."

"Busy day?" I asked, opening the fridge to pull out ingredients to make dinner. Spaghetti tonight, and every day until payday. What a glamorous life I led.

He shrugged. "The usual. I see you have logged two more souls today."

"Yep. That puts me at ninety-eight. You wouldn't mind rounding it up to an even hundred, right?" I asked with a voice as sweet as honey. He laughed—a gentle, slightly echoing sound. That creeping sensation of joy rose inside my body and I did my best to ignore it. Gabriel had that effect on human beings. Even though I had known him for two years, it was still really unnerving.

"If only the Good Lord would allow me to. You have done remarkably well this year. You are nearly past the mark to your salvation," he replied.

I didn't even bother to shrug. "Ring-a-ding ding."

He watched me with a considerate look as I went about filling a deep pot with water to cook the noodles. "Something troubling you, my dear?"

"Not at all." He closed the book and placed it back on the fridge, which was no feat for him since he was close to seven feet tall. Gabriel appeared in his human form because his angel form would have blinded me. He wore a navy Armani tux that easily cost more than my rent. An archangel with impeccable taste, oh my.

"Shouldn't you be happier about your progress?"

I sat the pot on the stove and turned the dial, watching the coils for the red glow. "It's hard to get worked up about the fact that even when my debt is paid, I still have to do this for the rest of my life because I'm the only one who can. I don't like having that decision made for me already, Gabe."

When I turned to face him, he had a curious expression on his delicate features. I shook my head.

"You don't get it. It's fine. You're a seven-foot angel in charge of delivering God's will. I wouldn't expect you to understand the mind of a twenty-one year old American girl."

I moved to take the spaghetti sauce out of the cupboard when I felt his large, warm hands resting on my shoulders. His face brushed my cheek, voice low and soft with kindness.

"Have faith, Jordan. That is all I ask of you and all you should ask of yourself."

He kissed my forehead, in the same spot as always—above my right eyebrow. Over the years, it had become a familiar gesture between the two of us. I felt the gentle brush of air as he walked past me and out the door. A lone golden feather drifted to the floor in his wake. I stooped and picked it up, twirling the holy object between my fingers. His pep talk hadn't worked, but I did love it when he left souvenirs. I tucked the feather in the top of my ponytail and went to gather the seasonings for the spaghetti. All three of them—seasoning salt, garlic powder, and onion powder—were sitting in a row on my counter. Had Gabriel done that while I wasn't looking?

Once again, I raked my gaze through the apartment for any sort of presence before reminding myself to calm down. Gabriel must have done it, because ghosts can't touch anything. Relax.

Still, maybe I should sleep with two guns underneath my pillow. A girl can never be too cautious.

CHAPTER TWO

"Order up for Tables 6, 10, and 14!" The head chef's voice beckoned me back to the counter where the steaming portions of fried chicken, grits, corn on the cob, and greens sat waiting for a hand to carry them to the customers. I finished refilling the sweet tea for a gentleman reading the paper on my left before heading back to where the chubby cook bellowed.

The Sweet Spot was a tiny but well-known Southern cuisine restaurant. Odd to have one in Albany, but it was pretty popular. The place was owned by Colton Banks – a South Carolina native who moved up North when he married a New York resident. I'd known him for going on three years and secretly felt a little proud of how the place had bloomed since we met. Not on my account, of course.

I scooped up the three plates and balanced them on my flat, round tray before gliding towards the tables. They were each labeled with little plastic outlines of the state of South Carolina. Corny but memorable, as Colton always said. Work hours were odd for me because I basically went through them with my brain turned off. The hand gestures of writing orders, carrying trays, and pouring drinks came unconsciously. No matter how fast the chef rang up orders, I could get them to tables, no sweat. Most people had a career or were in college in their twenties, but I was dancing the elegant dance of a waitress.

After the plates had been passed out, I set about clearing off the table of a couple who had just left. The pair was currently on the sidewalk giggling obscenities in each other's ears. Something in my chest ached as I watched them from the corner of my eye. I couldn't remember what it was like to have a life, let alone a boyfriend. Must've been nice.

"Jordan?"

I turned my head to the left to find my best friend and fellow waitress Lauren Yi waving her dishrag at me. She shook her head, biting back a smile.

"You were cleaning the same spot for like a minute. Something on your mind?"

I shrugged. "Not much."

"There's a surprise," she teased, her brown eyes flashing with mischief. That might have offended some people, but Lauren had an abrasive personality. She seemed like a bitch when you first met her but beneath the attitude was a richer, more interesting Lauren. Besides, how many Korean girls worked at Southern cuisine kitchens? Maybe I'd Google the statistics later.

"I'm just saying that you've been moodier than usual. Don't ask me how I know, I just do," she continued, holding up the salt and peppershakers while I cleaned underneath them. Maybe I should have told her the truth — that not twenty-four hours earlier the archangel Gabriel was in my kitchen marking off souls in my own personal Penance Book. She'd probably just rent me a nice white padded room and a jacket to match.

"Just tired and ready to call it a week," I said as earnestly as possible.

She wiped her brow, ruffling her pin-straight black hair. "Aren't we all? When's your shift over?"

"Soon. I've got a few stops to make and then I'm passing out for the weekend."

Lauren arched an eyebrow at me. "For a girl with no life, you sure have a lot of 'stops' to make. You're always late for work. What are you doing all the time?"

I met her eyes with a dead serious expression. "I'm Spider-Man."

She burst into giggles, slugging me in the arm before moving on to the next table. "Get back to work, you moron."

Her insult seemed to be just the pick-me-up I needed because I finished off my shift with a genuine smile. I waved good night to everyone and headed out of the door into the cool August evening. If I got lucky, I would spot another ghost to finish off my debt. Gabriel seemed to have confidence in me. I could only hope The Big Guy did as well.

Fifteen minutes later, with keys dangling in my hand, I walked up the short stairwell to my apartment only to stop halfway there. The cute guy from the park was leaning against the wall to the left of my door. Shock and fear rolled through me. How did he know where I live? How should I react? Could I get to the gun in time?

Finally, I decided to play it cool and continued up the steps as if nothing had bothered me. When I got closer, I could see him more clearly. He was even more handsome up close. His longish dark brown hair was parted down the middle, hanging low over his forehead and along the side of his neck. Intense sea-green eyes held my gaze.

He smiled at me with those full lips when I walked over. "Hi."

"Hi," I replied, not sure of what else to say. "Can I help you?"

"Actually, yes. Mind if we step inside for a chat?"

I glanced around in the narrow, empty hallway. No witnesses. Shit. "Uh, I'm not sure if that's a good idea."

The stranger raised his hands. "I'm not gonna hurt you, I swear. You can even pat me down if you want to."

I lifted an eyebrow. "You'd like that, wouldn't you?"

He grinned. "No comment. So how about it? I'll be quick, I just don't want an audience."

I took a deep breath. This was a terrible idea. I knew that. He probably knew that. Still, according to the law I couldn't shoot him outside of my property and claim self-defense so I might as well go inside. After all, I was a small relatively cute girl and he was a big strapping fellow. The cops would probably believe me over him if I claimed he assaulted me. Morally questionable but effective.

I stuck the keys in the door and nodded. "Yeah, come on."

When the door opened, he didn't try to rush me. He stepped inside and watched me close the door. I was careful not to lock it in case I needed to escape. I tossed my duster on the chair by the round kitchen table and headed for the fridge. The key was to act casual. The guy had no idea I owned a firearm, nor was he aware that I knew self-defense.

"So what's up? I saw you in the park the other day."

"Yes, you did. I was surprised." That made me look at him. He seemed serious.

"Why? Were you pretending to be invisible?"

The stranger chuckled, walking towards me. I froze, pulse thundering in my ears as adrenaline shot through me. He stopped a few inches short of actually touching me and murmured:

"You have no idea."

Still meeting my eyes, he reached up into the cabinet and brought down my favorite green coffee mug. "You were going to make coffee, right?"

The truth hit me like a lightning bolt. How could he have known where that was unless he had been in the apartment? I felt a paralyzing jolt of fear grow in my stomach and spread through my body like cold poison. Then, out of almost nowhere, I got angry.

"You—? You were in my *apartment*? How the fuck did you get in here? Why? Are you some kind of sick freak or something?" I searched for the nearest weapon I could reach. He didn't even try to defend himself as I discovered a dirty kitchen knife and brandished it at him.

"You and I have something in common, Jordan."

"You have three seconds to get out of here before I call the cops or stab you, not necessarily in that order." I held the knife inches away from his throat.

His smile widened into a smirk.

I narrowed my eyes at him. "I am *not* playing with you. Get. Out."

"Y'see, there's something you can do that other people can't."

"*Now*."

"And that's how and why I tracked you down."

"Time's up. Now get out!" I punctuated the last word by slashing at his arm. The blade met resistance but no blood came out. It just sort of…bounced off.

"I'm dead…and you can see me."

My mouth dropped open. "You…you can't be a ghost. You can touch things."

"I'm a poltergeist. I can touch whatever I want, whenever I want." He reached a hand out towards my cheek. I flinched, expecting to be hurt but instead it felt like touching some sort of metaphysical barrier. The skin on my cheek tingled, though not in the same way that a ghost passed by me. This sensation was more constant, as if energy were rushing from him to me.

"I need your help. I want to know what happened to me, and you're the only person in this entire city who can help me." His voice was gentler now. The teasing smile vanished, leaving his face vulnerable, serious, maybe even wounded.

I shook my head, taking another step back and kept a loose hold on the knife just to make myself feel better. "You were *stalking* me and now you're asking for my help? You're out of your damn mind."

"I don't *have* a mind to be out of. I can't remember anything. All I know is that you're the only person in Albany who can see and hear me. That's all I've got to go on."

"Give me one good reason to help you," I shot back, crossing my arms underneath my chest.

The poltergeist paused, softening his tone. "What if the reason I'm dead is that I did something terrible? I can't go wandering around for the rest of eternity not knowing. Wouldn't you want to know?"

Something in my chest stung when he spoke those words. He couldn't possibly have known about what happened to me, but the question wasn't lost on me. I often wished I hadn't killed an innocent man or that I could forget about it, but at least I was working to make up for it. If I denied him the same chance, what would that say about me?

"I...I can't guarantee anything, but I can give it a try," I said after a long, tense silence.

He sighed in relief. "Thank you."

A few minutes later, I had rummaged through my duster to find my notepad and the mystery dead guy had perched himself on the counter by the sink. My hands still shook a bit as I smoothed down the paper enough to write. How embarrassing.

"What's your name?"

"Michael. I can't remember my last name, oddly enough," he said, his brow wrinkling a bit with worry. I started the page.

Michael
Caucasian, possible Mediterranean background
Brown hair
Green eyes
6'1"
Athletic build
No accent
Apparently a poltergeist

"You're Jordan Amador, right?"

I looked at him in surprise. He pointed to the counter behind me where there was a stack of bills. "It was on your mail."

"Oh. Right. Yeah, that's me." I cleared my throat and started off with my official preliminary questions for a new spirit.

"When did you 'wake up'?" There seemed to be a prominent process where troubled souls would recover after their death either at the site or nearby hours, or sometimes days, later. They never immediately remembered how or why they died. In my experience, it took between twenty-four hours to two weeks for a ghost to remember his or her death. Perhaps Michael would have that sort of luck.

"About two days ago. I was lying on a bench outside of some sort of club."

"When did you realize you were dead?"

"At first, I thought the couple outside were just ignoring me, but then I started to notice they couldn't hear me no matter how I shouted. Even when you're ignoring someone, you flinch if they scream right in your ear. The weirdest part is that I could still touch them even though they couldn't see me."

He paused to chuckle. "Found that out the fun way, though. I flipped up this chick's skirt in the middle of the street just to test out the theory."

I rolled my eyes and wrote "horny dead asshole" below the last line. "Can you remember anything about your life yet?"

"Nothing more than my name so far."

I snapped the notepad shut and took a good long look at him from head to toe. "Based on your face and body, I'd say you're not out of your twenties. The clothes you died in are the clothes you're wearing now, and that makes it a little harder to figure out what you did for a living."

Michael wore a modest attire: a black button up shirt with the sleeves tucked back, dark blue jeans with a chain hanging off the back pocket, and black Timberland boots. The reason ghosts wore clothes was that their souls retained a self-image. Since human beings wore clothes at nearly all times, it was only natural that the way they saw themselves as spirits was represented that way as well. The fact that he had feet was what threw me off the most, which explained why I hadn't recognized him as dead sooner. I made a note of his wristwatch and the silver chain with a small padlock around his neck before moving on.

"By the way, how did you know you were a poltergeist instead of just a ghost?"

Michael shrugged. "Well, think about it. The definition of 'poltergeist' is 'noisy ghost.' I figured that's what made me different from a regular ghost since in most legends and stories, they can't touch stuff."

That actually sort of made sense. Hell, I'd only remembered what a poltergeist was because of the 1982 movie. Despite his somewhat immature behavior, the knowledge of the term suggested Michael may have been well-read when he was alive. It could come in handy later.

"Tomorrow, we'll try to find the place where you woke up and see if anyone has discovered your body. With any luck, your memory will return and we can find out your soul's final wish," I said as I set the pad on the counter.

He nodded, raking a hand through his hair to push it out of his face. "How…how do you know all this stuff?"

I let a small, tired smile cross my lips. "That's a long, complicated story. It's late. I don't want to get into it tonight so why don't you go wander off and I'll see you in the morning."

I started to walk away but he jumped in front of me, seeming confused. "Wander off where? And what am I supposed to do all night?"

That made me pause. There was no reason why I should have trusted him enough to let him stay in my apartment overnight, but then again I couldn't let him go around making trouble for other people. In the end, I just sighed and flourished a hand at the apartment.

"If you promise to behave yourself, you can just stay here. In the den. If you come in my room while I'm asleep,

I'm going to start researching ways to get rid of you." I ended this statement with a harsh glare.

He held his hands up in supplication. "I'll be a good boy. Scout's honor."

"I'll hold you to that."

With that, I sidled past him with great care not to bump into him. I wasn't ready to feel that odd sensation again. I shuffled off to the bedroom and shut the door with a sigh, feeling much more tired now that everything slowed down enough for me to process it. I kicked off my shoes, peeled away the skirt, and unbuttoned the shirt most of the way before searching for my nightclothes. Once I redressed, I flopped down on the bed face-first, allowing a frustrated groan to tear from my throat.

"I cannot believe I'm having a sleepover with a dead guy."

CHAPTER THREE

I smelled coffee. Coffee and bacon. What the hell?

My body reacted before my mind could catch up—poised at the door, gun in hand. Then, I remembered I had a houseguest and I let my arm drop. A *dead* houseguest.

After scraping myself off the bed, I threw on a robe, some ratty blue slippers, and stopped to check myself in the mirror. I was halfway through fixing my mussed black locks when I realized I had been preening for *a freaking dead guy*. I shook my head at myself and walked out of the room.

"I got bored waiting for you, so I decided to make breakfast," Michael told me, shaking the pan a little to get the bacon a nice even brown. He was a picture of nonchalance, as if it wasn't unusual that he was a dead guy cooking breakfast for a girl he hadn't known a day yet. It made my head hurt just thinking about it.

"Though I can't believe you don't have any eggs. Even poor people have eggs. That's just depressing."

"You're dead. What do you care?" I yawned, grabbing my mug and the fresh pitcher of coffee.

"I'm merely remarking upon the fact that you're pathetic."

I rolled my eyes. "Fine. Go rob a bank and get me some cash. Then you can have your damn eggs."

He clucked his tongue at me, turning off the stove. "We've got to work on your people skills. Sleep well?"

"No, but that's normal for me." After adding cream and sugar, I sipped away at the delicious beverage while searching for a plate to put the bacon on.

Michael watched me with his arms crossed. "Well, the good news is that I apparently know how to cook. Maybe that will help us."

"Yep, you're a regular Emeril Lagasse. Bacon *a la* bacon, with bacon garnish." I smirked when he scowled at me. We'd known each other for less than a day and we were already arguing. That had to be some kind of record for me.

"So I was thinking," I continued, biting into the first strip. "If you're a poltergeist, shouldn't you be able to change between being solid and intangible?"

"I tried that out last night. I'm not very good at it. It sort of...comes and goes," he admitted, staring at his outstretched hand as if it would change. Nothing happened. Poor sap. "So you've really never met something like me before?"

I shook my head. Michael scratched his head. "That's just...weird. I wonder why I'm not a regular ghost...or why I didn't just go to Heaven or Hell."

"I don't know either. I'll ask Gabriel about it the next time I see him." I moved to the kitchen table with the coffee and bacon, scooping up my notepad to review what I'd written last night.

Michael followed, sitting opposite of me. "Who's Gabriel?"

"The archangel? God's Messenger? Doesn't anyone read the Bible any more?"

"I had to make sure. What's he want with you? Do you two have a — wait for it — *heavenly* relationship?"

I rolled my eyes again. "He keeps track of all the souls I assist. I can't exactly just call on him. He's always in different parts of the world helping people."

"Oh, I get it. You help ghosts find their final wishes so they can pass on to Heaven or Hell."

"Exactly."

"Why? Did you just fall into this job, or was it bestowed on you by a higher power?" His tone was teasing, but already I began to feel uncomfortable with where the conversation was heading.

I kept my eyes on the paper and my voice as mild as possible. "We really should get going. I've got a long day ahead of me if you're gonna keep sticking around."

I stood and drained my mug, tossing it in the sink before heading back to my room. I threw on normal street clothes: purple t-shirt, black jeans, tennis shoes, and my trusty grey duster. The key to my existence was lying low and hoping nobody noticed me whispering to no one they could see. It truly was a wretched sort of life, but I had a price to pay and this was part of it.

When I came back out, Michael was waiting. "You're very trusting, you know. How do you know I'm not some sort of wandering murderous spirit?"

"Because they don't live around here. I've only seen an evil spirit once."

Michael's eyes widened as he walked towards the door with me. "What was that like?"

I opened the door, not meeting his gaze. "Don't ask. It'll give you nightmares."

"I don't dream."

"Be grateful for that."

He shut the door for me, arching an eyebrow. "You're just a ray of sunshine, huh?"

"I'm glad you finally noticed." I locked the door and then we started down the hallway. A couple of my neighbors walked up, waving briefly to me and walking straight towards Michael. He had to dodge behind me to keep from bumping one of them.

He shook his head, stuffing both hands in his pockets. "Am I ever gonna get used to this?"

"With any luck, you won't have to because we'll find out how you died and you can cross over," I replied, grabbing the Bluetooth I kept in my duster for this exact purpose and attaching it to my right ear. Otherwise, people saw me talking to myself and would think I was nuts. We made it to the sidewalk now where people were brushing past so Michael fell in line directly behind me to keep from hitting them. I couldn't feel his presence behind me because he had no body heat. The notion raised the hairs on the nape of my neck. Better not let him know it creeped me out. He might use it against me.

"And then what'll happen? Who determines whether I go to Heaven or Hell?" Michael asked. We reached my bus stop in a minute or so. Two people sat on the bench while Michael and I stood next to the sign.

I tilted my face towards him out of habit. "Gabriel told me that you go before the Father and Son. They weigh your life based on what you accomplished. It's not quite as black and white as in the Good Book."

"That's a relief. I'm getting the feeling I wasn't a very good little boy during my life." His expression relaxed. I made a mental note about his more serious behavior. It could be that he was starting to regain more of his personality traits. That would become helpful later on. Still, I smiled to keep him from worrying about my silence.

"What? Did the skirt flipping tip you off?"

He smirked. "Why? Jealous?"

"You wish."

"For all you know, I do. Maybe my final wish is to follow you around for all eternity." He leaned down to my height with a smug look on his face.

I narrowed my eyes at him. "I'll have you exorcised before I let that happen."

"Ooh, would you? I wanna see if it actually works." His voice was genuinely eager. What a weirdo. Luckily, the bus pulled up and I climbed aboard, sliding my bus pass through the slot. It was half past noon, so there were passengers everywhere, forcing me to choose a spot in the very rear. Michael walked on, flopping down next to me in the empty seat.

"I think the best thing about being dead is no longer paying for public transportation."

"You're just full of deep thoughts, aren't you?"

"Yep."

24

I sighed. "Focus, please. I need you to watch where the bus route goes and let me know when you recognize something so we can try to find your body."

"What if we don't?"

"I check the obituaries. If nothing turns up, I have to file a missing persons report and see if anything matches at the coroner's."

The bus lurched forward, its engine coughing to life and making it harder to hear his voice. "How many times have you had to do that before?"

"Not many. I have to be careful that the police don't get wise to me being involved with so many dead people. They might peg me as a suspicious character."

Michael peered into my face, making me lean back a bit. He had a strange lack of appreciation for personal space. "You *are* pretty shifty looking. It's the bags under your eyes and the fact that you're about ten pounds underweight."

I folded my arms underneath my chest, choosing to stare out of the window instead of facing him. "I don't look *that* bad."

"Maybe not. You're pretty cute for a girl who sees dead people all the time."

I resisted the urge to squirm in my seat from the compliment. I was wholly unused to them.

"Though I can't vouch for your fashion sense. What's with the man-coat?" He tugged at the edge of my sleeve.

I jerked it away reflexively. "Don't!"

His eyes widened at my reaction. The people in seats in front of me turned to look.

I cleared my throat, reminding myself to calm down. "It's…important to me."

Michael studied my neutral expression before nodding. "Got it."

No joke this time. Maybe he wasn't as thick as he looked. Ye gods. I started to apologize, but his hand shot out past my face, pointing.

"There! I recognize that club. I woke up down the street from here."

I tugged on the bus line and we came to a stop nearby. Michael followed me out as I hopped onto the sidewalk and fished for my notepad.

"Let your mind go blank and then just describe whatever comes in it as you look at this place," I instructed with my pen poised.

Michael let his eyes wander over the building, now mostly empty because it was the middle of the day and most people were at home or at work. "I remember there was music, some kind of emo-kid rock music playing when I woke up. The first thing I noticed was that it looked sort of chilly out here, but I wasn't cold. I just felt…faint. I felt like myself but somehow a little different."

He ran his fingertips across the aforementioned park bench, eyes searching the tattered wood for answers. "I got up to ask a girl next to me where I was, but she didn't answer me. When I touched her, she looked right at me but asked her friend if he was messing with her. That's when I figured she couldn't see or hear me. It should have bothered me more when I realized I had died somehow, but instead I just wandered down the street checking for proof. I flipped the girl's skirt up over there."

He pointed towards an ice cream shop two stores away with a faint smirk on his lips. "She freaked out. Thought it was the wind. I couldn't figure out what to do so I just starting walking in that direction."

Michael turned and walked, making me have to jog to catch up with his long strides. "I walked for most of the night, not knowing why but I knew I had somewhere to be."

"What happened after that?"

He stopped and I collided with his back. I rubbed the tingling sensation away from my nose, frowning up at him. A few people around me whispered and stared at my strange behavior but I ignored them. Michael hesitated, turning his face until just one side was visible.

"I saw you."

I stared. "What? When?"

"I think you were walking towards the bus stop that day. Something about you caught my attention. I don't know why, but I felt like I had to be near you. Still, I didn't want to freak you out so I made sure you didn't see me when you got on the bus, stayed in the background during the ride, got off one stop after yours. I crept into your apartment through the window and hid in the closet. After you went to bed, I had a look around to see if there was any reason I felt drawn to you. Nothing really came of it but I had nowhere else to go so I stuck around. The next morning when I poured your coffee, you seemed to notice but like most people, you sort of brushed it off. When you left for work, I trailed you for a while but then I realized just how insane my stalking had gotten and went to the park. That's when I figured out you could see me that time you walked past. I didn't understand what was going on but I figured you might be able to help me. I followed you back to the apartment. This time, though, there was a blond guy in your kitchen so I stayed away. I figured I'd wait it out until you got back from work the next night. That's why I was outside your apartment when we officially met."

Michael turned around, looking sheepish. I mouthed uselessly for a moment, trying to figure just what to tell him. "That is the creepiest goddamn thing that has ever happened to me."

He tilted his head, making an apologetic face. "Yeah, sorry about that. I had hoped you might find it romantic or something, but that was sort of a long-shot."

"Who am I, Bella Swan? That makes me never want to sleep ever again! Thanks, you creeper." I resisted the strong urge to shudder at the thought of him sneaking around my apartment while I slept. Good thing I didn't have a rocking chair or that would just be the end of my ability to relax at home.

He winced a bit. "Alright, I deserve that. What's your conclusion?"

I sighed, flipping through what I had written down. "Unfortunately, nothing you've told me suggests the nature of how you died. We're gonna have to check the obits. Come on."

Around the corner from the club, I discovered a newsstand and bought the available newspapers. Tossing the other parts of them aside, I found the proper section and began browsing through names and photos.

Michael hovered over my shoulder, bouncing on his heels with anxiety. "Anything?"

"I found one. I'll write it down and Google it later." I scribbled down a man named Michael who didn't have an accompanying picture. As I folded up the paper, he tucked his hands into his pockets once more.

"So now what?"

"We'll circle the block a couple of times to see if anything jogs your memory. Until I check this name, there's nothing more I can do." I hated the immovable truth in my words. This was the worst part of my "job" — waiting.

Two days left. Any more waiting and I was dead meat. Harrowing thought, really.

The poltergeist fell in step beside me, making sure to take in every detail he could about the block. This part of town was nicer than my side with its shiny boutiques, brightly colored neon signs, and clean, well-lit parking garages. The club Michael had woken up in front of, called *Devil's Paradise*, was pretty exclusive — they only let the trendiest of the trendy in to observe whatever band would be playing. It had previously occurred to me to ask the people inside if they had seen Michael before, but the success rate without a picture would be pretty low. Better to dig up a photo before banging on doors. It saved time.

"What are the chances that people I know have reported me missing?" Michael asked.

I thought about it. "Depends. If it's been two days, someone should have notified the authorities. Y'know, assuming you're a person of good moral character."

He touched his chest, feigning a wound. "Ouch. You think I'm a drug dealer or something?"

I snorted. "More likely a male prostitute."

He threw his head back and laughed, nearly making me jump. "That's rich. If that's what my life was like, I'm sad I died. I'm sure my clients will miss me."

"Or at least part of you." I let my eyes drift downward.

Michael shook his head, smirking. "Careful. You'll have me blushing soon."

We turned the corner in a comfortable silence. Not sure how that came about. Could it be that I was getting used to him? I could only hope I wasn't that desperate for companionship.

We passed a candy shop that made my stomach growl as I caught sight of fresh pralines and caramel apples. I rarely enjoyed sweets since I was on such a limited budget.

Michael noticed my longing gaze and offered a sympathetic look. "I think I'm going to miss getting a sugar rush."

"It's overrated. Still, I'd kill for a fresh caramel apple," I admitted, rubbing my stomach. The bacon and coffee had only gone so far. Real food would be a necessity within the next hour.

"Is your wallet really that tight?"

I resisted the urge to wince. "I'm on my own. The money I get is from the restaurant. Most of that goes towards rent and utilities. I make what I can out of the rest."

"You work for God. He can't cut you some slack in the employment department?"

That made me smirk. "You would think so. Anything familiar yet?"

"Nope. Maybe I really was a street…walker…" He stopped and then whirled around.

I stopped dead in my tracks, confused. "What is it?"

His eyes darted through the crowd wildly as if he were searching for someone. "I thought I saw something."

"Something or someone?"

"Someone. A man. He had dark hair. When I noticed him, something felt weird," Michael muttered, looking back and forth down the sidewalk.

I threw up my hands. "Feel free to specify at any time."

"I'm sorry, I just…" Michael shook his head a bit, still frowning. "Forget it. Maybe I'm seeing things."

He kept walking, careful not to bump into anyone. I couldn't help but feel worried. I cast my own gaze into the people on either side of me. It was clear to me that this street and whomever that mystery man was had something to do with Michael's death. Sometimes I had to take a ghost to more than one site to help their memory return but for him, this seemed to be a hot spot. Still, there was an uneasy feeling in my gut that I had never felt before when working on a case.

When I caught up with Michael, he was peering at the sign for a store called Guitar Center with a glazed expression. He didn't speak, but he stepped up to the glass and watched a brunette with purple bangs shelve different kinds of headphones. I had to step close to hear him whisper, "Chloe."

"Chloe?"

He blinked a couple times, snapping out of whatever vision he'd just seen. "Yeah. It's weird. Her face just sort of clicked in my mind. I think I knew her when I was alive."

"Couldn't hurt to ask." The door jingled to indicate my entrance, and I made my way through the aisle to find the girl. She was a little shorter and thicker than me with wide pink lips and too much mascara. Still, she smiled prettily when I walked over and welcomed me to the store.

"Can I help you?"

"Yeah. Is your name Chloe?"

"Mm-hm. What's up?"

I fought the urge to glance at the poltergeist to my right in confirmation. "I'm Jordan. Do you know someone named Michael? Six foot one, brown hair, green eyes?"

"Yeah, sure. He's a friend of mine. Does he need something?"

Uh oh. She didn't know he was dead. This little interview could get real bad real fast. I licked my lips and thought of the least harmful thing to do.

"Would you mind giving me his cell phone number? I have an important call for him."

"Sure, no problem." She glanced over her shoulder to make sure her boss wasn't hovering around before taking out her iPhone and showing me his number. I copied it down on the notepad. It was indeed a local cell phone number, and maybe the first bit of good news for the day.

"Ask her how she knows me," Michael prodded. Couldn't blame the guy.

"By the way, how do you know him?"

"Oh, he comes in here all the time to try out the new guitars. He practically lives here. His band plays on weekends over at that club down the way. Sometimes I drop by to see the performance, but he disappeared after the first big concert a couple nights back. He's always been like that, though. You interested in him?"

Naturally, my face went hot with a blush. Michael spared me a sly little smile.

I faked a laugh. "No way. He's dead wrong for me."

"Oh, real nice. Gimme a second to go make a rim shot on the drum set over there," Michael grumbled, crossing his arms across his chest.

I bit back a snicker and addressed the girl again. "Thanks for your help. I really appreciate it. I may need some more help from you pinning him down—"

Cue another immature chuckle from the Peanut Gallery. "—would you mind telling me the store hours?"

She gave them to me, no questions asked. Nice girl. I waved and left the store, heading for the nearest quiet spot. There was a clearing across the street with a few tables underneath a group of trees, so we scurried over the crosswalk to take a seat. I dialed Michael's number, putting it on speakerphone so I could write any new information down. Instead of ringing, the phone belted out lyrics to Oasis' "Falling Down." At the very least, the guy had good taste in music.

"You've reached the voicemail of Michael O'Brien. If you leave your name and number, I'll be sure to get back to you if I actually give a shit. Konnichiwa, bitches." *BEEP.*

I arched an eyebrow. "So you really were a charmer while you were alive."

Michael grinned. "Make fun of me all you want, I don't care."

"Why?"

"I know my last name now." For an instant, I didn't have anything to say in response. The statement was so simple, but he said it with such…happiness. Who would have thought that one little word could make his face glow like that? I masked my surprise by scribbling down what I had heard on the notepad and closing the phone.

"Well, we've got a name, a number, and a reference. Maybe today isn't a total loss."

He made a scornful noise. "Please, what would you be doing if you weren't out solving my death?"

"Lying in bed with a cup of coffee and a good book," I replied with a wistful sigh. He muttered something about being a drama queen under his breath while I stood and stuffed my phone in my pocket.

"Where to next, fearless leader?"

"Home. We've done a lot today and your mind needs to reset itself. Come on." We passed back the way we came but I kept an eye out for any unusual dark-haired men. Y'know, other than the one walking right next to me. Maybe I was just being paranoid again but ever since he mentioned the man, I had felt like someone was watching us. I hoped for once it was just my imagination. If only I could be so lucky.

CHAPTER FOUR

"So you don't have enough money to buy a caramel apple, but you can afford a laptop?"

I leaned over the side of the kitchen table, plugging the landline for the Internet into my laptop. Couldn't afford wireless yet but I was working on it. "It's called saving up. Considering the nature of my work, I knew I'd be needing one unless I wanted to schlep to the library every time I want to search for something."

I plopped down in my chair and opened the Internet browser, taking me straight to Google. Michael propped his elbow on the back of my chair, leaning in to see. I typed in "Michael O'Brien Albany NY 518 555-8762" and hit Enter. The page exploded full of entries. I read through the headlines that included pictures and none of them were the dead man standing to my left. However, one of them caught my eye because it had to do with the club Chloe had mentioned, Devil's Paradise.

Underground Band 'Throwaway Angels' Smash Hit in Devil's Paradise

"Gee, is there enough symbolism here for you?" I muttered. Michael snorted with laughter. I opened the article and began to scan through it, particularly the first couple paragraphs.

August 5th, 2010 – Local talent Throwaway Angels hits it big at club Devil's Paradise in Albany, NY. Tonight was the first performance to sell out tickets more than a week in advance for such a small establishment and the response through email, phone calls, and Tweets suggests that fans are begging for more.

The band, consisting of five members, is of the garage rock variety: showcasing strong vocals by the femme fatale Casey Beck and the hunky Michael O'Brien, dual guitarists Kate Levitz and Stanley Cooper, and drummer Martin Cunningham. Michael O'Brien founded the group over a year ago and had been strategically planning performances ever since until they were able to secure a gig. He has not released a statement as to whether or not they will do a follow up to their explosive concert.

"Well, this explains my Guitar Center visits," Michael said.

The rest of the article went on to describe which songs they played, which wasn't terribly useful, so I copied and pasted the article in a Word document for safekeeping. "If we're lucky, we can figure out an address from this information. If you really did that well at the club, someone will try to find you in order to get a statement or invite you guys back."

I paused, frowning. Michael tilted his head at me. "What's wrong?"

"I was going to say we need to contact your band mates, but…they probably don't know you're dead."

He shrugged. "For all we know, one of them did it. Think about it: with such a successful debut, what if one of these guys wanted to gank me to become the new leader of the band?"

I shook my head. "That'd be a damn stupid thing to die over. Playing at a football stadium during the Superbowl is worth killing for but Devil's Paradise in Albany? Not so much."

Michael raked his bangs away from his face with a sigh, his expression somewhat melancholy. "It's just a theory. Couldn't hurt to write the story in case it turns out to be true."

A small smile tugged at my lips. "Who are you? Richard Castle?"

He flashed me a roguish grin. "Only if you'll be my Beckett."

"I walked right into that one, didn't I?"

"A little bit, yeah."

I leaned back in my chair, stretching my arms over my head before pressing them over my eyes to think. The best course of action now would be to contact the writer of the article to see if they had a listed address for Michael. I'd hate to go snooping around his apartment if the killer was hanging about, but any other method would involve alerting the others to the fact that he was dead. It would be much harder to recover his memory and get him crossed over with cops covering all the angles of the case. Honestly, I should have just enrolled in the Albany police academy for all the trouble I went through with deaths in this city.

"What are you thinking, Beckett?"

I didn't bother telling him not to call me that. Instead, I removed my arms from my face to stare up at him from upside down. "I'm thinking we should contact the author of the article to see if we can get an address. With any luck, no one is there and we can figure out how to get inside."

"What if my body's in there?"

"We'll pretty much have no choice but to call the cops. Things will get sticky, but not impossible. Every day that passes is another day for you to potentially get your memory back." I sat up straight and scribbled down the email address of the article writer posted on the right-hand side of his name—Vincent Dreyfuss. I typed the most innocuous email possible asking for Michael's address to send him fan mail and hoped he would reply sometime soon. For now, we would have to wait.

"Now that we have some free time…" Michael sat down in the chair next to me, fixing me with a sobering gaze. "Why don't you tell me about how you got into this mess you're in?"

I lowered my eyes to the keyboard. "I'd rather not."

"Jordan." He spoke just my name with a tone that was both firm and gentle at the same time. There wasn't really a defense I had other than it was my own damn business. Part of me knew I needed to face my past at some point. After all, little harm could come from telling it to a dead man.

I let out a long breath. "Two years ago, I was home alone when some sort of demon came into my apartment and tried to attack me..."

Crazed teeth gnashed inches away from my face. The eyes rolled back until only the whites showed. Spider-like fingers strained for my throat. I screamed and ran towards the bedroom.

I slammed the door shut and dove for the nightstand, hands shaking as I checked the chambers to make sure the gun was loaded. The door flew open with a bang. A second bang followed. Then all was silent.

The phantom was gone, but in its place stood a man in a suit beneath his dark grey duster. His hair was black and his face was growing paler by the second. He reached out his hand. My panicked eyes spotted the scarlet speckled across the palm. The room had gone silent because the gun had deafened me. The barrel was still smoking and now I could see the hole I had put through the man's chest.

I couldn't breathe, but somehow I could still talk, and my lips were whispering one word over and over.

"No, no, no, no..."

The man said nothing as he fell to his knees in front of me, his azure eyes locked on mine as if he were trying to tell me something, but the strength was ebbing from him in crimson rivulets. I dropped the gun and fell to my knees as well. My fingertips grazed his face as if I could bring him back to life with one touch, but we both knew it was too late. He laid a rough, scarred hand to the side of my cheek where hot tears had fallen, his lips parting to whisper in a soothing voice.

"Don't be afraid. They're going to come for you, but please don't be afraid."

"I'm sorry, I'm so sorry, please..." I managed to gasp out in between sobs.

The man merely smiled and closed his eyes. "Don't be. I'm ready."

He swayed forward and I caught his heavy body, feeling his blood soak my shirt. He slid down until his face rested in my lap, drawing in a few more shallow breaths before going completely still, empty, lifeless. I sat there with my coated hands stroking his hair, still whispering over and over for him to forgive me.

Golden light poured in from all angles, nearly blinding me, and I could just barely see the outline of a man with wings.

When the light dimmed, a blond man stood in front of me with white-gold wings that stretched nearly from wall to wall of my small bedroom. His tanned body was wrapped in white linen and his skin seemed to possess an ethereal quality, glowing like he had some unique source of inner radiance. Blue eyes like twin suns shone down on me with kindness and empathy. A new feeling of shock and reverence gave me enough strength to speak.

"W-Who are you?"

"My name is Gabriel. I am the archangel of the Lord God." His voice had an echo to it that seemed to soothe and agitate me at the same time. The angel folded his wings into his back and knelt beside the dead man in my lap. His fingers hovered over the wound the bullet had left through the man's back.

"As I thought…he is dead."

More tears poured as I tried to explain. "I-I didn't know it was him. There was a monster chasing me. I got scared. I'm so sorry."

Gabriel's face fell into that of a pitying expression. "You are human. It was only natural for you to be afraid. However, the Father cannot overlook what you have done. The man before you is a Seer — one of the few humans in this world who can see angels, demons, and spirits. He was hunting the demon you saw a moment ago."

"Please, I don't want to die. I'll do anything to make this better," I whispered, bowing to the angel.

He touched the crown of my head in comfort. "There is something you can do to make amends, my child. You must take his place."

I looked up in shock. "What?"

"You are a Seer, Jordan. Your abilities had not awakened until just now. That is why the demon was drawn to you. Your time to serve the Lord is now. In order to pay for the crime of taking this man's life, you must help one hundred wandering *souls cross from this world to the next. If you do not finish this task two years from this day, I am afraid your soul shall be sent to hell."*

"H-How? How do I even know which people are spirits?" I stammered in protest.

"The dead have no feet to walk upon because they are no longer tied to the Earth. Your task is to discover how they died and help them fulfill their final wish. Do not fear, for I will teach you how to free their souls. After this is done, the soul will go to the next world and I will write down the name in the Book of Penance."

He held out his hand and a red leather book materialized, spelling out my name in gold cursive across the front. It managed to be both beautiful and macabre. Gabriel placed it by my side and carefully rolled the man over onto his back. He plucked a feather from his wings and pressed it over the man's heart.

"Rest in peace. The gates of Heaven are waiting."

I watched with wonderment as the feather dissipated into tiny flecks of light and felt warmth as something nearly transparent rose from the body. I realized with shock that it was the man's soul. He hung in the air between Gabriel and me for a moment before floating upward and out of sight. His body faded seconds later, leaving only the bloodstained clothes behind. My fingers closed over the grey duster, which was still salvageable in comparison to the shirt and pants.

"I shall be watching over you always, Jordan Amador. Do your very best and above all, have faith." He rose upward on those amazing wings once more and was gone.

"Wow," Michael murmured. "That's…pretty damn heavy. So did you ever learn the guy's name who you…y'know?"

I shook my head. "Gabriel said it wasn't important, but…"

I stood and walked over to the counter, opening the first drawer on my right. From it, I found a manila folder and tossed it to Michael. He flipped the cover open, reading the file name.

"Mr. N?"

"N as in unknown?"

"Geek," he said. Inside were several news clippings I had collected that told of a nameless man who performed exorcisms around the world and appeared at the scenes of a crime days in advance. No one knew anything about him or where he lived. He was as much a ghost as any of the spirits I had met.

"This guy was a serious bad ass. I hope you find out who he is someday."

"Me too."

He paused. "Wait, so you've been on your own doing this for two years? What about your family? Parents?"

"I never knew my father. My mother..." I took a deep breath. "They took me away from her when I was five. She was put in a psychiatric hospital and committed suicide not long afterwards."

"Jesus." He started to say more, but I just shook my head.

"The worst thing you can do is feel sorry for me. It's a small price to pay for my soul so I'll pay it."

"So what? You think you *deserve* to be completely alienated from every aspect of humanity because you accidentally killed someone?" The disbelief in his voice was nearly palpable. I merely shrugged.

He let out a bitter chuckle, raking a hand through his hair. "You're a piece of work, alright. There are a lot of things you can do wrong in this life, but killing someone in self-defense is not the worst crime ever committed."

I hardened my gaze. "That's easy for you to say. You don't remember your life. I highly doubt with your rock star status that you ever killed someone and sat there watching them bleed to death in front of you."

My throat tightened as the mental image of his blood on my hands flashed through my head. I brushed the thought away as quickly as I could. "I don't care if I never have to speak to another human being again as long as I can pay for my mistake."

"What's the point of saving your own life if you do nothing with it?" he asked, stunning me to silence. The truth in his words rang like bells through my head. He was right. The arrogant son of a bitch was right.

I closed my eyes and let my breath out slow. "We're busy enough trying to save your soul. Please don't try to save mine."

He didn't call out to me as I turned and went back to my room, shutting the door. I collapsed on the bed face first. There was no reason to listen to him. The only things that mattered were the last two souls that still needed saving. Faintly, I heard the front door open and close. I shut my eyes and told myself not to care.

My dreams were almost always nothing but fractured memories of the night I killed the man who saved me, but this time I didn't see my room. There was a long hallway with a white door and a gold knocker. I stood there in this pure isolation, transfixed as a soft voice spoke into my left ear.

"Open the door."

My head snapped around to look but no one was there. "Who's there?"

"Relax, my dear. Don't worry. Everything you've ever wanted…everything you're waiting for in this life…is beyond that door. The only thing you have to do is open it." The voice caressed my ears as if it were made of silk.

I felt relaxed, almost euphoric. My bare feet could hardly even feel the cold of the tile as I began to walk down the hall to the door. Black satin from the dress I wore curled around my ankles as I continued, one hand reaching for the elegant glass knob. My body came to a stop.

"Open the door, Jordan. You will suffer no longer. Don't you deserve to be happy?"

"Yes," I whispered, feeling the weight of its words. "I'm so tired."

I turned the knob and the door swung inward, exposing nothing but a vast darkness. From it, a hand wearing a black glove stretched towards me. Surprised, I took a step back. A tall Japanese man stepped out of the shadows, clothed in a black tuxedo with tails. His hair was midnight black and framed both sides of his pale face. He bowed formally at the waist, speaking with a seductive purr.

"Please come with me. I need your help. Yours and yours only."

He held out his hand, palm upward, with a patient smile. I had no idea who this man was, but for some reason, I believed him. I reached my hand towards his, but then hesitated. Something about his smile made the tranquil feeling retreat. He opened his eyes and I noticed that they were the palest blue I had ever seen, nearly white. Stranger still were his pupils, which weren't round but thin slits like a snake's.

"What's wrong, my pet?"

"Where are we going?" I glanced furtively into the dark abyss behind him that now seemed ominous. At first, all I could think about was disappearing with the gorgeous stranger, but now my surety had melted into uncertainty.

He smiled again. "What does it matter? Don't you want to be happy? Don't you want to be freed of your burdens?"

"Yes, but not if I'm walking in blind."

"I will be your eyes, your ears, your mouth. Rely on me only, Jordan. I am but your servant."

My fingers hung in the air, mere inches from his, but something in my gut told me to pull away. I pressed my hand to my chest, shaking my head.

"Please, just tell me where we're going."

The man's smile faded, leaving his once pleasant face colder than ice. "You have opened the door. There is no room for doubt or hesitation."

He grabbed my wrist and pulled me towards him. I screamed and tried to yank my arm free. I turned to run back down the hallway but it seemed to stretch for miles with no end in sight, no door on the other end to run through. The man folded my arms across my chest and held me against him with inhuman strength, his lips brushing my ear.

"Make no mistake. I will find you and you will help me. Your Father is not the only one with a plan."

He dragged me, kicking and struggling, backwards towards the darkness.

I woke up, groping in the dark for my gun when I noticed someone in front of my bed.

"Jordan, calm down! It's me!" Michael strode into the moonlight cascading in from the window opposite the bed. How long had I been asleep? I slid the gun back underneath the pillow and pressed my hands over my eyes, trying to slow my breathing. The effects of the nightmare still raced through my body like a drug. I hadn't felt such intense fear before, not since the night I killed that man.

"Nightmare?" Michael asked, casting a concerned look over my shaking shoulders. I rubbed my arms to settle the goosebumps and merely nodded, still too bothered to come up with a sarcastic remark.

"You have them every night, don't you?"

I glanced up at him, frowning. "How did you...?"

He pulled out the bottom drawer of my nightstand. I winced. There was a small glass and a large bottle of strong whiskey inside. One of the few perks of living next to a liquor store. "Just a guess."

"I really don't appreciate you snooping around me when I'm asleep," I grumbled, tossing back the covers. A quick glance at the clock clued me in to the fact that it was past eight. I'd been asleep for nearly six hours.

"Why didn't you wake me up?"

"We had a fight. I went for a walk. You were asleep by the time I got back so I decided to let you rest. That was before I knew about the nightmares, though," he said, brushing the back of his fingers against my cheek. The gesture made me jump. I then realized that there were tracks of tears drying on my skin. Shit.

I wiped my face and stood up, pretending not to care. "Well, you should have gotten me up. We still have work to do."

He was still staring at me with that soft expression. I let out a frustrated sigh. "Oh, don't give me that look. I thought we had mutual disdain for each other. Don't go ruining it by actually caring about me."

"It's high time someone did." His voice was hard to place so I couldn't tell if he meant the comment or not. I sifted my fingers through my hair and walked towards the door without answering, partially because I didn't know what to say and wasn't sure I wanted to continue the conversation.

"Did anything happen when you went for that walk?" I called over my shoulder, sitting in front of the laptop and tapping it awake.

"Not really. I went around the park a few times. Decided not to murder you in your sleep," he added with a small smirk.

"How kind of you. Aha!" I discovered that Vincent had indeed emailed me back.

Michael leaned over my shoulder. "I knew I wasn't the only person who says 'aha.' Is that what I think it is?"

"Yep. Your address." I copied and pasted the address into a Map Quest tab I'd opened and set about copying directions. Still hadn't gotten around to buying that printer yet.

Once I finished, I folded the paper and slipped it in the back pocket of my jeans, then went to the fridge to get a drink. "Hey, Jordan?"

"Yeah?"

"Did I thank you?"

I thought about it. "No, I guess not."

Michael gave me a small smile. "I will."

I couldn't resist a grin. "At least we know the movie quotes part of your memory is back. *Desperado*? Really?"

"Aw, c'mon," the poltergeist protested, adopting a faux hurt look. "I thought that sounded cool. It's classic Robert Rodriguez."

I took a long swig from my water bottle and replaced it on the shelf, shutting the fridge door. "If you say so. Hold on, I've got to grab something before we go."

Normally, I didn't need to resort to carrying the handgun with me but there was always the chance that his killer, assuming if there was one, was still in the vicinity. The gun itself was nothing fancy — a .38 Chief Special Smith & Wesson revolver. I had two copies of the permit for it: one in my home, the other in the lining of my coat. The inner pocket of the duster was just the right size for it to fit comfortably but still be able to be drawn easily. I didn't expect I would need to use it, but better safe than sorry.

"Do you really think I've been murdered?" Michael's voice was soft, but I still heard it from across the bedroom. He stood in the doorway with a rather solemn expression. Words failed me. Would he really want to hear the answer? If it were me, would I want to know if someone killed me? Maybe.

I took a deep breath. "I'll be honest with you. It doesn't look good. The fact that no one knows you're dead yet makes me worry that your death might have been intentional."

I stepped closer to him, staring all the way up into his face. "But if you want the truth, I don't think the reason you died was your fault. You're a pain in the ass, but you're a good guy. I'm sorry this happened to you."

He gazed at me for a handful of seconds before nodding and his hair slid forward into his eyes. For some reason, it was the first time Michael seemed human. He was always so amiable and confident that seeing him be vulnerable felt odd.

"Thank you."

"Come on. Let's go find some answers."

CHAPTER FIVE

We made good time—a half-hour ride on the bus followed by a five-minute walk to the building. The one bedroom apartment was on the third floor. The hallway housed bare white walls and grey carpeting with eight other rooms on each side. A couple of newspapers were curled up outside of the door. I tried the knob. Unlocked. Shit.

I motioned for Michael to be quiet and fished the gun out of my inner pocket. I nosed the door open an inch at a time until the light from the hallway shone in. The first room was clearly a den with a squishy, faded black couch and a glass coffee table covered in sheet music and magazines in front of a decent-sized television set. I took slow, measured steps to make sure my feet made no noise and checked behind the couch. Nothing.

Pausing, I removed the flashlight I'd brought just in case and held it parallel to the gun. The kitchen was clear as well, sporting only dirty dishes and opened cereal boxes. The last room was to my right. Probably the bedroom. I took a deep breath and turned the doorknob.

"RROW!"

I shrieked, nearly firing off a shot as a black cat scurried past my knees with an indignant meow. The animal gave me a curious look with its golden eyes. She had a red collar with the name "Bast" on it in white lettering. Only Michael would name his cat after an Egyptian goddess. I let out a relieved sigh before shoving the door the rest of the way open with my foot.

"You're lucky you didn't get shot, furball," I muttered, flipping on the light to the bedroom. Nothing in here, either. The bed was a queen-size with rumpled blue sheets and a black comforter. A bookshelf that sagged under the weight of its books had been shoved against the far wall. Pocketing the flashlight, I checked underneath the bed, but there was nothing under it but unwashed socks and lint. Why had the door been unlocked? Nothing appeared out of place like he'd been robbed. My gut told me something was up.

I checked the bathroom and closet before heading out of the room only to find Michael crouching in front of the cat.

"Jordan, you're not gonna believe this—the cat can totally see me."

I put the gun away. "No way."

"Yes way." He held his hand outstretched and moved it from side to side. The cat's head moved from side to side as well.

I knelt, rubbing the cat under her chin. "You guys really are half in and half out, huh?"

"What?"

"Nothing. C'mon, it's time to start looking for clues to who you are." I stood and brushed off my knees, sliding the gun back in my pocket. We split up. I went around the den to search for his wallet in case it was here instead of with his body and Michael disappeared into his bedroom. The television sat on top of a small cart with DVDs packed into it, everything from *Citizen Kane* to *Independence Day*. From the looks of it, Michael was nothing more than your average American guy. Across from the coffee table, I discovered a one-drawer file cabinet and opened it, hoping to find something interesting. The bulk of the files inside was sheet music, but the very last folder held something interesting: hospital bills and a page with a diagnosis on it.

"Michael, get out here!" I called.

He reappeared, jogging over to me. "Found something?"

"I'll say. According to this, you were badly injured in some sort of fight. You had a skull fracture and they treated you here in town. They say you suffered from retrograde post-traumatic amnesia."

Michael's eyes widened. "What? I thought amnesia wasn't even real?"

"As far as I know, it's possible. It's just extremely unlikely. The way I hear it you have to be both injured and have witnessed something emotionally traumatizing. The records say this happened a couple years ago." I frowned, trying to mull the new facts over in my head.

"So I was severely injured two years before I died? There's no way that's just a coincidence," he said, damn near reading my thoughts.

"Agreed. Did you find anything in your bedroom?"

"Nothing but clothes, books, and old pizza boxes. The room, though…it feels familiar. I knew where stuff was almost unconsciously. It was weird as hell."

"Good. You're making progress."

"Thank you, Dr. Phil," he said, pointing back to the file. "What else have they got on me in here?"

"You're twenty-four years old, your blood type is AB negative, and…damn."

"What?"

"Your parents aren't listed. Not sure if I can find your next of kin without reporting you missing, which we can't do since your body's not here." I let out a sigh. "I swear, I am just going to drop this case."

Michael laughed. "Wow, thanks."

"Oh, cut me some slack. I'm not a detective. I'm a damn waitress. Some of this stuff is beyond my resources."

"Hey, you're a pretty smart waitress. I doubt the average person could have figured out half as much stuff as you did."

I resisted the urge to frown. Again, compliments. Not used to them.

I flipped the folder closed and folded it enough to fit in one of my pockets. "Just…help me search for receipts. If we can figure out what places you frequent, maybe we can find out where your body is."

I sifted through the piles of sheet music and magazines on the coffee table, locating a handful of receipts in the process. Michael went into the kitchen to search there as well. I sat on the couch to go through them. The black cat hopped up next to me, pushing her head underneath my hand. I scratched the spot between her ears as I read them aloud.

"A few from McDonalds, Starbucks, Guitar Center…nothing too special. It's all stuff around this area. At the very least, we can take your picture around and ask if anybody's seen you recently."

"Sounds like a plan. Shouldn't we stop by Devil's Paradise tonight too?"

"Yeah. Your band might be there. Still, we don't know what they look like."

"This might help." I glanced up to see Michael holding a digital camera. He handed it to me, taking a seat. The cat crawled across my lap to settle on his. How unnerving. I started flipping through the memory card: pictures of the park, a couple of instruments, and at last Devil's Paradise.

"I think these may be photos from your performance the other night." The first picture of the club had a massive crowd in line outside. The next depicted a blurry but definite picture of Michael on stage with his band. He stood out in front beside a short brunette with a streak of white in her bangs. Behind him stood a tall black guy with a faux-hawk and a skinny blonde girl with short hair. I could just barely make out the drummer in the back—a dark-haired Hispanic guy. There were a handful of these pictures all taken from different angles but the date at the corner confirmed they had been taken August 5th, 2010.

"Alright, now at least we know who we're looking for," I said, standing.

Michael scooped up the cat and deposited her on the couch. She hopped to the floor and wandered into the kitchen to drink water from a bowl on the floor by the counter. I made a mental note to come back and feed her.

"Anything else you think we need?" Michael inquired.

I thought about it and then an idea hit me. "Spare key?"

"Oh. Sure." Michael opened the file cabinet and stuck his hand inside, bringing out a key that had been taped to the inside of the drawer. After a second, he realized what he'd just done and shot a surprised look at me.

"How'd I do that?"

"Habitual memory. I figured you'd react without thinking about it," I explained, stashing the key in my pocket. At least now we could actually lock the door.

Luckily, we'd gotten out in time to catch the next bus to Devil's Paradise. When we pulled up to the stop across the street, I began to regret coming here on a Saturday night. The line stretched down the block: Goth punks, girls in tiny skirts, and guys with faux-hawks. Two bouncers stood outside the double doors, eyeing each person before allowing them inside and refusing those who didn't make the cut. The white guy on the right had a neck as thick as a ham and a body like the trunk of a Redwood. The black guy on the left was easily over six-feet tall and could probably bench-press a Volvo. Great.

"I can see this being a problem," Michael said, letting his eyes scan over the long line. I raked a hand through my hair as I tried to figure out what to do. My outfit was far too casual to get me in. It wasn't like I could bribe the bouncers: I had maybe twenty bucks.

"Any bright ideas, rock star?"

"Prostitution?"

I sent him a hateful glare while he just held up his hands in surrender. "Sorry. I got nuthin.' There's no point in having me sneak in there because I can't talk to anyone."

"Wait, does that mean you figured out how to turn intangible?"

He stuck his hand out to touch the bus sign. It passed right through like magic. "Yep."

I nearly slapped my forehead. "You could have told me that earlier."

"You didn't—"

"If you say 'you didn't ask,' I am going to call that exorcist."

Michael closed his mouth and merely smirked. I resisted the urge to roll my eyes.

"Hey, Jordan!"

A female voice called to me from across the street. I spotted the girl from Guitar Center, Chloe, waving me over from near the front of the line. I checked for cars and then jogged over to her with a surprised smile.

"What are you doing here?" I asked.

She waved a hand at the club. "I came here to meet up with some friends. Are you still looking for Michael?"

"Yeah. I called the number you gave me but he didn't pick up."

Chloe frowned a bit. "Sorry to hear that. Do you want to come inside and see the band? I know at least two of them are here tonight. Maybe they know where he is."

"Yeah, that seems likely," I replied, indicating the huge line behind her.

Chloe flashed me a crafty grin. "You're with me. Don't worry about it."

I watched with shock as she tugged me in next to her and waved to the bouncers. Their stony expressions softened and they nodded for us to go in. When I turned to ask her how the hell she'd done that, she told me she had been the baby sitter for each guy's kids on weekends. Small world.

Inside, the club was deceptively large. The stage at the far wall had a band of six going in full swing, swallowing me in thrumming music as soon as I stepped through the door. The main room was separated into two parts: the immense dance floor packed with bodies and a surrounding area of booths where waiters were serving food. Chloe led the way up the stairs to the left. Michael trailed behind us, watching with wonderment as people passed right through him without noticing. I sort of envied normal people sometimes.

We approached one of the booths near the bar on our left where I recognized two of Michael's bandmates: the brunette with white streaks in her hair and the black guy with the faux-hawk.

"Hey, guys! Having a good time?" Chloe asked with a bright smile.

The short brunette groaned, leaning forward in her seat to shout over the music. "I would if they had a better band on stage. These guys are amateurs with a capital A."

The black guy shook his head at her. "Give 'em a break, Casey. Everybody's gotta start somewhere."

She shrugged, arching a thin eyebrow at me. "Who's the new girl?"

"This is Jordan. She's looking for Michael."

Casey snorted. "Aren't we all? I can't believe he up and left right after we had such a good premiere. Here, sit down."

She scooted over and patted the open spot to her right. I sat and Chloe took a seat opposite me by the black guy. He stuck out a hand, smiling. I took it.

"Name's Stan. Nice to meet you."

"Nice to meet you too," I replied, impressed by how friendly they all were. Michael may have been annoying, but he kept good company. Speaking of whom, Michael stood beside my side of the booth so he could keep up with the conversation. A waiter wandered by, asking for drink orders, but I declined. I knew for a fact how expensive alcohol was at popular clubs in the city. Besides, no sense in drinking while I was "working." Casey and Stan ordered beers while Chloe stuck with a tried-and-true Vodka soda. I wracked my brain for inconspicuous ways of asking what happened to Michael in the last few days.

"Does he always disappear like that from time to time?"

Stan waggled his hand in the "kind of" motion. "He sucks at communication. Sometimes I'll go three days without talking to him and then he'll call me the next day to chat for four hours."

"Same here. I haven't been able to keep up with him since I met him," Casey admitted, absently folding a paper napkin into triangular shapes.

"Why are you looking for him anyway? He's not in trouble, is he?" Stan pressed, adopting a somewhat wary look. Good instincts. Crap.

"No, it's nothing like that. I found something of his that I thought might be important to him. It's an old watch with his name on it. I would have brought it with me but I was worried it would get stolen in this crowd."

"Oh. I was starting to think you were a reporter," Stan said in a sheepish voice.

"Or a cop. Especially because of this," Casey pointed to the duster.

I managed a faint smile. "Yeah, I guess I do sort of look like a cop in this getup. Sorry if I made you suspicious."

Chloe waved the comment away. "Trust me, we're honestly shocked there aren't any warrants out on him."

Behind me, Michael snorted. "I'm loving the solidarity."

I cleared my throat to hide a laugh. "So you guys don't think he's in any trouble?"

"No more than usual. Last time I heard from him was after Thursday's performance when he left to head home. He always slips out the back door right after we finish so he can beat the crowd to the bus."

A red flag went up in my mind. This club happened to spill out into an alleyway that was dark, damp, and far away from the street. That would mean few to no witnesses for our potential killer. I hid the interest with a passive nod and made a mental note to check there as soon as I could get away from the group. I hoped that would be soon because the longer I sat here, the more horrible I felt that these guys didn't know their friend was dead. It wasn't like I could tell them his spirit was hovering not a foot away from the table. Besides that, there was no absolute proof. Not yet, anyway.

The waiter returned with the drinks, asking for food orders. Chloe ordered some wings but the other two declined since they'd eaten before they got to the club.

"Hey, where's the bathroom?" I asked Casey.

She pointed past my head to the right of the stage. "Go by the stage and hang a right. Good luck, though. The line's a bitch this time of night."

"Thanks. I'll be back. It was nice meeting you guys. Thanks for your help." They all waved as I retreated through the crowd. The bathroom was my cover. I'd only needed an excuse to sneak out of the club and didn't have a pack of cigarettes to use as a ploy. Michael and I passed the insanely long line to the Ladies Room and found one of the exits that spilled into the alleyway. Luckily, it hadn't been a fire exit so an alarm didn't go off. I stepped out into the dark and noticed that there wasn't a knob to let us back in. Smart. Didn't want anyone sneaking into the club without paying. I found an empty cigarette pack on the floor and wedged it in the door. If we got lucky, we could check the area before one of the bouncers noticed.

"What are we looking for? It's been a couple days since I would have been here." Michael watched me examine every inch of the concrete around us. The alley stretched a good ten feet and then turned into a right. Behind me, there was faint noise from the street, but its view was obscured by a large dumpster.

"True, but unless you were killed by an expert, they may have left some kind of evidence." I slipped on a pair of purple surgical gloves that I kept with me specifically for snooping purposes and flipped on my flashlight. The Exit sign above the door shed an eerie red light over the area but that was about it. Aside from the dumpster a few feet away, there was a trio of trashcans against the wall opposite the exit. Great. My favorite part of the job.

Breathing as sparingly as possible, I peeked into the trash and carefully sifted through, looking for traces of blood or anything that may have been on Michael's body when he left the club. Michael started to join me but I stopped him.

"What? It'll go faster this way."

I arched an eyebrow. "Michael, if someone happens to look this way, they're going to see trash floating in mid-air. That's not very inconspicuous."

"Neither is a hot chick in a grey overcoat with purple gloves sifting through garbage," he said, his voice flat. Damn. The man had a point.

"Just help me look around. And don't touch anything."

"Why?"

"Because shut up."

Sighing, Michael walked past me to inspect the bits of garbage that hadn't made it into the cans. I searched the three containers and found nothing out of the ordinary, which made me groan internally because that meant I'd probably have to check the dumpster. Did I like this guy enough to get that horrible smell in my clothes? No. Would I do it anyway? Maybe.

With a regretful moan in my throat, I stepped towards the dumpster, but stopped as my foot kicked something metallic into my line of sight. I stooped and picked it up, examining it in the dim light. A broken silver chain with a tiny padlock on it.

"Michael, come here for a second."

When he walked over, I held the necklace up to him. They matched perfectly. Hot damn.

"I'd say this is a clue," I muttered, inspecting the edges to detect any traces of blood. None. Still, this was definitely proof that something had gone down in this alley.

"Thanks, Captain Obvious," Michael said with half-hearted sarcasm, too busy staring at the chain to commit to sounding dry. "I'm guessing it snapped off in the struggle. Maybe I fell."

"Yeah. Judging by the fact that there's no blood around, I'd say whoever attacked you either broke one of your bones or used something quiet to take you out, like a syringe. The question is still why, though. As far as I can tell, you're not an incredibly important person."

He gave me a look. I winced. "No offense. I mean, your band is doing well but it's not doing *that* well. I'm starting to worry that we need to involve the police. There are some questions I can't go around asking without raising suspicion. You saw how your band mates reacted when I did."

"Yeah," he said. "I wish I could say everything's rushing back to me, but I'm only getting a feeling that I really did die here. Someone said something to me, and when I turned around, it happened. I just can't remember *what*, though."

"Don't stress too much about that. The point is to find out about your life and why you died. When we do that, your final wish should become clear. Come on. We'll do one final check and then go back inside. Your band mates might be getting curious."

We walked up and down the alley, as well as the one next to it that led to a dead end, but there wasn't anything else. Afterward, I carefully placed the necklace in my pocket and threw the gloves away. I poked my head into the door of the club. Nobody. Lucky us.

Quickly I removed the empty cigarette pack and slunk back towards the main area of the club with Michael behind me. The girls in line to the bathroom gave me funny looks but I brushed past them, heading for the booth.

Chloe had gone off meeting her other friends, as Casey told me. Shame. I wanted to thank her again for getting me in. I left my number with Casey and Stanley and said good night, happy once we were out of the flashing lights and pounding music. We reached the bus stop, which was thankfully devoid of other people, and Michael exhaled slowly, glancing at me.

"So what's the plan for tomorrow?"

"I have to take Linda to her funeral to speak to her Mom. I think that's her final wish. We might get lucky. If I get her to cross over, Gabriel will show up and maybe I can ask him for help. He's not allowed to directly help me solve cases by order of the Big Guy, but he can offer advice."

Michael shook his head. "What's that like, having an archangel drop by every once in a while?"

I shrugged. "It was nerve-wracking at first, but...I eventually got used to it. Gabriel's really easy to get along with. He's probably the closest thing I have to family. I guess being God's Messenger has something to do with that."

"Are you allowed to ask him questions about Heaven and Hell and stuff?"

"Sort of. There are rules. He told me he's not allowed to tell me anything that would reveal the 'true nature' of God or Heaven because I'm supposed to find out on my own when I die."

"So I take it you tried asking him about Mr. N?"

I lowered my eyes, forcing myself not to wince. "Yeah, but he said that's on the list of things I'm not allowed to ask him. He told me I don't understand now, but it's for a good purpose."

He made a soft, scornful noise in the back of his throat. "Can't be that good of a purpose if it means you have to have nightmares every night for the rest of your life."

That sounded like honest-to-God sympathy. I couldn't help but glance up at him. He met my eyes with a solemn look that made my breath catch for a second. There was something strangely compelling about his face when he stared back at me like that. It was a quality I had recognized in someone else, too. Gabriel.

His voice was quiet. "The bus is here."

I faced forward to see the rusty vehicle in front of us. Just like that, the spell broke and I climbed aboard, shaking off my thoughts.

CHAPTER SIX

"Ms. Catalina Amador, I'm sorry, but you're going to have to come with us."

My mother's shoulders tensed in response to the man's statement. I stood behind her, blinking up curiously at the scene before me. My mother had opened the apartment door with the latch still on it and through the crack I could see a man in a suit with two men in blue uniforms on either side of him.

At five years old, I had no clue who they were or why they were at our home. I tugged on my mother's skirt, whining, "Mama? Who is it?"

She pushed me away from their sight. When she spoke, her voice was harsh with anger. "I know what I saw, Dr. Merriweather. There is nothing you and your facility can do. There are powers in this world beyond your comprehension and they are the ones who have come for me today, not you."

The doctor sighed. "Ms. Amador, we are trying to help you. We don't want you to endanger yourself or your daughter —"

"My daughter is fine, you son of a bitch!" She spat, making me jump. I had never heard her speak like that. Her accent made her words burn like flames against my skin. Tears welled up in my eyes so I buried my face in her leg, trying to hug her.

"Mama, I'm scared. Why are you yelling?"

She rested a hand on the top of my head, whispering to me. "Don't cry, mi hija. It's alright."

"Ma'am, if you don't come out of the apartment I'm going to have to have the police escort you out. I have legal permission to admit you into the facility. Rest assured, your daughter will be taken care of and your stay will not be permanent." The doctor adjusted his large glasses over his nearly translucent face. My mother glared at him before turning to me and kneeling until our faces were level. The fury trickled out of her lovely features, filling my vision with her soft brown eyes.

"Listen to me. These men have come to take me away. I have to go with them."

I shook my head wildly. "Why? I don't want you to go! Don't go! Please don't go!"

"Por favor. Be strong. I love you. I love you so much. Never forget that." She hugged me tight, allowing me mere seconds to bury my face into her neck as I tried to memorize the feeling. I was sobbing by the time she pried my arms away and opened the door for the men. The doctor led her out of the room first but I ran, heading for my room to lock myself in. Someone grabbed my arms from behind, lifting me into the air. I screamed and kicked as hard as I could. The cop that picked me up had no expression, no face — just a blank void. I didn't want to go. I didn't want to go.

They put her in the back of a white van and started driving without telling me where we were going. I sat up front with the faceless men, calling for my mother over and over again. My eyes were swollen and red by the time the truck stopped, so I couldn't see where we were until they opened the doors. The building before me was huge and white like a hospital, but something about it seemed nothing like a place to help people.

The men led my mother away and dragged me into a tiny office with grey wallpaper and a massive white woman behind a desk. In front of her sat a Spanish woman with light skin and a deep scowl that only worsened when she saw me. Her brown hair had been pulled into a tight bun atop her head and her forehead had deep lines in it. I bawled and asked for my mother again, but they ignored me. The fat woman handed the Spanish lady a stack of papers in a folder and turned to me with a sickening smile.

"It's okay, sweetie. You're going to live with your Aunt Carmensita for a while until your Mommy gets better. She'll take care of you."

Aunt Carmensita grabbed my hand and pulled me out of the office without a word, ignoring my sniffling hiccups. Why didn't anyone listen to me? Where was my mother? I just wanted my mother.

My aunt dragged me to the parking lot where a dingy green car sat. She strapped me into the back seat and got into the driver's side. The car coughed to life and I became surrounded in the smell of gasoline, exhaust fumes, and the faint stench of vomit from the faded suede seats. We pulled out of the parking lot and lurched onto the street.

"Where are we going? Where's Mama? I want Mama," I piped up.

My aunt scowled. "Your Mama ain't coming, niña. She's gone loca so they put her in the house with all the other idiotas. Stop that crying. You're lucky. They were going to put you in a home if I hadn't come along."

"Mama's not loca! Mentirosa!" I wailed, scrubbing frantically at my tear-soaked eyes.

My aunt snorted, digging through her glove compartment until she came away with a half-empty pack of cigarettes and a lighter. She set the pack on the space between the seats, close enough for me to touch. She lit one cigarette and cracked my window open to let the smoke filter out, her voice flat with cruelty. "Está loca. Always been loca. If she had kept her mouth shut, none of this would have happened. Blame your Mama for this, niña. If I had my way, they would have taken you too but they didn't. Stop crying. You're gonna stay with me for a while and you will behave. I'll get that crazy out of you one way or another."

Finally, I'd had enough. Infuriated by her words, I grabbed the pack of cigarettes and threw them out of the window. She let out an anguished shriek.

"Morena del Diablo! What did you do that for?"

"Don't lie about my Mama! Don't!" My voice was so hoarse I could hardly yell but I managed it anyway.

"Just wait until we get home, niña. All the fancy men in suits in the world won't be able to help you then." She puffed angrily through her last cigarette.

"I don't care! Liar!"

I sat, fuming, as we drove through New Jersey until we reached a wretched apartment complex that smelled of urine. As soon as she parked the car, Aunt Carmen ripped me out of the seat and spanked me, shouting about how ungrateful I was, how I was just like my mother. I did my best not to cry out,

remembering my mother's words about being strong, but it
was hard to obey a woman I would never see again. Her blows
rained down on my head, neck, and back like hail until hot tears
were all I could see.

"Jordan?"

My eyes flew open as I heard someone say my
name. Michael stood over me with a worried expression.
He must have noticed how hard I was breathing. I wiped
the thin film of sweat away from my forehead and sat up,
eyes adjusting to the light spilling in from the window.

"I'm alright. What is it?"

"You slept right through the morning. I thought it
might be time to start moving." I glanced at the clock to
confirm this. Four o'clock. Damn, he was right. I had slept
for a long time. Then again, I'd stayed up well into early
morning going over his case, trying to find anything I
might have missed. One day left. Twenty-four hours to
solve Michael's murder or I'd burn in hell for all eternity.
No pressure.

"Why didn't you wake me up earlier?" I grumbled,
motioning for him to turn around while I got out of bed.
No pants. I felt more comfortable sleeping that way.

Michael obliged, answering without a single quip
about me being pantsless. Weird. "You looked like you
needed the rest."

"Eh. I'll rest when I'm dead," I said, collecting my
robe from the floor and putting it on.

Michael snorted. "I should find that funny, but it's
more disturbing than anything else."

I shrugged. "They can't all be winners. I don't
suppose you—"

"Made coffee?" He pointed to my nightstand, where
a steaming mug of liquid paradise sat. Was I so predictable
that a guy who had only known me for going on three days
could figure out my morning rituals? Probably. Oh well. I
drank the coffee anyway and walked towards the kitchen.

"What did you do while I slept?"

Michael gestured a hand at the table where the hospital papers were spread out. "Looking over what we gathered. I kept hoping my memory would come back, but the only thing I remembered was how to play a few songs on the guitar."

A smile touched my lips. "I have to admit I would pay to see you play one in public. People would freak out if they saw a guitar playing itself in the middle of the sidewalk."

He flashed me a grin. "Hey, don't tempt me. I almost went home to grab my guitar but then I remembered I'm invisible to normal people. I'd be on Youtube by morning."

I nearly choked on the next mouthful of coffee from laughter. "*The Mysterious Floating Guitar of Albany, New York.* Maybe it'd make it all the way to CNN."

We shared another bout of giggles that eventually descended into comfortable silence. Wait, comfortable? Ah, hell. I must be losing my marbles.

Michael seemed to notice this so he glanced around the kitchen, searching for dishes.

"Why don't you get dressed and I'll scrounge up some food?"

I shook my head. "Keep it up and I won't solve your murder just so you can be my butler."

He chuckled. "That's pretty cruel. You couldn't even pay me if you did that."

I paused. "Good point. You'd be my slave. Somehow, I like that idea even better."

Michael rolled his eyes. "Go get dressed, woman."

Smirking, I took another deep sip of the coffee and returned to my room. No casual clothes today. I wasn't going into the actual funeral, but I would be near the church. No sense in making the mourners worry about a woman showing up who no one knew, so it wouldn't hurt to blend in. That meant a black button up shirt, skirt, and flats. I'd wear heels, but I might be doing a lot of walking today.

I took a quick shower and got dressed, pinning up my hair in somewhat of a bun. Many women wore full makeup—lipstick, blush, foundation, mascara, the works— but I honestly hadn't learned how to put it on properly on account of who raised me. On my worst days, I wore foundation and eyeliner and that was it. Same for this instance.

Michael let out a low wolf whistle when I walked into the kitchen, which was pretty much the reaction I'd expected. "Don't you clean up nice."

"Thank you," I replied with a flat tone, swiping a reheated slice of bacon and toast from a plate. As I munched, I plopped down in front of my laptop and opened it. Needed directions to the funeral. The lack of car would be a problem, but I had enough money to spring for a cab.

"What exactly is gonna happen with the ghost girl?" Michael asked, hovering over my shoulder as I typed.

"When a spirit sees the person or thing that caused them to stay behind, they'll speak to it, and that's what allows their final wish to be fulfilled. Afterwards, they just disappear into the next world and Gabriel comes to write their name in the Book of Penance."

"Book of Penance?"

I pointed to the top of the fridge. Michael walked over and picked it up, flipping through to read the names written in black ink.

"Wow. You've helped this many in two years?"

"Don't sound so impressed. I've still got to solve your case by midnight on Monday or I'm going to Hell, literally."

He fell silent and then asked. "Do you always do that?"

I glanced at him, confused. "Do what?"

"Self-deprecate to push people away." The bluntness of the comment rendered me speechless.

"Yes," I murmured after a while. "I don't always do it on purpose. It's a bad habit I developed from being on my own for so long. Any other personal flaws you'd like to point out?"

"No. I figured we'd work on them one by one."

I flipped open my notepad and began scribbling down directions to distract myself. "So what? Are you my therapist now?"

He sighed. "If only. I'd get so much cash working on your ruptured psyche."

I arched an eyebrow at him. "Ruptured psyche? Only a musician could come up with something so poetic instead of just saying I'm effed up in the head."

Michael shrugged. "It's a gift."

"I'll take your word for it." I closed the notepad and drained the remainder of my coffee and scarfed down the bacon and toast.

"Let's go."

Ghosts are tricky bastards. They're intangible but they don't float through everything. I ended up getting Linda into the cab by instructing her to just hover above the seat or she'd sink right through it. Adult ghosts had better grasps on the concept of not going through everything. It was much harder to teach young ones. Needless to say, the cab driver had thought I was cuckoo for Coco Puffs for whispering incessantly to thin air. Michael had a fine time laughing at my plight. Jerk.

The good news was that we didn't have to travel for too long. The church where the funeral was held was about fifteen minutes from where I lived. I groaned when I looked at the meter in the cab, but I'd live. I told our driver to sit tight for about ten minutes and ushered the two dead people out of the back.

When we arrived, the procession had already lined up for the bringing in of the body. I felt my throat tighten as I saw the tiny white coffin housing Linda's body. The first time I had worked with a child's ghost, I'd cried at least three times: when I met him, when I saw his parents, and when I saw him cross over. Now I only got choked up at the funeral. It had been a rough couple of years.

The cab had let us out across the parking lot from the front of the church so nobody could see us yet. Good. I knelt in front of Linda and mustered an encouraging smile.

"Do you remember what's kept you here on Earth?"

Linda nodded, making her pigtails bob up and down. "I wanted to tell my Mommy something."

"Okay, sweetheart. Mommy won't answer you but she will feel your presence deep down. I want you to go inside and tell her whatever it is you need to tell her. I'll wait for you out here."

"Mmkay." The little ghost headed towards the long throng of family and loved ones until she disappeared from sight inside the sanctuary. I let out a long breath.

Michael stood next to me with a concerned expression. "This isn't your first time seeing a kid's funeral, huh?"

I shook my head. He sighed. "That's a damn shame. Y'know, as much as I bitch about being dead, I don't really mind. The world will survive without guys like me. Kids like Linda, though…makes you wonder if there's a greater purpose for stuff like this."

A small snort escaped me. "Gabriel always tells me to have faith. It's hard to do when you see little girls and little boys who have lost their lives. I can only imagine how her mother must feel. Maybe something like mine did."

Michael opened his mouth but I just shook my head again. "Don't say anything sympathetic or I'll cry, and I am damn sure not messing up my makeup today."

He closed it. "Hard ass."

"I try."

We spent the next five minutes or so in silence. I spotted Linda walking back towards the cab, looking the same as how she'd entered. So young. She seemed to understand that she wasn't normal, but I didn't know if she knew much beyond that.

I smiled at her again. "Did you tell her?"

"Yes. Thank you. What happens now?"

"Have you fulfilled your final wish?"

She looked up at me with her blue eyes. Something in them changed when I said those words. The childish air around her seemed to dissipate as she whispered, "Yes."

"Then you have nothing to tie you to this world. Your Father is waiting for you, Linda Margaret Hamilton. Cross over and walk the Earth no more."

A bright golden light surrounded her on all sides and she faded from view with a calm, peaceful expression. When the last speck of light disappeared, I knew she had gone to the next world.

"Wow," Michael whispered. "Is that what it'll be like for me?"

"Mm-hm." I knocked on the glass to let the cab driver know I was getting back in the car. He gave me a confused look.

"What the hell was that all about? You didn't even go in."

I spared him a thin smile. "I didn't need to. Drive back to my apartment, if you please."

He sighed and shook his head. "Whatever you say, lady."

We drove back into town until we reached my apartment. By then, the sun had already set and swallowed the city sky in a wave of navy. Not a bad day, all things considered. Especially if it was my last day with my soul free.

The door swung inward, treating me to the sight of Gabriel in my kitchen filling out the Book of Penance. As always, he was dressed in an immaculate, expensive suit and looked out of place in my crummy living conditions. I walked in and shut the door behind Michael, addressing the angel.

"You know, it wouldn't kill you to show up in jeans one day. You're making me feel like such a bum with those fancy threads."

Gabriel smiled and looked up. "Sorry. I'll try to remember next—"

He stopped in mid-sentence and I swear to God, all the blood rushed out of his face. It took me a second to realize he was staring at the poltergeist behind me.

"*Michael?*"

"*Gabriel?*"

My jaw dropped. I stepped back, looking between them to find completely stunned expressions on both their faces. It took me a moment to form a coherent sentence.

"Wait, wait, wait a damn minute. You two *know* each other?"

Michael ran his fingers through his hair nervously. "Yes. No. Shit, I don't know. When you said his name, I didn't notice but now that I've seen his face, it all clicked."

I turned on Gabriel. "Why do *you* know who he is?"

"Jordan, this is no mere ghost. This is the soul of Michael the archangel, Commander of God's Army in Heaven," Gabriel explained in an awestruck voice. He took a cautionary step forward.

"Brother, do you realize how long you've been gone?"

I pressed my fingers to my temples and massaged them, trying to keep up. "Alright. One of you had better start explaining something or my brain is going to explode."

Gabriel spared me a sympathetic look. "Very well. Two years ago, the Spear of Longinus—that which pierced the side of the Son and killed him—was discovered and brought into this city for an auction. Father knew what a dangerous weapon it is and therefore sent Michael to retrieve it so it would not fall into the hands of evil. The night of the auction, Michael disappeared."

"How could he disappear? Shouldn't one of you have been able to find him?"

The blond archangel shook his head. "No, Jordan, you don't understand. When I say he disappeared, I mean from existence."

I stared at him. "What do you mean from existence?"

"Before you brought him in here, I had no recollection of the archangel Michael. When I saw his face, everything came back to me at once, like some sort of shockwave. This is the work of something powerful, something that was able to bend reality so that history did not hold a record of Michael. It was only broken now that I've seen him with my own eyes."

I raked my fingers through my hair, sinking into the chair by the table. "But what the hell could do something like this? Make everyone in Heaven and Earth forget that Michael even existed?"

"I suppose we'll find out when we recover the Spear. In theory, it may have been the cause of all this because it holds so much power."

"You said you didn't want the Spear to fall into the hands of evil. Is there anyone specific you're talking about?" I asked.

Gabriel's pale eyes narrowed. "Satan has long coveted the Spear. It's been lost since the death and rebirth of Christ. Mankind has no idea the sort of might that rests inside that accursed object. There's no telling what the Fallen One could do if he got his filthy hands on it."

"Well, apparently he did because I'm dead. I've been this way since Thursday night."

Gabriel shook his head. "You're not dead. Angels cannot die. Your soul has been displaced. Despite whatever happened, your body was not destroyed. You were sent in a special body that allowed you to use all your powers rather than just some of them, like the one I am inhabiting."

I turned my head to look up at Michael. "Is any more of this coming back to you?"

He nodded. "I'm starting to remember my life before this happened. Not much, but it's there. I remember the auction and winning the Spear. I was leaving with it to report back to Heaven when someone attacked me. I hit my head pretty hard when I fell. I woke up in a hospital and couldn't remember anything. Since I couldn't remember I was an angel, I never used any of my powers or tried to contact Gabriel."

"Yes. Apparently, you believed you were human and therefore your soul didn't give off the aura of an angel, making it impossible for us to notice you," Gabriel said.

I frowned as another question came to mind. "Why didn't God tell you where he was? He's omniscient, right?"

"Father will not directly interact on Earth. He feels that humanity and the angels will reach harmony if we face our problems without His help. Aside from His orders, He will not act if it interferes with human lives."

The urge to frown was enormous. "I don't mean to blaspheme, but that's pretty messed up, Gabe."

He spared me a small smile. "I would like to agree, but I don't want to be disavowed of my rank."

That almost made me feel better. "Can you remember who attacked you and stole the Spear?"

Michael shook his head. "Not exactly. It was night. I couldn't see well. All I can say is that it was a man dressed in black."

Something clicked in my mind. "Did he have dark hair?"

"I think so."

"Michael, you mentioned a strange dark-haired man when we were walking yesterday. Maybe he's the guy that stole the Spear. Maybe he's the guy who kicked you out of your body. Gabriel, is that possible?"

"Yes. However, I am not entirely sure of why a demon would want an angel's body. They can't kill him. It's virtually indestructible. I get the feeling there is a larger scheme in the works. If that demon saw the two of you yesterday, then he has surely been trailing you and knows where this apartment is."

Fear climbed up my throat and made my mouth dry. "What should we do?"

"Don't panic," he assured me in a kind voice, causing a relaxing sensation to fill my body until I could breathe normally again. Gabriel strode over to the door and muttered something in another language under his breath, tracing his fingertips over the wood in the shape of the cross. He did it to all four sides of the door and to each of the windows in the apartment.

"I have blessed all the entrances to this apartment. Demons cannot enter a place that has been blessed by an angel. No matter what happens, you will be safe here." He touched the side of my face. I felt a little better.

"However, I would advise you not to leave until we're able to find out what this demon wants with Michael's body and where it is—"

"I can't stay holed up in this apartment, Gabriel," I insisted. "I have work tomorrow."

His face took on a more stern edge. "Jordan, I do not want to place your life in danger."

"I won't be in danger. I'll go to work and come straight back. You don't have to treat me like a child. I've managed to stay alive this long, haven't I?"

He stared me down for a long moment before sighing and reaching into his pocket. "I am beginning to wonder if stubbornness is a specifically human trait."

Michael smirked a little. "Nope, that's just Jordan."

"Hey, back off—!"

"Hush," Gabriel said, growing impatient with our bickering. He held up a black rosary and three vials of what appeared to be water.

I stared at him in confusion as he handed them to me. "I'm not Catholic, you know."

"I know, but these will protect you should a demon choose to attack. The cross hurts their skin and makes them vulnerable to injury. The holy water will as well. Carry these on your person every time you leave this apartment. I will be waiting for you when you return tomorrow. I have a few sources to check so I must depart for the night."

He glanced at Michael. "I am relieved you've been found, brother. Watch over her until I return. Stay vigilant."

"I will."

With that, he left. Silence folded around us for a moment or two, then I filled it.

"Well, that wasn't weird."

"Tell me about it," Michael said, slumping into the chair across from me. "This is so bizarre. I'm starting to remember who I was before this happened. I was so different from how I am now."

"How so?"

He winced. "Well, for one I didn't much care for humanity. I had spent so much time in Heaven that you all seemed like sheep to me: blind and dumb without guidance."

"I can't really fault you for that. We're not very smart or good-natured at times. What can you remember about your life when you thought you were human?"

Michael tilted his head a little, trying to remember. It was sort of a cute look. I immediately brushed the thought away. "I spent the first year trying to build a life out of pretty much nothing. I didn't know who I was or why no one knew me. One of the first things that got me back on track was music. I remember hearing an old man on a park bench play his guitar, so I decided to learn how to play. When I got good, I performed at local clubs until my band mates found me and we started the Throwaway Angels.

Obvious symbolism aside, it was the most fun I'd had since the incident."

He glanced at me with a sly smile. "Aside from meeting you, of course."

I rolled my eyes. "You're an archangel. You're not allowed to flirt with me anymore. Especially since I'm apparently a blind, dumb sheep girl."

Michael pouted, watching me rise from the chair to go put away the holy objects Gabriel had given me. "You're going to hold that over my head forever, aren't you?"

"Yup. Now come on. I want to hear more stories."

"You're inviting me into your bedroom? What was it you said about flirting?"

"One more smart ass comment and I'll have Gabriel ban you from my apartment."

"Yes, ma'am."

CHAPTER SEVEN

By the time I rolled out of bed the next morning, I hated myself. Michael's human and angelic life had been so interesting that I didn't kick him out of my room until well into morning. I had a seven-hour shift today that started at eight AM sharp. Yippee-skippy.

Michael tried to give me a serious speech about being careful, but I assured him I would be fine and that he didn't need to follow me there or back from work. I'd considered bringing the gun, but according to Gabriel, it wouldn't help since demons couldn't be eliminated by anything other than holy items. I wished I thought of asking him to bless the gun or the bullets before he left. Wondered if that would have worked. I decided to ask him when I got home.

The workday crawled by because my mind was so preoccupied with Michael and the Spear of Longinus. Something else nagged at the back of my mind, but it just wouldn't come to me. Figures.

Finally, my shift ended and I headed onto the street with an unnatural awareness of everyone who passed by me. A dark-haired man. Right. Because that was extremely specific and helpful.

Something scampered past my ankles — too big to be some kind of rodent. I stumbled, staring down in shock as I recognized the sleek black fur and familiar gold eyes. Michael's cat, Bast.

"Hey, you," I cooed, stooping to reach for her. "How the hell'd you get out of the apartment? You'd better come with me."

As if understanding my words, the cat mewled in protest and scampered down the alleyway to my left. Groaning, I broke into a jog and tried to catch up. The cat darted around a corner to the right and I followed, calling after it.

"Oh, c'mon! My place's not that bad!"

I rounded the corner, hopped over a few trashcans, and squeezed my way past a large dumpster. No sign of the cat. I went to the alley on my right, bending down to look behind the trashcans at the dead end.

"Bast? Where'd you go?"

A voice spoke directly into my left ear. "Looking for someone, my dear?"

A cold shock went up my spine. I whirled around, fists raised, only to stand there stupefied by the sight before me. There stood a Japanese man in a black tuxedo and matching gloves, smiling at me. It was the man from my nightmare. I hadn't even remembered it until I saw that pale face of his again.

"*You*…no, that's not possible," I whispered, my arms dropping to my sides like deadweight.

The man tilted his head at an angle. "Whatever do you mean, my pet?"

I shook my head. "You can't be real. That was just a dream."

"I assure you, Jordan. I am quite real. And like in the dream, I am in need of your assistance."

"Why? You're not dead, are you?" I glanced down. Polished dress shoes adorned his feet. The man chuckled, a sound that crawled up my spine like a feather being drawn along my skin. I shuddered.

"Not at all. I am here to offer you a choice."

My throat went dry. Fear welled up from inside my chest where my heart thundered from the adrenaline.

"What choice?"

"I know the deepest desires of your heart, Jordan," the man said in his most soothing voice. "You long to be freed of this burden of trafficking souls. You want to live your life free of the Father's bonds. I can help you take back your life."

I slipped my hand into the pocket of my duster and gripped the rosary tightly. Everything finally clicked into place.

"Nice offer, but no thank you...demon."

His eyes narrowed. Another wave of fear washed over me as he glared with those slit-shaped pupils that reminded me of some sort of reptile. I thought he was getting angry but he merely started to chuckle again.

"Well played, my dear. I am indeed under the employ of the Fallen One. Unfortunately, your refusal is unacceptable. I'm afraid I will have to remove you from this alley by force."

He stepped towards me, still smiling like a serpent. "You may scream if you like."

I took a deep breath and withdrew my hand from my pocket. "That won't be necessary."

I slammed my fist into his stomach with the cross lying across my knuckles. He hissed, pitching forward. Ignoring the pain crackling through my right hand, I kneed him in the chin and then brought the same fist across the side of his face. The force of the blow knocked the demon into the left wall of the alley, doubled over, nursing the wounds. He was still too close to the end of alleyway. As soon as I made a break for it, he'd be able to grab me.

A sudden sound caught my attention. I thought the demon had been coughing. He was...*laughing*. I took a cautionary step back as he pushed off from the wall. Blood trickled down his chin as a wistful sigh escaped his lips. "It's been so long since I've felt pain in this body. It's quite delicious, I must say."

Don't panic. Stay calm. I tightened my jaw and spoke with confidence I didn't feel in the least. "Want the second course?"

The demon lowered his hands from his stomach, allowing his voice to take an almost regretful tone. "As much as I do, I cannot stall the ceremony any longer."

The humor drained out of his face, leaving it clear with malicious intent. I slid my left hand into the other pocket, gripping the vials of holy water. As soon as he stepped forward, I threw two of them at him. He dodged to the right almost effortlessly. I brought my fist up again, but then he vanished. Too late, I felt his breath on the nape of my neck. A horrible, vise-like grip wrapped around my right arm. He twisted it behind my back and slammed me face-first into the brick wall. The vicious blow stunned me. Blood dripped down my forehead, hot and thick.

He ripped the rosary from my sore knuckles and tore off the duster. The demon held my arms behind my back with one hand, sliding the other around my throat and squeezing. I gagged, struggling with every muscle in my body, but to no avail. Tears overflowed down my face as the last gasps of air escaped my mouth.

"You could have made this so much easier on yourself," the demon murmured against my ear. "Then again, that is what I like about you, dear Jordan. You're a fighter."

The world bled out of my eyes and darkness pooled in its place.

A bright orange light peeled back my eyelids, making me groan. The color swirled in unsteady intervals until I blinked a few times. Sunlight. The faint heat probably meant I was outside somewhere. My arms ached with dull pain from being held above my head. I strained my neck upward to see that my handcuffed hands dangled from a hook sticking out of a concrete wall behind me. My aching body swung back and forth when the warm wind fluttered over me. Tiny grey pebbles on the ground shifted as well.

I let my eyes adjust. I was on a rooftop of a building, but not within the city limits. It looked to be somewhere on the outskirts, maybe an old factory in a foreclosed sector.

Michael's body lay on top of a stone slate, motionless and yet somehow still gorgeous. Next to it stood the demon.

"Ah, you're awake," he purred, fixing me with an amused stare.

The grogginess I had once felt retreated in an instant, leaving me cold with fear and confusion. The wind picked up as he strolled towards me with the patience I imagined a serial killer had when he knew his victim was helpless. My feet skimmed the ground as I struggled, trying to strain the chain of the handcuffs to see if I could bend it. No such luck.

He clucked his tongue and shook his head, making his black hair flutter. "I wouldn't do that. You'll only hurt your wrists."

"What do you care? Aren't you going to torture me some more anyway?" Raw pain rippled through my injured throat, making me sound hoarse.

He smirked. "Would you prefer a lie or the truth?"

"Who are you?"

He shrugged. "I have many names and many forms, for I have served my master well for eons. This body happens to be my favorite because of the fear it seems to inspire. However, to ease your curious mind, you may call me Belial."

"Great. Now that we've gotten that out of the way, what do you want with me?"

"You are a very special girl, Jordan." Belial stopped mere inches from me and reached his gloved hand towards my neck. I flinched when he touched my throat, stroking the delicate skin as if I were a cat.

"The blood running through your veins is that of a Seer. In order to make this ceremony work, I will need it to open a channel into Michael's body. Once that is done, I can inhabit it myself."

"What does a demon want inside an angel's body?" I managed to get the question out without a shaky voice. Gabriel would have been proud.

Belial dropped his hand. "Angels have the power of emotional influence over humans. Surely you have realized this, spending time with God's Messenger himself. In that body, I will be able to control as many of you as I wish in order to serve my master."

I shook my head. "What good will that do you once Christ comes back in the Rapture?"

He merely smiled. "What good will it do the Son to return to a world that is beyond his control?"

The icy knot in my gut hardened into a glacier. Gabriel had been wrong. This wasn't just about me and Michael—this was about the free will of the entire world. I forced myself to take slow, even breaths and think logically. Belial hadn't killed me yet. Every second I was still alive was a second I could potentially keep this from happening. My best course of action would be to stall him, keep him talking, until Gabriel could get here. Not my best plan, but it was better than nothing.

"How did you even find me?" I demanded. His thin eyebrows rose in surprise, as if he hadn't expected me to ask, but the venomous smile remained intact. The guy seemed to like the sound of his own voice, which could work to my advantage.

"That is quite the interesting story. Two years ago, my master informed me that the Spear of Longinus had surfaced. It was being sold in an auction in Albany, New York. Thus, I was given a human body and told to retrieve two things: the spear and a Seer. My master is often enigmatic, so he did not tell me what these were for. I went to the auction, only to be outbid by your precious Michael."

He sneered when he spoke the angel's name, his eyes glittering with hatred. "I later cornered him outside and we fought. I was about to finish him off when a group of people spotted us. My priority was the spear, so unfortunately I had to retreat and find the Seer my master required. But before I left, I decided to take the ever-difficult angel out of the picture. I commanded the Spear to erase his identity so that none of the other angels would be able to find him. However, I underestimated the might of the spear itself. It wiped him from the entire history of the universe, leaving me without memory of him either. Thus, I continued on my mission to find a Seer."

The smile widened into a grin. "That is when I knew our fates were intertwined, sweet Jordan. I had located a Seer to entrap by sending out a lesser demon as bait. These creatures aren't particularly smart. They only seek out human souls and feed off their fear. The Seer fell for it and chased the demon into the apartment of a young woman."

My entire body went numb. Everything became deathly silent except for the sound of his voice.

"Do you understand now?"

"You sent that thing into my apartment. You're the reason I killed that man," I whispered, my throat tightening as I fought back tears of hatred.

"Indeed I did. You killed the man I was going to use for the sacrifice. It's quite interesting when you think about it. If you had not slain him, he would be in this situation instead of you."

I wanted to scream. I wanted to yell and rip free of these handcuffs and tear him apart. This *beast* was the reason I had been alone for two years straight, the reason I had to spend day after day looking for lost souls, the reason I had been drinking myself stupid in order to calm down enough to sleep, the reason I woke up constantly every night because of horrific dreams. The rage burned inside my chest like a wildfire. I was so angry I couldn't even speak.

Belial sighed. "I made the mistake of leaving the area after you killed the Seer because you had not yet had your Awakening. I reported back to my master with the Spear. That is when he informed me that he needed a Seer in order to gain access to an archangel's body, which I had unknowingly lost. Things seemed problematic until I stumbled across him one night while searching through the city. I confronted him in an alley and captured his body. The only task left was to locate a Seer, and all I had to do was wait. Regular souls are drawn to your kind. So was Michael's. You can imagine my surprise when I discovered you were the Seer he found. I spread my influence and reached out to you in a dream to see if I could win you over. When you refused, I planted one of my sentries to wait for you and the angel in his apartment."

"Bast."

"My, you catch on quick. I kept an eye on you until you were most vulnerable, and you played right into my hands."

"So that's it? You're going to kill me and then what?"

"I wouldn't be so bitter if I were you, my dear. I have plans for your soul after you die."

"What plans?"

The demon stepped closer, filling my vision with those empty eyes. "I asked the master for your soul in return for my services. When you die, you will become my servant."

I licked my lips, trying to remain calm as best as I could but I could feel myself starting to shiver from the finality of his words. "Why?"

Belial chuckled. "You're too modest. I was not lying when I said I liked you. I will thoroughly enjoy bending you to my will. Besides, it would be much more fun than simply killing you."

"If it's all the same to you, I'd rather have my soul destroyed than be your pet."

"That reaction alone makes me wish I didn't have to kill you right away," he sighed, closing those thick lashes over his eyes.

I fought back another urge to shiver with a question. "How can you claim my soul? I thought everyone who dies is taken before the Father and Son to decide if they go to Heaven or Hell."

Belial's eyes lit up. "Excellent question. But what you forget is that your soul is already damned. We know about the contract you've made with Gabriel. You haven't collected the one hundred souls, so yours belongs to my master to do with what he will. In this case, it will be given to me."

I swallowed hard. "Why'd you wait until sunset?"

He stepped away, walking towards where Michael's body lay and picked up the Spear of Longinus. The wooden shaft of the spear had been snapped off. The tip looked sharp despite being worn with time. He stroked the blade almost lovingly, like a kid with a delicious piece of candy.

"The Lord's power works best in the light. At night, His power dims and mine grows. When the sun goes down, I will be able to perform the ritual at full strength. Take in the last of the sun, dear Jordan. When night falls, you are mine."

Panicked, I glanced at the horizon over the city. The dusky orange had given way to a dark navy blue. A sliver of the sun was still visible, but from here it looked as if it were dying—dragging down all the beautiful pinks, reds, and yellows down in its throes. I didn't have long, maybe less than a minute. Where the hell was Gabriel?

When I turned my head again, Belial stood right in front of me. As I stared at him, a strange sense of calm enveloped me.

"Are you afraid?" he whispered. I shook my head slowly.

The demon rested his gloved fingertips over my heart, testing my pulse to see if I were lying. "Why not?"

"Whatever happens…it ends tonight. I have no choice in the matter. There's nothing left for me but death or salvation. You have nothing left to scare me with."

"Then close your eyes and say a prayer, sweet Jordan. I will send you to sleep." Belial lifted the spear, its tip crusted with the blood of Christ, of Michael, and soon to be with mine. The sun finally disappeared from sight, wrapping the two of us in darkness. I let my eyes fall shut and words spilled from my mouth from memory.

"Our Father, who art in Heaven
Hallowed be thy name
Thy kingdom come
Thy will be done
On Earth, as it is in Heaven
Give us this day our daily bread
And forgive us our trespassers
As we forgive those who trespass against us
Lead us not into temptation
But deliver us from evil
For thine is the kingdom and the power and the glory,
forever.

Amen."

"Jordan!"

I opened my eyes to see Gabriel soaring over the edge of the building, his wings spread wide. Michael dangled from his arms, shouting my name. In that exact moment, Belial plunged the spear into the spot a few inches above my heart. Excruciating pain ate through my chest as my blood overflowed the wound, coating both the rest of the spear and Belial's hands. Agony climbed through my limbs like acid and stole my breath.

Hit too many arteries, I thought sluggishly. *I'll only have a few minutes before I die.* When this notion filled my mind, I should have panicked or cried, but I didn't. All I could think was, *I hope I get to say goodbye to Michael.*

"Thank you for your sacrifice, Seer. With this life blood, I will usher in the era of the Dark One," Belial said with an insidious smile. He ripped the blade out of my chest, turning to face the angel and poltergeist that had landed on the roof.

"Filthy creature!" Gabriel shouted, his beautiful golden wings flaring in anger. "Father should have sent you lower than the depths of Hell when he banished you and your wretched leader from the Heavens."

"On the contrary, archangel. He could not have given us a sweeter reward than to free us of His tyranny. Let me show you how your Lord has blessed me."

He rushed forward, almost too fast for my eyes to follow. Gabriel darted after him in a graceful arc, drawing the elegant sword from his waist and shouting at Michael over his shoulder.

"Attend to Jordan!"

Gabriel swung downward in a powerful stroke, but Belial met it with the tip of the spear, deflecting the blow. They moved with deadly, liquid grace, scattering gravel this way and that as they fought.

Michael raced around the other side of his body to meet me, his green eyes wide with panic as they fell across the wound.

"Jordan, stay with me. I need you to focus." He wrapped his arms around my waist and lifted me until my handcuffs came free from the hook. Michael sank to his knees and laid me on the ground, his hands hovering over the wound. Each inhale burned like hell. The blood that oozed outward took my strength with it.

I took a deep breath, struggling to speak. "I-It's not your fault. I know you did the best you could. Please…help Gabriel."

"I can't. Jordan, *you've got a hole in your chest.*"

I managed a small smile. "Guess that means I'm not going anywhere. Go."

He clenched his jaw and closed his eyes momentarily before starting to stand up. "Don't die. I'd hate to have to miss you."

I let my head roll backward just in time to catch sight of Michael racing towards the battle between Belial and Gabriel. The angel had managed to drive the demon farther away from the body, but he had a cut on his cheek, arm, and over his left knee from the spear. The demon hadn't fared much better. Even from here I could see the tears in his suit that had been marred with blood.

Belial reached back to swing, but Michael grabbed his arm, shoving his palm upward at the demon's elbow. Belial's arm broke with a sickening crack, and the demon roared with pain. The spear flew from his grasp, landing a few feet away from Michael's body. Gabriel's sword flashed as he slashed his blade across Belial's chest, slicing a gash down his front. The demon let his broken arm go limp at his side and grabbed Michael by the throat with his other hand, throwing him at Gabriel. The angel reacted only a second too slow, moving aside on reflex. Belial ran for the spear, sweeping it up and slamming it into the chest of Michael's body.

I cried out as something boiled within me, as if my very essence were being torn apart. It burned so badly I couldn't breathe. I could only writhe on the floor, feeling salty blood well up in the back of my throat.

A light shot up into the sky from Michael's body, nearly blinding me. I could just barely see Belial's face, a mask of fiendish glee, as Michael's body arched upward on its own. He let the weapon clatter to the rooftop and hovered over the blinding light: bruised, bloodied, and ecstatic.

"Master will be so proud," he said, leaning forward to climb into the light. The demon's fingertips brushed over the area above the wound when he stopped in mid-motion. His body jerked forward as Michael ran him through with the spear, twisting the end for good measure.

"Go to hell," Michael spat, stepping back to let Belial's body fall. The demon hit the roof with a solid sound, painting the gravel black with his blood. He drew in a couple shallow breaths, his voice wet and thick with hatred.

"Savor...your victory now, archangel. I will return and take what is mine."

With a final gurgle, the demon went still. Gabriel and Michael hurried over to me, kneeling on either side of my trembling form. Gabriel snapped the chain of the handcuffs with ease, but I couldn't really feel it. The pain had receded and with it came numbness. I could barely breathe anymore. I had lost too much blood.

"Can you save her?"

Gabriel scanned the wound. "I should be able to seal it up."

He plucked a feather from his wing and started to lay it over the gash, but I caught his wrist. "Don't."

Gabriel's mouth fell open. "Jordan, what are you —"

"If you heal me, the portal to Michael's body will close," I said through shallow breaths. "Let him go back."

Michael shook his head. "No. No, I won't do it. I will *not* be responsible for your death, Jordan!"

"It's not your choice to make. I have to make things right. This is the only way to truly atone for the life I took."

"Jordan, there is no way to know if the Father will accept this in place of the hundredth soul you owe," Gabriel said in a pleading voice. Now that he was so near to me, I could feel waves of worry pouring off the angel and flowing inside me. So much compassion. I had never felt such a powerful sensation before.

"I know. Finish it."

He raised his eyes up to Michael, whose face had crumbled into something between anguish and disbelief. My limbs were shaking badly, but I still reached up and touched the side of his cheek to make him look me in the eye. The strange metaphysical energy of his poltergeist form spilled across my tired skin and gave me enough power to speak clearly.

"This is what you were born to do, Michael. You're an archangel. The people in this world need you more than I do."

"What if I need you?" he whispered, almost as if he were ashamed of what he was saying.

I smiled. "That's the most…beautiful thing…"

He pressed a finger over my lips before I could finish the *V for Vendetta* quote and returned the smile, though it was weak around the edges. "You watch too many movies. Goodbye, Jordan."

His lips pressed to my forehead, a strangely soft tingle, before he got up and walked over to his body. Gabriel brushed the hair from my face and kissed the back of my hand, his lovely face heavy with regret.

"I will treasure you always."

"Back atcha, Gabe."

I didn't see Michael enter his body. I *felt* it. It felt like sliding beneath the warm covers of a bed after a long day — safe, comfortable, alleviating. Death swept me up into its arms and carried me away to darkness where there was no pain, no suffering, and not a care in the world. I couldn't have asked for more.

BOOK TWO: IN MEDIAS RES

Under his gloomy power I shall not long
Lie vanquished; thou has given me to possess
Life in myself forever, by thee I live,
Though now to Death I yield, and am his due
All that of me can die, yet that debt paid,
Thou wilt not leave me in the loathsome grave
His prey, nor suffer my unspotted soul
Forever with corruption there to dwell.
-*Paradise Lost*, John Milton

CHAPTER EIGHT

I had been expecting great leaping flames, sinister cackling, and maybe Peter Stormare dressed in all white to greet me in the pits of hell, but that didn't happen. The first indication that I was alive was that I could see the ceiling fan of my bedroom. Then, like a tidal wave, I felt pain. *Everywhere.* My bruised hand, my punctured chest, my sore arms—the agony hit my poor senses all at once. I closed my eyes and just lay there until the sensory overload receded.

I gathered my arms beneath me to sit up. It wasn't easy but I managed to prop my back up against the headboard. Michael sat in a chair to my right with his head resting on the mattress, slumped over asleep. Then, I noticed that his hand, which had been resting near mine, was emitting heat. Michael was alive. *Alive.*

Then why the hell was I?

I reached out towards him just enough to brush my fingertips over the back of his hand. Michael grunted and rolled his head to the side, peeking up at me through a waterfall of brown hair. A sleepy smile tugged at his lips.

"You're awake."

I cleared my throat a few times until I could speak. "You're alive."

He stood and perched himself on the bed, brow furrowing with concern. "How do you feel?"

I shrugged one shoulder, immediately regretting it as my chest wound stung. "Like I've been choked, stabbed, and handcuffed."

"It could have been a lot worse," Michael murmured, tugging aside the bloodstained button up shirt to reveal the heavily bandaged part of my chest.

"I know. Why wasn't it? I thought I died."

"You did," he said in that same soft voice. "But after Father saw what you did in order to restore my life, He decided to wipe your debt clean."

"So…when I die…I'm not going to Hell?"

Michael finally smiled. "You're not going to Hell."

A rush of relief flooded through me from head to toe. I lay my head back, resisting the urge to cry. "Thank God."

"You bet I did."

It took a minute or so before I could regain composure. When my eyes were dry and my throat clear, I spoke up. "That reminds me. Does this mean you have all your memories back?"

The smile waned. "Yes. I remember everything about being an archangel, but…it's sort of bittersweet."

I tilted my head in question. "Why?"

"The Michael you knew is now just a small fraction of who I am. I will never be him again." His voice held such regret in it that I reached out and touched his hand, trying to choose the right words to express how I felt. As annoying as his poltergeist self had been, I did like him deep down. I hadn't even considered the fact that regaining his body and all of his memories would change his personality.

"Who you are and who you were are the men that I owe my life to. You can never disappoint me, Michael." My words had the kind of truth I expected from someone like Gabriel. I wasn't the smartest or most eloquent person. However, judging by the relieved expression on the angel's face, I made my point well.

"Thank you. For everything. Your faith is something no one can replace."

I waved the comment away. "Knock it off. Just because you got your body back doesn't mean you get to sweet talk me."

Michael laughed. As with Gabriel, the joyous feeling filled my chest and erased the aches and pains that had previously resided there. I caught myself wishing he would never leave and cursed my vulnerable state.

Just then, Gabriel walked through the door with a dark-haired Hispanic man I didn't recognize. They were both wearing street clothes: Gabriel in a black sweater and dark blue jeans while the stranger wore a grey button-up shirt and black slacks.

I lifted an eyebrow. "I'm digging the casual look on you, Gabe. Be careful or one of these Albany girls might make off with you."

The handsome angel blushed, to my delight. "I'll be quite careful. Jordan, this is Raphael. He's going to be treating you."

"Raphael? As in archangel Raphael?"

Gabriel nodded. I squirmed in my seat. "Geez, I'm really getting the star treatment, aren't I? Why are three of God's archangels wasting time with a waitress?"

Raphael spoke with a surprisingly deep voice that had a hint of a Spanish accent in the background. "You don't give yourself enough credit. You made an important sacrifice. You are entitled to a bit of attention."

That made me smile. "Fantastic. You wouldn't mind bringing me something to eat, would you?"

"Certainly not. Michael, mind showing me around?"

"No problem." Giving my hand a final squeeze, Michael stood and led Raphael out of the room in search of food. Gabriel sat beside me and began inspecting the many bandages adorning my body.

"What happened to Belial?"

Anger flickered across Gabriel's face at the mention of the demon's name. "We burned his body, but unfortunately the Spear of Longinus did not kill him permanently. Demons are very hard to destroy. Their souls are simply expelled from their bodies and return to Hell where their wretched leader gets them new ones."

"Guess I'll be needing a lot more crosses, then," I said, trying not to wince as he checked my chest wound.

He nodded with a grim expression. "Many. Michael was immensely concerned with your condition. He even went before the Father and Son to plead on your behalf."

My jaw dropped. "Plead what on my behalf?"

"I think she might want to hear this from me, Gabe." I spotted Michael in the doorway with a glass of ice water and a Nutra-Grain bar. Raphael entered behind him, glancing between us with a worried look. I eyed Michael's careful expression as he walked towards me with the food. He very pointedly did not look at me as he handed the items over.

"Hear what?"

"Based on the persistent nature of the demon Belial, I asked the Father to remain at your side until we have determined he no longer wants possession of your soul."

I sputtered in mid-swallow of the water. "What?"

Michael cleared his throat. "It was the logical thing to do."

"*Logical?* Michael, you're an archangel. You can't just hang around my stuffy little one-bedroom apartment!" I exclaimed, resisting the urge to throw the health bar at his head.

"I'm not moving in with you and I won't be abandoning my post as Commander of God's Army. I'll just be continuing my job here on Earth alongside you."

I gave Gabriel a pleading look. "There is no way The Big Guy agreed to this, right?"

Gabriel coughed into his hand. I noticed the upward twitch of his lips. The damn angel was trying not to laugh. "He found it to be an acceptable proposition. I'm quite sorry."

I palmed my forehead, trying to wrap my head around this ridiculous idea. Well, at least this put an end to the problem of being alone. Lord knows I had never thought it would be ended by way of archangel.

Gabriel spoke up, interrupting the uncomfortable silence. "I can see the two of you will need time to adjust to this change. We will be back tomorrow to check your wounds, Jordan."

The two left the room in a hurry. Smart angels. I took a deep breath, licked my dry lips, and tried to figure out where to start.

"I'm not sure if you noticed, but I'm not much of a people person, Michael. It won't be easy with you hanging around me all the time."

He took a seat at the foot of the bed. "Do you want to know why I volunteered to do this? Other than the whole 'there's a demon trying to get you' thing?"

"Yeah, that'd be nice." I hadn't meant to sound so mean, honest, but I suddenly remembered Michael's words before I died. They rang clearly in my head, almost mocking me: *What if I need you?* As silly as it sounded, I felt embarrassed and defensive. Did he still feel that way or was that just the other Michael?

"I may have only been with you a week, but I feel I can do more here than I thought. Yes, it's true that you are smart and tough and independent, but you've been alone for so long. I owe you my life. This is the least I can do."

I wanted to protest, but I remained silent because he was right. I'd been doing things on my own as soon as I got old enough to leave my aunt's apartment in inner city New Jersey. She had been cruel because I reminded her too much of my mother. She already had two kids and a distant husband to worry about. Nearly all of the growing up I had done as a person, I did so alone.

That didn't mean I could accept it. "But I barely know you."

Michael spared me a soft smile. "Then I guess we'll have to get reacquainted."

He stuck out his hand. "Michael the archangel, Prince of Heaven's Army."

I finally sighed and took it. "Jordan Amador. Welcome to my world."

CHAPTER NINE

The first order of business was calling work. The incident had caused me to miss two days. Gabriel came up with the cover story: I had been violently mugged and would be recuperating for two weeks minimum. Colton sent Lauren over to check on me (and probably confirm that I wasn't lying) and she nearly fell apart when she saw my condition. She told me she knew relatives who would fly over here from Korea and hunt down my attacker, but I managed to convince her not to do it. Strangely enough, it was one of the sweetest things anyone had ever said to me.

Michael posed as an at-home nurse assistant in the daytime hours. I told Lauren I was deathly afraid of hospitals, so they had discharged me. When he left to get me more food, Lauren asked for his number. I'd laughed so hard I nearly reopened my stitches.

Speaking of those, Raphael had actually treated me while I had been unconscious. It turns out that he couldn't bring me to full health because of the massive strain I had already gone through. Raphael worried that using all of his healing powers might push my body past its limits.

At the moment, we were in my bathroom with the door shut—me perched on the side of the bathtub with Raphael sitting in a chair across from me. His hands were warm and firm against my skin as he tested my temperature, examined the bruises, and moved the joints in my injured hand. Everything still hurt, but not nearly as bad as when I first woke up. I probably should have felt more uncomfortable being shirtless in front of a man I had only known for two days, but Raphael kept me distracted with conversation as he worked. Plus, angels weren't attracted to human beings so there was no sexual tension to be had, much to my relief.

"So does Michael have any of your healing abilities?" I asked.

He offered me a faint smile. "Michael is more of a fighter than a healer. I've had more experience in this area."

I arched an eyebrow. "Aren't all archangels sword-toting badasses?"

He chuckled — a warm, rolling sound. "Not exactly. He is the more proficient strategist when it comes to fighting. It has always been that way."

"If that's true, do you really think he'll do a good job of taking care of me?"

I could tell the question surprised him. He paused, mulling the thought over. "Each archangel has strengths and weaknesses. As God's Messenger, Gabriel interacts easily with human beings, but lacks the hardened nature of a warrior like Michael. As God's Healer, I have extensive skills in treating the bodies and souls of humans so I lack the desire to harm others. Michael is the superior commander, but he has spent the least amount of time on Earth. I believe this is why Father sent him to return the Spear of Longinus to its proper place. I think that is also why Father agreed to let him stay on Earth with you. There is much more he can learn here than in Heaven."

"You didn't answer my question."

Raphael grinned, tossing the small pile of old bandages in the wastebasket before standing. "Yes, Jordan. I think he will do a fine job taking care of you, and vice versa."

I frowned. "How could I possibly take care of an archangel?"

His brown eyes twinkled as he spared me an enigmatic smile. "How indeed."

I shook my head and offered him my hands, which he took to help lift me to my somewhat shaky feet. He opened the door and held me steady to walk back to my bed. He could have just picked me up, but I insisted I could get there myself. Stubborn? Who, me?

From my bed, I could see into the kitchen where Michael stood at the stove cooking something. He even wore an apron, which made me giggle. I'd have to make fun of him for it later.

Raphael handed me a glass of water before zipping up his leather bag. "That should be all for now."

He hesitated, his brow furrowing in a slight frown. "Are you sure you don't want me to heal your back?"

Discomfort curled through my stomach in a cold wave. I didn't like that he'd seen them—my scars. It raised a lot of questions, and none of them I wanted to answer. "No. I'm alright."

"Very well. I will be dropping by a few times a week to check on your progress. Make sure not to put too much stress on your body."

I nodded. "Thank you. I owe you my life."

He smiled. This time, I could feel a different emotion than with Gabriel and Michael. An overwhelming sense of calm washed through me. I felt safe in his presence.

"Think nothing of it. Good night, Jordan."

With that, he turned and left, nodding to Michael before leaving the apartment. It made me realize this would be the first time I was alone with the new (or would that be old?) Michael. Just how much of the Michael I knew was in there? That was the million-dollar question.

I searched the top of my nightstand for the remote control and turned on the TV. Midway through *Transformers*, Michael appeared with a bowl of chili and a spoon. I couldn't stop staring.

"Do you realize how weird it is that you're an angel who knows how to cook?" I pointed out, hoping my question would mask the sound of my stomach growling.

Michael shrugged, handing me the bowl, spoon, and napkin he'd brought with him. "Man's gotta eat."

"That reminds me—what kind of body is that? Is it like Gabriel described?" I continued, tasting the first spoonful. Oh, Lord. It was delicious. The urge to shovel in several mouthfuls was intense.

"It's…a little hard to explain," he admitted, sitting on the edge of my bed. The little blue apron was gone. I missed it.

"This is a hybrid body: half-human and half-angel. I look human to blend in with everyone else, but I can still use my abilities."

"So where are your wings?"

"They'll appear if I concentrate hard enough."

I considered asking him to show them to me, but I figured that was a little personal. "What kind of abilities do you have?"

"Seeing spirits, something similar to super strength, influencing emotions and will power…those sorts of things."

"Are the demons the same way?"

Michael's eyes narrowed a bit. As with Gabriel, the angels really didn't like it when I mentioned their evil counterparts. It was understandable: Belial had been the foulest creature I'd ever met, dead or alive.

"You could say that. They too have human bodies, but demon souls. Belial is Satan's personal favorite of all his minions. He's the most resourceful, since he's spent the most time on Earth. It's hard to keep track of him because he switches among his own line of human bodies every so often."

A shudder crawled up my spine when I thought about his creepy smile and lifeless eyes. "Can he possess anyone?"

Michael shook his head. "Two souls can't share the same body without one of them being expelled. That's why possessed people are so violent. The two spirits fight for control. A demon only uses that tactic if his original body is in danger of being destroyed."

I lowered the bowl. "Belial mentioned something about a lower class demon he sent as a lure for Mr. N. How is it that things like that can walk around in our world?"

"Trust me, it wasn't supposed to. As Gabriel said, Father has not directly interacted with the human race since the Transfiguration of the Son. It's the same with Satan. He isn't allowed to make his presence known to mankind. Instead, he sends his minions out to corrupt. To counter his actions, Father implements everything through the archangels. Sometimes He will give specific orders, but in general we travel between Heaven and Earth keeping peace."

"So what happens when I help souls cross over to the other side?"

"The archangel Uriel escorts the souls up to the gates of Heaven for judgment."

My eyebrows rose in surprise. "Damn, I guess Milton really was onto something when he wrote *Paradise Lost*."

Michael flashed me a grin. "He had a little help."

I rolled my eyes. "Be more vague."

"I can try."

Ignoring this, I moved on to my next pressing question. "How did you guys find me after Belial kidnapped me?"

"That's a bit more complicated. When you fell out of consciousness, you entered a state that can be tracked. Because you're a Seer, your mind sends out certain kinds of energy that we angels can feel, and so we followed it to where you were."

I considered his words. "Maybe that's how Belial was able to find me in the first place. The first time I saw him was in a dream. I wish I had remembered it earlier."

"Well, at least you know now."

"Can I ask you something else about him?"

"If you must."

"Why are his eyes like that? Like a snake's? I've never seen anything like it before."

"It's the mark of an archdemon. There are only five of them, if you recall—Belial, Mulciber, Moloch, Mammon, and Beelzebub. They consider themselves to be the Princes of Hell, as they were Satan's most loyal followers before the Fall. Only Seers and angels can see the mark. To the average person, his eyes look normal."

Feeling sufficiently full from the chili I'd devoured, I reached out to place it on the nightstand, only to wince as another wave of pain spread through my upper torso. Michael stopped me in mid-motion, putting the bowl down for me. My lack of mobility annoyed me to no end.

"So what do you suppose we're gonna do for the next ten days that I'm stuck in this bed?"

"I thought you'd ask me that," he replied, reaching for the floor by the foot of the bed. He held up a plastic bag and dropped it next to me on the bedspread. The thing was nearly bursting with books of all sizes.

I lifted an eyebrow at him. "You sure know how to thrill a girl."

Michael rolled his eyes. "It's more enriching than T.V. Besides, there's some good stuff in here that you might find…therapeutic."

He glanced at the closed drawer of my nightstand, frowning a little. I couldn't blame him. My alcohol dependence was unhealthy and I knew it, but so far I hadn't found a better way to cope with the nightmares. Couldn't afford the therapy, and the very thought of Alcoholics Anonymous intimidated me.

To distract myself from this notion, I picked up a thin green book with a familiar title, reciting the first stanza of "Do Not Go Gentle into that Good Night" from memory.

"A Dylan Thomas fan, I see," Michael said with a grin. "Maybe you're not such a heathen after all." I fought the urge to make a face at him and pointed to the bookcase on the left side of my bed that was piled high with books:

poetry, classic literature, contemporary novels, and pretty much anything I'd been able to get my hands on.

Before he could respond in an undoubtedly smartass way, I spoke. "Don't you have somewhere to be? You are an up-and-coming rock star, remember?"

I paused, considering my words. "Wait, are you still going to live the way you did when you thought you were human?"

"I thought it over and decided it would be the easiest way to coexist here on Earth. Hiding in plain sight, I suppose."

He grabbed the remote and shut off the television before scooping the book out of my hands, which confused me.

"Relax. I'll read it for you. I've been told I have a soothing voice."

"Somebody lied to you."

Michael sighed. "I'm beginning to regret our arrangement already."

"Join the club. We have milk and cookies, and go on cookouts every Friday."

"Jordan?"

"Yes?"

"Hush."

After Michael read through most of Walt Whitman's *Leaves of Grass*, I fell asleep. The nightmares came, but I only woke up once during the night. Michael had slipped out of the apartment by then. It was harder to fall asleep the second time, but I managed.

I woke when I heard movement in the kitchen. Groaning, I buried my head beneath the pillow until my body stopped throbbing with pain. I ventured to take a peek. Michael had kindly left the bedroom door open, and I could see him laying plastic bags full of groceries on the counter. Almost immediately, my mood perked up. He'd bought me food? Hell, maybe I could get used to this.

My dry throat begged for water so I obliged, draining the rest of the glass that had been sitting on the ever-crowded nightstand. I cleared my throat loud and calling out "Hey" to Michael.

He glanced over at me. "Morning."

"Morning. Is it weird that I have a hard time picturing you in a grocery store?"

He gave me a cryptic smile. "There's a lot you're gonna have to get used to with me. Anyway, roll over. I have to make sure you didn't bleed through the bandages during the night."

I turned over, propping my back against the headboard. I'd ditched the ruined button up shirt for a dark purple one—man's sized so I wouldn't be exposing too much. Sure, he was an angel, but I couldn't help wanting to be modest around him anyway. Maybe because he was my friend now. Thankfully, the wound was high on my chest, so I could still wear a bra underneath.

I started to unbutton the shirt myself but he told me not to since one of my hands still had a magnificent bruise across the knuckles. Lucky me, though, because it didn't hurt that much any more. The purplish skin had grown stiff, but I could tell it was beginning to heal, as was the circle of bruises around my throat. With Raphael's continued treatments, they would fade within days.

Michael waved his hand in front of my face, making me jump. "I asked you if you were hungry."

Damn, I hadn't realized how hard I'd been thinking. He'd finished checking the bandages without me even noticing. "Yeah."

He tilted his head a little. "You okay?"

"Yeah, I'm fine. Why?"

"You're chewing your bottom lip like you do when you're trying not to frown."

I stared at him in shock. "How could you have possibly noticed that about me? We've known each other for like what? Three days?"

Michael merely shrugged. I shook my head. "Go get me food."

After a moment, I added the word "please" and Michael cracked a smile. "I think that's the first time I've ever heard you say that."

"Don't get used to it."

"Always a charmer, aren't we?" With that, he loped off to the kitchen. I watched him go with a strange sort of bemusement. I couldn't understand how Michael rolled with the punches the way he did. My personality was naturally cranky, but for some reason he didn't seem to mind. I wondered if the patience came from being an angel.

Somewhere during my musing, I caught a whiff of how I smelled and nearly gagged. My body had been in such a delicate condition that I hadn't been able to shower since the incident. Unacceptable. I tossed the covers back and set my feet on the floor, firmly resolved to fix this problem. My legs burned with pain after I stood up and several ligaments cracked, but it wasn't too bad altogether. Huzzah.

I shuffled my way over to the dresser in front of the bed and gathered some undergarments from the corner of the drawer. Really needed to wash my clothes soon. Maybe I'd guilt my new bodyguard into doing them for me. I managed to reach the bathroom without toppling over or anything when Michael called from the kitchen.

"What kind of food are you in the mood for?"

"The edible kind." I yelled back. "It'll have to wait until after my shower."

A pause. Hurried footsteps. Michael appeared in the doorway with a frown. "Wait, what?"

I pointed at the tub. "Me. Shower. Now."

"Jordan, you really shouldn't be moving around that much. Your stitches might tear. Can't this wait a little longer?"

"The day I can't wash my own ass is the day I don't need to continue living," I said, flipping on the faucet. Water rushed into the tub—a relaxing sound in itself.

He sighed. "You have a point. But don't take a shower. You shouldn't be standing for any long period of time. Take a bath and don't let the water soak into your wound. I'll be out here if you need any help."

I paused. There was just no way I could let that one go. "Would you *like* to help me bathe, Michael?"

To my amusement, he cleared his throat and wouldn't meet my eyes. "Not what I meant."

"Honestly, it would make the entire experience more bearable." I could feel the grin taking over my lips and didn't fight it. Hell, it was the most fun I'd had in a while. Apparently, the new Michael could get flustered. Interesting.

He shot me an accusing look. "You really are shameless, aren't you?"

Was it my imagination or was he blushing? Ha! "It's all part of my charm."

Michael shook his head and shut the door without replying. I allowed myself one small giggle before adjusting the water's temperature and shedding both my clothes and the bandages.

As the tub filled, I took a good look at myself in the mirror. There was really only one word for what I saw: yikes. The stitches were still visible on my chest, where ugly mounds of light brown flesh had gathered around the wound. Whenever they came out, there would definitely be a large, jagged scar in its place. A ring of bruises marred my neck and a sizeable one peeked out from beneath my hair where my head had hit the wall in the alley. I felt another surge of anger towards Belial. It was one thing to hurt me emotionally, but the bastard had physically marked me. Gabriel said there was no known way to destroy a demon soul.

I was sure as hell going to find one someday.

With my hair down I looked a lot like my mother. She had been from Madrid while my father was black, origin unknown. That was just about the only thing I knew about my father. He'd left before I was born. As for my mother, she was an entirely different story. One I didn't like to revisit often.

After the tub filled, I took my sweet time lowering myself into the smooth porcelain and soothing hot water. My injuries stung, but it was heavenly after I settled in. I lay my head back and just went still. Got to enjoy the little things in life.

My thoughts started to drift as I lay there, making sure not to let the water hit my chest wound. How long would Michael stay with me? Is this how cohabitation worked — a constant exchange of banter between two people? Or was our situation unique? Hell if I knew. The last relationship I'd been in ended in tatters. We'd never even made it to the moving-in stage. How did people do this on a regular or even permanent basis? Then again, who was I to complain? I had an archangel at my beck and call. You'd think I would be more grateful. Then again, attention from anyone, especially men, made me defensive. Stupid, but true.

I drained the tub and climbed out, drying off slowly on account of my stiff limbs. The underwear took an annoying amount of time to put on, but I managed. Finally, I wrapped myself in a thick navy robe and called for Michael.

Once more, I sat on the edge of the tub, staring at the opposite wall as Michael sat in a chair he'd gotten from the kitchen and redressed my chest. I kept the robe bunched around my waist, hiding everything at navel level and lower. He hadn't been this close to me before we'd known each other so I started noticing little things about him, like how he smelled. His scent was a mix of Old Spice deodorant and some sort of sweet aftershave. Unlike Gabriel or Raphael, his fingertips were rough from playing the guitar. I'd never noticed how large his hands were up until now.

"Something on your mind?"

I glanced at Michael. "What do you mean?"

"Well, it's been five minutes and you haven't insulted me yet. I'm getting worried." His green eyes sparkled with amusement.

I scowled. "It's not all about you, y'know."

He chuckled. "My fault. Still, what's on your mind?"

I searched for something to say because it wouldn't be appropriate to admit I'd been thinking about the way he smelled or how big his hands were. "Not much. I was just thinking how long it's been since I've had someone around all the time."

"No boyfriend?"

I winced. "Once. Terrell Molding. It...ended badly."

"What happened?"

"We had been dating before the incident with Mr. N. As you can imagine, things got rough afterward. I knew I couldn't tell him what I'd seen because he wouldn't believe me, so I pushed him away."

"That must have been hard for you." His voice was soft with sympathy rather than pity. A small part of me felt relieved by that.

I shrugged and then winced because it still hurt. Gotta stop doing that. "I got over it. It wouldn't have worked out in the long run anyway."

"What makes you say that?"

"He wanted the American dream: a beach house in Hawaii, a white picket fence, two kids, and a dog. Despite everything around him, he still held on to the illusion that people are good and life is sweet. We were from two completely different worlds."

Michael was silent. "I don't think that's the problem."

"What do you mean?"

"It's still the same world, but you two just saw it differently."

"I guess that's true."

"Now that you've gotten your life back, will you try to make things work with him?"

That caught me off-guard. "W-Well, I didn't really consider it, no."

"Why not?"

"Who are you? Dr. Phil?"

"Jordan, for once, just answer the question."

"I...I never felt like I was good enough for him, alright? He was on track to become a pediatrician and he came from a large, successful family. I couldn't stand the thought of going home to his family in California with my background."

"Background?"

"I already told you what happened to my parents. I didn't even go to college. His whole family comes from a prestigious line of African descent and I'm mixed. They weren't very happy with that."

"Why should they matter at all if you loved the guy?"

"No one ever said I loved him." My voice was small and defensive when I spoke. I hated that. He didn't speak at first—just finished the last bit of my bandages and tugged my robe closed.

I shook my head. "I guess that's a pretty stupid reason for not trying, hm?"

"Want to know what I really think?"

"Knock yourself out," I said, avoiding eye contact because it made me feel too vulnerable.

Michael leaned forward in his chair and brushed a lock of hair behind my ear to catch my attention. "I think you're way harder on yourself than other people are, and you shouldn't be because there's nothing wrong with you that's beyond saving."

Before I could reply, he stood up and offered me his hand. "Now come on. Your food's getting cold."

CHAPTER TEN

"You ready?"

"Yeah."

"You sure?"

"Did I stutter?"

I had been expecting a right cross. Instead, I got kicked in the stomach.

My body crumpled like a paper doll. I couldn't help clutching the injured spot with both hands, as if that would dull the pain. It wormed up from my abs to my chest, blossoming outward to my limbs. Still, I couldn't stay in the same place or he'd hit me again, so I threw myself to the side as he tried to trip me. I came up on one knee and brought both forearms up as his right leg came down, heel first. I blocked the blow and punched him in the back of the knee.

Jared hissed and danced two steps backwards, hopping on one foot. "Damn. Good hit, Jor."

"Thanks," I rasped, rubbing my midsection. I'd be bruised later. Michael wouldn't like that. Then again, that was why I hadn't told him about this little session of mine.

Jared offered a hand and I took it, grateful as he pulled me to my feet. After a moment, I could breathe normally and returned to a defensive stance.

A couple people had stopped to watch us. I shot them hard looks, which made them wander off and pretend like they hadn't been staring. I understood them, though. It wasn't every day that a big black guy and an average height mixed girl with a bandaged chest and scars trained in a gym. Though I suspected they wanted to make sure he wasn't wiping the floor with me, which he was.

Jared was a fourth-degree black belt. I hadn't even had official martial arts training. Everything I knew about self-defense, I learned from him shortly after I moved to Albany two years ago. We met at the gym, and since he knew I couldn't afford lessons, he took pity and taught me whenever he had free time.

His brown eyes wandered down my upper body and he paused, giving me a concerned look. "Need a break yet?"

I wiped the sweat off my forehead. "Nah. Maybe in about ten minutes or so. What's the verdict so far?"

He relaxed his 6'3" frame and I knew I was in the clear for at least another five minutes. Jared wasn't the type to attack without warning. "Your reaction time has taken the biggest hit, if you ask me. The advantage you usually have over me is speed, and that's nowhere present from what I've seen. For instance, when you raise your arms to block, it's not very solid. I could break through it if I wanted to."

I winced. "Got it. Anything I can do to fix that?"

He shot me a disapproving look. "Oh, I don't know, bed rest like your damn doctor recommended?"

I rolled my eyes. "Thanks, Mom."

Jared sighed. "Fine. If you swear up and down that you want to improve...yoga."

"Yoga."

"Yes, yoga."

"Can you really see me in a pair of tights bending myself into a pretzel?"

He rubbed his goatee, adopting an amused look. "Y'know, it's not a bad mental image."

I flipped him off and he laughed. "I mean it, though. It'll get you limber without stressing your body out too much."

"I'll take it into consideration. Now let's go again."

He sank into a defensive position. I launched myself at him, aiming kicks at him since my upper body strength had taken most of the damage from Belial's attack. Jared blocked my blows with expert ease, hopping out of the way when I tried to trip him. I aimed a chop at his throat when I found an opening, but he grabbed my wrist and twisted my arm, throwing me over his shoulder. I hit the mat with a solid thud, groaning as pain flooded up my spine in a startling rush.

Jared stood over me with a neutral expression. "You okay, tough guy?"

I waved a hand to dismiss the comment. "Sure. I'll let you know when my dislocated vertebrae pops back into place."

He chuckled, but then the grin disappeared when he spotted something over my head. "Uh, were you expecting company?"

"No. Why?"

Jared pointed. "Because there's a tall guy heading this way who looks like he wants a piece."

I tilted my head up to see Michael storming down the aisle between the mats with a death glare aimed in my direction. Great. Busted.

"What the hell are you doing?" he demanded when he was within earshot.

I sat up, rolling my shoulder to make sure it hadn't popped out of alignment when Jared tossed me. "What does it look like I'm doing?"

"You told me you were going grocery shopping."

I glanced around. "Hm. Must've gotten lost on the way there."

Michael closed his eyes and I swore, it seemed like he was counting to ten. Instead of hurtling another pissed-off comment in my direction, he turned to Jared and stuck out a hand. "Sorry. I'm Michael. I'm attempting to be her at-home assistant."

Jared shook his hand and then glared at me. "You failed to mention that, Jor."

I stood, bending down to touch my toes. In top form, I could press the pads of my fingers to the floor, but in my current state, I could barely brush the ground. Shit.

"You didn't ask."

Jared sighed. "Yep. Under the bandages, you're still the same hardheaded moron as always. Guess I'd better get out of here."

He started to leave, but then pointed at me with a stern look. "Don't call me until you're cleared with him, y'hear?"

I saluted him. "Sir, yes, sir."

Jared shook his head and headed towards the locker room. Michael rounded on me as I grabbed my water bottle from my corner of the mat. "How long have you been doing this behind my back?"

I drank about half the bottle before answering. "Why? It's only going to make you madder when you find out."

"Jordan, I told you that you would have to take it slow for a while. Forcing your body to recover is only going to make things worse."

"I'm not forcing anything. I'm preparing."

He narrowed his eyes at me. "For what?"

"For whatever the hell is coming for me next. I don't want to get my ass handed to me again, thanks." I turned away, heading towards the locker room as well. Usually, I'd take a shower because the gym here had pretty nice facilities, but the stitches couldn't be under a showerhead until my skin healed. I'd have to head home and take a bath.

Michael followed me. "So what? Do you not understand the concept of a bodyguard?"

"I don't want to be saved. I can take care of myself."

"Yes, because it worked so well last time."

I whirled on him, poking a finger in his chest. "Don't go there. You're not gonna like where it ends."

"And where is that? A hospital? Because that's exactly where you're headed at this rate."

I threw up my hands. "You don't understand anything, do you?"

"No, I don't. So explain it to me."

"This isn't the time or the place, okay? Let me get my crap and then you can continue lecturing me on the way home. Sound good?"

"Sounds perfect," he growled.

I stalked into the locker room and let out a groan of pure frustration. My anger distracted me enough that I couldn't remember the combination to the lock, so I just stood there and pressed my forehead against the cool metal, trying to calm down. I hadn't wanted him to find out. I really hadn't. He was supposed to be at band practice all night, so I'd snuck out of the apartment for a quick lesson. He must have gotten back early. I was never going to hear the end of it.

"Man trouble?"

I glanced to my right to find a blonde girl looking at me with a mix between amusement and sympathy. I let out a snort.

"You have no idea."

One frosty, silent bus ride later, Michael and I arrived at my apartment. I took the longest bath possible to avoid the upcoming argument and redid my own bandages. They weren't as neat and perfect as when Michael or Raphael did them, but they did the trick. The time alone gave me a moment to cool off and at least attempt to act like an adult.

A succulent smell greeted my nostrils when I left the bedroom. Something with tomatoes and broth. My stomach growled comically loud in response.

Michael stood in front of the stove where a big silver pot sat. He ladled some kind of soup into a bowl. Even though I was sort of mad at him, I still wanted to eat the food he'd made.

"Is that for me, or do I have to apologize first?" I asked.

"The great and powerful Jordan Amador knows how to apologize? I'm shocked."

I contemplated kicking him in the shin. No. I was going to be mature about this if it killed me. "Well, if you get down off your high horse, maybe you'll be able to hear it."

"I really should have believed you when you said you weren't a people person."

"Yup."

Sighing, Michael handed me the bowl. I dug up a spoon from the drawer before heading to the kitchen table to eat. The soup was indeed tomato-based, but I tasted a hint of basil among the shrimp, clams, and mushrooms in it. I hadn't tasted anything this good in months. Maybe I should apologize.

Michael sat across from me and we both ate in stagnant silence. When the last bit of soup disappeared, I decided to make the first move.

"How'd you find me?"

"Your phone went straight to voicemail, so I checked the grocery store and the surrounding area. When you didn't turn up, I thought about where you might go to blow off some steam. Then I remembered you had a gym membership."

"Am I that predictable?"

He allowed a small smile to grace his lips. "Only to me."

I glared at him. "Ego isn't a good look on you."

"Thanks, that's sweet." The amusement bled out of his face, leaving it serious but with a softer look than before. One thing I did like about Michael is that he didn't seem to hold grudges, even when I was in the wrong. Not that I'd ever admit it out loud.

"So what's really going on here, Jordan? You know it's dangerous to put that much strain on your body."

"I don't think it's something I can explain to you."

"Try me."

I lowered my gaze to the table. "Look, can we just drop it for now? I'm not really in a sharing mood."

"Fine," he said, and the annoyance in his voice made me feel guilty. "There's another reason I was looking for you. There was an incident this morning that I think we should look into."

"What's that?"

"A local museum was robbed. The thief took nine different pieces and killed two guards, injuring a third."

"I'm assuming there are ghosts involved."

Michael shook his head. "No. This has the mark of a demon on it."

A chill trickled down my spine. I met his eyes, hoping he hadn't seen me shiver. "Which demon?"

"I don't think it's Belial," he replied in a gentler tone, and I relaxed a bit. "But I do think it's something we should investigate, in case there's something bigger in the works."

"What makes you think it's a demon's work?"

"The items that were stolen are part of a new exhibit of cursed weapons. Scythes, sickles, machetes, spears, you name it. Most of them were imported from Europe. Some things can gain power when they are the cause of several deaths. You've probably heard of myths like James Dean's car or the Hope Diamond, right? If an object is directly responsible for a large number of deaths, eventually it can become powerful enough to harm even an archangel. We can't let them get out of the city, or any of the angels stationed on earth are in danger."

"So what's the plan?" I asked.

"I think we should talk to the injured guard and see what he has to say about the break-in, and then find out if anyone tried to fence the stolen property."

I eyed him. "That sounds like something only the angels would need to do. Why do you need me?"

"The questioning I can handle, but talking to someone who fences stolen valuables isn't my department.

Demons in that bracket won't talk to me, but they might talk to you."

"So I'm a honey trap, then?"

He paused and then flashed me a winsome smile. "If you don't mind."

"As long as I don't have to wear heels, I'm fine with it. When is this going down?"

"We'll talk to the guard tonight, just to make sure the demon doesn't try to make a move. I've ordered someone to watch over him, but better safe than sorry. We can start looking for potential criminals once we're sure the demons are involved."

Michael and I both stood, gathering our respective jackets. "Now there's a phrase I don't hear often enough in my life."

The archangel held the door open for me with a grin. "Welcome to my world."

CHAPTER ELEVEN

As we strolled into the hospital, I couldn't help thinking about Maroon 5's "Harder to Breathe" because I was having a difficult time staying calm. I had been kidnapped and beaten senseless by an agent of Lucifer, and yet the white coats the doctors wore scared me just as badly. The men who had taken me from my mother wore those same damned lab coats. Every time I saw one, it awakened a dormant fear inside me — fear that I'd be dragged away from someone I loved again, fear that I'd be placed into the waiting hands of another horrible person. It would never truly go away.

Michael's shoulder bumped mine, which shook me out of my thoughts. I glanced at him. "What?"

"You're frowning."

"Am I supposed to be smiling right now?"

He faced forward, looking at our reflection in the elevator doors. "No, but you look like you're about to bolt at any second."

I watched the digital numbers change one by one as we rose up to the right floor, fiddling with the rosary in the pocket of my leather jacket. Somehow, the beads had a calming effect on me. "I'm fine."

"Hard ass."

A tiny smirk touched my lips. "Stop thinking about my butt. You're an archangel."

He grinned, but didn't reply.

The elevator bell rang and the doors slid open, revealing the shiny linoleum floor and baby blue walls of the recovery wing. I took a deep breath and followed the archangel out, resisting the urge to readjust the fake press badge clipped on my lapel. Imitating the press was much less dangerous than imitating a police officer or federal agent. It had been Michael's idea. I suspected he had been watching *Supernatural* recently. It amused me to no end, especially considering the fact that he was a dead ringer for Jared Padalecki.

We walked down the hallway towards Robert Sterling's room with confident strides. However, I noticed something odd along the way.

"Where are the angels you asked to keep an eye on him?"

Michael came to a stop in front of Sterling's room, frowning. "Good question. I called them on the way here and they said everything was quiet."

"Am I the only one getting a rotten feeling right now?"

"No, you're not." He glanced down one end of the hallway while I examined the other. Among the doctors and nurses, I spotted a brunette woman in pink scrubs walking towards us. Our eyes met and she stopped about ten feet away. Her face went blank. I had seen that look before, but not on a person. It was the look of a big cat right before it struck — pupils dilating, nostrils flaring, lips parting to reveal its fangs.

"Michael."

He followed my gaze and his spine straightened like a yardstick. He pushed me behind him as the demon walked towards us in a slow, hip-swinging stride with a sly smile on her lips.

She stopped less than a foot away, staring up into Michael's face. "My, my. Humanity looks good on you, archangel."

"You have ten seconds to get in that elevator and leave this place," he said, and the look in his eyes was unlike anything I'd ever seen before. Rage, pure and simple.

"And if I don't?"

"You'll leave in a body bag."

"Ooh. Pretty sexy talk coming from you. Sure you can deliver on that?"

"Five seconds left."

"Sounds tempting, but I'm on a deadline. The guard bites the big one so you idiots can continue scrambling around in the dark. I thought this would be a boring job, but since you brought your little pet along—" Her brown eyes settled on me. "—I think we're gonna have a good ole time."

"Time's up. Decide."

"Gladly."

Her left arm swung so fast I almost didn't see it. She drew a silver dagger from the small of her back and slashed Michael's chest. He caught her wrist and swung his large fist at her head, but she ducked. She wrenched her arm free and dropped into a back roll. When she came up, she held a .9mm Glock.

"Gun!" Michael called out to the hospital staff just as the demon opened fire. He shoved me into the room opposite Sterling's.

I slammed the door shut as gunshots echoed through the hall, kneeling to make myself less of a target. There was no one in the room except me, so I didn't have a panicking person to talk down, but there was still an armed rampaging demon right outside my door and my gun wasn't handy. Perfect.

I pressed my cheek to the door and closed my eyes, listening to the commotion and trying to ascertain what was happening. I heard frantic shouts and footsteps, and the shots weren't heading towards the elevator and the stairs. She wasn't trying to get away. This demon was hellbent on completing her mission, which meant she'd have to get Michael away from Sterling's room. The best way to do that was threatening the innocent.

My phone buzzed in my pocket, scaring the shit out of me. I fumbled with the device, relieved when I noticed it was Michael.

"Are you okay?"

"That's a dumb question."

"No, smart ass, I meant are you hit?"

"No. What's the plan?"

"She's trying to draw me out. That means she's gonna head for you."

"I figured."

"Got any weapons on you?"

"Just the rosary," I said, crawling towards the empty hospital bed and checking to see if I had anything to work with in the meantime. Nothing but a damned bedpan.

"They called security, but it'll take at least ten minutes for the cops to get up here. Here's what you're going to do: lock the door and stand beside it. The second she kicks it down, hit her with everything you got. That should distract her enough for me to take her out."

"Got it. And one more thing."

"Yeah?"

"Don't let her kill me or I'll haunt the hell out of you." I hung up and grabbed the thankfully empty bedpan, pressing my back against the wall next to the door. I closed my eyes and breathed slowly, trying my best to remain calm. Silence permeated the air. I watched the light beneath the door until a shadow fell across it. Showtime.

The door cracked in half when the demon kicked it, sending splinters flying in all directions. I swung at her face with the metal bedpan, landing a blow on her forehead. Her head snapped back. It gave me a couple of crucial seconds. I swatted at her right hand, knocking the gun across the room. She recovered with a vicious backslap that sent me careening backwards toward the hospital bed sans my trusty bedpan.

"Mm, you've got some bite to you, human," she smirked, marching towards me with deadly intent. The dagger glinted in her hand as she raised it. I waited until the last second to duck. The blade bit through the thin mattress. Just as it did, I kicked at her right knee. She screamed as it dislocated her kneecap, crumpling her to the ground.

"You little bitch!" She tackled me, straddling my body as soon as it hit the floor. She slammed my head into the linoleum. I cried out as pain lanced through my skull. She tried to stab me but I grabbed her arm, stopping it mere inches from my throat. She bore down harder and the tip of the dagger crept closer. My muscles strained and my entire body broke out in cold sweat. I used every ounce of strength, but it wasn't enough. I couldn't hold her off any longer.

A shadow fell across the demon's face. She glanced up for a split second. Michael stood in the doorway. He kicked her square in the temple and she smashed into the adjacent wall. The sheer force knocked her out like a light, and the dagger clattered to the floor next to her.

Michael offered me a hand. I accepted it, rubbing my neck as I stood. "Cutting it a little close there, pretty boy."

"Sorry. My timing was off. Are you okay?" He pushed my hair back, examining my cheek where the demon had hit me. The skin ached, meaning I probably had a bruise on its way.

"I'll live. You, on the other hand…" My eyes found the oozing cut the dagger had scored across Michael's chest, from his hipbone to just below his right pectoral, exposed by the tear in his t-shirt. Blood had seeped into the cotton, painting the white dark red. I hadn't seen that much since Belial stabbed me. It made my stomach clench.

"It's shallow. I'll be alright," he said, brushing past me to the floored demon. He knelt and picked up the dagger, his green eyes roving over the weapon.

"This is one of the missing items from the museum. Looks like we've got our confirmation of the demons' involvement."

"Do you think she's the one from the break in?"

"Maybe."

"Why just maybe?"

He shook his head. "This doesn't smell right. If she did this on her own, she wouldn't feel compelled to kill the guard. She could just fence the stuff, take her money, and leave town. Coming back to eliminate the witness means he saw something they didn't want him to. She's under orders."

The elevator bell rang. I heard several authoritative voices — the police. Michael cursed under his breath and dropped the dagger next to the unconscious woman.

"She's in here!" He called out. The police rushed in, checking to make sure we were both okay before surrounding the demon. They cuffed her and dragged her out of the room. They took our statements and gave us contact numbers for future involvement in the case. As expected, the dagger was taken into custody as evidence for the heist.

The doctors and nurses on the wing went back to taking care of the startled patients in other rooms. They checked on Sterling, who agreed to let us see him provided that we cleaned up a bit. One of the nurses began dressing Michael's cut but got called in to help a patient who had started coding. She seemed conflicted so I showed her my card proving that I was First Aid certified. Satisfied, she left it to me instead.

I hadn't seen Michael without a shirt before. It sounded absurd, but I felt a bit nervous as I mopped up the blood that had dripped onto the waistband of his jeans. I never saw him work out, but his muscles had the kind of definition that suggested he lifted weights and played sports in his spare time back when he thought he was human.

"Well, this is a role reversal," Michael said, breaking up the tense silence.

I tossed the soiled gauze aside, reaching for the Neosporin. "Don't get used to it. I have lousy bedside manner."

He chuckled and it sent vibrations all the way up my arm as I rubbed in the ointment. It made me shiver. I prayed that he didn't see my reaction. "No argument there."

"All kidding aside…you mentioned that these weapons can hurt angels. Will you be able to heal this yourself?"

His expression sobered. "I won't know until we get home. Can't heal myself here. Too many witnesses."

I pushed his arm a little higher before I pressed the bandages on until the wound was covered. I then taped them down as neatly as I could. "Here's hoping for the best. Any other aches and pains, Mr. O'Brien?"

"No, Nurse Amador, I'm fine. Thanks."

"You're welcome." I started to back up but he caught my shirttail, tugging me closer. He touched the side of my face. A streak of nervousness shot through me until I felt a cool tingling sensation on my skin. He was healing the bruise. It hadn't quite shown up on my brown skin just yet so no one would notice. I tried to focus on this thought, and not how I could still smell his cologne from this close, or how nervous I felt with him shirtless and only inches away. *Calm down, woman.*

I cleared my throat as his fingers fell away from my cheek. "Thank you. Let's go talk to Sterling and get the hell out of here."

"Amen." He stood and pulled on his jacket, zipping it up to hide his bare chest. I felt a small amount of disappointment at the sight and then promptly ignored it.

There was a nurse checking Sterling's vitals when we walked inside. She told us to keep it brief and make sure not to agitate him before she left.

He looked to be over six feet tall, with broad shoulders and a bit of a beer gut. He had started to go bald on top, but everywhere else the hair was brown and curly. Relief spread across his face when he saw Michael.

"Hey. Talked to the cops?" he asked with a hint of a Boston accent.

Michael nodded. "Yeah, they're gonna leave someone on this floor for the next couple days, just to be safe. Can you tell us what you saw at the break-in?"

Sterling shook his head. "You're not gonna believe me."

Michael offered the guy a smile. "Try me. I've seen some weird stuff in my time, and so has she."

He nodded to me. I stepped forward, not wanting to be impolite. "I'm Jordan. Nice to meet you."

Sterling raised an eyebrow. "You're the girl who helped catch that bitch?"

"Guess you could say that."

"Thanks. I owe ya one."

"No problem. So what did you see?"

"Three of 'em. Two men and a woman. Highly trained. See, it was my birthday and so a couple of the guys stuck around to keep me company since I got stuck with a graveyard shift. We were playing cards, shootin' the shit and whatnot, when the security feed went offline. The whole system just crashed. At first, we thought it was a blackout, but then when we went to go check, the lines were cut. They took out my buddy Jim when he went to check the electricity. Brooke and I went to check on the exhibits, and that's when we found the other two. My superiors tell us we're supposed to hang back and try to contain the situation without engaging, but we thought we might get a raise if we caught these guys on our own. Brooke went in with his nightstick on the guy. He..."

Sterling closed his eyes and his voice wavered. "...didn't make it. I thought I had the girl on the ropes, so I hit her with my taser. She laughed it off like it tickled or something. Threw me against the far wall and then shot me in the shoulder. They were about to finish me off when the cops showed up. When the uniforms saw me on the ground, they opened fire. None of them were close enough to see, but I was. The bullets…they hit. I saw the blood. But it didn't stop them. They just left."

He glanced at Michael. "Of course, the cops said it was the shock from all that pain that distorted my vision. Made me remember things wrong. Maybe that's true. But I still ain't gonna forget it any time soon. Print whatever the hell you want in your article. I don't care either way. I've still gotta bury my friends."

I laid a hand on his shoulder. "I'm sorry. I've seen someone I care about die, and it's not easy. Make sure you get some help, okay?"

He nodded. "You guys had better beat it. I could use some sleep."

"Alright. Thanks for your cooperation, Mr. Sterling. Stay safe."

We waved to him and the nurse before leaving. There was an older lady doctor in the elevator when we walked in. She studied the looks on our faces before speaking.

"Long night?"

Michael and I answered in unison: "You have no idea."

The fight with the demon left me drained, so Michael dropped me off at the apartment to rest before getting ready to track down the fence.

Unfortunately, Michael's theory proved true. He couldn't heal the cut with his energy, meaning it would remain until his body naturally repaired itself. Definitely a bad sign. We'd have to find those weapons and quickly if we wanted to keep the other angels safe.

I hopped in bed with a novel and read for a while. I didn't remember falling asleep, but apparently *Frankenstein* had enough dark charm to send me off for a short nap. Judging by the dim streetlight peeking in through my window, I guessed it was sometime after seven o'clock. An eerie sort of twilight had fallen across my room and the young white boy standing at the foot of my bed.

"Whoa!" I shouted. "Who the hell are you?"

The boy blinked his large brown eyes at me. "Jacob."

I tried to breathe normally and tilted my head so I could see next to my bed. The boy had no feet. Ghost. A huge sigh escaped me. I let go of the gun and slid my hand from beneath the pillow.

"Well, congratulations for scaring the crap out of me, Jacob," I told him, pressing a hand to my chest as if it would help my heart stop racing.

Jacob gave me an apologetic look. "Oh, um, I'm sorry. I dunno why I came in here. I just sort of...did."

"You're a ghost, kiddo. You didn't find me on purpose. It's sort of like an instinct."

His eyes widened. "I'm...dead?"

"Yes," I said. "I'm sorry."

He stared at the floor for a handful of seconds before lifting his head to look at me. "Why am I still here, then?"

I opened my mouth to answer, but the front door opened and Michael stepped inside. It took him about three seconds to spot the boy by my bed. He rushed over, his brow furrowed in a frown.

"Who's the kid?"

"This is Jacob. He's a ghost."

He sighed, which was odd. Did he honestly think a child would hurt me?

"Have ghosts ever followed you home before?"

I shook my head. "No. They always see me on the street."

"Right." Michael knelt so he could be eye-level with Jacob.

"My name is Michael. I'm an archangel."

Jacob's face brightened with surprise. "Really?"

Michael chuckled. "I know. I don't look like one, but I am. You need my help if you want to pass over to the next world."

"Hey, he was my ghost kid first."

He looked at me then, genuinely shocked. "Jordan, you don't have to do this any more."

"I know that. I actually want to help him. This ability isn't going to go away, so I might as well use it."

Michael studied my face. Then he smiled. "Alright."

If I didn't know any better, I'd have thought he was proud of me. Good thing I knew better. I tossed back the covers and stood up, ignoring all the parts of my body that complained, and set about searching for my notepad. "Okay, Jacob. Why don't you tell me the last thing you can remember?"

"Well, I was outside some sort of building. It wasn't an office or a skyscraper. It looked sort of like a hospital."

I nodded, having found a pencil and my worn notepad, and started scribbling what I knew so far.

Jacob
Appears eight or nine years old
Caucasian
Brown eyes
Brown hair
Remembers hospital or building that looked like one

"Do you remember how far you walked to get here?"

The boy shook his head. "I lost track of time. Something just told me to walk away and when I finally stopped, I was here. I'm sorry."

"It's okay. Your memories will start to come back after a while."

"What happens then?"

"We'll find out what your final wish is and you'll cross over to the other side." Michael jumped in this time.

Jacob still appeared anxious, not that I blamed him. "What if I'm not ready to go yet?"

I glanced at Michael and he understood the look. "It's natural for you to be worried about crossing over, but I promise it's a better place to be. You won't have to worry about anything ever again, and you'll be loved for all eternity."

Jacob's shoulders relaxed. "Okay."

"Follow me." I headed towards the kitchen. My laptop lay on the table. Its blue light occasionally glowed in the dark, beckoning me to find my answers. Michael flipped the light switch on and automatically began clearing away dishes and leftover food. Strange behavior, since his own home had been a pigsty.

After everything on the computer had been set up, I went about my normal researching route. My initial information gathering always started with a document I had compiled of local hospital morgues. I could weed out some of them, considering the fact that Jacob had gotten here on foot. The kid didn't remember how far he had walked, but I couldn't imagine it had been more than half an hour. Even without his core memories, he would have noticed if it took an hour or more to "find" me.

The hardest part of my cases was locating pictures. Jacob was a child so he wouldn't have any ID even if we found his body. The best course of action to take would be to call the hospitals and ask if anyone with Jacob's description was in their morgues. Hopefully, something would turn up.

"What happens now?" Jacob asked.

I brandished my cell phone. "The fun part of my job — phone calls."

Michael sat a mug of fresh instant coffee in front of me with a sympathetic smile. "Happy hunting."

"Thanks." I took a deep sip of the delicious beverage and dove in.

An hour later, I set the phone down and stretched my back with a miserable sigh. All those numbers and I still hit a dead end. At the very least I knew one thing — Jacob had not 'woken up' outside of a hospital. The morgues were still open, and none of them had a kid with his name or description. Most of them told me to call back the next day to double check. I'd most likely end up doing that just to be thorough, but the chances of finding anything were slim.

"Alright, so if you didn't 'wake up' outside of a hospital, where the heck were you?" I muttered to myself, peering at my laptop as if an idea would spring from the screen. Jacob stood to my right, chewing his bottom lip.

"I wish I could tell you something more helpful," the boy offered. "I'm sorry."

"It's alright. You have to walk up some blind alleys before you find where you're going. I've got an idea — why don't you go in my room and watch some TV? Maybe something on the local channels will jog your memory. Michael, would you turn it on for him?"

"Sure." He followed the boy back to my bedroom. I drummed my fingertips on the tabletop, trying to figure out another angle to look at this case. The newspaper stands were closed by now, but I could still check the obituaries online. They wouldn't be up to date just yet, but most of the names present would be recent. I connected to the local website and searched again. I found a couple of Jacobs, but they weren't children. Well, no one ever said this job was easy.

"Hey." I tilted my head back to find Michael smiling down at me. "Any luck?"

"Nope. Shame, though. Cute kid."

"Yeah," he said with a regretful smile.

I straightened up and closed the laptop, sliding in my seat so I could look at him. "Why did you seem so agitated when you came in? Is there something you're not telling me?"

The smile disappeared, replaced with a neutral expression, and he didn't answer. Not a good sign.

I pressed on. "Is there something you're not *supposed* to tell me?"

Michael ran a hand through his hair, brows furrowing. "Not exactly. I'm just…worried. Jacob isn't dangerous, but I don't like that he came into your apartment instead of finding you on the street like the other ghosts. It bothers me."

"Why? You know Gabriel blessed this apartment. If he were a threat, he wouldn't be able to get in, remember?"

He plopped down in the chair next to mine. "I know. I guess this whole thing with Belial made me paranoid. And it doesn't help that there's a rumor of another major player in town."

"Agreed," I admitted. "But as long as I'm in here, we can relax a little."

He smiled. I cocked my head to the side. "What?"

"I think that's the first time you've said 'we'."

My eyes widened a bit. How the hell did he notice stuff like that? He just kept catching me off-guard.

"Lighten up, Jordan. You don't have to be dark and tormented all the time."

I squirmed in my seat, avoiding eye contact. "I'm not very good at being anything other than grumpy."

He rose from his seat. "That's what I'm here for. Maybe some of my traits will rub off on you."

"...I'm going to ignore the sexual connotations of that sentence just so my brain won't explode."

"How deep in the gutter does your mind have to be to think that sounded perverted?"

"...I refuse to answer that question."

"Just help me clean up the kitchen, will you?"

"I don't know. Will anything 'rub off on me'? ...don't you dare throw that dishrag at me."

Afterwards, we went to my room to check on Jacob. To my surprise, he was floating cross-legged over the bed, turning those large eyes on us as we entered. Most young ghosts couldn't figure out how to do that.

"Did anything come back to you?" I asked. He shook his head.

"Well, Michael and I need to go somewhere so why don't you stick around until we come back?"

"Okay."

I swiped my leather jacket from the closet and shut the bedroom door behind us. "Alright. Let's go hunt us some demons."

CHAPTER TWELVE

I didn't know much about the Albany criminal underbelly, but I had assumed deals went down in dive bars and smoke-filled billiard halls. The notorious Julius Fenton did not reside in either of these places. Instead, he was a manager at the Build-A-Bear workshop in Crossgates Mall. I wish I was joking.

Michael circled the inside of the mall as my back up. Fenton would be able to sense him, but we had heard that he worked both the angel and the demon circuit, so for the right price he would sell us the information. It wasn't exactly against the rules for demons to be stoolies, after all. Sin was sin. Didn't matter who they betrayed.

The mall closed in an hour, so I straightened my shoulders and walked into the shop, keeping an eye out for anything suspicious. Cute little girls and boys tugged their mothers and fathers by the hand, their new best friends ready to be stuffed and clothed. It felt too weird for words.

An Asian boy in his teens smiled at me as I walked up to the register. "Hi. How can I help you?"

"I was wondering if your manager, Mr. Fenton, was in?"

"Sure, he's in the back getting ready to close up. I'll grab him for you."

"See," Michael said from the link in my ear. "Was that so hard?"

"Your sarcasm is really not helping me," I muttered, tapping my fingers on the counter as I waited. We had borrowed the miniature microphone and ear bud from one of Michael's cop friends. It made me feel like I was in an action flick, waiting for Arnold Schwarzenegger to burst in and beat up the bad guy. I watched way too many movies.

The boy returned with an older Japanese fellow with grey hair and deep frown lines in his forehead. Furthermore, he didn't have the same uniform as the kid. His navy suit was expensive and pressed to perfection. Not what I expected. Then again, were demons ever predictable?

His brown eyes widened as he spotted me. "What can I do for you, young lady?"

I took a deep breath. "I wanted to talk to you about a specific order for an important client."

He searched my face for a long moment and then waved a hand. "Sure. Come with me. I'll just be a moment, Kevin."

I followed him to his office in the back, wiping my sweaty palms on the legs of my jeans as I went. No one jumped out to grab me. That was definitely a first.

He closed the door behind us when we reached his office and took a seat, eying me. "So you're the Seer."

I didn't know how to respond, so I waited for him to say something else.

He tilted his head a bit and continued. "Thought you'd be taller."

I bristled. "I'm average height, thank you very much. Should we get down to brass tacks?"

Fenton spread his hands. "What do you want? Clearly it's not to take me in, or you'd have brought the pretty boy with you."

"Okay, I changed my mind. Shoot him," the archangel said. I almost smiled. I was the only person allowed to call him that, apparently. Instead, I kept my face blank. "We want to know if someone tried to fence the museum items stolen yesterday morning. We're prepared to make a generous offer if you cooperate."

"Oh? Have the archangels gotten so desperate that they would directly fund an illegal operation?" He folded his hands on the desk and tapped his thumbs together.

"I wouldn't put it that way. More like choosing the lesser of two evils."

"How so?"

I shrugged. "Well, they could either pay you, no muss, no fuss, or kidnap you and torture the information out of you."

Fenton tossed his head back, letting out a bark of laughter. "An angel? Torturing a demon? I'd like to see that."

"He keeps this up, and he might," Michael growled in my ear. I bit my lip to stop a second smile. The grumpy Peanut Gallery was not making this any easier.

"The offer's on the table. What d'you say?"

The demon dug his pinky finger inside his ear, giving me nothing but a cool look for a handful of seconds. "Well, my pockets are a bit light these days. Ten thousand bucks and I can give you what you need."

"Which is?"

"The occupation of the person who ordered the break-in. I'm not exactly in the know these days, but I do keep my ears open."

"So they didn't try to fence the weapons to you?"

"Nope. Didn't try with any other of the low level fencers in town either. They want the stuff here in Albany for a reason."

"And that would be…?"

He smirked. "Money first, *jou-chan*."

I scowled at the term. I'd watched enough anime to know what it meant—the equivalent of "young missy." I dug into my jacket for the already-signed check from Gabriel. I wrote in the amount and handed it to him. He took a moment to verify its validity and then spoke again.

"Word is that there's an archdemon in town. Not sure who yet. He or she has plans to bump off the pretty boy to give our side the advantage. All I know is they're a doctor."

"What kind of doctor?"

"Don't know. Don't much care. None of my business anyway."

"We just paid you ten grand for some vague crap that anyone could have said. You've gotta give me some kind of details."

Fenton's eyes narrowed and Michael chimed in. "Easy, Jor."

I tried again, keeping my voice level. "Is it Belial?"

"No. He's still down below after you and the angels smoked him."

Some of the tension in my back relaxed. I was safe for now. "Do you know when any of this is going down?"

"Before the week's out. I'd be careful if I were you, *jou-chan*."

"Thanks." I cocked my head to the side, murmuring into the mic. "Anything else you need me to ask?"

"No. That's good enough. Let's not test our luck."

I left the office, letting out a relieved sigh as I exited the shop. Michael met me at the food court and we headed outside into the cool night air.

"Is it really okay to pay off a demon? Sounds sketchy even to me."

Michael clucked his tongue. "O, ye of little faith. It's not a normal check. It's got a microchip with a tracker inside it. The second he goes back to his lair to store it with all his other ill-gotten gains, a strike team'll take him out. He won't go away forever because he's got good lawyers, but it'll keep him off the streets for a while."

"Impressive. So what now? All we've got is confirmation, no real details."

"I'll start digging to see what I can find on his doctor claim. In the meantime, we'll help Jacob cross over tomorrow."

"Busy week."

"Isn't it always?"

He nudged my shoulder, giving me a fond look. "You did good in there. Maybe you should've been a cop instead of a waitress."

"Nah. Outfit's too uncomfortable."

Michael raised his eyebrows in surprise. "When were you in a cop uniform?"

I flashed him my most mischievous smile as I flagged down a taxi to take us home.

"A lady doesn't kiss and tell."

Jacob was exactly where we'd left him when we got back to my apartment. His eyes found mine when I walked in the bedroom, tossing my jacket on the bedspread.

"Any luck with your memories?"

The boy shook his head. "Sorry."

I sat on the edge of the bed, grabbing the remote to turn off the TV. "Well, there's no rush. Hopefully we can get more things done in the morning. In the meantime, you're welcome to stay here."

He adopted a curious expression. "What will we do until then?"

"We'll make Michael read stuff to us."

With that, I turned to the angel who was currently giving me a dirty look. "Right?"

Michael smiled, but I could tell I'd annoyed him. "Why not?"

Inwardly cackling, I climbed onto the bed. Jacob hovered next to me, seeming interested in the books Michael removed from the bag.

"Any requests?"

"Hmm...why don't we start with the *Odyssey*?"

"Do you have *any* idea how long that is?"

"Guess you'd better get started then, huh?"

Defeated, Michael seated himself on the side of the bed and cracked open the book. I settled in, closing my eyes as he began reading. Some small part of me couldn't help but think: *I could get used to this.*

Thunder roared overhead, shaking the bedroom walls like an earthquake. Rain smacked the windowpanes and the glass trembled. They weren't the only things shaking in this room. Darkness pervaded every inch of my vision, but I could feel – and what I felt now was unlike anything else. Heat, firm skin, thin cotton sheets, and strong muscles.

Soft lips devoured my throat, climbing higher to the spot where my jaw met my ear. Strong arms wrapped around my back, holding me upright and pressing me against a man's smooth chest. His hands stroked the length of my spine. Shivers rolled down my skin. I buried my fingers in his hair. I couldn't see him, but something about his touch felt familiar. I wasn't afraid. In fact, I felt safer in his arms than I ever had in my entire life.

He grabbed my waist and rolled us over, crawling above me. His lips found mine in the dark and the kiss sent shuddering waves of pleasure down my body. My hands slid up to his shoulders and wrapped around the back of his neck. My thighs parted. Then, complete and utter bliss. Even without sight, we somehow moved together as one. Seconds before I reached the edge, lightning split the skies, giving me a brief glimpse of the man above me. Brown hair. Full lips. Green eyes.

Warmth brushed my cheek. I stirred, tilting my face away from it. It was probably just sunlight. Which meant it was morning. Boo.

I lay motionless on my left side, unwilling to move a muscle since my bed was so warm. Surely I could grab another hour or so of sleep. I curled my legs in a bit to get more comfortable, but frowned when I felt them touch something foreign. Not a book, which happened sometimes. This 'something' was warm and alive.

I cracked one eyelid open and found myself staring Michael in the face. He was lying next to me, eyes closed, with the book resting below his chin. That wasn't the most pressing thing, however. Sometime during the night I'd scooted closer, and his hand rested on the curve of my hip, almost possessively. Each time he exhaled, it spilled hot air across one side of my face. I stared at him for a minute,

trying to figure out how to react. Then the dream
rushed up to the surface of my mind like a tsunami. I felt
my entire body tense as I realized who the man in it had
been. *Son of a bitch.*

Michael made a small sound in the back of his throat
and opened his eyes, looking right at me. Neither one of us
moved. I ventured to fill the awkward silence first.

"Um. Hi?"

The archangel smiled in a sleepy fashion. "You
always know the appropriate thing to say in social
situations."

"I am human, after all."

"I keep forgetting," Michael said, sliding his hand
away from my waist as if it were nothing unusual. He
rolled over onto his back and yawned, stretching his tall
frame. I ignored the admittedly nice view and instead
forced myself to sit up, wondering where Jacob had gone.
The thought didn't last long, because all I could think
about was the fact that I just had an incredibly dirty dream
about an archangel and then woke up accidentally
cuddling with him.

"Jordan?"

"Huh-what?"

He gave me a confused look. "I asked if you were
hungry."

Apparently not for food, a little voice cackled in the
back of my head. I promptly told it to shut up and just
nodded. He stood and left the room in search of breakfast. I
watched him go and concluded that I was definitely going
to Hell.

The clock read half-past noon, confirming that we'd
stayed up for most of the night reading Homer. I couldn't
remember which one of us had fallen asleep first. That was
when it hit me.

I didn't have nightmares last night.

For a moment, I just sat there with my mouth
slightly agape. For the first time in two whole years, I'd

slept through the night without waking up bathed in sweat or crying. For the first time in two years, I hadn't needed the strong whiskey in my nightstand to help calm me down enough to rest. Why now? Was it because of Michael?

"Jordan?"

I glanced upward to see Jacob standing in the doorway. On reflex, I smiled at him so he wouldn't worry about how I had looked a second ago.

"Hey, kid."

"Is something wrong?" he asked.

"No, everything's fine. I think today we'll take you around the city to see if you recognize anything."

He nodded, and then wandered back towards the kitchen. I slid to the edge of the bed and stood, stretching. By now, my right hand no longer hurt and the stiffness in my neck had decreased significantly. I could feel the bandages beneath my shirt shifting as I moved. Michael would have to change them soon. That would be especially interesting after that vivid dream.

After choosing an outfit from my closet, I started to shove the hangers back towards the rear, but then my hand touched something covered in plastic. Strange. I hadn't gone to the dry cleaners in a while.

I pulled it out. It was Mr. N's duster. I thought I had lost in the alley when Belial attacked me. Pleased, I stripped off the plastic and ran my hands over the clean fabric, fingertips brushing over the places where the sleeves had been sewn back together. Something warm unfurled in my chest. Somehow, this was probably the nicest thing anyone had ever done for me.

Still, seeing it made me feel too vulnerable so I placed it back into the closet and gathered my undergarments to go take a bath.

Twenty minutes later, just when I finished putting my underwear on, I heard Michael knock on the door and open it before I could grab my robe.

"Hey, I—" He stopped in mid-sentence.

I picked up my robe from the floor and slid it on, facing him.

"Yes?"

"Jordan...your back. Why didn't you tell me?" He shut the door behind him and motioned for me to turn around.

I sighed, allowing the soft wool to slide down enough to expose my lower back. Along the base of my spine were faded brown scars—some long and thin like string, while others were thick and twisted like snakes. Michael hadn't seen them when he wrapped my chest because I'd made a point not to lower the robe enough for him to notice. I knew he'd ask about them.

"Belial didn't do this, did he?"

I shook my head. "No."

"Then who?"

My voice came out soft. "Aunt Carmen."

He took in a sharp breath. I shivered as his fingertips traced the nastier looking ones closer to my backbone. "She couldn't hit me where people might see. Didn't want someone to call the cops on her."

"Jordan..."

I shook my head and pulled the robe up, tying it. "No. I'm tired of talking about me. I want to hear something about you for once."

My eyes found the silver chain around his neck with the tiny padlock still intact. "When did you get that back?"

Michael seemed like he wanted to argue, but he merely sighed. "Raphael fixed it. He's always been good with his hands."

"Is he the one who sewed up my duster?"

"No, that was me. I figured you'd want it back, since he meant so much to you."

Again, a warm spot filled my stomach. How could he stand to be so sweet to me all the time? "Thank you. Seriously."

"You're welcome."

I gestured to the necklace. "Where did you get it?"

His green eyes flickered with an unknown emotion as he wrapped a large hand around the padlock, almost as if it were a reflex. "I bought it from someone not long after I lost my memory."

I sat down on the edge of the tub and motioned for him to continue. Michael grabbed the First Aid kit from the sink and pulled up the folding chair that had been pushed into the corner, rewrapping my chest as he told me the story.

Michael hated clothes shopping, but felt it was a necessary evil after the incident. The police had recovered his wallet and Visa card, meaning they'd also found where he lived. Turns out the same person who robbed him and knocked him out also emptied out his apartment. After a long call with the bank he got the identity theft straightened out, but that still left him needing to buy all new furnishings and clothes. He hadn't been able to find out where his substantial savings had come from since he didn't have a job yet. He assumed he was an orphan who had been left an inheritance and left it at that.

After getting turned around a couple times, he located the men's sections and started shifting through the endless sea of blacks, blues, and browns. The entire situation seemed humorously absurd. He had no clue who he was so what sort of clothing defined him? Jeans? Slacks? Shorts? Pin-striped suits?

"Can I help you, sir?"

He heard a female voice from behind him. A woman selling men's clothes. Well, of course. He prepared to tell her to leave him alone, but ended up rooted in the spot like a moron. This girl was flat-out gorgeous. He didn't even notice what she was wearing, because her smile blew the rational part of his brain right out the back of his skull. Dark brown hair, grey eyes, long lashes, smooth ivory skin – he wondered if it was even legal to let girls like her out in public.

After a moment he realized he hadn't answered her question, so he cleared his throat and offered her a smile. "You can start by not calling me sir."

She chuckled. "Sorry. I'm supposed to say that to everyone. What are you looking for?"

Michael threw up his arms. "To be honest, I have no clue. I'm supposed to be getting a new wardrobe, but I have no idea where to start."

"Well, don't worry. I'll definitely help you get there. My name is Diana."

She offered a slender, manicured hand. He shook it. "Michael."

No matter how many times he said it out loud, it felt weird to him. He supposed it was because he didn't have any physical recollection of someone saying his name: no mother, no father, no teasing children at school, no over-zealous big brother hanging the syllables over his head in an obnoxious way. It was just a name. Like he was just a man.

"Michael. I like that name. Were you named after anyone in particular?" She asked as she pushed aside a few suit jackets.

He brushed his fingertips against the sizeable bump on the back of his head.

"Honestly, I don't know."

"Well, there's your problem right there. How can you know where you're going when you don't know where you've been?"

Her question stopped him in his tracks. "What do you mean?"

"I'd have trouble trying to pick out a wardrobe too if I didn't know who I was already. I mean, think about it. The stuff that happens to our parents and to us when we're young are what make us what we are. Now, most people don't think there's much to a name, but I think it sets a sort of precedent." She tossed a couple of jackets over his arm. He watched her, enraptured as she continued to explain.

"There are some names that have a destiny like...Butch. With a name like that, you have to grow up to be a bodyguard or an athlete. Guys like Calvin and Theodore have to be those well-groomed guys in those sweater vests you see all the time. The Georges and Marks of the world have to be engineers and scientists or bankers and lawyers." Four dress shirts: two light blue, one black, one light green. She pressed three white into his hands before smiling that nuclear smile again.

"But you got lucky. Michael is one of those names that can mold to meet any need."

"How so?"

She shrugged, beckoning him to follow her to the pants section. "Think about all the Michaels in the world. You've got Michael Jordan, famous basketball player. Michael Jackson, King of Pop music. Michael Buble, fantastic crooner. Michael Phelps, Olympic bad ass. And if you want to forget about all the pop culture, there's what the name itself means."

"What's that?"

Diana handed him a pair of shoes, dropping her voice as if she were telling him a secret.

"God-like."

"That's a bit of a stretch for me, don't you think?"

She shrugged, grabbing two felt boxes with cufflinks in them and a silver necklace with a tiny padlock around it. "I don't know. If you're anything like God, then I certainly don't mind going to Heaven."

He laughed. "I think you're giving me way too much credit."

"Maybe so," she chirped. "Take these jeans and shirts and try it all on. See how everything fits and let me know when you're ready for check out." She gave him an encouraging push towards the changing room. A peculiar girl, to say the least.

Thirty minutes later, he had a respectable pile of clothes that fit and started counting out all the bills to pay for the stuff. Diana rang up the items with smooth, practiced movements, humming under her breath as she went. He didn't know the tune, but he knew it would probably stick with him for the rest of the day.

"Your total is $440.50."

He glanced back down at the money his hands. "I'm a little shy of that. Do you think you can take a couple things off?"

"Sure. What do you want to put back?"

"Maybe one of the cufflinks. The necklace too."

She pouted. "Oh, keep the necklace. I think it would look good on you. Besides, I think you need it."

"What makes you say that?"

She leaned in, running a fingernail across the shimmering silver. "Well, my mom told me people who don't know themselves can have their hearts stolen easily. This necklace has a padlock on it so it'll protect you. You'll always have a little reminder to keep your heart safe."

He smiled. "That's very corny, you know."

"I know."

"Alright, keep the necklace and ditch the cufflinks."

Pleased, she removed the items from the list and he handed her the money. She bagged everything for him and left the necklace out, surprising him by taking it out of its little velvet case and slipping it around his neck. She looked at the finished product with a satisfied grin.

"There. You're all set."

"Before I go, tell me something."

"Sure."

"What does your name mean?"

Her grey eyes widened, seeming luminous in the bright lights overhead. "I...don't actually know. I've never looked it up before."

"Oh? Alright, how about I come by tomorrow and I'll tell you what your name means? No cheating and checking online tonight."

She studied him for a good long while until he felt worried she would blow him off but she finally nodded. "Okay. My shift is over at six. Don't be late."

"I won't be. Thank you, Diana."

She winked at him before turning back around. "Have a nice day, sir."

I watched as Michael pulled away from me and closed the small, transparent box holding my First Aid supplies. "And? What happened when you came back the next day?"

Michael stood up and placed the kit back underneath my sink. "She wasn't there."

I frowned. "Why? You two seemed to have hit it off pretty well."

"She was killed in a hit-and-run the night before." His voice was so quiet I barely heard it over the sound of the water rushing from the faucet as he washed his hands.

I closed my eyes. "I'm sorry."

Michael shook his head, leaning forward to put the finishing touches on my bandages. "It's alright. I'm glad to have met someone like her at all, even if our time was short. Before then, I had no clue where I was going or what I was going to do. She helped me take the first step. That's why I don't judge humans as harshly as I once did."

"Although..." His eyes wandered down towards my back. "Sometimes it's hard to resist the urge."

"I can't imagine anything tempting you, Michael."

When he met my eyes this time, it felt different. I couldn't have explained it if someone asked me to but it just...*was*. For a couple of seconds, my view of Michael trickled from angel to human being all from one slight crinkle above his brow, a faint tilting of his lips downward, the quick bob of his Adam's apple in his throat, and an emotion in his sea-green eyes that had no business being there. Worse still, my fuzzy mind worried my own eyes reflected the same thing.

"You'd be surprised," he murmured, before straightening up so fast that I swayed a little in my seat. The trance shattered around us, and the tension crumbled with it. For now, anyway.

"You didn't tell me."

"Tell you what?"

"What does Diana mean?"

He paused in the doorway, his shoulders tensing. I thought about apologizing for prying, but as my lips parted so did his.

"Divine. It means divine."

He didn't give me a chance to reply, just cleared his throat and raised his voice to a more normal tone. "You need to eat. I can take Jacob around town today."

"I'm going with you."

He sighed, flashing me a weary look. "I thought we agreed you were going to take it a little easier since the hospital fight."

"Look, I appreciate the concern, but I'm healed to the point where I can walk around without pain or stiffness. Besides, you're going to need my insight on this one."

"I can handle this one. You've already done enough. I'm supposed to protect you and you almost got your head smashed in by a demon. You need to stay home and get better."

"I know what you're trying to do, Michael. I'm a big girl. I can't just hide here all day. I have a life. I have sins to atone for, even if your boss says my soul is freed. I have to hold myself accountable for what I've done."

Michael narrowed his eyes at me. "And what if Belial is standing on the other side of that door?"

At the mention of the demon's name, a cold shock went up my spine. The skin on the back of my neck tightened as if he were behind me, laughing that dry laugh in my ear. I steadied my breath and stood, stepping closer to Michael and giving him a challenging smile. "Well then, I guess it's a good thing that you'll be there to protect me."

Michael studied me for a long moment, seeming to realize the aggravating truth of my words. He reached up and unclipped the necklace from his neck, thoroughly confusing me. "I was right, you know. You are stubborn."

I merely shrugged. This time, it didn't hurt. Hurray. "It's one of my best—what the hell are you doing?"

He gripped my left arm and wrapped the necklace around it until the chain stretched tight across the skin of my wrist, leaving the padlock to hang down near my palm. He then lifted it up and kissed it. The combination of his warm lips and the cold metal made goosebumps pop up across my skin before I could yank my hand away.

"What was that for?"

"I put a special mark on the necklace. I can locate it no matter where I am. As long as you're wearing it, I know where you are."

I stared at him. "...did you just Lo-Jack me?"

"Maybe. Now come on. We've got work to do, remember?"

CHAPTER THIRTEEN

This is not good.

My fingers wrapped themselves into fists and clenched, digging my nails into my palm. Breath came in shaky gulps that I tried to hide by clenching my teeth. The vibrantly green grass looked awful soft and friendly between the frayed edges of my black Reeboks as I tried in vain to get control of myself. What, you may ask, spawned this particular panic attack? We followed Jacob through town until he found where he'd woken up.

In front of a psychiatric hospital.

Lovely.

Michael tugged me aside and blocked the view of the cheerful white sign indicating the name of the mental hospital. Not that it helped. "Jordan, look at me. Are you alright?"

"Yeah," I told him with a high, false laugh. "Doesn't everyone do their Lamaze breathing in front of an insane asylum?"

My joke didn't seem to make him feel any better. He gripped my upper arms and made me look up at his face. "You don't have to go in. You know that."

I shook my head. "My ghost kid. My job. I'll be fine, I swear."

"I don't believe you."

I unclenched one hand and patted him on the arm. "That's because you're smart."

Thankfully, the panic attack was only momentary. My breathing slowed. The cold sweat down my back evaporated. I felt the fear retreating into the depths of my mind.

Jacob had a worried look on his face, mirroring Michael's. "What's wrong?"

"Nothing, kiddo. We're fine. Now that we're at your site, are you remembering anything else?"

"Yes. There was a lady inside. She had dark hair and glasses. I remember seeing her."

"There must be a children's wing here, right? Do you think this woman is the reason you didn't cross over?"

Jacob's nose wrinkled in concentration as he tried to remember. "Maybe."

"Was she a doctor? A nurse? A secretary?"

The boy shook his head. "She was in a suit, not scrubs. I don't think she was a physician."

"Hospital management, sounds like. Alright, I need you to concentrate and tell me if she had any outstanding features."

Jacob closed his eyes and took a deep breath, remaining silent for a long moment before replying. "She was kinda pale...her hair was really long and curly...and she had a white name tag that said Dr. Vulcan on it."

"Vulcan?" I said in disbelief. "Eh, maybe she's a Trekkie. Good job, Jacob." I scribbled the name down on my notepad and squared my shoulders, facing the sidewalk leading up to the white and somehow ominous building.

"Let's find your doctor."

The receptionist at the bottom floor front desk was young—maybe seventeen or eighteen. Probably some kind of intern. She looked up at us through red bangs as we approached.

"How can I help you?"

"We were hoping to see if Dr. Vulcan was available today."

The girl turned to her computer and started typing away, blue eyes scanning the screen. "Do you have an appointment with her?"

"No. I was hoping you guys did walk-in appointments," I said. Trust me, I wasn't an expert on psychiatric hospitals, but if they were anything like clinics then we may have been in luck.

The redhead did some more reading before answering. "Actually, she's just finishing up rounds. I can send you up to her office if you'd like."

I breathed a sigh of relief. "Yes, that would be fantastic."

The receptionist took down information for both of us and pointed us to the left wing of the building. My shoulders wouldn't relax as I walked through the pristine hallways with men and women in lab coats brushing past me. Michael wordlessly slipped his fingers between mine. Part of me wanted to protest because I usually didn't like being touched, but I didn't say anything because it actually helped calm me down. His hand was solid and warm and real. I needed that right now.

Dr. Vulcan had a nice corner office with a rear view of the estate. We sat in the plush leather chairs in front of her desk. I tried to keep my leg from bouncing up and down from nervous energy, but I couldn't until Michael laid his hand on my knee for a brief moment. Jacob wandered around the room, staring at the towering bookshelves along the walls behind me. Even I had to admit they were impressive. How had she managed to cram so many medical books in there?

After a moment, a blonde woman appeared, catching our attention. "Excuse me, Dr. Vulcan has asked to meet you on the bottom floor. Exactly what kind of help are you looking for?"

Michael glanced at me and I nodded, indicating that I'd answer. "I have someone who might have been through here before—a little boy named Jacob."

The woman nodded. "Well, she might remember who that is. Her files of past patients are in that file cabinet right there. I can send someone to open them for you, but he will need your information to gain access."

I turned to Michael, murmuring. "You take the kid to see her. I'll stay here and stall in case she's not the right one for his final wish."

He stood. "Be careful."

I saluted him. Michael and Jacob went out into the hallway and the blonde lady promised that someone would come by to help me in a minute. After sitting back down, I closed my eyes and took slow breaths, reminding myself that this was a completely different hospital and nothing horrible would happen to me here. Michael would help the kid cross over and then we could go home — the light at the end of my panic-ridden tunnel.

"Miss Amador?"

I whirled around to see a tall man in an expensive black suit standing in the doorway. Even more impressive than his height was the long ebony hair he'd pulled back into a ponytail going down his back. Thick-rimmed glasses obscured the color of his eyes from me as he smiled.

"You need access to the files, right?"

"Uh, yeah." I said, walking over to the cabinet and preparing to lie through my teeth.

He reached into his pockets, searching for the keys. "Would you mind answering a question for me?"

"Sure."

"Does this smell like chloroform?"

Before I could move, he withdrew a white cloth and pressed it over my face. A muffled scream escaped me, but I knew it wasn't loud enough to attract anyone from the hall. The tall man calmly wrapped his arms around me to keep me still as the drug took effect. My body went weak and rubbery as I slipped into unconsciousness. For the second time in my life, a psychiatric hospital would be the death of me.

How poetic.

My head throbbed. It felt like my brain was trying to hammer its way through my skull and into the outside world. A pained groan crawled out of my throat and escaped my dry lips. As I regained consciousness, I realized I was lying on a bed of some kind. The mattress had way too many springs in it so they poked my spine like needles. My eyelids fluttered for a second and a wave of nausea hit. I pressed my palm to my forehead as if it would help. That was when I realized the necklace around my wrist was gone.

"Sleep well?"

I heard a purring baritone voice from the corner of the white room. My eyes shot open. Ignoring the nausea and dizziness, I frantically pushed myself up to a sitting position. There stood the longhaired man who came to unlock Jacob's files. He leaned his lanky frame against the far wall, smoking a cigarette. The black suit stood out stark against the pristine paint behind him.

I swallowed hard and tried to get a bearing on where I was. No windows. The door didn't have a knob, either. From what I could tell, this was either an operating room or somewhere they put the patients who were a threat to themselves or the hospital staff. It was also rather small — no more than an eight by eight foot room, not much bigger than the bathroom in my apartment.

The man continued to watch me with a cool expression. The eerie patience on his face made me realize I hadn't replied to his comment. As if I really knew what to say to the man who had just kidnapped me. I went for the casual approach.

"You're not allowed to smoke in hospitals."

He chuckled deeply enough to shake his broad shoulders. I took a moment to analyze his weight and strength. Could I take him? Most likely, no. Would I try it anyway? Hell yeah.

"You're right, I suppose. Still, I can't help loving these things." He flicked the cancer stick to the linoleum floor and stomped it out.

"Humans come up with the most wonderful things to destroy themselves with."

A red flag popped up in my mind. Please God, no. "Pardon?"

The man walked towards me and fear wormed its way up my stomach, settling in my chest. He had a heavy presence about him that confirmed my suspicion.

"I'm hurt, Jordan. You don't recognize me?"

My whole body tensed. He leaned over the bed until our faces were level, placing his arms on either side of me. I had to ball my hands into fists to keep them from trembling. I looked into his eyes. They were a chillingly blue hue with reptilian pupils. I'd seen them before.

"Belial."

He tilted his head to the side, and a sheet of that fine black hair slid across the side of his face. It brushed my cheek and made me flinch. "Did you miss me?"

"Not particularly." I hated how afraid my voice sounded.

The demon smiled in a way I imagine a snake would at a mouse. "I suppose not. There's no need for you to be scared of me this time. If I was going to kill you, I'd have done it while you slept."

I licked my lips, mind racing to think rationally. "Like I believe that. Killing me while I was unconscious wouldn't be any fun. You'd want to do it while I was awake and screaming, right?"

His sadistic smile widened. "My, my. We are getting to know each other, aren't we?"

"If you're not going to kill me, then would you mind getting the hell out of my personal space?"

"Why? Am I making you uncomfortable?" He tilted his head so that our lips were almost touching.

I took a deep breath, preparing to deck him if he dared kiss me. "No, I just hate that cologne you're wearing. My ex-boyfriend used to wear it."

Belial's eyes widened like I'd surprised him. He stood to his full height, letting out another one of those creepy chuckles. "You really are an interesting girl."

Now that I had my personal space back, the tension slid out of my rigid spine. I rested my feet on the floor. Whatever happened, I needed to be off this bed. It was clear that the demon had designs on my soul, but my body was a whole different issue. Better to play it safe. Or as safe as I could with a creature from Hell that wanted me to be his pet for all eternity.

"I aim to please," I said. "Now get to the point. If you're not going to kill me, what do you want?"

The smile remained intact, unnerving the hell out of me. He could give the Joker a run for his money with that thing. "The same thing I wanted before, my dear. Your soul."

I glanced around the bare room. "I don't see another spear lying around. How are you going to pull that off?"

"Persuasion." To my surprise, he began unbuttoning his suit jacket, revealing a cobalt blue dress shirt beneath it.

I lifted an eyebrow. "No offense, but nudity is not going to win me over."

Belial let out an amused snort after he tossed the jacket aside, rolling up the sleeves to the shirt. "As appealing as that sounds, that's not what I'm going to do. I thought I'd give you a fair chance to fight for your soul. If you win, I'll let you go. If I win, you agree to go through a ceremony that will bind us together for all eternity."

There it was. He had a trap, a plan, and I'd played right into it by coming to this hospital.

I stood and crossed my arms underneath my chest. "Do you honestly expect me to believe a demon would keep his word? What makes you think I'd agree to something like this?"

"Because, dear Jordan, you are running out of time." His voice made a cold and slimy feeling glide down my spine.

"What do you mean?"

"Right now, my associate Mulciber is torturing your sweet Michael with the weapons she stole from the museum. She intends to kill him. If you want any chance of saving him, you will play my game."

All the blood rushed out of my face. I knew that name. Mulciber, the demon in *Paradise Lost* who had been responsible for building Pandemonium. The last time I'd seen Michael, he had walked off with Jacob to see Dr. Vulcan. Had that been Mulciber? At the very least, it explained her strange last name. Mulciber and Vulcan were both the name of a Roman god. Figures. An archdemon would compare herself to a god.

Belial smirked. "Do we have a deal?"

I answered him with a right cross, which struck him straight in his smug mouth. He rose to full height and touched the blood on the corner of his lips. He licked it away — a slow, intimate gesture that made me shiver. It was a silent threat, a violent promise, a precursor to something truly terrible.

"I'll take that as a yes."

I let a hateful smile form on my lips, trying to contain my rage enough to remember my self-defense lessons. "You like pain, right? Come a little closer and I'll give you all you can handle, you son of a bitch."

The demon nodded. "I sincerely hope you will."

Belial had height, reach, and weight on me, so I knew there would be no point in attacking him first. I needed to use his body against him. That would be the only way I could beat him and get to Michael. Still, the longer we waited the closer, he came to death. The cold fingers of fear caressed my stomach, but I ignored them. I told myself he was an archangel who could handle himself.

Belial left his arms at his side and began to circle me. I kept my eyes on his posture, waiting for him to betray any kind of movement, and mirrored him to keep him in my line of sight. His left fist lashed out, aiming at my face. I parried it, forcing his arm downward and hitting him in the chin with the back of my fist. It hurt, but not nearly as bad as it would later, for both of us.

He rubbed the spot, amused. "Not bad."

In a flash, he aimed a high sidekick at the left side of my chest. I brought up my forearm and blocked it. Pain crackled down the side of my arm, but it was better than getting hit in the face. The blow knocked me off-balance, giving him the chance to knee me in the gut. Quickly, I blocked it and thrust my palm upward, aiming at his nose. His head snapped back, allowing me a couple crucial seconds.

I slammed my one fist into his solar plexus and hit him with a powerful roundhouse kick in the same place. He stumbled backward, clutching the spot and trying to breathe. I darted forward to finish him off with a two-handed hit, but at the last minute he grabbed my wrists and whirled, slamming me into the wall behind him. The back of my head hit, stunning me. In an instant he pinned my hands, and stared down at me with a patronizing look.

"Give up?"

"Not hardly," I spat, sliding my right leg forward. I kneed him in the crotch. He hissed, loosening his grip on my arms. While he was distracted, I shoved my foot into his stomach and pushed him away, ignoring the painful bump I could feel rising on my skull.

Belial let out a rush of breath and nodded in my direction, seeming impressed.

"It seems I underestimated you, Jordan."

I shrugged one shoulder. "A lot of people do that."

"Very well. Perhaps I should treat you as an equal."

Uh oh. I didn't like the sound of that.

Belial unbuttoned his shirt a little more. "You do realize that I could just threaten everyone you've ever loved. I could make some grand speech about how they would die in horrible fashions: torn apart, drowned, strangled, stabbed. But that wouldn't work on you, would it?"

I focused on his seemingly harmless movements, waiting for the inevitable attack. "No, it wouldn't. There's no reason to think you wouldn't just kill them anyway after you have my soul."

Belial nodded, fixing me with his predatory gaze. "Exactly. So that argument would be useless to pursue. However, there is the question of Michael."

As soon as he spoke his name, I felt another wave of worry roll through me. How many minutes had we wasted? Where was he? Or was Belial just bluffing?

The demon moved so fast that I almost didn't see it. Left jab, right cross, uppercut, left hook. I moved in close so some of them would miss, trying not to make a sound as his knuckles grazed my upper arms. Before I could add space between us, he kneed me in the stomach and slammed his forearm into my back. I hit the floor. I stayed there for a second, trying to block out the pain.

"Do you see how weak he makes you?" Belial said with a sigh. "The mere mention of his name and your defenses drop. I find it rather upsetting, don't you?"

Once I could breathe again, I pushed up from the ground and faced him.

"What are you getting at, demon?"

He came at me again, this time trying to trip me. I let my body fall backwards and went into a back roll, coming up on my knees. He kicked at my face and I blocked, grabbing his foot to throw him off-balance. Mistake. He executed a perfect kick to the side of my head with his other foot. I managed to move mostly out of the way, but it still connected, knocking me onto my stomach again. I'd have a nasty bruise on my face if I got out of this mess alive, not to mention I'd accidentally bitten my tongue.

Belial knelt in front of me, watching patiently as I tried to shake off the pain.

"Deep down, you know what I'm talking about. You know that if you join me you will never have to worry about another person again."

I spat out a mouthful of blood. "What are you talking about?"

"I know you worry about the people at your job, your waitress friend, even your horrible aunt. You fear they will be targets because of your ability as a Seer. As much as you try to feel nothing, you are a compassionate woman, Jordan. You can never truly forget about them."

"You don't know shit," I growled, standing abruptly. I knew it was stupid to try to catch him off-guard but I didn't have much of a choice. He was wearing me out little by little, and time was slipping away as he talked. I poured it on with all my energy, using my agility to drive him backward. He blocked my blows with ease, acting as though he were humoring me.

"I know more than you think, my dear. Just as I know that you've figured out what's going to happen at the end of this fight."

Belial caught my right arm and punched me in the stomach. My body crumpled forward, leaving me almost limp in his grip. Pain exploded through my entire midsection and straight down my legs like bolts of lightning. He flung me backwards onto the bed and held my arms down, staring into my contorted face. He sighed and watched me writhe beneath him as if disappointed.

"You knew when you first hit me that it would end up this way, and yet you still fought. You foolishly reasoned that you could beat me even though you know I am five times stronger than you are. Why is that, Jordan?"

"Go to Hell," I managed to hiss through gritted teeth.

Belial grinned. "Still stubborn, I see. I'll let you in on a little secret."

He leaned down until his lips were level with my ear, making me shudder as his hot breath touched my skin. "There is a part of you that wants to give in to me. It was there when we first met in your dream, and it is still there even now. You may think me a monster, but if you were honest with yourself you would realize that my monstrosity just might be that thing you have been searching for. How long do you think you can hide the darkness of your soul from the archangel? How long before he realizes the sin you carry in your heart is not worthy of his love?"

The weight of his words made me feel raw and empty inside. In his own sick way, he was telling the truth. Just hearing it made me feel ashamed of myself. I shook my head, trying to free my arms from his vise-like grip, but it was useless. "And I suppose you're any better? I've read the Bible, Belial. Spoiler alert: you lose. So I'd rather let you beat the crap out of me than give you my soul."

His voice came out a whisper. "Even if I could help you find out about your mother?"

I froze. Belial lifted his face mere inches above mine, waiting for me to react.

"What about my mother?"

"You have spent your whole life loving her, and yet you know nothing about the last days of her life. If you agree to be mine, I will help you find out the truth about her and about the unfortunate man who saved your life. Isn't that what you want, Jordan?"

He sounded so terribly convincing. I slowly realized that I actually wanted to believe him. I knew that Michael and Gabriel had orders not to tell me about Mr. N, but maybe, just maybe, this demon knew about the both of them. Was the truth about my mother worth my soul?

I took a deep, slow breath and met those pale blue eyes. "What exactly would happen if I agreed to this ceremony?"

Something inhuman slid across his face. I'd seen desire before, and this seemed like a dark cousin of the feeling. For the first time, I truly noticed the demon beneath the handsome exterior, and it frightened me down to my core. His hands relaxed on my arms a bit, signaling the fact that he thought he'd finally gotten to me.

"It's quite simple. Just as your Michael can mark things, so can I. We would exchange blood and you would pledge your soul to mine. You will be my servant and I will be your master."

Belial lifted one hand and cupped my chin in a surprisingly tender gesture, his voice dropping to a seductive tone. "And believe me, it does not come without certain pleasures."

He kissed me and I let him. His mouth was hot and tasted faintly of blood, both mine and his—somehow just like I thought a demon would taste. After a moment or two, I broke from his rose-petal-soft lips enough to speak.

"If I do this, will you let Michael go?"

He dropped his mouth to my throat, kissing the skin as he began to unbutton my blouse. "The archangel is no concern of mine. He and Mulciber are on the basement floor where there are no cameras. It seems we both got what we wanted."

"Seems so," I murmured, shivering as he spread the cloth away from my chest. He tore off the bandages one by one, leaving little stinging patches on my chest. His eyes found the mound of scar tissue where the spear had stabbed me. Belial ran his fingertips over the stitches, tracing them down my bare stomach. He lowered his face and then his lips followed the line his fingers made while he unbuttoned his own shirt, exposing more ivory skin. He licked my navel slowly and then rose up enough to look me in the eye again.

"Is this everything you wanted?"

"Not quite," I whispered, trailing one hand down to the clasp of the bra. He watched hungrily. My fingers closed around the item tucked within the cup. I withdrew Gabriel's feather from the inside of my bra and stabbed Belial in the chest.

He screamed as it seared his skin, burning as if I'd placed a red-hot poker against him. I slammed my knee into his side so that he rolled off the bed and fell with him, landing on the floor astride his waist. He convulsed below me, writhing with pain and cursing me with every breath he could draw.

"Tell me how to get out of this room or I'll burn you alive," I demanded, shoving the feather in deeper for emphasis.

He cried out, gasping for air. "Lying bitch!"

I spared him a mean little smile. "I learned from the best. You weren't going to hold up your end of the bargain anyway, right?"

He glared up at me, his large hands closing around my waist and squeezing to the point of bruising. "I should kill you."

I jabbed him in the chest again. He growled in pain, letting me go. "Likewise. Now tell me."

"Keycard…in my left pocket…" he ground out.

"Move one inch and I'll shove this thing right out the other side of you."

I lifted up enough to slide my left hand into his pocket and found a keycard. Surprise, surprise. Demons were really honest when you threatened to burn holes through their chests.

"Stay on the floor. If you try to attack me, I'll make sure it stays in you this time."

I kept a careful eye on him as I removed the tip of the angel feather and stood up, making sure he didn't follow me. I slid the keycard through the slot next to the door and it popped open with a click. Belial spoke just before I opened it all the way.

"You just proved my point, you know," he rasped, pushing up on one arm to fix me with a spiteful stare. "Your soul is as black as mine and you know it."

I glanced at him over my shoulder enough to send him an ice-cold stare. "I'll learn to live with it."

I closed the door behind me and didn't look back.

CHAPTER FOURTEEN

The basement floor was cold, damp, and empty. I had to swipe the keycard in the elevator just to get to it. Like I'd thought, there were hall closets and places used for storing medical supplies and patient files, but no one was on the floor except for me. It did not bode well.

However, I could hear some kind of commotion at the end of the hall coming from the last room to the right. The walls were concrete and hadn't been painted over, so they were dark grey, almost like a dungeon. My skin sang with tension as I crept closer to the room. I could hear something and it sounded like...chains.

The door was like the one I had encountered with Belial. Only a key card could open it. This one had a window, though. Dim white light poured outward. Well, I hadn't come all the way down here for nothing. Better take a quick look.

I pressed my right side into the door and slowly lifted up enough to see inside. What I saw made my mouth go dry.

Michael was chained to the far wall with what looked like the restraints used on patients in a hospital, except they were crusted over with some sort of red substance that may have been blood. His shirt had been torn off and deep gouges covered his formerly perfect skin. From here, I could see his bloody lip and a bruise marring his left cheek. God in Heaven, what had happened to him?

Just then, I heard a woman's voice so I eased over until I could see the opposite side of the room where Mulciber stood. She was breathtakingly beautiful, or would have been if she didn't have a completely sadistic expression on her pale face. Her smile was toothy and her eyes held the kind of malice you only saw in horror flicks. She wore a cream-colored tank top and navy skirt. Pretty good fashion sense for a psychopathic monster. Still, the thing that bothered me most was the object in her hand that looked like a hand-held sickle.

Mulciber hummed as she walked toward Michael, her lipstick glimmering as red as the blood on his chest. "Know where this one's from?"

Her voice was thick with a French accent. Michael summoned enough strength to spit in her direction. She clucked her tongue, shaking her head.

"You have such bad manners for an angel, *mon ami*. Anyway, this little number is responsible for forty-three deaths in Scotland—ten of which were children. They say every drop of blood it spilled is still soaked into the handle. It goes for about $20,000 on the market. Think it'll be more or less effective than the blade before it?"

Michael glared at her. "Enjoy it while it lasts, demon. It only makes Judgment Day that much sweeter when we wipe your wretched kind from this world."

Mulciber chuckled—a malevolent sound that gave me the creeps even through the metal door. "Your kind is so confident about the end of this war. It won't much matter if you win in the end. I promise you, archangel, that you will not leave this place alive."

He let out a bitter laugh. "I find your lack of faith disturbing."

She batted her eyelashes at him, lifting his chin with the curved part of the blade.

"Nonsense. I have faith in plenty of things. Like your little human pet, for instance."

Michael's eyes widened. "What are you talking about?"

"You silly fool. She's listening to every word we say. Isn't that right, *ma cherie*?"

The door whooshed open, spilling me onto the floor in front of them. Shit. I lay there for a second, cursing my carelessness while the demon laughed.

"I'm glad you could join us."

I pushed to my feet and balled my hands into fists, murmuring to Michael. "I'm sorry."

Michael didn't speak to me, instead addressing Mulciber. "She has nothing to do with this, demon. Let her go."

"Oh, but she does, dear Michael." Mulciber stalked towards me, placing a long-fingered hand on my shoulder.

"I've been trying all this time to get your little boyfriend to show me his wings, but he just won't cooperate. Perhaps you can provide him with some incentive."

She twirled the sickle in her hand. I suspected it was meant to intimidate me. Boy, was she in for a surprise.

"Sorry, but he hasn't shown them to me either. Looks like neither one of us are worthy."

"Oh, what a pity. I guess we'll just have to keep trying." She slid away from me and brought her arm up to slash him, but I called out to her first.

"What would it cost me to keep you from killing him?"

She paused, tilting her head at me in question. "Cost, *ma cherie*?"

"Everything with you demons seems to be about gaining something. What can you gain from killing Michael?" It was a dumb question but I had to buy us some time. She didn't know I had the feather, but I would have to get close to use it. If I tipped her off, she'd tear me to pieces. Either way, I wasn't about to let her cut him again. Not on my watch.

"Why, one less soldier to fight the war for good," Mulciber said casually as if she were describing the weather and not the destruction of God's Army. "With Michael gone, a less experienced angel will have to lead the forces. There can't possibly be a thing you possess that is worth more than that."

"So you're like Belial, huh? Just one thing in mind?"

She snorted. "Please. Belial is the most shortsighted of us. You see how easily I made a deal with him to get the angel while he just went for your pathetic little soul. I'll never understand why."

"Because I killed Mr. N."

Mulciber blew a lock of curly hair off her forehead, seeming bored. "Mr. Who?"

"The Seer who worked for God on Earth. Six foot two, black hair, blue eyes, scars on his hands, face, and neck. I killed him two years ago."

Her brown eyes expanded. "*You* did that?"

I nodded. A shiver ran up her body, ending in a long exhale. "*Ma cherie*, I could kiss you. That man was such a pain in my *derriere*. I met him at the psychiatric hospital in Jersey all those years ago. Part of me regrets never getting the chance to tear his lungs out and watch him suffocate."

The breath in my lungs evaporated. I managed to choke out, "Jersey?"

"*Oui*. You see, I am a traveling psychiatrist. I go from place to place and corrupt as many souls as I can in these hospitals because all they ever need is one little push. In Jersey, I had finally gotten my hands on a Seer, but that man came to visit and tried to keep her out of my clutches. I had been in charge of finding one in order to complete the abduction of an angel's body, but because he intervened, I lost her. What ever was that poor woman's name?"

"Jordan, don't," Michael whispered, his worried eyes fixed on my shaking shoulders.

"Catalina Amador."

Mulciber stared at me. "How did you know that?"

"She was my mother."

Michael shut his eyes and hung his head. Mulciber's face lit up with a fantastic smile. She clapped her hands together as if I had just told her Christmas was coming early this year. "I cannot imagine anything more wonderful than this! I have killed the mother of an archangel's human pet. Can it really get any more delicious?"

"Yes," I whispered, reaching a hand towards the surgical tray behind me where a machete lay. "It can."

She was standing too close to me to dodge as I snatched up the weapon and swung at her head. In my fury, I'd aimed high, at her smirking face — a foolish mistake that would certainly cost me. She froze, her wild black tresses hiding her features for a second, and then slowly turned back towards me. The tip of the machete had cut into her right cheek, leaving a trail of crimson down her chin that splashed onto her neck and collarbone. She now wore a thoughtful expression as she touched the wound, and then glanced at me.

"You are bold, Seer. Foolish, but bold."

I gripped the machete's worn wooden handle, my strength renewed at the thought of murdering this filthy creature with my own hands. "I get that a lot."

Mulciber lowered her stained fingertips, eying me. "Are you challenging me, *ma cherie*?"

Behind me, Michael struggled against his bonds to no avail, his voice an urgent hiss. "Jordan, don't—"

"You bet your ass I am," I shot back, ignoring him. I didn't need to hear a warning. I knew what I was about to do was stupid and pointless, but I hadn't come all this way to leave my mother's murderer in one piece nor would I allow this demon to kill the man who had taken such good care of me.

She twirled the sickle again. "Are you saying you are willing to die to defend the archangel?"

"It's not exactly on my To Do list, but yeah. I am."

She smiled then, seeming satisfied with my answer. "Very well. I will allow you the chance to die for your angel."

"Mulciber, let her go. You have what you want. You don't need to do this," Michael interrupted as she sank into a ready stance with her weapon.

She chuckled. "You're sweet, *mon ami*, but it's too late. Her fate is out of your hands."

I saw her high-heeled foot take one step forward and then she disappeared.

Seconds later, I felt her breath on the nape of my neck and the sharp pain of the sickle slicing down my back. I cried out, whirling and swinging the machete. She ducked my blow, kicking me in the stomach. I slammed against the opposite wall, smearing blood across it like a sickening mural. She could have killed me with that swing, but she didn't. She wanted to play with me, just like Belial, but this wasn't for keeps. She didn't have a fifth grade crush on me — she wanted to wear me down and tear me apart while Michael watched, helpless, powerless, and miserable. But I'd chosen this path. I wasn't going to die with a whimper, but a roar.

I pushed away from the wall, blocking out the pain from my injured back. Luckily, she hadn't sliced all the way through my shirt, but it was mostly trashed, exposing the scars. I'd have a new one if I made it out of this mess in one piece.

Mulciber wiped my blood off of her sickle, waiting for me to come to her. "You must tell me how it feels, *ma cherie*."

"How what feels?"

As soon as the last word left my mouth, I leapt for her, swinging. She blocked and I aimed a kick at her kneecap, but she spun around behind me. I turned again, bringing the machete up to block her next blow. My knees buckled under the strength of the hit, but they still held.

She smirked down into my face, still calm, still evil, still waiting. "To know that you are going to die and that God has the power to save you, but chooses not to. It must be excruciating."

I pushed her away from me with the weapon, pleased when the tip of the machete slashed a hole in the bottom of her blouse. Still didn't reach flesh, but at least I'd hit something.

"That's where we're different, demon. I don't lament the fact that He won't intervene. I dealt with that when I was a little girl."

"Then why do you fight? Why do you give your life for their side when they have allowed you to suffer as you have?"

"Because I know deep down that one day their side is going to send you packing with your tail tucked between your legs," I sneered.

She narrowed her eyes. I'd managed to bruise her ego. Bully for me. "That is going to cost you."

She attacked. I could barely keep up with her movements, frantically blocking as many slashes and hacks, wincing as sparks bounced off my skin. She aimed low and sliced into my right thigh. I managed not to cry out this time, instead using the opening to shove the machete into her left shoulder.

She gasped, shocked that I'd injured her, and grabbed the blade to yank it out, cutting her hand in the process. I backed off, circling behind her with a slight limp. Hot blood ran down my injured leg. I started to feel faint. She hadn't punctured my femoral artery, thank God, but I could tell the cut was deep. I wouldn't last long in this state. I needed to end this. She was still too far away to reach. If I ran at her with the feather, she'd run me through in a heartbeat. I'd have to lure her in somehow.

"I commend you, Seer," Mulciber said, her voice now cold rather than mocking. "No human has ever managed to injure me twice." She switched the sickle to her right hand, leaving her left arm motionless.

"I have grown tired of playing with you. Say goodbye to the archangel."

I couldn't help glancing at Michael. Through the fight, he had been watching with growing panic in those sea-green eyes. I felt rather selfish for making him be a witness to my death a second time. I could only hope he'd forgive me for my actions. However, something changed when he met my gaze. Mulciber stood only a few inches in front of him, and I understood what was about to happen seconds before it did.

Michael shoved both feet into the demon's back, catching her off-guard and catapulting her towards me unguarded. I didn't hesitate. I shoved the machete through her ribcage, beneath her right breast. She went rigid, choking. I twisted the blade a little, making sure I hit something vital.

"You were saying?"

Then, all at once, she smiled toothily at me and grabbed me by the throat. "Almost, but not quite."

I gagged as her pale, steely fingers cut off my air supply. She lifted me and shoved me against the far wall. My feet dangled inches off of the floor, my body weight making me suffocate even faster. She grabbed the machete with her left hand and yanked it out, splashing blood over us both, and let it clatter to the floor.

"I'm impressed, *ma cherie*. You and the angel are almost of a single mind. Too bad it is not enough to save you. All your faith is in vain."

The world had started to go black around the edges, but one word rang clear through my mind. Faith.

With one hand, I grabbed the demon's wrist, distracting her attention as I managed to wheeze out one thing.

"Faith is the substance of things hoped for and the evidence of things not seen. Tell me if you saw this coming, *ma cherie*."

I withdrew Gabriel's feather from my back pocket and slammed it into Mulciber's chest. She screamed in pain, dropping me and crumpling to the floor. I should have demanded that she let Michael down but I didn't. I just kept digging the feather in deeper and deeper, watching her squirm with relish. She tried to claw at my arms, but I couldn't even feel the scratches. I wanted her to burn in fires hotter than any Hell. I wanted her to feel every second of pain she had caused me and my mother and Michael and the man I'd never known. Burn, baby, burn.

Her eyes rolled back into her head and that was when I knew she was dead. Her chest was a ruin of black where the feather had burned clear through to the bone, evaporating the space where her heart should have been. I leaned down until my mouth was level with her ear and whispered:

"*Vaya con Dios*, bitch."

I tucked the feather back into my pocket and limped over to Michael, who wore a grim expression on his face. I found a stool in the corner and picked up the sickle. I used it to saw through the chains connected to the blood-soaked restraints, talking to distract myself from the horror of what I'd just done.

"What are these things? Why can't you get free?"

"Demon's blood. She sacrificed one of her underlings to make them. Demon blood is one of the most powerful substances on earth. Even this body can be trapped by it. Only demons and full-blooded humans can break through the bonds, not angels."

Finally, I sliced through the second restraint and he fell, leaning his back against the wall for a moment to regain his strength. "How did she manage to trap you?"

"I was told she would meet us in the basement. Just as the elevator doors opened, I felt the presence of an archdemon. That's when he attacked me from behind with the restraints and Mulciber dragged me down the hall into this room."

I frowned. "He? Who's he?"

Michael's face got very cold. "Why don't you ask him yourself?"

He slipped his arm around my waist and then closed his eyes, concentrating on something I couldn't see or hear. A great wind rushed through the room like we were at the center of a hurricane. It blew so hard that the stool in front of me clattered over on its side and went flying. To my surprise, it hit something invisible before finally smacking the far wall. Seconds later, Jacob faded into view with a sullen look on his face.

"That's not fair!" he cried, glaring at Michael.

I glanced between the two of them with shock. "What's going on?"

"Jacob isn't a ghost. He's a malevolent poltergeist masquerading as a ghost. He was hired by Mulciber and Belial to lure us here," Michael explained.

My jaw dropped. "But he's just a kid, I mean…why? Why would you do something like that, Jacob?"

The boy's face thinned out in anger, making him seem less like a child and more like a monster. "Why? Because human beings are the worst things in this world and in any world!"

"What are you talking about? I don't see how we could be any more ruthless than the demon you just helped try to *murder* someone," I spat.

Jacob's eyes narrowed. "When I was eight, my father murdered my mother right in front of me. He didn't care about anyone but himself. I loved her more than anything in the world and he just took her from me like it was nothing! The cops didn't believe my story so I waited until they all left and killed him in his sleep but it wasn't enough. It would never be enough for what I lost. I dedicated the rest of my life to getting back at humanity. They put me in foster homes and I killed those parents one after the other and made it seem like someone else did until some stupid housewife got lucky and pushed me down the stairs right before I could off her. My soul didn't pass over because I still want to cause as much pain and suffering as my father caused me. Does that answer your question?"

Christ. I'd met some pretty horrible people recently but this kid took the cake. That story had gushed out of him like blood, as if he'd been hoping to bring it up because he hated us so much. "So I guess you don't ever intend to cross over to one world or the other?"

"Not if I can help it," the poltergeist sneered, reaching for the sickle I'd dropped. Before I could move, Jacob ran at us.

I tensed for a fight, but Michael held out his left hand and spoke one word.

"Enough."

Jacob stopped only inches from us. Fear widened his eyes as his body began to fade away as if he were made of sand that the wind was blowing away. "W-What's happening to me?"

"I can't send you to Hell and I can't send you to Heaven," Michael said. "There's a place for souls who take advantage of their lives after death. It's called Purgatory."

Jacob thrashed and shouted curses at us in midair, but eventually his screams died down and he disappeared from sight.

"Geez," I mumbled, shivering. "Is he gonna be there for all eternity?"

"No. When Judgment Day arrives, he and all the other souls trapped there will be judged just like the rest of humanity."

"Maybe by then he won't be so angry."

He didn't reply. Instead, Michael moved closer, encircling me with his arms.

I stiffened, confused. "Michael, what...?"

"Shh," he whispered. "I'm sorry."

"For what?"

"Everything."

For some reason, the quietness of his voice and the simplicity of that one word made all the horrible events in my life come rushing back to me at once. I wrapped my arms around his neck and felt every ounce of fear, sadness, and anger that I'd brushed off in order to be strong enough to escape Belial.

For the first time in two years, I cried. I cried for my mother, I cried for the man I'd killed, I cried for Michael, and I cried for the life I'd never have. My legs wouldn't support my weight any more so we sunk to the floor. Michael said nothing, simply holding me. I couldn't remember how long we sat there, but he never let go as long as we did. Thank God for him.

Then, gradually, the tears stopped. Maybe it had happened because I hadn't truly dealt with any of what had been done to me recently, but I was glad to be done with it. Relief poured in around me like warm water— relief that I was alive and had saved the man I could arguably consider to be my best friend. I took a deep shuddering breath and lifted my head, wiping my face clean and smiling at the angel in front of me.

"If you ever tell anyone I cried in front of you, I'll make you wish you were never born."

Michael smiled back. "Your secret's safe with me. Seems like you saved my life again."

I shrugged, clearing my hoarse throat so I wouldn't sound like Carol Channing any more. "At least I didn't get stabbed in the chest this time."

He brushed his fingertips over the fresh bruise where Belial had kicked me. "At least."

"So does this mean you owe me?"

"I suppose so. What did you have in mind?"

"Can I...see your wings?"

Michael nodded, his voice gaining a little humor. "I think you may be worthy of it now."

He closed his eyes in concentration, and then the air around us stirred. His wings sprouted from his back and stretched nearly from one wall to the other. I could only stare in awe. They were beautiful. Gabriel's wings had a golden sheen over the white. Michael's shone as if someone had mixed silver and pearl together to create a new color.

"Michael, they're...amazing," I murmured. I resisted the urge to touch one just to make sure it was real, but I felt that might have been a little too intimate a gesture.

"Thank you," he said. When I looked back at him, I noticed our faces were far too close together and that my hands were still resting on his shoulders. That strange tension from before returned in full force, making me far more aware of his body and how we were sitting than I should have been.

"Jordan?"

"Hm?"

"I'm going to have to owe you another favor."

"For what?"

"This." He tugged me forward enough to kiss me. I should have been shocked and appalled. I wasn't. Everything that had been wrong with Belial's kiss seemed to have been righted by Michael's. His lips were soft and full and warm. He kept it chaste, no tongue, but made up for it by gently drawing my bottom lip between his and sucking. It couldn't have lasted more than a handful of seconds yet I felt time slipping into oblivion. My fuzzy brain tried to come up with a comparison of what he tasted like. I could think of no other word than euphoria.

Michael drew back first and rested his forehead against mine. I caught my breath and licked my lips, trying to summon enough strength to talk.

"You're going to get in big trouble for that, huh?"

"Definitely."

"Worth it?"

"So worth it."

With that, he grinned and stood up, offering me his hand.

"Let's go home."

CHAPTER FIFTEEN

"You two just can't stay out of trouble, can you?" Raphael sighed as he inspected the nasty bruise on my forehead.

I shrugged. "No good deed goes unpunished."

"Obviously. You've gotten in more trouble in one week than I've been in for a hundred years," Gabriel mused as he dabbed a cotton ball doused with rubbing alcohol on Michael's cuts. He didn't seem to find it painful, but maybe he was just being manly about it. Figures.

"Just lucky, I guess."

"Better lucky than smart," Gabriel said. I stuck my tongue out at him and he chuckled.

"I suppose we should thank you for at least getting rid of Mulciber for a while. There's no sign of Belial, either."

I froze. "Does that mean Michael has to leave?"

Silence fell. Michael's face was blank, but I noticed that his shoulders tensed just a bit.

Gabriel spared me a faint smile. "Normally, yes. However, considering you've angered Mulciber I think it's safe to say you'll still be needing his protection."

"Oh. Right." I felt a flush of heat across my cheeks. If Raphael or Gabriel noticed, neither of them said anything. Fabulous.

"That's two demons in one city. Maybe you need to move, Jordan," Michael said, his eyes sparkling as they met mine.

"Please. I'm not going to let two measly archdemons run me out of town. There'd have to be at least…four."

Raphael finished cleaning and treating my wounds, patting my shoulder. "With your luck, it'll probably happen."

He grinned as I glared at him. "Thanks for the confidence boost, Raph."

"My pleasure. Almost finished, brother?"

"Yes. He's got a hard head, after all," Gabriel replied.

Michael rolled his eyes. "If you have something to say, just say it already."

Gabriel finished wrapping the gauze around his chest and put it back in the First Aid kit before standing. "Be careful. That's all."

"I'm pretty sure we won't get in anymore fights any time soon," Michael told him, rubbing his bruised cheek with a rueful expression.

Gabriel's blue eyes twinkled. "I wasn't talking about fighting."

We both stared at him with wide eyes, but he merely nodded to both of us and followed Raphael out of my bedroom without saying another word.

The awkward silence started to grow so I sighed and flopped down on the bed with a groan. My eyes fell across Michael's neck—now noticeably empty.

"I'm sorry Belial took the necklace. I know it was important to you."

The angel shook his head. "It...couldn't be helped."

"Can you sense where he put it?"

"Not really. It's out of range. He must have thrown it away. Don't worry about it."

I paused. "But doesn't that mean you don't have anything to protect your heart any more?"

He met my eyes, a slow smile touching his lips. "Guess I'll have to risk it."

The eye contact felt far too intimate. I had to glance away. "Well, we're certainly not going anywhere for a while. Want to do some reading?"

"I had something else in mind," Michael said, sitting next to me. I swallowed, trying very hard to keep my mind out of the gutter.

"And that is...?"

He held up a DVD case. *A Walk in the Clouds*. Oh, thank Heaven. "Your less-than-subtle best friend Lauren insisted we should watch it."

I shrugged. "Eh. Put it on."

Michael got up and turned the TV and DVD player on while I stared at everything in the room except his rather muscular bare back. No sense in being immature. So we'd kissed. Big whup. Didn't mean I was going to act like a fifth grader about it.

I nearly yelped as Michael turned the lights off and crawled next to me.

"Just so you know," I said in a mild tone. "That kiss was a one time thing."

"Really? That's too bad, 'cause I have something for you."

Surprised, I couldn't help but glance over at him. He leaned across me, his face drifting dangerously close to mine. Instead of kissing me, he reached for something on the nightstand and brought it up to my face. It was a caramel apple.

"You're welcome," he murmured with a secretive smirk. Slowly, I took the apple and unwrapped it, bringing the delicious treat to my lips.

"Bite me."

Michael was strongly reprimanded for what was described as "fraternizing" with a human being. The Big Guy let him off with a warning since we didn't go past first base and it was understandable that we were both incredibly vulnerable at that point. Gabriel and Raphael knew about it afterwards and didn't make a fuss, but I sometimes caught them smiling at us without saying anything. I decided to just let it slide. Shit happens, whether it's demons having designs on your body or angels stealing smooches. It's not a part of life — it's just a part of *my* life.

However, there was a bit of good news to come from our messy business at the hospital. Gabriel got a tip from a demon stoolie that Mulciber and Belial wouldn't be returning to Earth for a period of time. Their boss was rather ticked off that neither of them were able to complete their missions. Mulciber didn't kill Michael and Belial didn't secure the Spear of Longinus. I personally found the thought comforting, but not after Gabriel reminded me this would only further their desire for revenge once they finally returned to this world. I enrolled myself in a riflery class as well as a martial arts one to get better skills for my next grudge match with Belial, assuming he has enough chivalry to challenge me to a duel again.

It turns out that Jacob had been able to enter my apartment because Gabriel hadn't made the blessing of my apartment specific to spirits, just demons. He refined it as soon as we told him what happened and apologized for not being careful enough. I tried to convince him it wasn't his fault, but I got the feeling he didn't believe me, God bless his heart. We were even anyway. He'd been the one who told me years ago that demons were susceptible to the feathers on an angel's wings because they were so pure that it burned them. I owed Gabriel my life and aimed to find a way to make it up to him someday.

Michael started training me in some of the arts Mr. N had been practicing like how to ward off malevolent spirits and perform exorcisms if need be. He wasn't crazy about the idea of bringing me deeper into the supernatural world but he got better as the weeks passed. If anything, he felt more confident about me going to work on my own now that I knew how to defend myself from a demon attack.

Speaking of which, I finally got to go back to work, only to not do much the first day because the whole staff threw me a Welcome Back party. Lauren even brought her sweet little daughter Lily to see me. I couldn't believe how big she'd gotten. Michael had been right. Life had been passing by, whether I noticed or not.

Michael's band has been doing well throughout the city. He got gigs more and more often, and I actually went with him to many of them—sometimes just so he wouldn't worry about me and sometimes because I liked hearing him play. He even had groupies now. I found it utterly hilarious watching him try to slide past them to get to our table at the club. Maybe it was a little mean, but after all, I was only human.

BOOK THREE: THE BEAUTIFUL DESCENT

Thou wilt learn in time
The truth, for time alone reveals the just;
A villain is detected in a day.
-*Oedipus Rex*, Sophocles

CHAPTER SIXTEEN

"You're being stubborn, you know."

"I know."

"I thought we agreed on this issue."

"Seriously, Jordan, it's not a big deal."

"I beg to differ."

I crossed my arms beneath my chest and narrowed my eyes at Michael as he sat comfortably across from me in the booth. Truthfully, this setting danced on the border of ridiculous.

First of all, I couldn't even remember the last time I'd been out to lunch with a guy, and certainly not one this good-looking. The man certainly wasn't hard on the eyes, but by now I was quite immune to his appearance. Practice.

Second of all, I hadn't been outside of Albany in damn near forever. My life was oddly self-contained, maybe even confined, to my apartment, the restaurant, and the park. Sure, I'd been to the homes, workplaces, and graves of many ghosts, but none of them had been cause for me to vacate the city's towering structures. Clean air. Green grass. Critters. It was friggin' weird.

Third of all, discovering how my mother spent her last days before the demons got her murdered was the final nail in the crazy coffin. It would be worth the four-hour drive and the many weeks it had taken to save up to pay for food and gas. Except for some reason, Michael insisted on paying for this meal, even though we had arranged for him to pay for the rental car and hotel. Therein lay my current dilemma.

Our perky waitress Krystal appeared, smiling as she caught the tail end of the argument.

"Newlyweds?"

I adopted an insulted look. "He wishes."

Michael chuckled. "How can I not when you sweet-talk me like that?"

My eyes immediately rolled and she giggled before continuing onward. "Can I get you two anything else?"

"No, you can bring us the check."

The blonde waitress reached into her frock and withdrew the bill. I reached for it but Michael snatched it out of her hand, flashing me a challenging smirk. I kicked him in the shin.

"Ow!" He winced, rubbing the injured spot. "Why am I being punished for being a gentleman?"

"Because I'm not a lady, dammit. Now give it here."

"You paid for breakfast in Atlantic City. It's only fair."

"Since when has fair ever been a factor in this relationship?"

Krystal glanced between the two of us. "...are you *sure* you're not married?"

"If by 'married' you mean me hating him, then yes."

Michael rolled his eyes and handed her his Visa card. "Here you go."

"Thanks, I'll be right back." She walked away, shaking her head with an amused look on her face.

I sighed and leaned my head backward, trying to stifle my irritation. At least the meal had been good. I hadn't eaten pancakes in ages. Michael had offered to make them once, but I declined the offer because it was too damned domestic. Our arrangement had been going on for nearly two months now. It didn't need to become any more complicated.

"How far are we from our destination?"

"Not far. Maybe another hour's drive," Michael said, his voice less humorous this time. We didn't have much of a plan for when we arrived in New Jersey, but that had never stopped us before. We were nothing if not determined.

I sat up straight and regarded him with a bemused look. "If I didn't know any better, I'd say you sound worried."

His brows knit together in the beginnings of a frown. "For good reason."

His green eyes lowered their gaze to the spot over my heart where a faded scar lay hidden beneath my black t-shirt. I had gotten the stitches out, but the skin was still a light brown that didn't match the rest of my chocolate complexion.

Two months. It'd be two months in a couple of days. I tried not to think about it too much.

"Don't get your feathers all ruffled," I scolded. "We're being much more careful than we were before."

"Being careful is never enough. You know that," Michael replied.

I shrugged. "Being worried isn't going to help any either."

He seemed to take my words to heart this time, but it didn't matter because Krystal reappeared with Michael's debit card in one hand and a tray full of empty glasses balanced on the other.

"Thanks for coming out. Have a nice day!"

"You too." I slid out of the booth and stretched my arms above my head, patting the pockets of my grey duster to make sure everything was in place. Just when I turned to go, Krystal's tray started to slide out of her hand. Michael miraculously caught it in mid-air, saving the dishes from peril. He handed it back to the relieved girl, who sighed heavily and said:

"Thanks. You're an angel."

I laughed so hard that Michael had to shove me out the door.

By the time we reached the hotel, the day had wound down into sunset and the city seemed to swallow us whole. We'd have more time to take in some of the sights and local culture after I had a shower. This October day was as sticky as the candy that would be passed out at the end of the month.

I breathed a sigh of relief when Michael opened the hotel door with his keycard, causing a blast of cool air to hit my face. Hurrah. The cream-colored walls and burgundy comforters were almost as inviting as that air conditioning so I shuffled inside with my suitcase and kicked the door shut. Michael gravitated to the queen-sized bed closest to the door since he was technically my angelic bodyguard so I dumped my stuff on the other mattress before collapsing face-first onto it. Michael let out a faint groan as well before silence enveloped us both. Once the sweat coating my spine dried, I rolled over and kicked off my Reeboks.

"How far is the place from here?" I asked.

"Ten minutes, or so MapQuest says."

"Good. Means we won't have to roll out of bed until noon or so tomorrow." The socks came off next. I wiggled my toes on the fuzzy white carpet and sat up on the edge of the bed. Michael was sprawled on his back with his long legs trailing onto the floor. The urge to giggle rose in my throat. When he wore khakis, he looked like an enormous brunette stork.

"Sounds like a plan. Might give us some time to take in the sights, too."

A frown tugged at my lips. "This isn't a vacation, y'know."

He shrugged, raking the hair out of his eyes so he could meet my gaze. "I know. But it wouldn't be the worst idea in the world."

I spared him a sarcastic smirk. "Yeah, because we all know what that idea was."

The archangel rolled his eyes. "One day you'll appreciate the sacrifices I make for you."

"Sure, I will. Dibs on the shower." He groaned as I unzipped my bag to get out my clothes.

"Oh, c'mon, I drove for four hours. The least you could do is let me shower first."

"I offered to drive and you declined."

Michael finally sat up, scowling at me. "I'm a guy. We have things about driving."

"Well, too bad. Ladies first." Having gathered my clothes, I headed towards the bathroom, but he called to me before I got there.

"I thought you said you weren't a lady."

I stopped and glared at him. The archangel had the most infuriating smirk on his face. I contemplated taking another shot at his shin.

"I am when it suits me."

The accursed smirk widened. "And when is that?"

I flashed him a very mean smile. "You'll never see it."

Before he could supply another snappy comeback, I slipped into the bathroom and shut the door. A few weeks ago, he might have talked me out of taking my shower first but I'd caught on to his methods by now. Sure, Gabriel was the most eloquent of the archangels that I had met, but Michael had a strangely compelling way of arguing. Hell, that was how he'd ended up accompanying me in the first place.

The hot shower left me in a much better mood than before. Maybe I had just needed the alone time. Michael was great and all, but I hadn't been close with an attractive male aside from Gabriel in a while. It took some getting used to.

I redressed in comfortable clothes—a plum-colored t-shirt and black Capris. It took nearly an entire minute of adjusting my hair before I realized I was *preening*. What the hell. I shot myself an annoyed glare in the mirror before stomping out of the bathroom in a huff.

Michael had stripped down to a white tank top, proof that he too felt a little hot under the collar. His eyes tracked my movement across the room, but he didn't say anything. That was a first.

The television spouted information about the weather and current events, which didn't surprise me. Michael would want to know what kind of environment we'd traveled into and if it was any better or worse than Albany. If we were lucky, though, we'd only be here for a few days. It all depended on whether the psychiatric hospital had held onto the full records of my mother's stay. I had called ahead and requested patient information but they needed to bring legal documentation — in my case, a copy of my birth certificate — to confirm that I was her daughter in order to access the files.

"Shower's all yours," I said unnecessarily. Some part of me enjoyed pushing Michael's buttons and I couldn't tell if it was a good or bad thing. He stood, tossed me the remote, and began searching through his duffel bag for clothing.

"What's the plan for the rest of the night?"

I shrugged, eyes locked on the TV screen. Ooh, *Castle* rerun. Nice. "Order a pizza and sleep?"

His back was facing me but I could hear the smile in his voice. "Great. Something new and different for us."

Wonder if I could set his head on fire with my mind. Nah. "What would you suggest then, Mr. O'Brien?"

"We're in a new city. The least we can do is have dinner somewhere."

I paused. "Why does that sound like a date?"

Michael turned and arched an eyebrow at me. "Is there something you need to tell me, Jordan?"

I spared him a cold look. "Ha-ha."

He flashed me that million-dollar smile and I snorted, waving in the direction of the bathroom. "Stop flirting with me and go take a shower, pretty boy."

His soft chuckle lingered even after he disappeared into the bathroom. Stupid sexy angel.

CHAPTER SEVENTEEN

We ended up wandering around town on foot just to save on gas. The slow pace wasn't as annoying as I thought it would be, now that the humidity had crept off into the night. This city had a relatively small population and it showed: the streets were busy with people, but the traffic and general noise was low. Music drifted through the air from a nearby club, punctuated by occasional cheering from whatever game was on inside the sports bars. Girls hung together in groups outside of the movie theater, giggling as cute boys walked past them. The environment felt comfortable, maybe because I'd become so used to the vibrant but sometimes impersonal city of Albany.

Plus, there was always the amusing pastime of people watching, which became especially fun when I went out with Michael. The archangel was somewhat aware of his effect on the opposite sex, but no more than that. He missed the longing glances sent at him from married women, the flirty smiles from single women, and the nervous snickers passed between teens and tweens. I found myself smirking at the hate-laden glances they sent me when we strolled by them. It was one of the unspoken benefits of being in the company of a good-looking guy.

"Hungry yet?"

Michael's voice jolted me out of my petty thoughts. I shook my head. "Nah. Maybe in another hour or so. Besides, it seems like we've got company."

I jerked a thumb backwards to the willowy blonde in a red sweater and black skirt who had been trailing us since we left the hotel.

Michael's dark eyebrows rose in surprise. "When did you notice?"

"About a minute or two after we left the hotel."

A slow smile touched his lips. "Would it be wrong to say I'm a little proud?"

I rolled my eyes. "I have been doing this whole ghost thing for two years, you know."

"Point taken."

The average person wouldn't have noticed, but we did walk a little faster. The back of my neck tingled as if I could feel her stare from here. The nasty business with Jacob taught me to be much more cautious around spirits. Fortunately, Michael had taught me a few chants that would hold an evil spirit at bay, but the potential danger still hung over me like mist — thick, almost palpable.

Crickets and frogs serenaded our entrance into the park. Like the main streets, there were people, but the place wasn't crowded. Most of the visitors had gathered at the shore of the placid lake. The cuter couples were skipping stones on the silver water and watching the ripples fragment the moon's reflection. Nice date spot.

Michael and I headed for a more secluded area along the winding trail lit by the occasional lamppost. Thick foliage enclosed us on both sides of the path, making the place seem much more private than public.

We stopped in front of a park bench and turned towards the specter. She continued towards us with a calm expression, her pale but pretty face betraying nothing.

I casually slipped my hands into the pockets of my grey duster, checking that the blessed rosary was still in place, before speaking up.

"Can I help you?"

She jumped, shock evident in her voice even through the light British accent. "You can see me?"

"We both can. My name is Jordan and this is Michael. We noticed you've been following us for a while."

The woman winced. "Sorry, it's just that…something told me to follow you."

"It's an instinct that all human souls have. You're drawn to people who can see ghosts. That's what Jordan is," Michael said.

The woman's shoulders relaxed and she let out a relieved sigh. "Thank goodness. I've felt so lost and alone."

"It's alright. We're here to help. What's the last thing you remember?" As I spoke, I rummaged through the inner pocket of my duster for the ever-present notepad and pen. Michael had a better memory than me, so he didn't need one. Higher brain capacity, I supposed.

"Well, I was standing outside of a restaurant. I think it was an Applebee's or something. I couldn't remember how I'd gotten there or how long I'd been there. Someone walked right through me and that's when I realized I wasn't alive."

"Do you remember your name?"

"Marianne."

I began my list.

Marianne
Appears to be in her mid-to-late twenties
Red sweater, black skirt
Blonde hair
Blue eyes
British accent
Woke up in front of Applebee's

"Anything else? Can you think of your last name or your address?"

She shook her head. "But there is this."

Marianne reached inside the sweater and pulled off a gold necklace, holding it out. Michael and I stepped forward, though not close enough for her to touch us, and examined the oval locket. On one side, there were the initials M.R. and below them, the initials J.A. On the other, there was a photograph of a very young Marianne and a Middle Eastern boy. They couldn't have been older than six or seven.

I wrote down a few more thoughts on the paper. "Alright. We'll start working on your case tonight and see what we can come up with. If we're lucky, it won't take long."

"What about them?"

"Them who?"

Marianne pointed behind us. Michael and I turned. My mouth dropped open.

There were at least ten ghosts standing behind us. Holy shit.

They didn't seemed organized or menacing. There were six men, three women, and one child all dressed differently, but each with the same needy look in their eyes.

I cleared my throat, my gaze traveling from one specter to the next. "This isn't normal, is it?"

"Not in the least," Michael replied, his green eyes wide. Ghosts never tended to appear all at once. On average, I encountered one every two to three weeks in Albany. The odds that ten of them would gather in New Jersey around Michael and I were incredibly improbable. Then again, no one ever said my job made any sense.

"What should we do?" I asked.

Michael ran a hand through his hair—a nervous habit of his. "I don't think we have much of a choice but to try and help them."

A sigh escaped me. "I had a feeling you'd say that."

To them, I said: "Alright, folks, single file line. I need names and anything else you remember."

Fifteen minutes later, a third of my notepad was filled with the personal information of nearly a dozen ghosts. We wouldn't be able to help them tonight, so I sent all of them but Marianne away. Once they had gone, we walked back towards the front of the park.

"Well, that wasn't weird," I said, stuffing my notepad in my pocket. It was then that I noticed the rosary wasn't in there. I paused, patting myself down but it was nowhere to be found.

Michael stopped walking when he noticed what I was doing. "What's wrong?"

"I think I dropped the rosary back there. Wait here, I'll be right back." I jogged back up the trail, searching the gravel in the dim light of the lamps above me. When I reached the park bench a couple minutes later, I found it on the ground. Just as I stooped to pick it up, someone appeared in front of me.

I caught a look at his face and felt the blood drain out of mine.

"Terrell?"

My ex-boyfriend's dark brown eyes widened to nearly epic proportions. "Jordan? What are you doing here?"

"I…I'm here for family issues. What are *you* doing here?" I asked, hating that my heartbeat had tripled in the last five seconds. Unfortunately, his good looks hadn't faded in the least. His skin was a rich mahogany, teeth perfect and white, full lips softening his square jaw darkened by the presence of a goatee. His six-foot frame was encased in a navy suit jacket over a black shirt and blue jeans. I felt woefully unattractive in my comfortable, but unimpressive get up.

"Doctor's conference," Terrell said, the shock melting into a pleasant expression. "I'm here until Wednesday. Man. It's crazy seeing you like this. How long's it been?"

I shoved my hands in my pockets so he wouldn't see them shaking. "Two and half years or so."

"Sounds about right. Looks like they've been good to you." A sly smile tugged at the edge of his lips. The blood in my cheeks heated up.

I shuffled momentarily, trying to regain composure. "I was just heading out of the park so…it was good seeing you."

"Oh, come on, you're not using that weak line on me, are you?" he said, arching an eyebrow.

I winced. "What do you want me to say?"

"Jordan, it's been almost three years. The least you can do is let my buy you dinner so we can catch up."

Deep inside, I felt my resolve beginning to crumble. Damn him. This man was the only person on Earth I couldn't say no to.

"I dunno if that's a good idea…"

He paused. "Oh, wait. Are you seeing someone…?"

I shook my head. "No, but I don't want to make things complicated."

"It's dinner, not a week in Hawaii. Tomorrow night, the Dynasty, eight o'clock. Don't be late." With that, he flashed me another brilliant smile and kept walking. I stared after him for a long moment before turning around and returning to Michael and Marianne waiting for me. When I reached them, Michael was scanning the crowd with a slight frown on his face.

"Something wrong?"

He shook his head. "No, I just got an odd feeling all of the sudden. Ready?"

I thought about pressing him to explain what he'd felt, but decided to do it later. "Yeah. Let's head for the Applebee's and see if anything rings a bell for Marianne."

It didn't take long to get there, but luck still wasn't on our side. The staff didn't recall seeing anyone with her friend's description, but they let me have all the last names that started with A. We headed back to the hotel to begin the tedious search process to see if anything turned up.

Twenty minutes on Google proved fruitless until I managed to get lucky with the eighth name on my list of potentials. The guy in the photo's name was Jameson Micah Arlo. He'd used his middle name for the reservation. He worked at an orphanage outside the city limits. We couldn't call to meet with him because it was after visiting hours and all the kiddies would be asleep, so we'd have to arrange a meeting tomorrow. I gave Marianne instructions to meet us tomorrow in the afternoon. Like most ghosts, she felt worried about leaving our presence while we slept, but I assured her a walk the city might help her memory return.

With a groan, I toppled over backwards on my bed, eyes dropping closed. The cool cotton of the comforter felt great. Peace at last. Not that I'd keep it that way.

"So what was with the ghost party in the park?"

"That I don't know," Michael said. "I've never seen anything like it before. I left Gabriel a voicemail asking if he'd encountered something similar."

"I don't suppose it's Christ's Return, is it?"

He let out a small chuckle. "Ah, no. Trust me, you'll know when that happens."

A grin touched my lips. Well, he had a point. Revelation painted a much more vivid picture of the Rapture, after all. I wasn't the best Christian, but I did know the basics.

"Is there anything that could cause such a large collection of souls?"

Michael paused before replying. "Perhaps a holy item being discovered? Not something like the Spear — something that has more of a connection to mankind. The spear represented man's sin. It would have to be something…purer."

I sat up, the grin evaporating as a thought occurred to me. "And what are the odds it would appear the same time we're in New Jersey?"

His green eyes radiated the same concern as my brown ones. "Impossible."

A sigh escaped me. "For once, can I just have a normal week?"

Michael spared me a faint smile. "Apparently not. How 'bout I pick out somewhere nice to go tomorrow night to make up for it?"

"Can't. I have plans."

Up went the angel's eyebrows. "With whom?"

I pointedly did not look at him as I answered, choosing to sift through my suitcase for my nightclothes. "Terrell."

"Terrell? You mean ex-boyfriend, white-picket-fence Terrell?"

"The same."

"When'd you run into him?"

"When I went to grab the rosary in the park."

"Oh."

An awkward silence fell. I ignored it.

Michael took a moment before speaking again. "Are you sure that's a good idea?"

Funny how he echoed me having not been there when it happened. "It's dinner, not a honeymoon in the Bahamas. Wasn't my idea in the first place."

"But you still agreed to go."

I shot him a sarcastic look. "Yes, I did, Captain Obvious. Is there a problem?"

He stared back at me for a second before adopting the phoniest smile I'd ever been graced to see on this Earth. "Nothing would make me happier than to see you two together."

I shook my head. "You're an awful liar, Michael."

The angel cleared his throat, seeming a bit embarrassed. "In all seriousness, I am actually thinking about your welfare. You two do have a pretty rough past."

I gathered my clothes up, heading for the bathroom. "I'll be fine, trust me. If I were impressed by knights in shining armor, I would have fallen for you."

He frowned at me. "Ouch."

I batted my eyelashes at him. "Sticks and stones, Michael. Sticks and stones."

CHAPTER EIGHTEEN

Something tickled down my chest. I couldn't see it. There was cloth over my eyes — a blindfold. I should have panicked, but I felt oddly calm. I was lying on silken sheets that cradled my body as if they were alive. Weird.

The mysterious object brushed over my throat. I shivered, reaching up to undo the blindfold, but a soothing male voice stopped me.

"Not yet."

I felt compelled to listen to him, so I lowered my arms and lay motionless. The air stirred over my face and then I felt it again — across my forehead, over my nose, past my lips. I realized after a moment that it was a feather. Its delicate ridges dipped past my collarbone and caressed the scarred flesh on my chest; a soothing gesture. Moments later, I felt the warm breath of someone's mouth and then soft lips. The kiss lasted only seconds, but it felt longer. My mind was spinning from the simple pleasure of it.

The man withdrew. I reached up to undo the blindfold as he cupped my chin, stroking my skin. My eyes opened, focusing slowly. As they adjusted, I could see the silhouette of wings stretching wide from the man's bare back. But there was something wrong. His wings weren't silver but midnight black, and the tips were singed as if they had been held over a flame. The man's face faded into view and it was one I knew very well: alabaster skin, long jet black hair, serpentine smile, and eyes so pale blue that they were almost white, making the thin pupils at the center seem even more reptilian.

Belial smiled that cold smile as he closed the inches between us. "Did you miss me, my pet?"

My lungs filled with air and I screamed.

I awoke with a jolt, panting, cold sweat dripping down my spine like icy fingers, reaching for my mouth as if I could still feel the demon's lips. *Shit.*

I heard Michael stir in his bed, awakened by my gasping. It took him only seconds to notice I was not in good shape. He tossed back the covers and hurried to my side, his voice still gravelly from slumber.

"Jordan, what's wrong?"

I just shook my head, still not coherent enough to talk. He reached out to touch my shoulder.

"Geez, you're shaking."

I swatted his hand away just as his fingertips brushed my skin. "Don't! Don't...touch me."

"Alright, I won't. Just tell me what you saw."

I kicked the covers off my legs and walked over to the mini-fridge on the floor, wordlessly opening it. Michael spoke from behind me.

"What are you doing?"

"Getting a drink. What does it look like I'm doing?" I snapped, slamming the door shut after I found a comically small bottle of alcohol.

He stepped close to me, trying to take it out of my hands. "You don't need it."

"The hell I don't," I growled, tightening my fingers around the neck of the bottle. When he couldn't pry it away, he grabbed my shoulders and held me still.

"Jordan, look at me."

Finally, I stopped trying to wriggle out of his grasp and met his eyes. There wasn't irritation or impatience in them—just concern. He spoke again, his voice quiet and measured.

"You don't need it."

Something painful welled up in my chest, but I ignored the sensation as best as I could. Seeing me cry once was enough. Instead, I threw up my hands.

"What do you want me to do? I can't deal with this shit every night."

Michael watched me before touching the side of my cheek, brushing the hair out of my eyes. "Then let me do my job."

Gently, he took the bottle and set it on the table behind me, tugging me forward enough to wrap his arms around me. Part of me wanted to resist and argue with him more, but the other part wanted to sink into him and forget the horrible dream as quickly as possible. In the end, I just stood there—neither hurting nor helping the situation. After a few deep breaths, my heart rate slowed and the adrenaline drained out of my tired body until I was back to my normal, cantankerous self.

"I don't think hugging me is part of your job description."

He was tall enough that I couldn't see his face with my own pressed to his shoulder, but I could tell he was smiling by his tone. "Last time I checked, hugging wasn't a sin."

A tiny smile found my lips. "Obviously you're doing it wrong."

Feeling admittedly better, I pushed away from him and sank back onto the bed, tugging out the loose knot I'd tied my hair up into so I could run my fingers through it. Nervous habit.

Michael sat next to me, but didn't touch me this time. I appreciated it.

"What did you see?"

I couldn't help but wince. "Belial."

"It's not the first time, is it?"

I shook my head. "Ever since the fight at the psychiatric hospital, I've had nightmares about him. Still, this one was much more…vivid."

A cold shudder rolled up my spine as I thought about him kissing me, how he had manipulated me into thinking he was someone else. Bastard.

Michael let out a long breath, leaning his arms on his long legs. "I know it sounds corny but…you know I'd never let him hurt you again."

I nodded, fingers combing through my hair until it was untangled enough to fit back in a ponytail. "I know."

"Is there anything you want me to do?"

A thought popped into mind — something I'd forgotten about for a while — that time he and I had fallen asleep in bed together and I didn't have nightmares that night. Somehow, his close proximity seemed to cancel my bad dreams. Why, though? Maybe I'd ask Gabriel about it.

"No," I said out loud. "I'll be alright."

A tiny voice in my head whispered that I was an idiot, but I told it to go die in a fire. Our relationship had crossed so many lines at this point, and there would be no reason to keep at it. He was an archangel, for Christ's sake, not a teddy bear.

I climbed into bed and flopped down on the pillow face up. Michael took the hint and went back to his own, hesitating before getting in.

"Good night, Jordan."

I sighed. "Let's hope so."

I expected to wake up in a cold sweat, buried underneath the fluffy white comforter, but something was different. There wasn't a damp imprint of my body on the mattress. Quite the opposite, actually. I felt warm. Inexplicably so.

There was a firm weight down my back and along my waist that seemed to keep the cold of the hotel room at bay. Even with my mind barely conscious, blind pleasure filled me. I felt...safe. Not really a familiar sensation with my lifestyle.

A content sigh slipped past my lips. I snuggled deeper into my comfortable spot, reaching over my waist to pull the covers in tighter so I could make myself a cocoon. I touched something smooth. Not the blanket. Firmer. Confused and still mostly asleep, I tried to stretch but my heels brushed against a pair of rather large bare feet. A muscular chest met my spine, melting into it perfectly. Definitely male.

Wait, what?

My eyes flew open. I sat up in my bed to find Michael lying asleep next to me with one large arm draped across my hips.

I scrambled backwards in a flustered panic, remembering it was only a Queen-sized bed seconds too late. I tumbled off the edge and hit the floor, which knocked the wind out of me. However, the enormous thud woke up the intruding archangel.

"Jor?" he croaked in his ultra-deep morning voice, peeking over the edge of the mattress.

I stood up in a flash and shrieked, "What the *hell* are you doing?"

He frowned. "Making sure you didn't crack your skull?"

I ground my back teeth. "Not that, jackass. Why are you in bed with me?"

Michael raked the hair out of his face so he could see me better. "Oh. Jordan, you were tossing and turning the entire night. I couldn't keep waking you up or you'd never get any rest—"

"—so you just thought there's no harm in crawling in bed with me? Have you lost your mind?"

He continued looking confused. "We've shared a bed before. What's the big deal?"

"What's the big deal? You had my permission when that happened."

"I was just trying to help."

I pressed my fingertips against my temple. A headache was forthcoming. The hot blood rushing through me felt liable to pop out of my neck at any second. "I'm not a child. I can handle a few bad dreams by myself."

Finally, he got irritated. "So what? We're just going to pretend like you weren't about to start drinking last night because the nightmare freaked you out so badly?"

"Sounds good to me."

He shook his head. "Denial isn't going to help you get better. I'm sorry if I made you uncomfortable and invaded your privacy, but I didn't know what else to do. You were in pain."

"Fine. Let me enlighten you. Life is pain. I'll get over it."

He glared at me. "So if the same thing were happening to me and I told you to just back off and forget about it, what would you say?"

That shut me up for a couple of seconds. He had a point. Sort of. Not that it mattered because he was clearly missing the big picture. "Michael, you've been on earth long enough to know that there are some lines you just shouldn't cross. Last night was one of them. If you don't see that, then we have nothing else to talk about."

I stalked off to the bathroom, not answering when he called after me. The door slammed shut between us — louder than a gunshot. I stood in the middle of the room and wrapped my arms around myself.

I still felt warm.

Damn him.

Thirty minutes later, we were both dressed and out the door to head to the psychiatric hospital where my mother's records would be. I didn't expect to find much — after all, it had been eighteen years. I was lucky the hospital was small enough that they hadn't deleted the files. The backups were our only shot.

"Can I ask you something?"

"No."

Michael ignored me and continued anyway. I was still a bit mad at him but at least he hadn't tried to bring the argument up again. "How come you didn't do this sooner?"

I thought about blowing him off, but telling him the truth at least kept my mind off our spat. "I wasn't able to leave my aunt's place until I was sixteen. I'd gotten a job at fourteen and hid money around the apartment. When I had enough, I ran for it and hitched a ride to the first thing smoking out of Jersey. An old woman drove me to Albany and that's where I decided to set up shop. Her name was Selina Lebeau. She let me rent the room above her candy store while I got another job. Took me forever just to be able to afford basic household stuff. Got lucky one night at the restaurant when I met Lauren and she helped get me a full time job there. I just couldn't save up enough to get back to Jersey, no matter how hard I tried. Why do you ask?"

He shrugged one shoulder, concentrating on the road ahead rather than looking at me. "She's important to you. I knew there had to be a reason why you hadn't done it before now."

Further talk was hindered by the fact that we'd pulled into the parking lot of the psychiatric hospital. Like last time, I felt the creeping sensation of a panic attack coming on: muscles tightening, pupils dilating, cold sweat, and rapid breathing. I gripped the side of my car door and closed my eyes, breathing in and out slowly until the symptoms faded. This time, there would be no faceless men dragging me away from my mother, nor would Belial or Mulciber be waiting for me. I had to believe that with all my heart, or I'd never get out of this car.

Finally, I opened the door and stepped out, squaring my shoulders and doing my best not to wince as I looked up at the sparkling white hospital, stark against the bright green grass and the vibrant blue-sky overhead. Cheerful place. I wasn't buying it.

The automatic doors whooshed open, sending a blast of frigid air against my skin. I shivered and glanced about the lobby. Pristine baby blue walls, linoleum floors, and framed pictures of smiling people. It felt oddly like walking into an eye doctor's office.

I brushed the thought aside and walked up to the front desk where a black guy sat with a phone tucked against his shoulder. He smiled when we walked over, lowering the receiver.

"Can I help you?"

"Yes. We have an appointment with a Dr. Reginald," I said.

He faced the computer in front of him, typing in a few things. "I see. I'll send a call for her. Make sure you have your paperwork ready. Please have a seat over there."

He pointed to the plush navy chairs in the carpeted waiting room to my right. I withdrew the paperwork that had been folded up in one of my inner pockets and sat down. Michael took the seat to my left. Silence fell over us as the minutes crept by, punctuated only by a clock ticking on the wall and the typing of the male secretary. Anxious energy began to build in my nerves. It wasn't until Michael touched my left leg that I realized I had been bouncing it up and down.

He flashed me a reassuring smile and leaned over a bit to murmur something to me. "If you don't stop doing that, I'm going to staple your foot to the floor."

A challenging smirk touched my lips. "Try it and die."

The angel adopted a haughty expression. "Is that a threat, mortal?"

"I most certainly hope it is."

"I could take you blindfolded with one arm tied behind my back."

I arched an eyebrow. "Is that how they did it back in your time, Grandpa?"

"Ouch. That's a low blow."

I would have replied but then a short Asian woman in her forties walked over, offering her hand.

"Hi, I'm Dr. Reginald. Are you Jordan Amador?"

I stood, accepting her firm handshake. "Yes, ma'am. This is my friend Michael O'Brien. He's here for moral support."

She paused, pointing at him and then me. "Michael…Jordan?"

I couldn't help but smile a bit. I'd gotten used to people making that reference over the past couple months. "Yeah, I know. It's weird."

She grinned at my admittance. "Nice to meet you. If you'll follow me, we'll get started."

Dr. Reginald led us past the front desk and down the hallway of the employees' offices, meaning that all the patients were on the upper three floors. She opened the door to the stairwell and we followed her to the basement, which was even colder than the sub-zero first floor.

"Pardon me if I have a little trouble with the files," the doctor said, taking a set of keys out of her pocket. "It's very rare that we have past relatives coming in to find information about loved ones."

"It's fine," I assured her.

"May I see your information?"

I handed her the file containing my birth certificate. She scanned it briefly and handed it back to me, turning to unlock the door. Inside, the room was filled with row after row of file cabinets, all with elaborate letters and codes for organization. Must have been hell to have to catalogue things this way.

"Our recent patients' information is in our computers upstairs, but everyone who was at this facility from ten years ago or longer has hard copies. We keep them in case the state or federal government needs them." Dr. Reginald 's dark eyes scanned the rows until she recognized the one we needed to be on. We approached a worn out black file cabinet and she opened it, mumbling to herself as she looked through the folders' tabs. I chewed my bottom lip, but at last she found the right manila and pulled it out.

"Here we are. There's not much on there—just your basic profile and how long she stayed at this hospital," she said, handing it to me.

My hands shook the tiniest bit as I opened the folder, coming upon a grey document with my mother's name, former address, marital status, and so on. A picture was paper-clipped in the top right corner and it made my breath catch to see her face again. *Morena*, just like me. Staring into the photograph was like looking into a mirror of an older, much stronger reflection of myself. After a moment, I tore my gaze away from my mother's brazen brown eyes and instead read through the information.

"Wait, this says that she was never legally released from the hospital because she ran away. I thought my mother's body was found here?" I asked, frowning.

Dr. Reginald's brow furrowed as well as she stepped on my left side, since Michael towered over my right, and scanned the profile. "That's odd. If you want more clarification, you'd have to see if there's a police report attached."

She turned the page and I read it out loud: "Found three blocks away from psychiatric hospital with a deep laceration in her rib cage that suggest it was self-inflicted. No signs of struggle. The weapon was found in her chest cavity with her fingerprints and the prints of another unidentified dead man on it. Her male accomplice fled the scene. Male accomplice?"

Behind that page, I found a rough sketch of a dark-haired man in his late thirties with a thin scar over his right eyebrow and another peeking up from the collar of his shirt on the left side of his neck. I couldn't breathe.

It was Mr. N.

Beneath his picture, in an untidy scrawl, was a name.

Andrew Bethsaida.

Andrew Bethsaida was the name of the man I killed.

My throat tightened upon seeing his face again. I swallowed hard a couple of times before speaking to the doctor.

"Do you have a profile on this man?"

"He was brought in as a consultant later on during your mother's stay at the hospital. He specialized in schizophrenia, paranoia, and other psychological problems in people with multicultural backgrounds. However, if you aren't his next of kin then I'm afraid I can't divulge his personal information." She sounded regretful, as if she noticed the distraught look on my face.

"It's...okay. I just wanted to know. Would I be able to get a copy of this file?"

"Sure, I'll get that for you upstairs."

"Thank you. One more thing — is there a chance that she had any personal items put in storage here?"

Dr. Reginald paused, thinking about it. "Most likely, no. The policy is to keep a patient's things for about a year and then either donate them or throw them away. However, I did see something on the other page."

She flipped back to the first sheet and pointed down at the bottom.

"It says here that her personal belongings were forwarded to this address."

"God," I whispered.

Michael touched my shoulder. "What's wrong?"

"That's the address to my Aunt Carmen's apartment."

CHAPTER NINETEEN

"Are you sure you don't want me to go in with you?"

I heard what Michael said, but my eyes were fixed on the dilapidated apartment building, stretched tall and dank against the cloudy sky. Brick and mortar never seemed more daunting than on this place. Not even children scurrying back and forth on skateboards and scooters made it appear any less awful. The air here wasn't like that of the quaint part of Jersey that we'd left. This place smelled of cigarette smoke, filth from the nearby open manholes, and exhaust from old, overworked cars. A defeated atmosphere hung about, unwilling to dissipate as if it were some sort of permanent fog. There was no panic attack this time because I wasn't afraid of my aunt's home. I *hated* it.

After a while, I realized I hadn't answered him so I took a deep breath and unlocked my car door. "Yeah. I won't be long."

I didn't spare him a glance as I got out. Seeing his face would make me chicken out and want to stay there, or maybe beg him to drive me the hell out of here. I couldn't do that. My mom deserved better.

I walked across the cracked sidewalk and into the courtyard that split the building into two sections. The building itself had four floors and last time I checked, hers was on the second. Part of me prayed that she wouldn't still be living here but I knew my luck wasn't that good.

I ascended the stairs and walked to Room 234, raising my fist to knock on the door. My hand hung in the air above the faded forest green paint for a long moment until I worked up the nerve. Two knocks. Nothing. Three, this time. Nada. Four knocks.

The ancient doorknob turned. I stepped back and stared into the face of Carmensita Durante.

Her eyes were grey, but not the same kind of grey as a cloudy sky. They were dark and dirty like cigarette ash. Smoke curled up from the lit coffin nail clutched in her bony hand. She hadn't aged well. Her skin was yellowed from years of chain smoking and hung from her skull like a turkey's jowls. Her hair was all grey and pulled into a tight bun. Her clothes were simple as always: pink blouse with a scoop neck, black skirt, and faded blue slippers. The only thing that had changed about Aunt Carmen's demeanor was that she was shocked to see me.

"*Hola, tia,*" I said, shoving my hands in the pockets of my duster. My fingers wrapped around the rosary self-consciously. Sure, she wasn't technically a demon, but there were plenty of times during my childhood that I thought her to be inhuman.

In mere seconds, the surprise trickled out of her aged face to be replaced with the same harsh stoicism I'd seen for years.

"*Hola, chica.* It's been a long time, no?"

"Yes, it has."

She tapped ashes from the end of her cigarette, crossing one thin arm beneath the other and taking a drag on the cig. "What do you want?"

I licked my lips, trying to figure out the most delicate way to ask. "I was at the psychiatric hospital looking for things about Mom. They said they forwarded the rest of her things to you. Can I take a look?"

Aunt Carmen stared at me for a long moment before blowing out a stream of smoke inches away from my left cheek. I didn't flinch. She grunted at me and opened the door all the way. "Fine. Come in."

I stepped inside and immediately shut down all my senses. Cigarette smoke permeated anything vaguely resembling oxygen in this apartment. To my surprise, a few things had changed. The old tan couch made of scratchy cotton had disappeared and a green couch sat in its place, though the usual stains and burn holes were there. A dirty

glass table covered in magazines sat in front of it,
reflecting images from the large TV propped up on a set of
phonebooks nearby. The kitchen was to my right, but I
could only see the fridge and part of the counter from
where I stood. Past the den lay the bedrooms. I hoped she
wouldn't make me go back there to see her husband Rico,
provided that he was even home.

Aunt Carmen brushed past me and grabbed a small
glass from the coffee table that had an amber liquid in it. I
didn't even need to guess—Jose Cuervo. Her favorite kind
of tequila. Such a charming woman.

I took a deep breath and forced myself to speak up.
"Where are her things?"

She drained the glass and set it back down before
answering. "It's been eighteen years, *chica*. Do you really
think I kept them all? I sold all her valuable stuff and threw
the rest out with the garbage."

Anger flared up my body so fast that I got dizzy. I
clenched my hands into fists and reminded myself it was
unwise to punch an old woman in the face, even if she
deserved it. Instead, I just shook my head.

"Cold bitch," I spat.

Her bony hand lashed out and hit my right cheek,
leaving a patch of my skin stinging. It made me flinch, but
not stumble.

"Don't you dare speak to me like that in *mi casa,
morena del Diablo*! I took you in when you had nowhere else
to go, *puta*," she shot back, eyes narrowed to slits.

"Forgive me if I'm not grateful," I growled back.
"But you weren't exactly Surrogate Mother of the Year. If
it's all the same to you, I'd have rather been raised by
wolves. They'd have been cleaner and nicer than you ever
were."

She spat contemptuously at my feet. "You think
that's funny, eh? What else would you have done if not for
me? Found your deadbeat father? He didn't want you any
more than your *loca* mama—"

I took a step forward, putting myself mere inches from her face. The anger boiled hot in my stomach and flowed down my arms like a scalding tidal wave.

"Don't you call her that again in front of me or I will break you over my knee like a twig, old woman. Now do you have anything from my mother in this shithole you call a home or not?" I snarled.

She didn't back down, just stared at me with scorn. "On top of the bookshelf there is a picture. You may have that," Aunt Carmen said, pointing to her left. Against the wall was a short wooden shelf where pictures of her children and other ancient magazines had been stacked.

I walked over and knelt, seeing a picture frame that had been turned over. I lifted it and found an 8x10 inch photo of my mother when she was close to my age. Even this horrible place couldn't lessen her beauty. Slowly, the rage subsided and I could think straight once more.

I picked it up and headed for the door. Aunt Carmen decided this was a good time to start in on me like she used to before I left.

"Go on, go! Leave the only family you have, selfish brat! We live like *cucarachas* in this place without enough food or clothes, but that doesn't bother you, does it? You aren't good for anything, *niña*. You never will be. You're gonna end up like your pathetic mama someday and I won't be there to even take enough time to spit on your grave."

I yanked the door open and walked out, only to find myself face to face with Michael.

"I told you to wait downstairs," I said, my voice quieter than I intended.

Michael's face had a stoic quality to it that led me to believe he'd heard either most or all of our conversation. "Sorry."

I shook my head and turned my back on my aunt, beckoning the archangel. "Let's go."

"Just a second." To my surprise, he brushed past me and walked over to one rather surprised Aunt Carmen, offering his hand.

"Michael O'Brien. I just had to meet you."

She spared him a suspicious look, shaking his hand once as she eyed him. "You got something to say to me?"

Michael flashed her a stunning smile, the kind that made women weak in the knees, and tucked his hands in the pockets of his jeans as he shook his head.

"Y'know, there were a lot of things I thought I'd say to you if we ever met, but I never thought that I'd say thank you."

My eyes widened. Aunt Carmen's did as well. "'Scuse me?"

Michael continued on in a calm, polite voice, though the smile evaporated into nothing, leaving his handsome face serious as a heart attack. The air around him seemed to fill to the brim with static. I could feel the waves of anger flowing out of him in my lungs, in the back of my throat, in the pit of my stomach, as if our bodies had melded into one.

"I said thank you. If it weren't for your cruelty, your cowardice, your selfishness, and your ignorance, then the woman standing behind me might not have come to be. It's not your fault that your mother treasured your younger sister more than you and showered her with love and praise. I know how that must have made you feel. You became bitter and resented the both of them, so as soon as the opportunity presented itself, you leapt into action to betray your sister. When the hospital called to hand custody of Jordan over to you, it was like Christmas morning, wasn't it? What better revenge on Catalina then to break her daughter beyond repair? But then something happened, something unexpected. That girl you worked so hard to destroy grew up and became the very person you hated the most. She is beautiful, kind, intelligent, and full of life. I've been around for a very long time, Mrs. Durante.

Her kind of radiance is rare in this world. So I hope for your sake that you someday have enough sense to ask for her forgiveness because if you don't...there is a place waiting for you where they won't take as much pity on you as I have. You have a nice evening, ma'am."

With that, he turned around and walked down the hallway. Before I followed, I noticed the utter shock on Aunt Carmen's face mixed with a very human expression of fear, perhaps remorse. Served her right.

I caught up with Michael after a few paces, matching the stride of his long legs. We walked in silence towards the steps, serenaded by the crickets and car horns surrounding the dingy apartment complex.

"You didn't have to do that."

"I know," he replied, descending the stairs with me at his heels.

I sighed, mostly because I knew I could never stay mad at him. "Thank you."

Just as we reached the last few steps, my shoe snagged on the rusted railing and I pitched forward. Michael whirled around and caught me in a blur of motion. For a handful of seconds, his large hands suspended me above him and I stared down into his face, breathless, my head fuzzy with thoughts it had no business entertaining. A slow smile touched those full lips and I felt the vibrations from his chest as he spoke since we were pressed so close together.

"You're welcome."

CHAPTER TWENTY

"As a Seer, you don't possess what the average person would consider 'magic.' It's more a manipulation of energy through speech. When you acknowledge the true nature of something, you are able to unlock its abilities."

Michael paced back and forth in front of me as I sat in the grass on top of a small, secluded hill in the park. In the latter part of August, the heat slackened its moist grip on the city, leaving cooling breezes and pleasant atmosphere. I waited until he finished his small speech to respond.

"Now, in English, if you please."

He rolled his eyes at me, but grinned anyway. "Fine. In Layman's terms, you're going to be defending yourself through speech, not some kind of mystical mumbo-jumbo. I'm going to teach you how to channel your energy so you can protect yourself."

"See? Was that so hard?"

"Not as hard as it's going to be," Michael said with a sigh, plopping down in front of me. He crossed his legs and regarded me seriously with those green eyes of his.

"Gabriel has already exposed you to some of the language I'm talking about. When you invoke a spirit's crossing over, you're accessing a kind of verbal power. There are three basic versions: to heal, to defend, and to attack. For example, Raphael's greatest strength is in healing incantations, which is how he was able to bring your body back to life after you were stabbed. Gabriel's greatest strength is in defending, which you haven't seen yet, but trust me when I say it's impressive. My greatest strength is in attacking, but we won't get to that until you've had experience with the first two. It's dangerous if you try to utilize the energy untrained."

"What exactly will I be saying to access this power? Bible verses? Ominous Latin chanting?"

He grinned. "More or less. There's no need for the Latin, in actuality. It only works if the person has faith. There are hundreds of religions, but they all draw strength from the same source. Therefore, the one most relevant to you is Christianity,

and since you understand the Bible in English, that's what
you'll speak. The same would go for a Hindu Seer and so on. It's
the belief that counts."

Michael scooted a little closer. "Close your eyes."

I did. "Now keep breathing slowly and tell me if you can
feel what I'm doing."

I arched an eyebrow, though my eyes were still shut.
"This isn't going to be one of those awkward moments that
changes our friendship forever, is it?"

He sighed again. "Jordan."

"Sorry."

After I had been slowly inhaling for about fifteen seconds
or so, I felt a strange sort of warmth surrounding me. It wasn't
exactly physical — it simply felt as if the air around my body had
risen in temperature. Then, something within my chest
responded to the heat and sent wafting waves of coolness towards
it.

"Do you feel that?"

"Yes."

"This is what I was talking about a moment ago. You've
been emitting this kind of energy at an unconscious level and
that's what draws the ghosts to you. It calls to them, like it does
to anything that isn't purely human."

I opened my eyes. "Demons too?"

His expression hardened. "Yes, unfortunately. The Fallen
don't have as many powers as the angels, but they did retain
many of their old ones after the War in Heaven. It's why we've
had so much trouble fighting them."

"So this energy I'm feeling now…is that why I can sense
your emotions sometimes?"

He gave me a surprised look. "That's exactly why."

"So what does it feel like to normal people?"

"Since you're a Seer, you feel it directly. To them, it's
more like a…mood. If I were to influence, let's say, one of my
bandmates, they would feel a change in mood and wouldn't know
why. It's not exactly a kind of control, although I could force that
on them."

"And that's why the demons wanted your body."

213

He nodded. "The demons could incite rage, hatred, violence — any sin they could think of — over human beings. It'd be mayhem."

"Is there anyway to block it?"

"For normal people, no. For you, yes. You can draw your energy back into you and form a sort of shield. Here, I'll show you." He straightened his back and shoulders, resting his large hands on his knees.

"I'm going to try and influence you. When you start to feel it, try to wrap the energy around yourself as protection."

I shut my eyes again and reached deep down until I felt that odd cool sensation once more within my grasp. When the warmth tried to reach me, I concentrated on twisting the energy around me. It began to seep through the cracks so I raised my hand, which seemed to give my power more physicality. The heat receded after a moment or two, leaving goosebumps on my bare arms.

"Good. I'm impressed." Michael smiled, his voice genuine instead of teasing like usual. "From now on, we'll practice this every morning until you've got the hang of it."

I pouted. "Aw. When do I get to do the cool stuff like shooting mind bullets?"

He grinned again. "You have much to learn, young Padawan."

"If you start in on the Star Wars quotes, I am leaving."

"Fair enough. Now that you've got the basic feeling down, we can start on defense incantations. Before you say anything, you have to have drawn the energy around you, much like you did just a moment ago, and say 'In the name of the Father, I reject.' This causes a metaphysical barrier between you and whatever's coming at you. It's not going to be very strong the first time you do it, but the more you practice, the stronger the barrier becomes. Give it a try."

I cleared my throat, feeling vaguely silly as I repeated his words. "In the name of the Father, I reject."

After I spoke, I felt the cool, invisible energy crystallizing around me.

Michael nodded. "Good. If done properly, it can buy you enough time to fight back, retreat, or come up with another plan. You have to remember that it's not permanent. The only person who can sustain one for long is Gabriel."

"If he can do that, why didn't he form one to protect me when Belial attacked?"

"You can't form shields for others because the energy doesn't work that way."

"That sucks."

He smirked again. "Yeah, it does."

"Are you any good at shielding?"

Michael shook his head. "That's why I got my ass kicked by Mulciber."

A shudder went down my spine at the mention of her name. Evil soul-sucking bitch. I hoped she was rotting in Hell where she belonged. "Why didn't attacking her with your energy work?"

"The weapons she had been using on me were resistant to those kinds of attacks. They pretty much bounced right off of her. You have to understand that there's sort of a hierarchy of demons. Mulciber is among the most powerful. Belial is the so-called favorite of their little 'family,' but she's the brains of the outfit."

"What can you tell me about...Belial?" His name left my mouth like a whisper. Part of me still felt hesitant about saying his name, as if he'd hear it and appear. I may have been a brave fool at times, but I did not want to see him ever again.

The archangel paused, thinking. "Not much. You read Paradise Lost, right?"

"Yeah."

"It's pretty accurate on that account."

I shivered a little, rubbing my arms. "'Belial, in act more graceful and humane; a fairer person lost not Heav'n; he seemed for dignity compos'd and high exploit: but all was false and hollow; though his Tongue dropt Manna, and could make worse appear the better reason, to perplex and dash maturest counsels. Book II.'"

His eyes softened their gaze on me. All at once, I felt
my shield crumbling because of my lack of concentration.
Calming waves of emotion flowed out of Michael into me. For
once, I didn't mind. I honestly needed it.

He opened his mouth to say something sympathetic, but I
interrupted. "What can I use to attack?"

Michael shook his head. "Your power is too raw for that
right now. It could be dangerous."

"To whom? You're an archangel," I pointed out.

"No, that's not why. Attacks take more energy out of you
than defense or healing. If you use too much, you'll end up
drained. I'd rather not carry your unconscious body out of the
park," he added, arching an eyebrow.

I fought the urge to frown. "Alright, good point. Let's
keep going with the defense, then. But the mind bullets had better
happen eventually or I'm calling shenanigans."

"One more comment about 'mind bullets' and I'm taking
away all your Tenacious D CDs."

"You're no fun."

"We're here."

Michael's voice interrupted my thoughts, and I
realized that my mind had drifted off to memories of the
past during our silent car ride back to the hotel. After we
collected Marianne, we'd be heading to the orphanage for a
meeting with Jameson. That would at least be a step in the
right direction to solving the mystery of where all these
ghosts had come from.

Speaking of which, the timid ghost was waiting for
us outside of the lobby when we rolled up. She glided
straight through the back door of the car without
hesitation. Some ghosts picked up on the odd phasing
thing quickly while others, often children, took some work.

I withdrew the directions I'd gotten out of my back
pocket and read them aloud as Michael weaved his way
back onto the main road, though Marianne's hovering
above the seat behind me was awfully distracting.

Around twenty minutes later, we arrived at the
orphanage—a large, four-story brownstone building

settled on its own few acres of land outside of the city. There had been light rain earlier, so the ground was slick and the children weren't out in the playground out front. We drove into the parking lot around the left side of the building and got out. The plan was simple — we'd be interviewing Jameson pretending to be novelists while Marianne completed her final wish. It sounded a little creepy, but then again my job involved helping ghosts, so that was a given.

Thankfully, even with the disturbing deception, everything went smoothly and we helped her cross over. Still, I couldn't help feeling bad for Jameson, because he would never know how she felt about him.

"You okay?" Michael asked after we were both back in the car, strapping in for the ride back into town.

"Yeah, I just…" I took a deep breath. "It's a shame he didn't get to find out she was in love with him. It sounds like she carried it with her for a long time. I wish she had been able to tell him before she died."

He nodded, starting the engine. "Unprofessed feelings tend to eat at the soul. It's not healthy."

"Yeah. People really should just say how they feel."

Our eyes met. Silence spilled between us for a paralyzing few seconds before I cleared my throat and grabbed the directions from inside the glove compartment.

"Right. Let's get the hell out of here," I muttered, mentally chiding myself for letting such a stupid thing out of my mouth. Just as I retrieved the directions, the picture frame of my mother tumbled to the floorboard. As I scooped it up, my fingertips brushed against something bulky and rectangular in the back of the frame. What the hell?

I put the papers down and flipped the frame around, running my hands over the back until I found a thin seam at the bottom, so thin that I could only squeeze two fingers inside. When I pulled, a small leather-bound notebook no larger than the palm of my hand slid out.

"What is it?" Michael asked as I flipped it open. Inside, there was curly cursive writing on small sheets of tablet paper in Castilian Spanish, my mother's native language so it was only natural she would write in Spanish.

"I think it's a diary."

Michael leaned across the seat to see. "Your mother's? What's the date?"

I read the date at the top, though it took me a moment. She had taught me Spanish and English as a child, but I rarely spoke it so I was a bit rusty. "If this is right, then it's after they took her to the psychiatric hospital."

I turned more pages, finding that entry after entry, starting from the day they brought her in to the day the file said she died. A thrill went through me. This is what I had been searching for all this time. Answers.

CHAPTER TWENTY-ONE

August 5th, 1993

I am no fool.

I know why I have been brought here. They can pretend all they want that they want to help me, to heal me, to save me from myself, but I can see right through their lies. I was only able to procure these bits of paper from them because they hope I will willingly divulge my innermost thoughts to them. Each night, I take one sheet and hide it for safekeeping. Thus far, they have not caught on. I am not sure if I will be able to keep my writings safe from them forever, but I have learned that there is always hope even in the darkness.

I don't know where to start. I am writing merely to keep myself sane. I don't expect to be able to see my precious Jordan again, but should you ever find this, my daughter, know that I love you more than anything in the world. I had hoped to explain these things to you when you were older, but I fear I will be gone before you grow up and so I will divulge them here.

The year you were born, my powers came to fruition. I developed the ability to see the dead spirits walking the earth. The archangel Gabriel came to me and explained the order of things. There are twelve bloodlines in this world that possess the ability of Seers — the bridges between humans and Heaven. This power passes down through the generations of the original Twelve Disciples: Simon-Peter, Andrew, James the Son of Zebedee, John, Philip, Bartholomew, Thomas, Matthew, James the Son of Alphaeus, Thaddeus, Simon, and Judas. Not every son or daughter of these disciples has the gift — only a select few receive them. It is usually those with souls that are pure and untouched by the ways of man. We are charged with the task of helping the spirits who are left behind to reach the afterlife. We are few, but we are faithful.

It is for this reason that the people in this institution have imprisoned me. My sister, Carmensita, bore witness to my ministrations helping spirits cross over and called the authorities to take you away. She did not receive the gift and so she did not know, or care, that I was helping the ghosts. However, this is not the only reason I have been brought here.

Long ago, Gabriel warned me that someday the demons might become aware of my existence. They are as cunning as they are cruel. This is why I left Spain to come to the United States. I decided to stay mobile – to live in a city for a certain amount of years and then move in order to keep my presence under the radar, as they say in America. I do not know which particular demon or entity has overseen my capture, but I will do my best to find out and escape this place. I will keep this journal safe and record what I have found periodically, should it prove useful for my escape.

August 8th, 1993

It has been three days since my imprisonment. I have learned little, but I have at least learned something.

The head doctor is called Dr. Vulcan. I did not deduce that she was one of them until she smiled at me and I could see the cruelty, the evil, the hatred in her eyes. Whenever I am in her presence, I feel trapped. She has not revealed to me the reason for my capture, but I suspect she wants me to play some part in a plot against humanity as well as Heaven.

During my weekly sessions, they send in people to counsel me. This usually consists of asking me questions about my past in order to understand how I conjure up the so-called 'hallucinations.' They are just humoring me. I smile and give them nothing. It is probably not the wisest idea. I know that they will start to get nasty soon. I can feel it in my bones. But I will endure. I am an Amador and I am not afraid.

August 10th, 1993

The monsters have dropped their human masks and shown me their true faces. I will not detail the things they do to me because I will not give them the satisfaction of knowing they hurt me. I am stronger than that. I will endure.

Gabriel has finally contacted me through my dreams. We discussed an escape plan based on the small amount of information I have been able to gather. At this time, he cannot extract me because of the demons' numbers in this place. If he went for a direct assault, the demons would most certainly kill me rather than let me fall into the hands of the angels. He has learned this from experience. Instead, he said he will find another method, one that has less risk involved.

He also told me that he does not know why they chose now to abduct me, but that he will find out and he will find a way to free me. His kindness is what got me through their torture today. I do not blame him for being unable to help as of yet. The angels are charged with the safekeeping of both Heaven and Earth. They cannot put themselves out in the open because it is against the rules their Father made. But I have faith in Gabriel, in God, and in myself.

I will endure.

August 12th, 1993

The demons brought in a specialist today as their previous attempts to extract information have been fruitless. His name is Andrew. I do not think they know the truth, but I do. When he walked into my room this morning and looked at me with those dark blue eyes, I felt something.

Hope.

I cannot explain why, but I know this man is not here to hurt me. He did not ask me about my past or about my 'hallucinations.' He asked who I am. When I talked, he listened. He didn't write anything down. He didn't patronize me. He didn't look down his nose at me like the Americans do when they hear my accent. He is calm. He is steady. He is different.

Though I do not trust him fully, I have decided to cooperate somewhat. It may be one of their tricks, but if there is one thing I do trust, it is my own instincts. My powers only take me so far. I can only depend on myself in here and that will not happen if I have doubts.

Let us hope that I am right.

August 14th, 1993

The demons feel more confident with my cooperation and so they allow me more 'privileges' than before. I am not constantly restrained in my room. They allow me the luxury of a few books. It is almost an acceptable existence except for one thing. They will not let me see my daughter. I fear for her more than I fear for myself because I know the hatred my sister has for me and how she will project it onto Jordan. Jordan is a strong girl. I have to tell myself that every second I am here and not with her. I have endured unspeakable things in this place, but I worry she will endure worse. She does not deserve it. She never will.

Gabriel contacted me again and revealed that Andrew is on their side. They received word that the demons wanted someone to gain my trust to fool me into cooperating with them. He has been sent to monitor my stay here and unravel the secrets the demons are keeping. I do not know how successful he has been in this endeavor. I do know, though, that when he smiles, I feel safe. It is a strange feeling. Our time has been so short and yet I find myself relieved when he shows up for our sessions. It is foolish, but it is one of the only things that keeps me going.

August 15th, 1993

Andrew and I seem to have reached some sort of comfortable level now that I know he is not one of the demons' ploys. I have not met many charming men in my life, but he is one of the few. He often answers my questions with questions – a trait of both intelligent and infuriating men. When he's feeling generous, he tells me a little bit about his life.

Currently, he does not know about any other Seers in the states. Based on what I've heard, he is one of the most skilled Seers there has ever been. He has been helping ghosts cross over for nearly three decades, and he has had some vicious encounters with demons as well. He does not like to talk about the scars – especially not the one above his eye – and so I do not prod him about them, but I know he probably got them from protecting someone. However, beneath the charm, I sense there is more. He has no family and no ties to anyone because of his valuable abilities. He openly admits that coming to this hospital puts us both at risk, but he never backs down from a challenge. He is the one who told me that Dr. Vulcan, the head psychiatrist, is actually the demon Mulciber in disguise. The only reason he has been allowed access to the hospital is because he has mastered his powers to the point where he can pass himself off as a normal person.

When I asked him if he regrets his gift, he merely shrugged and said that it was a life, nothing more, nothing less. I told him that wasn't much. He smiled at me and said 'It's enough.'

Maybe it is.

August 16th, 1993

Is it possible to find light in the darkness?

August 17th, 1993

For the first time since I've been here, I was allowed to go outside. I had forgotten about the wind and how it feels in my hair and on my cheeks. I actually cried. Shameful. Andrew was the one who convinced them to let me have some fresh air. We were only allowed out for ten minutes, but that time alone made the shackles feel loose, almost nonexistent. Maybe this kind of serenity means my time here is drawing to a close. I do not know. What I do know is something inside me has changed, and not because of my imprisonment here. It is because of Andrew.

He gave me a rose today. I want to blame my happiness about this fact on the isolation and the desperation I've experienced in this little slice of Hell, but when he held my hand for that brief moment, I knew I had found myself again. Holding his hand reminded me of my former husband, Lewis, before he became a bastard, when we were young and in love. God help me. I am not capable of love. Or at least I thought I wasn't. It would be better for me to forget. I cannot.

He calls me Cat.
I wish I didn't love that about him.

August 18th, 1993

Something is wrong.
I believe that the demons are going to make a move soon. Today, they claimed that my behavior implicated signs of suicidal tendencies and so they placed a security guard in my room for 'safety reasons.' Furthermore, I did not have a session with Andrew today. They told me he had other arrangements. I cannot remember ever feeling so afraid. All I can think about is whether they have caught on to him and hurt him, or worse. I cannot escape by myself to look for him.

However, there was one ray of hope. When the men came in for my daily examination, they gave me a glass-less picture frame they said was from Andrew as part of my therapy — a photo that had been confiscated from my wallet. It was my senior portrait from high school. It seemed only for sentimental reasons, but just after they left I found a scrap of paper hidden behind the frame. I waited until nightfall when the guard left for a brief break and read it in the moonlight. There was no name, only a poem. It took me a moment to recognize it as W.H. Auden's "Song IX." I used to read his poems when I was learning English.

I do not know if this is a warning or a confession, but I know it is important and so I have kept it close by. I believe that whatever reason they have chosen to abduct me for is going to come to fruition tonight. I cannot explain why. It is just a feeling in my gut.

There is nothing left to do except wait. If this is my last entry, then so be it. I have led a good life. I have seen many wonders. I have laughed. I have cried. I have loved. I have…lived. Our Father gave us no greater privilege than that.
Catalina Amador

It took me a moment to realize that the car had stopped because we arrived at the hotel. My mind had been completely engrossed as I read the letters out loud.

Silence filled the car, seeming to highlight the stillness that had come over me when I read the last one.

Then, slowly, Michael unbuckled his seatbelt and leaned across, brushing his fingertips against my left cheek where hot tears had trickled down my face.

"I'm sorry," he whispered. "I am so sorry, Jordan."

A faint smile touched my lips as I lowered the diary into my lap. "Why? It wasn't your fault."

"If I had been there…maybe I could have prevented this…"

I shook my head, wiping my eyes. "We could sit here all day talking about what we would have done if we had been there. The past is the past. There's nothing we can do about it now."

"That doesn't make it hurt any less." His voice held such regret that I wondered if the letters had upset him more than me. I closed the diary and touched his hand, finally looking into his concerned face.

"Michael…it's okay. All I wanted on this trip was to find the answers for myself. I've done that. It's not pretty, but it's what I needed."

He wrapped his fingers around mine, strong and warm, and nodded. "Okay."

After giving my hand one last squeeze, he opened the car door to get out. I unbuckled the seat and climbed out, gathering the picture frame, diary, and papers I'd gotten from the psychiatric hospital.

I needed something else to think about, and soon. There was so much information to absorb. Upon glancing at my watch, I realized I only had a short while before my…*meeting* with Terrell. That did the trick alright. The mere thought of which made my pulse double and my palms start to dampen. Damn him.

We went back to our room, which was considerably chilly due to our absence, and Michael sat on the bed while I stared intently at my suitcase and wondered if I should change clothes. I mean, it wasn't a date. No way in hell. So

I shouldn't change. Or should I? I thought about calling Lauren to ask—since she was the only female presence in my life who knew things about men—but decided against it. It was a one-time occurrence, no need to change. Right?

"Are you okay?" Michael's mildly amused voice broke through my thoughts, making me jump a little.

"Hm?" I said.

He glanced at the suitcase. "You're been standing there for almost a minute with the weirdest looks on your face."

I cleared my throat and zipped the suitcase closed, trying to seem nonchalant. "It's nothing."

"Right." Michael reached down on the other side of his bed and withdrew his acoustic guitar—a gorgeous wooden one with a brilliant polish to it. He practiced three or four hours a day, and our trip was no exception. I stood in front of the mirror applying a bit more eyeliner while he began plucking at the strings and adjusting things accordingly.

"How long do you think you'll be out?" I caught on to his casual tone. He was trying way too hard not to sound interested. It was kind of adorable, in a way.

I hid a smile, picking up my comb. "A couple hours."

"Want me to order something?"

"Just for you. We're getting Chinese."

"Oh. Bring me back a Fortune cookie."

I paused, glancing at him. "You're an angel. Do you really believe in those things?"

Michael smirked. "Who says I believe in them? Maybe I just want to read the messages and add 'in bed' to the end of them."

I dropped my comb. He chuckled. I tossed him a dirty look and checked one more time to make sure my hair looked presentable before walking to the bed to get my duster. By now, I had started to recognize the melody he was recreating—a tune I'd heard on an old Guy Ritchie film. "Golden Brown" by the Stranglers. Good song.

"Call me if something comes up," I said, my hand on the doorknob.

He nodded, watching me with a rather guarded look.

"I'll be here."

Earlier during the day, I had looked up the restaurant to find it only about two blocks away, so there was no need to ask Michael to drive me. Besides, he already seemed displeased with my agreement to go—though he just wouldn't admit it—and I didn't want to put him in that position. I wasn't sure if his disapproval was a result of being protective, or if it was something more personal. Frankly, I didn't want to entertain either thought, so I walked down the street, careful to make sure I hadn't been followed by anyone dead or alive, until I reached the Dynasty.

The Chinese restaurant was tucked between a barbershop and a Subway and the inside was dim but with a quiet atmosphere. There were beautiful paintings on the walls of emperors and warriors and miniature chandeliers hanging above each table. The tables themselves were covered in forest green cloth that went well with the dark carpet. There was a short line at the front so I had to wait. Terrell was waiting for me at the center table. He smiled and waved when he saw me. My pulse skyrocketed. This was such a bad idea.

"Table for one?" the maitre'd asked, catching my attention.

I shook my head, pointing. "I see my party, it's fine."

He smiled. "Enjoy your date, ma'am."

I narrowed my eyes at him. "It's not a date."

He raised his eyebrows at the sudden hostility. I muttered an apology before I walked to the table. Terrell offered to pull my chair out but I declined, scooting up to the table on my own.

"You're early," I pointed out, having nothing better to say.

Terrell shrugged. "I had nothing better to do and I was honestly looking forward to this."

I felt my suspicion rising. "Why? Last time I checked, people usually aren't eager to see their ex-girlfriends unless it's for lascivious purposes."

He chuckled, sending a shiver down my spine. Damn that laugh of his. It was like having someone trace a finger down my back. He could advertise Old Spice commercials with that voice if he wanted to. "Lascivious? You've been reading, haven't you?"

"Guilty as charged."

The waitress came by and asked what I'd like to drink. I ordered tea and flipped open my menu, happy to find an excuse not to look at Terrell any more. The food was pretty standard for a Chinese restaurant. I always ordered the same thing anyway.

"Would you like to order your food now or do you need more time?"

I glanced at Terrell, who shook his head. "I'm ready if you are."

"General Tso's chicken, shrimp fried rice for the side, and Moo Goo Gai Pan," I answered, handing her the menu. Terrell gave his order as well, the same thing he always got even when we were dating — orange chicken and rice.

"I see your tastes haven't changed over the years," he said, dark brown eyes glittering in the dim lights.

I squirmed in my seat, resisting the urge to plunge my hand into my duster pocket to touch the rosary. It had become a nervous habit of mine.

"Guess not." Silence fell. Awkward R' Us.

"You look good, Jor." His tone softened, not so teasing this time around.

I felt my cheeks filling with heat. "Thanks. You too."

"And here I was thinking you didn't notice," he replied, grinning.

I finally felt comfortable enough to glare at him. His grin only widened.

"And there's that infamous glare. Still as scary as the last time I saw it."

"Thanks, I've been working on it." For the love of God, where was the food? I needed to stuff something in my mouth before I said something even stupider. Thankfully, she came back soon with the steaming piles of chicken and vegetables, though by now my stomach had turned into too many knots to truly enjoy the meal. He chose chopsticks while I stuck with a fork. Didn't have much practice with them as of yet.

"I don't get it."

Terrell glanced upward from his chopsticks, one thick eyebrow raised.

I shifted in my seat, spearing a steaming hot mushroom on my fork before continuing. "Why...are you being so nice to me? We didn't exactly leave on pleasant terms."

He didn't answer right away. He set down his chopsticks and folded his hands on the table like he used to when he had something serious to say. Seeing his old habits, his body movements, felt surreal, like slowly remembering the lines to a movie you've seen a hundred times.

"I've had a lot of time to think about what happened," Terrell said finally.

"At first, I blamed it all on you. The way you shut me out...it made me feel like we'd never really known each other and like you didn't respect me enough to tell me what was wrong."

His words made me wince because I knew everything he said was true. To him, I'm sure that I came across as a heartless bitch, especially since it had seemed to come from out of nowhere. In all honesty, it had. With Mr. N dead and my transformation into a Seer complete, I destroyed any remaining links to my old life. Unfortunately, Terrell had been part of the destruction.

"But as time went on, I realized that there were some things I could have done better. After you left, I didn't go after you. I could have tried harder to help you but I didn't because I was still angry. Seeing you again like this…it's got to be for a purpose."

I shook my head. "Not everything is like that, Terrell."

"Everything has its place, Jordan. You might be too afraid to admit it, but you know it's true."

At last, I met his eyes. His held a certain conviction in them. My poor little idealist. He'd never change.

"I'm not afraid of anything," I replied, my tone stiff and defensive even to my own ears. A small smile tugged at the edge of his lips.

"Why didn't you dress up tonight?"

"Why would I? This isn't a date."

"So a man and a woman who were once romantically interested in each other go to a restaurant to have dinner…and it's not a date?"

I cleared my throat, feeling a wave of heat rise to my cheeks. "Exactly."

Terrell shook his head. "That's what I'm talking about. You won't admit this is a date, or at least similar to a date, because you don't want to think about me that way."

"What way?"

The amused look on his face caved in to a more serious expression — one that made my stomach flop. "You know I didn't ask you out just to catch up."

I glanced away. "Don't know what you're talking about."

He sighed. "Fine. I get it. It's not like I expected you to leap into my arms or something. I guess what I'm trying to say is that I don't believe in coincidences. There's no way that we'd be in the same city at the same time in the same park if it wasn't for a reason. Forgive me if I'm an idiot for trying to make something of it."

Terrell lifted his right hand to signal the waiter. Guilt gnawed at my gut and I reached out, touching his left hand still resting on the table. "Wait."

He hesitated, giving me a considerate look. I exhaled. "I'm not trying to run you off. It's just...weird. I don't like thinking about what happened between us. It took me a while to stop worrying about you. I'm sorry."

Slowly, he smiled again and flipped his hand over so our fingers were intertwined. "Then, if you don't mind, why don't we just be honest and get through the weirdness together?"

That made me chuckle. "You always did have a way with words."

"Thanks for remembering."

"My pleasure." He squeezed my fingers and let go, returning to his orange chicken. Feeling a tad more comfortable, I ate the stray mushroom on my plate.

"So who's the guy?"

I coughed, nearly swallowing the mushroom down the wrong pipe. "Come again?"

He gave me an incredulous look. "I'm a doctor, if you recall. I can read people, and I'm getting a vibe off of you that you have a boyfriend."

I stared at him. "There is no way in hell you can know that."

Terrell shrugged. "Well, there's also the fact that you smell a little like AXE cologne, and as much of a tomboy as you are, that's not what you'd wear."

My shoulders relaxed. "Oh. Well if you knew that, why'd you still ask me out?"

He flashed me a grin. "I wouldn't be me if I
didn't think I could steal you from him."

I rolled my eyes. "You wish. You're half-right. I have
been traveling with a guy, but he's not my boyfriend."

"Good. That saves me the trouble of putting the
moves on you."

I kicked him in the shin and he laughed. The room
got a little warm when he did. Dammit.

"Alright, so why is your just-a-friend guy traveling
with you?"

"I needed a little help covering the costs. Besides, he
knew it'd be hard for me. I'm actually in town looking for
information about my mother."

Surprise stole across his face. "What kind of
information?"

"Anything I can find. There's not much, but I finally
got the chance to visit the psychiatric hospital she was in."

He leaned forward. "Did you find anything?"

"A bit. They still had her profile. I had to go to my
aunt's place to get the last of her things."

Terrell's handsome face darkened at the mention of
Aunt Carmen. "I doubt that went well."

A bitter smile crossed my lips. "It didn't, but…at
least the trip wasn't a total disaster."

"So when are you heading back to Albany?"

"Not sure. I have a couple more things to take care
of, and then we'll go back in a day or two."

"Well…" he said, rubbing the back of his neck in a
self-conscious sort of way. "If you're not too busy, I need
an escort to this event tomorrow night. Black tie affair."

My breath caught in my throat. Shit. Talk about a
blindside. I licked my lips and thought about it. Well, I
could go. The only thing on my schedule tomorrow would
be helping those ghosts we met in the park. I actually did
want to go with him. I'd forgotten Terrell's ability to draw
me to him. However, why was I hesitating?

At last, I shook off my thoughts and nodded. "I guess another night out wouldn't kill me."

"Great. If you need help finding a dress, give me a call."

I had to grin. "I also forgot what a metrosexual you are."

He flicked a bit of rice at me and I ducked, giggling. A nearby waiter gave us a weird look, but I ignored him. After all, this was the most fun I'd had all day.

From there, the not-date sort of glided along on its own. We talked about his job and how things had been going at the hospital he worked at. Working in medicine had always been interesting to me, but it wasn't something I could do. Granted, people's lives were as dependent on him as their afterlives were on me, but his job required so many hours and sweat and blood and tears. It had to be something he loved or it would run him ragged.

We also talked about his family, but only for a moment. I'd met his mother and father only once. It hadn't gone well. He had a younger sister named Grace, though, and she took a shine to me. He said she was doing well, much to my relief. Anyone with a family that judgmental needed all the luck life could get them.

An hour crept by before Terrell glanced at his watch and groaned. "I gotta get back. We start early tomorrow."

I spared him a sympathetic look. "Sorry to hear that."

He shrugged. "It's cool. Company's paying for this trip anyway."

Luckily, he had cash so we wouldn't have to wave down our almost non-existent waitress to pay the check. I didn't argue about paying for the meal because I knew it'd be fruitless. I could have talked Michael out of it, but not Terrell. He'd been born and bred a true gentleman, and therefore would never allow a lady to pay the check. I thought that was rather archaic thinking, but sweet in its own way. Not that I'd ever tell him or Michael that, ever.

Night had stretched out its limbs and painted the sky black, leaving Jersey to be lit by streetlamps and car headlights. The city itself seemed to be in motion. I stuffed my hands in my pockets, staring determinedly at his chest. If I looked into those dark eyes from this close, he'd surely steal my soul.

"Thanks for dinner. It wasn't nearly as disastrous as I thought it'd be."

He chuckled. "You're welcome. The dinner tomorrow is at seven o'clock sharp. What hotel are you staying in? I'll pick you up."

I told him and he copied it down into his Blackberry. We stood there in a brief awkward silence, trying to figure out the most appropriate way to say goodnight. I had been considering the fail-safe handshake, but he leaned in and kissed me on the cheek, voice soft in the cool air of night.

"Night, Jordan."

I watched him walk away towards his car, and the lingering sensation of his lips on my skin didn't leave until he pulled out of the parking spot and disappeared down the road. My hands fumbled for my cell phone as I shuffled down the sidewalk and collapsed on a nearby street bench, praying for the person on the other end to pick up.

"Hello?"

"Tell me I'm an idiot for going on a date with my ex-boyfriend."

A pause. "What ex-boyfriend?"

"Terrell."

Another pause. "No way. Tall, dark, handsome, pediatrician, cut-like-Morris-Chestnut Terrell?"

I palmed my forehead. "Do I know any other Terrell's, Lauren?"

"Hey, I had to be sure. What the hell is he doing in Jersey?"

"Medical conference. We bumped into each other at the park and he asked me to dinner. He just left."

Lauren let out a rush of breath. "Damn, girl. How are you holding up?"

"He just kissed me on the cheek. This is the first time I've breathed in like two minutes."

"I figured as much. I don't get it. I thought the two of you didn't leave on good terms."

"We didn't but…I don't know, Lauren. It seems like he's not mad anymore."

"Well, two years is a long time to think about your relationship," she admitted. Then, all of the sudden, her voice became rather indignant.

"Wait a minute, I thought you took Michael McSexy with you?"

I rolled my eyes. "Would you stop calling him that?"

"I'll stop calling him that when it stops being true," Lauren asserted in an irritated tone. "Anyway, is he or is he not with you?"

"Yes, he is. And that has nothing to do with Terrell," I shot back.

She groaned. "Is it really so terrible that he's sweet on you, Jordan?"

I raked a hand through my hair, trying my best not to sound exasperated. "I've told you before that it wouldn't work out. It's too complicated."

"Oh, and hooking up with your ex who lives in another state is not?"

She had me there. Dammit. "I'm not saying that's what I want."

"Then what *do* you want?"

Her question stopped me in my tracks. "I don't know. I honestly don't."

She paused again. "Well, now's a perfectly good time to find out. You know I only want what's best for you. This sort of chance doesn't come along every day."

"I know," I said. "But how the hell am I supposed to find out what I want?"

"If I knew, I'd tell you. All I can say is sleep on it. Maybe tomorrow morning you'll wake up with an answer."

"I hope so. Thanks."

"My pleasure. Talk to you soon."

"Bye." I hung up and pressed the phone to my lips, thinking. She'd been right. If you asked me yesterday, I would have said I'd never think about getting back with Terrell. Today, however, being with him and feeling so at home around him made me reconsider a few things. On the one hand, he knew nothing about my ghost helping, the death of Mr. N, or the demons gunning for me. Being with him would put him in grave danger. On the other hand, he wanted a home, a family, and a life. A long time ago, I had wanted the same thing. We were leagues apart, and yet somehow still reaching for similar goals. God help us.

My feet felt heavy as I dragged myself into the closest bar and plopped down on the stool, signaling the shaggy-haired bartender with a ring in his eyebrow. He raised said eyebrow at my expression.

"Long day?"

"You have no idea."

Walking home with five Heinekens coursing through my system proved amusing. I swayed so much on the sidewalk that at one point I gave up and played an imaginary game of hopscotch. The funny looks I'd gotten were plentiful, but I was in too good of a mood to care. Thank God our room was on the bottom floor. Not sure if I could handle stairs in my state.

After dropping the card once or twice, I managed to slide it in and kicked the door open with my foot. Michael immediately glanced over at me from the foot of his bed. He wore a grey tank top and faded blue jeans. Some part of me loathed how good the archangel looked day in and day out. For once, I'd love to see him disheveled, even the slightest bit.

"I thought you'd be back hours ago. Where'd you go?" He asked, tossing aside the book he'd been reading — *Proven Guilty* by Jim Butcher, I noted somehow — and standing up.

I hesitated letting go of the door since it seemed to be the only thing keeping me upright. "Bar down the street from the restaurant. They serve really good tequila shots."

The archangel's green eyes enlarged as they raked over me. "What?"

I flashed him a grin and shoved the door shut with my heel. "Kidding. I don't drink tequila. Had some beers. No biggie."

Michael sighed, sweeping the dark hair off his forehead and giving me a critical once-over. "Great. How many beers is 'some'?"

"Five. I'm *not* drunk," I insisted, poking him in the chest. It felt so very nice and warm that I leaned into him. All at once, my knees gave out, and he made a small noise of surprise, catching my arms so that I wouldn't slide down onto the floor.

"Sure you aren't," he grumbled as I snuggled the side of my face against his broad chest. So many muscles and yet I never saw him go to the gym. Damn perfect angel.

"I guess I can just yell at you in the morning, since you're not gonna listen to me now. In the meantime, you need to sleep this off." He scooped me up in his arms, bridal style, and carried me towards my bed. Being in his arms was comfortable. When he got to the mattress, he balanced my entire body in one arm and pulled back the covers. Even I had enough clarity left to be impressed by it.

Michael deposited me on the bed and began to pull back, but my arms were stubbornly locked around his neck. He paused, arching an eyebrow.

"You can let go now."

I shook my head. "Mm-mm. Comfy."

He let out a nervous chuckle, settling his knees on either side of me so he wouldn't have to hunch his six-foot-one frame over my body. "Could you try using words with more than two syllables?"

I exhaled, pressing the side of my forehead into his neck. Like his chest, his skin felt warm and smooth, with the light scent of whatever soap he'd used in the shower. Some sort of AXE brand, like the one Terrell said he could smell on me. I preferred the Old Spice Michael normally wore, but it worked for him.

"You think I'm an idiot, huh?"

Some of the tension in his shoulders eased. "Sometimes."

"No, I meant about seeing my ex. I shouldn't have seen him. Can't have him anyway. Not good enough. Besides, nobody wants to date a crazy lady who sees ghosts." My voice grew softer with every sentence.

Michael let out a small sigh, but I could hear the smile. "You never know. I hear the crazy ones are the most fun to date."

At last, a grin found its way to my lips. "Like you'd know."

"Well, I was human for a long while."

I let my head drop to the pillow, filling my vision with Michael's smirking visage. "You ever sleep with anyone?"

His eyebrows shot upward in surprise. "No, I…didn't get into a relationship. I didn't think it was a good idea. I couldn't remember who I was and I doubt many girls would understand that."

An interesting thought materialized in my head. "Was I your first kiss?"

He watched me with a careful expression. After a moment, he closed his eyes and his voice lost its emotion.

"I think you should get some rest."

"Why?"

"Because it's late and I don't think it's very healthy for me to be around you like this. I might end up breaking rules that are in place for your protection," he whispered, eyes smoldering with something that made shudders trickle down my back. Normally it would have made me nervous, but tonight I wasn't. What I saw in Michael's eyes was the opposite of what I'd seen in Terrell's. Terrell wanted me because he thought I'd be a good wife and mother. Michael wanted me because…he wanted me. No ulterior motive or future plans. He knew we'd be screwed up if we tried to have a relationship. I knew it too. The only problem was that neither one of us seemed to accept that fact just yet.

Evidence of the latter began to rise as I lifted my face enough to brush a small kiss on the corner of his lips. "What if I don't want you to protect me?"

Michael let out a long exhale. "Jordan."

I didn't know if the alcohol made me do it or if it was my own selfish desire, but I kissed him again and he didn't move away or tell me to stop. God. His lips were so soft. The tension that had been there when he laid me down returned to his back and shoulders, which I felt coiling beneath my fingertips like mattress springs. We stayed pressed together for a long moment until he let out a low sound—a groan of pleasure—and slipped his tongue past my lips. Just like that, I felt something metaphysical between us snap, and then my entire body became engulfed in an almost palpable heat. It ate at my skin like fire devouring a log, dizzying, torturous, and amazing. All at once, I realized it was his desire. He'd been holding it back from me. I'd never known just how powerful his feelings were when they manifested into physical forms.

His fingers wrapped around my forearms and lowered them from around his neck, pinning them against the pillow on either side of my head. He sighed into my mouth—a warm rush of breath—and broke the kiss, his

voice several octaves lower for reasons that made
goosebumps roll over the skin along my throat.

"Sleep."

He let go of my arms and climbed off of the bed. My
eyelids began to droop almost immediately. I didn't fight
the creeping darkness. As my mind started to drift, I could
just barely hear Michael's voice—low and soft in the quiet
room.

> *"The angels are stooping*
> *Above your bed;*
> *They weary of trooping*
> *With the whimpering dead.*
>
> *God's laughing in Heaven*
> *To see you so good;*
> *The Sailing Seven*
> *Are gay with His mood.*
>
> *I sigh that kiss you.*
> *For I must own*
> *That I shall miss you*
> *When you have grown."*

"A Cradle Song" by W. B. Yeats. With that, he
disappeared into the bathroom. I fell asleep just as the
spray of the shower reached my ears.

CHAPTER TWENTY-TWO

Morning didn't arrive gracefully. It slapped me in the face with an open palm, or at least it felt like that on account of the massive headache reverberating through my skull. I groaned and pressed my face into the pillow, blindly hoping its coolness would soothe my pain. No such luck.

A handful of minutes rolled by before I felt well enough to lift my head. Inch by inch, I withdrew from the pillow and tilted my face to look at the other bed. Michael wasn't in it. The clock read half past noon. Where had he gone?

Suppressing another moan of pain, I forced myself to sit up and ran my fingers through my incredibly mussed black hair so I could see. I shuffled over to the table against the far wall and found the Advil. Three pills would do the trick, or at least make me numb enough not to care. I drank some water from the sink to get them down and eyed the tepid water with distaste. Ice dispenser down the hall. Field trip.

My clothes from last night were still on, so I just slipped on my shoes and stuffed the keycard to the room in my pocket before leaving. The yellow-tinted hallway showed no signs of life. People in New Jersey liked to sleep in. My kind of town.

As I walked closer to the area where the ice dispenser and vending machines were, I could hear a familiar male voice. Confused, I peeked around the corner and spotted Michael facing the wall opposite me, speaking into his cell phone. The reception in the rooms was awful so he had to make calls out here. Good sense told me to go around the corner and tell him good morning but his next sentence stopped me.

"I know He wants to see me, brother. What was I supposed to do? She was drunk."

My heart nearly skipped a beat. Wait, what was he talking about? I flattened myself against the wall and tried to remember last night. I had a few beers and went back to the hotel room. Michael had carried me back to the bed. We had a little chat and I...kissed him. Christ.

I palmed my forehead, feeling the blood rush out of my face. Idiot. Lauren had told me before that I got a bit slutty when drunk, and obviously she'd been right. Now the Big Guy wanted to have a little discussion with Michael all because I couldn't keep it in my pants for one night. Shit.

My attention reverted back to the phone call. Gabriel's calming voice wafted to my ears. The call wasn't on speakerphone, but the volume was relatively loud.

"*I don't blame you for that, Michael. You know I don't.*"

"That makes one of you. This wasn't supposed to happen."

"*It's a test, Michael. One that you should take very carefully.*"

"She's not a test, she's a person. You know that better than I do."

"*Of course I do. Your situation is the test. All of the angels here on Earth have dealt with the desires of man except for you. It's something we have to overcome. You will do the same in time.*"

I heard him sigh in a frustrated sort of way. "That's just it, Gabe. I...part of me doesn't want to overcome it. Part of me wants what I know I can't have. What can I do about that?"

"*I can't give you a definite answer, brother. However, ask yourself this question: which part of you wants her – the angel or the man?*"

He took a deep breath and let it out slowly. "I don't know."

"*When you do know, you'll have found the solution to your problem.*"

"I'll take your word for it."

"Please do. Remember, this isn't just about the two of you. Your duty as Commander hangs in the balance as well. As much as you care for Jordan, you can't forget that. Your heart's never steered you wrong before. Listen to it."

"Yes, brother. I will."

"Good. Take care."

I hurried back down the hall and slipped inside the room, heart hammering in my throat. No. This wasn't the time to have a freak out. I slowed my breathing bit by bit and squared my shoulders. Gabriel was right. Michael wasn't just a charming bodyguard. He was Commander of God's Army in Heaven. He would exist forever in that role and there was nothing either of us could do to change it. It didn't matter how I felt about him. I wouldn't be responsible for him jeopardizing his mission. We both had a job to do in this world and we were damn well going to do it.

The door opened and Michael appeared just as I began gathering my clothes to go take a shower. "Oh, you're awake. I thought I'd have to scrape you off the mattress to get you up."

"We have a lot of stuff to do today. Figured it was time to get moving." I kept my voice professional and without emotion.

He shut the door and brushed past me. I nearly stumbled trying to make wider space between us as he passed by.

Michael blinked at me, confused. "You alright?"

"Yeah, I'm fine. I'll be out in a little while." Without another word, I shut myself in the bathroom. Well, that had gone well. I just needed a stuttering problem and Tom Cruise and I'd be all set.

Today was going to be a long day. Definitely, definitely going to be a long day.

"So where exactly are we meeting this guy?"

"Just through here," Michael replied, beckoning me as he found the right alley. The rain had finally left the city alone, but the concrete was still slick underfoot. I was happy to be wearing my Reeboks. I felt sorry for the ladies strolling around in pumps today. It was hard enough to stay upright in tennis shoes.

"Gabriel said that our contact would meet us outside this bar around three o'clock."

I hopped over a partially disintegrated cardboard box, breathing in through my mouth as we passed by the overflowing dumpsters on both sides of the brick walls. We came to stop in front of the knob-less metal door that led to a local dive bar.

The ghosts we interviewed earlier today had revealed startling news. Several of them were not from New Jersey, which didn't sound that shocking at first until we found out they were from across the country — one even hailed from Michigan. Two others were from Illinois. They all said the same thing: they felt compelled to walk to New Jersey, to where we were, but they couldn't explain why. Their needs to cross over had been pushed to the background of their residual minds. Gabriel and Michael agreed — there was a holy item involved.

"If that's true," I said. "What are we bargaining for this information? Nothing important, I hope."

"Not that I know of. Gabriel told me this particular demon doesn't want money or power or any of the usual bribes." He started to say more, but the door flew open and a tanned, spindly man strolled towards us. His head was shaved bald and he had a long, narrow nose with brown-blonde eyebrows, giving his face a severe look in the afternoon sun. Other than the frown lines in his forehead, he didn't seem all that intimidating, especially since he wore an unbuttoned black dress-shirt, white t-shirt beneath it, and jeans. He didn't bother checking the alleyway since it was long and hidden from the main roads on both sides.

Secluded. Dangerous. Sounds like somewhere a demon would like.

"I'm guessing you're my contact, right?" the man said, revealing that he had a thick Australian accent.

Michael's face had become unreadable. "Depends. What kind of information are you selling?"

The demon smirked. "We don't discuss that until we discuss my fee."

Michael cocked his head to the side. "What exactly is your fee?"

The man rolled his neck, the thin smirk elongating. "A fight."

Michael stared at him. "Excuse me?"

"Nothing like a good scrap every now and then. I don't really get one of good caliber these days. Humans are all soft little meat-jackets. Ya look like ya can put up a good one, for an angel," he added, his upper lip curling with a sneer.

Michael's jaw twitched, but he didn't say anything rude. "We don't have time for this. There has to be something else you want."

"Well..." The demon's blue eyes fell on me and an unpleasant light flickered in them. "If ya don't want to fight me, let me give ya girl here a kiss."

In an instant, my spine stiffened. I sent him a nasty glare. "Trust me, you don't want any of this, pal."

He grinned wide enough to bare teeth. "I'll be the judge of that, love."

The demon reached for me. I went for the gun holstered at the small of my back, intending to draw and maybe blow off one of his toes, but Michael appeared between us in an instant.

"Touch her and I'll feed you that hand finger by finger," the archangel growled.

The demon laughed, an arrogant bray that echoed down the empty alley, and stepped back with his hands held up in surrender. "Now that's more like it. Gimme a good fight and I'll give ya the information. Deal?"

"Deal." Michael shrugged out of his leather jacket and tossed it on the ground behind him, leaving him in a cream long-sleeved shirt, jeans, and boots. Except for his height, he didn't seem all that scary until I noticed the murderous expression in his eyes.

I touched his arm, murmuring his name, and he glanced down at me. "You're not fighting for my honor, y'know. Calm it down, pretty boy."

His shoulders relaxed a little bit at the use of "pretty boy" and some of that righteous fury drained from his face.

"I know."

"Good. Now be a dear and wipe the floor with this moron."

Michael spared me a wicked but dazzling smirk. "Will do."

The archangel straightened his posture as he turned to face the demon, who had shed his wrinkled outer shirt. He spread his legs in a wide stance and raised his fists to chest level.

"So who, exactly, do I have the honor of fighting today?"

Michael went with a side stance. "Michael."

"Mm. I thought it was you. The pretty one."

Michael's jaw twitched again. I pressed my back to the wall, safely out of range of either man. I didn't want to be anywhere near this demon when the archangel snapped.

"I'm not sure if you'll be much of a threat without that fancy sword of yours, but let's see what you've got." The demon rushed him, turning into a t-shirt-clad blur, but his speed meant nothing. Michael brought his right foot around in a perfect spinning side kick—which struck the demon right in the nose and floored him in half a second. My jaw dropped. So did the demon's.

He sputtered on the ground as blood blossomed from his nostrils down into his mouth, blue eyes wide with shock.

Michael lifted an eyebrow, his voice flat. "Was that an acceptable answer?"

The demon spat blood onto the ground and grinned, wiping his mouth clean with his forearm. "Ain't that a bitch? First blood goes to the angel. Looks like Luka's got his work cut out for him."

"Maybe Luka should stop referring to himself in the third person before he gets kicked in the face again," I said with a sweet smile.

He tossed a dirty look in my direction, which made me smile wider, and scrambled to his feet in an attempt to regain at least an ounce of dignity. Too late for that.

All at once, the demon seemed to change as he faced Michael this time. He rolled his shoulders, causing a few ligaments to crack, and resumed the stance he had before, but it was slightly different — more solid, more balanced, and definitely more serious.

He darted forward. Michael met him in mid-stride, blocking a vicious punch aimed at the angel's throat. Michael grabbed Luka's wrist with one hand and seized him beneath the arm, whirling and throwing him over his shoulder.

The demon twisted his body in mid-air and landed in a crouch — a movement that looked eerily inhuman. In an instant, he lunged towards Michael again, this time leading with a side kick that shoved the angel back into the brick wall behind him. Luka immediately closed the distance between them, sending a flurry of punches at his face and upper torso. Michael dodged to the side and kneed Luka in the stomach, hard enough to gain room to move away from the wall.

Luka flew into a series of kicks that were so fast I had trouble following them — front kick, crescent kick, a high one aimed at the shoulder, another aimed low at the knees — and Michael avoided them with liquid grace, blocking the ones that were too fast to dodge.

Luka finally managed to catch his left foot behind Michael's right ankle and jerked him off-balance, wrapping an arm around his neck to choke him. Michael threw his head backwards, knocking it against Luka's already damaged nose, and elbowed him in the gut. Luka collapsed against the wall and shook off the momentary pain, his face white with anger. Michael wore a placid, almost serene expression, maybe because he had the demon on his last legs. Luka spat out another mouthful of blood from his ruined nose and closed in, his muscles coiled tight with tension.

He faked a high kick, causing Michael to jerk backward involuntarily, and kneed him in the groin, grabbing a handful of the angel's hair and forcing him to his knees. Luka threw his arm around his neck and squeezed. Michael dug his hands into the demon's forearm, struggling to get free. I took several steps forward without noticing, my hand reaching for my gun.

Then, Michael grabbed Luka's right hand and broke his thumb. The demon screamed in agony, letting go. The archangel grabbed him by the arm and slammed into the concrete face-first, forcing him into an arm lock.

"Yield," Michael ordered, shoving his knee into the demon's spine so he couldn't get up. Luka let loose an unearthly growl, glaring daggers at the angel over his shoulder.

"You son of a—"

Michael tightened his grip, causing another stream of curses to leave the pinned demon. "I won't tell you a second time."

"Alright, ya bloody bastard! I give!" Luka snarled. Michael narrowed his eyes before slowly releasing him and taking a couple steps back. Luka rolled over and cradled his injured hand.

248

"Great. This'll take weeks to heal. I s'pose I owe ya an apology, but I can't exactly offer ya a handshake."

Michael nodded once. "For what it's worth, your form was excellent."

Luka snorted. "Don't need your compliments. What is it ya wanna know?"

Michael exhaled and the tension in his body finally relaxed. "Jordan and I have been observing extremely unusual soul traffic in this city. We encountered a large group of ghosts in the park, some from completely different states. They have no recollection as to why they traveled so far or why they felt compelled to come here. We believe that a holy item is involved."

Luka paused. "There's been rumor that the boss has something new in the works. Not quite as grand as stealing an angel's body, either."

I made a scornful noise in the back of my throat. "You're gonna have to be a little more specific than that."

Luka switched his gaze to me instead. "He said he wants to create something, rather than take what was never his to begin with. Ya can quote me on that. Ya said something about the ghosts being drawn to one spot, right?"

"Yes."

"Well right there, you're lookin' at something small. The larger holy items affect the living and the dead. If it's only affecting the ghosts so far, it'll be something that's connected to death. Most likely, it's something like the True Cross."

I gaped. "The Cross Jesus Christ was crucified on?"
Luka nodded. "The very same."
"But I thought it was never recovered."
"It wasn't. But that don't mean someone didn't find a piece of it."

I glanced up at Michael, who wore a deeply worried expression. "Is that really possible?"

"Perhaps. Last I heard, the True Cross was destroyed in order to prevent either side from utilizing it. However, I did not oversee its destruction. It was entrusted to one of the twelve disciples. If he was not careful enough, a piece may have survived."

Michael nodded to Luka once more. "Thank you for the information."

Luka shrugged. "Thanks for the fight. It's been ages since I've gotten my ass handed to me. Pretty refreshing."

I lifted an eyebrow. "Are all demons psychotic, violent perverts?"

Luka tossed me a feral grin. "Only the lucky ones. Later, love."

He knocked twice on the door to the bar and it opened, leaving us alone in the alley to absorb what he'd told us.

Michael scooped up his leather jacket and said nothing, instead heading back the way we came. It wasn't until we reached our hotel room that he spoke. "If Luka was right, then we're going to be on high alert for an attack. Satan does not directly interfere on Earth, and that most likely means he'll be sending Mulciber or Belial along to do his dirty work."

I rooted through my suitcase for the small First-Aid kit I'd packed. "And if all of this is going down in New Jersey the week we just so happen to be here, then that probably means it has something to do with me, doesn't it?"

Michael sighed. "Probably."

"I figured as much." I walked over and pushed him so that he sat down. He stared up at me in question. I pointed to his left cheek where a small cut lay beneath his eye.

"You're injured."

"It'll heal by itself."

"Not if it's infected. Hold still." I poured a bit of alcohol on a cotton ball and pressed it to the wound. He winced a bit. Maybe he'd been sucking it up.

"That was pretty impressive. Remind me to never pick a fight with you."

"Not that you don't do it anyway."

I rolled my eyes. "Oh, don't even go there. You give me lip all the time and yet you threatened to dismember a man for touching me."

He scowled, looking away as I opened a Band-Aid. "That's different."

"Sure it is." I pressed the Band-Aid to his skin and dusted off my hands.

"Any other injuries I need to know about?"

"Not sure." Before I could say anything, he yanked off his shirt and walked over to the bathroom mirror. I cleared my throat and concentrated on putting the small pack of cotton balls neatly back into the First Aid kit. If I ignored the shirtlessness, maybe it wouldn't affect me. Maybe.

"Mm. Doesn't look too bad," Michael noted. Out of the corner of my eye, I could see him touching a couple of bruises on his perfect washboard abs. Er, his abs. *Pay attention, Amador, he's talking to you.*

"He was tougher than he looked."

"Well, if he actually lived in Australia at some point, he had to learn how to fight. Everything on the continent tries to kill you." I closed the kit and setting it aside to dig deeper in the suitcase. Later tonight would be my second not-date with Terrell and I had packed an outfit in case Michael and I went to dinner somewhere nice. Or so I thought.

When I got to the bottom of the suitcase, I didn't find a modest burgundy dress with sensible straps and a high neckline. What I found instead was the slinkiest, revealing-est, attention-getting-est black dress I had ever seen in my life.

"What. The hell. Is *this*?!" I seethed. The Neiman Marcus tag was still on it. I had never set foot in a Neiman Marcus store in my life. But I knew someone who did. Someone busty, Korean, and annoyingly forward.

Michael gave me a confused look. "What's wrong?"

"This is *not* the dress I packed. This is the kind of dress you wear when you want to get molested on the ride home from prom!" I shouted, shaking the dress with emphasis.

Michael coughed, attempting to hide a chuckle, and walked over to examine it. "How'd it get in there?"

"My *ex*-best friend. She must have repacked my suitcase before we left," I grumbled, tossing the offensive article of clothing on the bed in defeat. I didn't have enough money left to get a different dress and I wasn't going to ask Michael for any. He'd done enough for me already. Meaning I'd have to squeeze into this thing and be Terrell's arm candy for the night.

"What exactly is the problem anyway? Why do you even need a dress?"

I hesitated. I forgot that I hadn't told Michael about the not-date tonight. Fantastic. "Oh. Terrell invited me out again tonight to escort him to some black tie affair."

Michael stared at me. I fidgeted. "Stop that."

"I'm not doing anything."

"Yes you are. You're mentally judging me."

He frowned. "How would you know that unless you subconsciously knew you were doing something unwise?"

I crossed my arms beneath my chest. "I don't have to answer that question. It's not a big deal. It's one stupid event. We'll be leaving Jersey soon enough and it won't matter anyway."

"You heard what Luka said. Something is going to happen soon. Do you really want to be out on your own tonight when Belial or Mulciber could be hiding around any corner?"

I glared at him. "I can take care of myself, Michael."

"No one's asking you to!" he yelled, making me jump. The angel turned away, raking his hand through his hair with a haggard sigh.

"Look, Jordan, you're not alone any more. It's my job to protect you while I'm here and I can't do that if you keep pushing me away."

"That's the problem, Michael," I shot back. "You have more responsibilities to your boss than you do to me. You taught me how to defend myself, how to heal myself, and that should be good enough. You can't keep babysitting one little human when you have an entire cosmos to worry about."

He faced me again, those green eyes boring into mine as if he could see straight through me. "Are you saying you want me to leave?"

My chest tightened. I hadn't expected him to say that. I bit my bottom lip, glancing away. "That's not what I mean."

"Then what do you mean?"

"Since when have I ever known what the hell I mean?"

He touched my right cheek, making me face him. "You do when it counts."

Staring up at him, shirtless, vulnerable, and wounded, I felt like I couldn't breathe. He had a knack for picking my walls apart brick by brick. It bothered me.

He took a step closer, casting a shadow over me.

"Stop," I mumbled, fixing my eyes on the floor. He brushed a lock of hair behind my ear, sliding his warm hand to lift my chin so I'd have to look at him.

"Stop what?" he murmured.

"Looking at me."

"Why?"

"That's how Terrell used to look at me before we kissed."

His lips parted to say something but I pushed past him, gathering up my duster from where it lay on the bed next to the dress.

"Get dressed. We have more ghosts to help."

CHAPTER TWENTY-THREE

In the three hours before I had to be ready for the event, we managed to cross two of the ghosts over to the other side. They were both locals of the area and had relatively simple final wishes. It didn't do us much good, though, because we found another two ghosts not soon after—one of which had come from Canada. Michael called Gabriel again and he told us he would meet us at the hotel later tonight to discuss what we were going to do. Thus far, the plan would involve trying to find the sliver of the True Cross—whether the demons had gotten their hands on it or not. I didn't like that plan. We needed a new one. There was no telling what they could do with that kind of power.

The silence in the hotel room was thick, stifling, and uncomfortable when I came out of the bathroom in the slinky dress. Luckily, the back didn't dip down low enough to expose the bra band or the scars. Through the grace of God, I had managed to work the tiny blow dryer attached to the wall so my black hair was fluffy and glossy around my shoulders. I never wore it down except for special occasions. Lauren said it made me look girlier, which was why I rarely did it.

I could feel Michael's eyes on me like twin points of heat on my spine as I slipped the rosary around my neck. He had every reason to be upset with my leaving, and I knew that, but it didn't change my decision. To be honest, I didn't want to go all that badly. I merely wanted to close the chapter on Terrell in the most definitive way I knew how. This way, we would have a real goodbye instead of me running out of his life like a coward.

"The dress looks good." Michael's voice was measured. I could only imagine what he actually thought, and thinking about it made me even more uncomfortable than I already was.

"Thank you."

"So I don't suppose I need to repeat the fact that this is a bad idea."

I closed my eyes, taking a deep breath. "Nope."

"Good to know." His tone overflowed with irritation. I thought about explaining the closure issue to him, but I'd feel silly saying it out loud. Instead, I put the finishing touches to my eyeliner and capped it, tossing it in my purse.

"Are you done?"

"I suppose I am."

I zipped the purse in one quick motion. "Y'know, this passive-aggressive shit is getting kind of old, Michael."

"Is it? Would you prefer the direct approach?"

I crossed my arms beneath my chest. "And what's that?"

Michael stood, walking until he towered over me, though not as much as usual because I was wearing high heels. "I could make you stay here if I wanted to."

I shrugged, feigning indifference. "Go ahead, big man. No one's stopping you."

He snorted, shaking his head. "Always have to have the last word, don't you?"

"It's one of my best traits," I sneered, snatching up the purse and heading for the door.

He called after me. "I thought the dinner wasn't until seven o'clock."

I paused with my hand on the doorknob. "It's six-forty-five. I'm gonna need a drink before the night's over. Don't wait up."

I slammed the door behind me, heading for the back of the building that led out into an alley and down to a local bar. The night air was cool rather than cold, soothing the tension flowing through my skin. I kicked the door shut and exhaled, standing in the dimly lit alley and trying to figure out why I had a lump in the back of my throat. We had a fight. Big deal. It was perfectly normal. Okay, that was a lie. Most people wouldn't manage to piss off an angel who was trying to protect them. I needed to apologize when I came back. He liked chocolate. Maybe I'd get him a Lindt bar as a peace offering. *Hi, honey, sorry I made you mad by running off to a party with my ex-boyfriend to avoid thinking about how you're getting under my skin.*

I choked on a laugh at that last thought. "He's gonna kill me for this."

I began walking down the alley, my heels clicking a funky staccato down the corridor, when I felt an itching tightness between my shoulders as if someone were watching me. I glanced behind me, only to be greeted by darkness and the distant wail of sirens. I turned and kept walking, this time a little faster, but the same tense sensation continued. I stopped.

All at once, the hairs on the back of my neck stood up. I no longer had the sneaking suspicion that something was watching me—I *knew* it. Cold sweat gathered on the small of my back and the itchy sensation of fear mixed with adrenaline hummed beneath my skin.

As if on cue, I heard a low growl seeping outward from the dark corner of the alley behind me. Probably a stray dog. No need to panic.

Squaring my shoulders, I turned around with a harsh expression on my face, prepared to out-stare the animal, and simply froze in place. The pair of eyes glaring at me from the shadows were a bright, almost hellish red. Last time I checked, dogs didn't have glowing eyes.

Its claws scraped against the concrete as it approached and finally walked into the dim light overhead. I had been half-right. The thing was shaped like a dog but it was unlike any canine I'd ever seen. On all four limbs, it had to be at least four feet tall and was covered from head to toe in shaggy black fur. Saliva dripped from its open jaws in globs, framing the razor sharp fangs. It almost distracted me from the acrid smell of sulfur that permeated the air and the steam that appeared to be rising from its very skin. There was no doubt in my mind that this thing had been sent specifically for me. I was damn sure it was not of this world. I'd fought something like this before.

It was a hellhound.

I swallowed to wet my suddenly-dry throat as the muscles coiled around the beast's shoulders when it prepared to attack. Well, being scared wasn't going to do me any good. Tossing off the cumbersome purse around my shoulders, I clenched my hands into fists and drew my energy out from where it rested inside me. My mouth formed an unpleasant smile.

"Alright, Scooby. Come get some."

Snarling, the beast lunged straight for me in a deadly arc.

"In the name of the Father, I reject!"

The hound smashed into me with what felt like the force of a Mack truck, taking me right off my feet. I slammed into the ground on my back, hands blocking my upper body. The shield had worked. The creature snapped at me with its huge jaws, but an invisible force kept it from touching me. Still, it had me pinned beneath its huge body and the shield wouldn't hold forever. I needed a plan and fast.

Grimacing, I summoned as much strength as I could and shoved my arms up into the thing's face. The shield forced it several feet away from me. The hound scuttled against the ground to get back on its feet. It gave me a couple of seconds to think. I needed to be on the offense.

I split my shield into several shards the way Michael had taught me and threw out my hands.

"Strike!"

One shard flew through the air like an arrow just as the creature raced towards me. The attack sliced down the right side of its body, spilling black blood onto the ground, but it kept coming. I threw myself to the side too late as it jumped at me. Its claws scored deep scratches across my right arm. Pain lanced through me as if I'd been burned with a red-hot poker. Shit!

The hound regrouped, rushing me again. I threw another two shards at it, this time slashing its left front paw and part of its spine. The beast stumbled as it ran but still crashed into me. I hit the ground again, knocking the air out of my lungs, too stunned to put up another shield. The hound snapped at my face but I rolled, crying out as one of its paws grazed my stomach before I could get away.

I felt something wooden beneath my shoulder. I glanced downward at the pile of trash I'd fallen into and found a broken broom handle. As the hellhound prepared for its final attack, I ripped the cross off my neck and shoved it into the tip of the splintered wood. The hound leapt, razor-sharp teeth aiming for my throat. I thrust the handle up into its massive chest.

The improvised stake pierced its shaggy hide and a sharp hissing sound emitted from where the cross buried itself in its insides. The hound convulsed in its death throes, still trying to bite me. My arms were too busy holding the stake to stop it from biting one side of my neck. I cried out again as its fangs scraped my skin, spilling blood. Just when I thought it would tear out my throat, two impossibly strong hands wrapped around its jaws and pulled them apart until I heard the loud snap of its skull cracking.

The great creature went limp and collapsed beside me, dead. In seconds, it disintegrated into ashes, leaving a steaming black stain on the ground. Michael reached down and helped me up, his face losing its righteous fury to give way to concern. It wasn't until I was standing unsteadily on my feet that I realized he had rushed out of a shower to help me. He was clad only in a towel. Huh. Interesting.

"You're hurt," he said, green eyes raking over my form.

I managed to shrug. "You're naked."

Ignoring me, he tugged my uninjured left arm across his shoulder and carefully walked me back inside. Naturally, the gouges didn't start hurting until we got in the rear entrance of the hotel, on account of the air conditioning. The adrenaline had worn off, leaving me shaky and scared shitless. Still, I managed to keep it together as Michael slid the key in the door with his left hand, his right still wrapped securely around my waist to hold me steady.

"How'd you know I was in trouble?" I asked.

"I felt the hellhound's presence. Whenever something with energy from Heaven or Hell is on Earth, the angels sense their presence," Michael told me. The door opened and he helped me inside, kicking it shut and hurriedly settling me down on the bed. He grabbed one of the fresh white towels on the sink and wet it. He knelt in front of me and began cleaning the wounds.

"I thought creatures from Hell couldn't appear on Earth."

"They can't. Hellhounds are usually just stray dogs that the demons use their influence over to corrupt them into monsters. It's sort of a loophole." He pressed the towel a little harder into my neck, causing me to hiss and his brow to furrow even deeper.

"I'm alright," I asserted, taking the cloth from him to mop up the blood. It seemed almost a shame for all that pure white to be marred with crimson.

He frowned at me. "How are you anywhere *near* alright, Jordan?"

I shrugged again, regretting it as the claw mark on my shoulder stung. "You taught me well, after all."

Michael shook his head. "Don't try to change the subject. I shouldn't have let you go out on your own. It was stupid of me."

It was my turn to frown this time. "What? Am I your pet? You don't run my life, Michael."

His gaze hardened. "That's not what I meant. You told me before that you'd be careful and now look at you. You almost got eaten by a hellhound all because you wanted to go on a date with your ex-boyfriend."

I pushed his hand out of the way when he reached for the towel, standing up. He stood too, appearing worried that I'd topple over from blood loss but I didn't. My anger had somehow given me enough strength to glare up at him.

"It wasn't a date—it was a meeting. Besides, why should you care?"

"Last time I checked I was your emotional support," he retorted a mildly sarcastic voice. "I can't perform my duties if I don't know the whole story."

A tired sigh escaped my throat. "What do you want me to say? I don't know how I feel about him any more than you do."

"Then why are you pursuing this relationship at all?"

My mouth fell open. "You—you're the one who asked me if I would ever consider getting back with him! Are you really giving me lip after you suggested it?"

Michael's face became stubborn. "Oh, great. So you ignore everything else I say to you except when it comes to this guy. That makes a lot of sense."

"This isn't about you, Michael."

His eyes narrowed slightly. "On that we agree."

His words stopped me. I had another angry retort prepared, but something stopped me. It was the way he said that last sentence and how waves of irritation seemed to pour off of him like a warm cloud of cologne that made me realize a startling truth.

"Michael…are you jealous?"

Silence spilled around us. Then, slowly, his expression began to recede from angry into something much harder to place. The frown disappeared and a very strange smirk touched his lips as he ran a hand through his dark, damp hair.

"Jealous, huh?"

He walked towards me. Normally, Michael was an open book of emotions: happiness, sadness, humor, compassion—all of them he wore on his sleeve like badges of honor. This walk I had not seen before. There was something in his body language that made my throat dry and my palms sweaty. He stalked towards me with the grace I only saw on National Geographic channel in the powerful movements of a lion on the plains of Africa—a predator closing in on the helpless prey.

Unfortunately, I didn't have a plain to run around on, so I backpedaled until my bare back pressed into the wall, the towel slipping from my slackened grip and onto the floor. My pulse skyrocketed when he stopped mere inches away, staring down at me with an unfamiliar heat in his gaze. The angel had vanished and the man stood in his place.

"My purpose on this Earth is to serve my Father and protect mankind from evil. It might not seem obvious, but I'm continuing my mission through protecting you, Jordan."

He lifted an arm and pressed his palm against the wall to the right of my head, his voice uncharacteristically soft. "In order to do this, I've had to train myself not to feel the same human emotions that you deal with on a daily basis—greed, gluttony, wrath, sloth, pride, envy, and lust."

When he said lust, the other arm rose to parallel the first on the left side of my head, effectively trapping me. I couldn't look away from the intensity in his eyes. Words died in my throat—words that should have gotten me out of this dangerous situation. Distantly, I realized Michael wasn't using his influence on me. This was the sheer power of his presence.

"So when you ask me if I'm jealous, you already know the answer because part of me is human. What you should be asking me is *why* I'm jealous, considering I have no right to be. Terrell is a good man. He could give you a comfortable life, keep you safe, and treat you well. I should want that for you. I should be willing to step back and let you live your own life. I should remember my place as an archangel under God's direct orders. Why do you think I can't do that, Jordan?"

I swallowed, imploring my lungs to fill with air enough to answer the question, though for the life of me I couldn't keep from stammering. "I-I don't know."

His face drifted close enough that I could smell the faint scent of his shampoo and the sweet spice of his aftershave, close enough that I could feel the warm air from each breath across my neck, close enough that goosebumps rolled over my arms from the thrill of being so near a handsome, nearly naked male body.

"I think you do know. You know exactly what I'm thinking right now, because you're thinking the same thing, even if you don't want to admit it to yourself."

I closed my eyes in an attempt to regain composure. "We should…probably patch me up. Don't want to die from blood loss."

"You're right. Hold still." Confused, I opened my eyes again to see him leaning towards the claw mark the beast had left on my collarbone, seeming as if he were going to kiss it. I pressed my palms against his chest to stop him, regretting it as my fingers came in contact with his firm skin.

"What are you doing?"

"It's faster if I use my healing energy."

"Y-Yeah, but when Raphael did it he used his hands," I insisted.

He smiled that secretive smile again. "True, but you made me angry. Consider this your punishment."

Before I could say anything else, he lowered his mouth to my collarbone and kissed the torn skin. I hissed, flinching as it stung, but then something else happened.

The cut tingled as if he'd poured rubbing alcohol over it, grew cold, and the skin re-knit itself as if it had never been damaged. No more blood, no more pain, no more mess. I hadn't been awake to experience this kind of rapid healing the first time. During our sessions, Raphael had merely run his hands over the wounds and they gradually closed up. Michael's method was nothing like his, probably for good reason.

There were three areas of scratches left on my body: the ones on my neck, the ones of my upper stomach, and the ones on my inner right forearm. My heart thudded inside my chest like an animal trying to escape its cage, but I had been trapped. Michael lifted my arm in one hand and trailed his lips across the delicate skin, sending goosebumps all the way to my fingertips. I could feel tremors going up my spine from the sensations and from the knowledge that he was doing something so intimate on purpose — dragging my very human desires out from depths of where I'd locked them in my mind. Damn him.

Now that the wounds on my arm had disappeared, he reached for the knot at the base of my neck that held up the dress. I panicked, afraid of what would happen if I let him. I caught his wrist, whispering his name. He held me with his heated gaze, his tone low and soft.

"Who don't you trust? Me or you?"

My lips barely moved. "Both."

"I'm not going to hurt you."

I shook my head. "That's not what I'm afraid of."

"What are you afraid of?"

I swallowed hard. "Not being able to stop."

A look went through his eyes that made my breath catch. "Let me worry about that."

He tugged the knot loose. I didn't stop him. The front of the black dress crumpled until the front lay a few inches above my waist, exposing my upper body clothed only by a black strapless bra. Michael's gaze could have burned a hole through solid steel and it was aimed at me. God help us both.

Time seemed to slow as he leaned over my neck and kissed the first scratch, sending waves of warmth through me that made my eyes flutter shut. He sighed and then inhaled the scent of my skin as if it supplied him with air to breathe. My knees nearly gave out as his tongue flicked across the second scratch, simultaneously agitating and soothing it. My hands came to rest on his broad shoulders, feeling the heat that seemed to permeate us both. One more left. Those soft lips caressed the third mark and made it disappear, leaving only the clean line of my throat for him to explore. He kissed over my pulse, the edge of my jaw, so carefully, as if he were sure I'd shatter from too much pressure.

I gasped as he lowered one hand to the dress and tugged it down several more inches, until the cuts on the upper portion my abs were exposed. Michael dropped to one knee and slid his hands over my waist, holding me still as his hot breath curled across my stomach. When his mouth passed over the wounds, my breathing became strained and weak. That same boiling metaphysical warmth from the last time we'd kissed flooded over me in a sudden rush, erasing whatever hesitance I had left. After the cuts closed and he stood to full height, I knew there was no turning back. Now or never. Now sounded very attractive.

Michael didn't hesitate either. In an instant, his body pinned mine against the wall and he kissed me, but it was different from before. This was a *kiss*. Eyes closed, lips parted, breath unsteady, tongue tracing a tantalizing line across my bottom lip. I had never in all my life been kissed like that, not by Terrell and not by any other temporary boyfriend I'd acquired. At first, his large hands cradled my cheeks to hold me still but the deeper the kiss became, the lower they sank. Down my neck, over my shoulders, brushing the sides of my bra, and finally settling on my hips. My knees were getting weaker and weaker by the second as his fingers drifted down into the crinkled half of the dress and just barely grazed my thighs.

Just when I thought I'd collapse, he wrapped his arms around the back of my legs and picked me up, raising me to his height. I ended up suspended in the air with Michael's lips trailing a line of heat down to the spot where my cleavage began. I honestly didn't give a shit about the consequences, especially not when I felt one of his thumbs caressing the delicate curve between my inner thigh and hipbone. My thighs acted on their own, encircling his waist, driving a muted hiss of pleasure from the both of us. The towel did him no justice. He was definitely the Commander for a reason.

All at once, there was a loud knock at the door.
Shit.

Michael moved first because I was too, ahem, distracted. He lifted his face enough to look me in the eye. I had to remind myself we had company because his gaze still held enough lust to eradicate all of my will power.

"I should probably answer that, hm?"

My voice was practically breathless. "Probably."

He seemed to think about it for a moment before sighing and lowering me to the floor. Finally embarrassed, I pulled the dress back up and fastened it, trying not to think about the fact that Michael watched me with a sort of defeated expression. I opened my mouth to speak, but he leaned down and kissed me, quick, firm, and luscious, before answering the door.

Gabriel stood there in all his cock-blocking blond glory with a dead serious look on his angelic face.

"Trouble. Follow me."

Michael barely had enough time to throw on his clothes. All I could do was toss off my heels and replace them with Reeboks before we followed Gabriel out the door. I didn't know if he had deduced what we'd been doing in our hotel room, but either way it didn't seem to matter. His brow was set firm in a frown—a look of determination I had only seen once, on a rooftop while he fought the demon Belial. Gabriel was always smiling, always serene, always kind. Seeing him like this scared me.

"What's going on?" Michael demanded, trying to catch up with his brother's quick pace through the lobby of the hotel. When we got outside, Gabriel stood still on the sidewalk and pointed to his left.

"Look."

I stared about, watching pedestrians walking up and down the streets. "Look at what? What are you—"

Then I saw them. People were walking in the same direction Gabriel was pointing, but that wasn't the strangest part. Some of them wandered into the streets and cars passed right through them. My jaw dropped.

There were at least fifty ghosts walking down the street.

"God…what's going on?" I whispered, eyes searching through the dead masses for a head count. I had been right. So far, I counted fifty-two ghosts.

"Something is calling to these spirits. I believe it is the sliver of the True Cross." Gabriel said.

Michael's jaw clenched. "I know for a fact none of the angels acquired it. Which means—"

"—one of the demons got their hands on it. We must move quickly. Follow them."

We jogged through the crowds, trying to catch up to see just where the ghosts were heading. Each one I passed had a blank, almost dreamy expression, as if their minds were far away.

"I don't get it," I said as I followed the angels. "Why would the True Cross Sliver attract so many spirits?"

"The True Cross is a bridge between the living and the dead." Gabriel said. "Christ gave up human life and died on that sacred wood so it is symbolic of humanity in both aspects. The dead are drawn to it because it is where he conquered death itself."

We rounded another corner. The ghosts had led us into the park. We followed the gravel path through the woods to the lake where an entire hoard of ghosts gathered. There had to be over a hundred here already.

I squinted as we came down the hill. A man in a tuxedo stood by the edge of the lake with his back to us. I brushed through the crowd of ghosts, ignoring the cold sensations their forms rippled across my skin. With a start, I realized I knew him.

"Terrell?"

He turned. "Jordan? I was wondering where you were. You weren't at the hotel and you didn't pick up your phone, so I came here looking for you."

"Jordan!" Michael called.

I waved a hand at him to dismiss the worried tone in his voice. "Don't worry, I know him."

I turned back to Terrell. "Look, I need you to get out of here. It's not safe."

"Get away from him," Michael ordered, his hands balling into fists.

I glared at him. "Michael, this isn't the time for that. We've got bigger problems right now and I don't need you getting overprotective—"

"Jordan, *listen to me*. That is not your ex-boyfriend."

I stared at him. "What are you talking about? I've been seeing him all week."

Terrell wrapped one arm around my shoulders, cradling me against the front of his body, and leaned down to whisper in my ear.

"And thus, I clothe my naked villainy with old odd ends stolen forth from holy writ, and seem a saint when most I play the Devil."

I recognized that quote. Shakespeare. "Terrell, what's going on?"

He kissed the shell of my ear and spoke again. "I'm afraid I haven't been completely honest with you…my pet."

A cold shock went through me. No. Impossible. Absolutely impossible.

"I want you to know that this façade was not the reunion I had planned for us, but it was suitable for my needs. If I had things my way, I would have taken my time in seducing you and getting you to trust me, but these aren't reasonable times and the Master grows impatient."

Terrell's normally warm voice had become bone-chillingly cold. It held a disgusting element of arrogance to it that he never had before. His words seeped into my skin like poison, filling my veins with a sickening feeling. It couldn't be. It just couldn't.

I shook my head, too numb to turn around and see his face, the face I had kissed a thousand times, the face that promised me the world, the face that wanted two kids and a dog and a white picket fence. "Can't be you. Two souls can't share a body. It's not you."

"You're quite right, Jordan. That is exactly why I killed him and took his body."

Just as he spoke, the tip of a blade pressed into my spine, right at the small of my back. The air left my lungs. I just stood there. My lips barely moved enough to form the words.

"You killed him."

The archdemon sighed in a melodramatic way. "He was necessary. I wouldn't have been able to manipulate you otherwise. It was tedious, but I spent our time apart studying his every move, his thoughts, his gestures, until I could copy them exactly. If it's any consolation, he died an honorable death. He would have made you proud, sweet Jordan."

Numb. All numb. Head spinning. Stomach churning. Eyes dim. Dead. My ex-boyfriend was dead

because of me. I killed him. I killed Terrell. Blood was
on my hands once again. So much blood.

"Jordan…" Michael took a step forward.

Belial jabbed the knife into my back, making me
flinch and the angel freeze in place. "One more step and I'll
split her in half. We only need her blood, not her life. Why
else would we send the hellhound?"

Gabriel's blue eyes narrowed. "We?"

Belial chuckled. "Yes, we. You know I am nothing
without my right hand man. Well, woman. Mulciber?"

The other demon approached from the edge of the
woods to our left, walking calmly towards our little
Mexican standoff as if it were nothing more than a picnic.
Her new body came in the form of a Vietnamese woman
with long, dark hair and brown eyes set in a round face. I
was still too numb to care about her sudden appearance.

"My, my. We have quite the reunion going on
tonight, do we not?"

"You have exactly five seconds to let go of her
before I tear out your spine, demon," Michael growled,
green eyes narrowed to slits. Gabriel whispered his name,
placing a gentle hand on his arm.

"Such brave words, angel. We both know there is no
way you can extract the girl without hurting her. Therefore,
I can do anything I want while you just stand there like
whipped puppies." She stroked her long fingers up and
down my left arm. Goosebumps rose as her red fingernails
began digging in, creating painful welts.

"What do you want, beast?" Gabriel spat, taking a
step forward as well.

Mulciber's pale face broke into a triumphant grin.
"Oh, I *have* what I want."

She reached into the pocket of her black Armani
pants suit and withdrew a tinted glass vial. Through the
light from an overhead lamp, I could see a tiny piece of
wood no bigger than a needle inside it.

"Tonight is the fall of man and angel. Tonight, we will conquer life and death in one fell swoop. Tonight, we wage war against the Heavens and spit in the face of God. Tonight is all about revenge — sweet, glorious revenge. Starting with you, Seer."

She grabbed my chin, making me look at her face, nearly inhuman with rage. "You took my favorite body from me. By your hand, your arm, you took away my victory. And so I will take away yours."

Before anyone could move, she grabbed my left arm and shoved her palm against my elbow, shattering it. I screamed, convulsing in Belial's arms. He held me upright as my body lurched forward, weakened by the pain that shot through my upper torso. Bile rose in the back of my throat. Too much. I would pass out from shock soon.

With a wordless roar, Michael lunged at Mulciber, his fist cocked to pummel the daylights out of her. She tossed the vial to Belial, who let go of me enough to catch it.

"Do it!"

Michael tackled her off her feet, grabbing her by the throat and slamming her to the ground. Gabriel leapt for me, but Belial raised the blade to my neck, stopping him.

"Move another inch and I'll flay her jugular," Belial sneered, popping the vial open with his thumb. Gabriel met my eyes and a look passed through them that I somehow understood. He was going to try something. I needed to be ready. I pushed past the aching feeling of loss in my chest and blocked out the pain of my ruined arm, waiting for him to make a move.

Belial used the tip of the knife to slice a neat line across his cheekbone. He held the vial up to it so the blood would run inside. The sliver burned a bright white color, nearly blinding both me and Gabriel. Belial used the distraction to slash one side of my neck. Blood poured forth and he held it to the vial as well to let it flood over the sliver. He lowered the knife a fraction from below my throat, giving us an opening.

I elbowed Belial as hard as I could in the sternum and dropped to the ground, giving Gabriel the chance to kick him in the chest. Belial flew backwards, head over feet, and landed near the shoreline of the lake. The vial went flying into the midst of the ghosts behind us, spewing light as if it were a supernatural sparkler. As Gabriel helped me stand, I felt some horrible power building only feet away where the vial landed. What had they done?

The ghosts turned to face the vial and a huge pillar of light exploded upward, creating a maelstrom in their midst. Wind tore around them into a funnel and sucked their bodies into it one by one until they all disappeared. Then it expanded. The people who had been in the park scattered at the sight of the twister. Gabriel wrapped his arms around me, protecting me from the debris that slapped against us. It surrounded the area in a huge tornado as if acting as a barrier to the outside. I had seen tornadoes before but this was nothing like them. It didn't move on towards another side of the park. It stayed where it was, trapping us inside the dangerous torrent.

I peeked through a gap in Gabriel's arms to see a man standing where the spirits had once been. He was naked and easily over eight feet tall. His skin was deathly pale and his hair was black and slicked back from his face, the cheekbones sharp, nose narrow, brows thick. I couldn't see his eyes because they were closed, but I knew he wasn't human. Gabriel unwrapped his arms from around me, his face slack with shock.

"What...what is that thing?" I whispered.

Its eyes opened and they were opaque with no irises, no sclera, nothing but twin orbs of black. Seconds later, wings stretched from its back but something was horribly wrong. The archangels' wings were white with sheens of gold, or silver, or bronze over them, but this creature's were blood red and singed at the ends.

"It can't be. This shouldn't be possible," Gabriel murmured, the blood draining from his face, leaving him damn near as pale as the thing in front of us.

Behind me, Belial chuckled. I whirled around, drawing my energy around me in case he decided to attack, but he wore a joyous expression, his hands spread wide.

"Thank you, Jordan. You have handed us the victory once again."

"What are you talking about, demon?" I snarled.

"We have tried for centuries to beat the angels at your own game and every time, we have been unsuccessful. Arrogant though we demons are, we have come to one final conclusion. There is no equal for God's angels. And so, we decided to create one."

As if on cue, the false angel landed beside Belial, training its empty eyes on the two of us. Fear curled up through my stomach, washing away the agony from my broken arm. I had faced death before — twice, in fact — and yet it paled in comparison to the stare of this abomination.

Gabriel pushed me behind him, murmuring under his breath. "You need to get out of here."

"I'd love to, Gabe, but I don't think Naked McEvilGuy is going to let me make a run for it," I replied through a grimace.

He seemed to realize the truth in my statement, but he didn't like it. Neither did I.

"Very well. Draw up your shields. Things are about to get…messy."

"Messy?"

Before he could answer, the false angel lunged for me, one huge hand outstretched. Gabriel shoved me out of the way and its fist punched a gigantic crater in the ground, scattering gravel, dirt, and dust into the air. I scrambled backwards with my good arm, swallowing hard, but there wasn't enough time to react because Gabriel shouted: "Michael! Now!"

The archangel appeared behind me and raised his hand to the sky. "Celeste!"

Thunder roared and clouds materialized above us. The sky seemed to explode with activity. I shielded my eyes, just barely able to see a gigantic lightning strike hit the false angel. The sound of the electricity connecting with its flesh made my ears pop and the hairs on my arms stand to attention. When the bolt disappeared, there was only a huge plume of smoke coming out of another even larger crater.

I shook my head, holding out my hand for Michael to help me up. "No way it's that easy."

He set his jaw, stepping towards the hole. "It's not. But that's not what the bolt was for."

Some of the smoke cleared and the moonlight caught upon a long, silver object stuck in the ground. A sword. Its handle had beautiful patterns beaten into the metal, images depicting angels soaring and demons falling in their wake.

Michael plucked it out of the ground. I had read about it before in *Paradise Lost*. It was the sword that cut the side of Satan and helped them win the war in Heaven.

When his hand closed around the hilt, the metal shone brilliantly. In a flash of movement, a silver liquid flooded up over his arm, his shoulder, his upper torso, down his body to his feet until he was covered from head to toe. Seconds later, it solidified into a sleek armor, with patterns and markings that matched the sword. It was similar to the type of armor that Roman and Spartan warriors once had—separate pieces that were solid yet light enough for quick movements. He turned, looking at the sky.

Another huge gust of wind whipped through my hair. Dozens of angels, all different sizes, male and female, landed behind us: armed to the teeth with swords, spears, lances, and axes, their snow-white wings flaring. Among them, Raphael stepped forward, radiant in a dark bronze helmet and armor, and carrying twin short axes.

"Jordan, you should not be here," he scolded softly, brown eyes filled with worry as they fell across my injured arm and the blood dripping from my neck. I was panting and shaking so hard that I could barely manage to shrug my uninjured shoulder.

"So I've been told."

Sheathing his axes, he laid his gloved fingertips on my arm and throat. I felt coolness enveloping the damaged areas, soothing the pain until the gash on my neck vanished and I could move my fingers again. I flexed the muscles in my arm and winced.

"That is only a temporary fix. I will need more time to mend the bones completely."

"Assuming we survive this."

He flashed me a bitter smile. "Indeed. Get somewhere safe."

I shook my head. "They'll only chase me. Give me a weapon."

"I don't have time to argue with you."

"Whether I leave or stay, I'm dead," I replied, my voice hard with resolve. "I'd personally rather go out fighting,"

Raphael stared down at me for a long moment before handing me one of his axes, which took a moment to balance in my hands. He motioned to two male archangels behind me — a pair of dark-haired, olive-skinned twins.

"Ithuriel, Zephon, stay close to her." The two angels nodded.

Raphael joined Michael and Gabriel where they stood in front of the crater, weapons poised. Across from us at the edge of the lake, Belial had acquired his own suit of armor: not nearly as intricately decorated as the angels, but the black metal looked as frightening as the demon himself. He raised a hand and scores of demons trudged out of the lake. Their dingy armor, weapons, and burnt grey wings dripped water as they came to a stop behind him.

Mulciber came up beside him with her face bloodied and bruised from Michael's assault. It made a grim smirk touch my lips. She too had summoned a dark brown armor and a whip made of fire, flickering light across her filthy mahogany-colored wings. They weren't kidding when they said they wanted a war.

The smoke cleared and the false angel rose to its feet from a crouch. Patches of burnt skin sloughed onto the ground, exposing muscle and cartilage, but the damn thing still stood.

Belial lifted twin katanas above his head, smiling that serpentine smile that did not suit Terrell's face at all. "Well, Prince of Heaven's Army, doesn't this seem familiar?"

Michael's eyes narrowed from beneath the brim of his silver helmet as he spoke. "For proof, look up and read thy Lot in yon celestial Sign where thou art weigh'd and show how light and weak if thou resist."

Fury flooded across the demon's features in a rush. "Don't you *dare* spit those words back at me, you arrogant fool! You struck down my Master once with that sword and I will make sure you pay back every drop of blood."

Belial motioned forward with his katanas. "Rain Hell upon them!"

The war began.

CHAPTER TWENTY-FOUR

The demons released a battle cry that shook the ground beneath my feet and hummed through my bones. They ran at us, weapons raised, armor gleaming in the moonlight, and every inch of my body tensed at once. I gripped the axe in my hands, and it seemed to grow lighter on account of the fresh adrenaline coursing through my veins. God help me.

The first wave of demons slammed into the front lines, surrounding me in a cacophony of noise: metal scraping metal, blades slicing flesh, blood splashing through the air. The two angels whom Raphael had assigned as my guardians flanked me, making a triangle facing outward so no one could sneak up behind us.

My eyes locked onto an approaching demon, a hulking man carrying a broad sword. He swung at me in a powerful but slow movement, allowing me the time to dodge and slice into his kneecaps with the axe. He screamed and collapsed to the ground, dropping the weapon. Zephon plunged his lance into the demon's neck, killing him. One down, hundreds to go.

Bodies wriggled and writhed around me on all sides, making it hard to concentrate, but I forced myself to widen my focus to anything wearing the wrong color armor headed in my direction. I parried a blow from another demon, struggling to hold off the sickle mere inches from my skin, and called out: "Strike!" My energy shard went straight through his forehead, killing him instantly, and I kicked him out of the way.

As I continued fighting, I could just barely hear the sound of the archangels fighting the false angel. Every time it struck and missed, the ground trembled like a miniature earthquake. Out of my peripheral, I spotted Gabriel floating overhead, his golden wings flapping to keep him aloft, his thin sword already black with demon's blood. He went into a straight dive and slashed at the false angel's right arm, slicing deep into its skin, but it was still too tough to cut through completely. The false angel batted him away with a vicious swipe, sending him spiraling into the air. It swung its massive fist down at the ground, where I noticed the glinting armor of Michael. I felt a sudden rush of concern, but the angel blocked the blow with his sword, shouting out attack incantations. Large wounds appeared on the creature's wide chest and blood spurted forth like a fountain, but still it stood.

Not far away, Raphael was locked in battle with Belial, swinging his axe as if it weighed no more than a pencil. Belial fought back just as fiercely, the sickening grin replaced with an utterly cold, murderous expression. But that wasn't what worried me. Where was Mulciber?

"Jordan!" I whipped my head to the right as Ithuriel called my name, his brown eyes wide as he pointed his rapier at something beside us. I followed his gaze and saw the tip of the flaming whip latching around the neck of one angel, throwing him into a group of others. It made a small clearing among the melee. Mulciber marched towards us with death in her eyes—a look that was meant for me and only me.

Ithuriel and Zephon stepped in front of me, blocking most of my body from view. Ithuriel sheathed his rapier and drew a bow from his back, loading it with three golden arrows. He released and they whistled through the air in a deadly arc. She flicked her arm and the whip slashed two of them in half, but the third hit the weak point in her armor at the shoulder. She flinched, grabbing the offending dart and throwing it to the ground. Blood dripped down her brown armor, but she kept coming.

Ithuriel kept shooting, stepping back to usher us to retreat as she got closer, slapping away the arrows as they came.

"Get ready!" He shouted to his companion, shouldering the bow and retrieving his rapier as she got within range.

She aimed for me, but Zephon blocked the blow with his lance, twisting the end of the whip around the blade and yanking. She flew forward and he punched her in the face, flooring her.

Hissing, she leapt back onto her feet, clutching her end of the now useless whip, and kicked his legs out from under him. He went into a back roll, coming up to grip his lance, but she jerked her wrist and the whip ripped it out of his grasp. It landed in the grass several feet behind her.

Ithuriel came at her next, his rapier raised, leaping in close to keep her from using the whip again. She used the handle to block him, moving almost too fast for the eye to see. Zephon joined his partner, armed with a blade that had been tucked in his belt as a back-up weapon. I continued fending off the demons that managed to break through to us, trying to keep an eye on their battle when I could. It wasn't until I heard their sharp cries of pain over the roar of war that something went wrong.

I turned. They were both on their knees, clutching identical shoulder wounds. A dagger had sprung from the handle of her whip—an obsidian-tipped blade. Judging by the pain on their faces, it must have been poisoned. She stepped towards me. Ithuriel reached for her, but she kicked him away, knocking him senseless.

Zephon grimaced, trying desperately to get to his feet. "Jordan, get out of here!"

I hacked and slashed at the demons in front of me, making a path for myself, but I didn't get very far. I didn't have enough ground to retreat to, and she was almost to me. I squared my shoulders and clutched the axe, raising it.

"Fine. You want me dead, bitch? Bring it."

Mulciber smiled sweetly back at me, her voice like poisoned honey. "Gladly."

She slashed at me with the whip. I shouted, "I reject!"

The weighted tip of the weapon ripped through my shield as if it were paper, but it gave me enough space to roll to the side, aiming for her already injured shoulder. She turned away at the last minute, making my axe miss and sink into the ground. I yanked it out of the dirt, wincing as my injured arm burned with pain, and faced her again.

"How adorable," she purred as she circled me, her hand twirling the handle of the whip. "I see the angel has taught you how to attack and defend. It won't work on me, my dear. I'm a new animal."

"On that we agree." I lunged forward and aimed for her head. Mulciber blocked me with her forearm and the blade sunk into the metal, crumpling it. Well, at least I'd hit her. She shot me an insolent glare, surprised that I'd at least managed to get through to flesh.

"Well done, Seer. I will play with you no more. It's time to die."

She aimed for my neck. I brought the axe up, but the tip of the whip wrapped around the handle. She pulled with inhuman strength, yanking it out of my grip. Shit!

I scrambled backwards, checking the ground for any loose weapons. Just as she raised the whip again, I found a discarded sword and blocked her next blow, wincing as sparks flew into my face, nearly blinding me. She laughed and kept coming, shouting above the sounds of dying all around us.

"What a piece of work is man!" Mulciber exclaimed, punctuating the quote with another powerful blow. My arm had begun to throb with pain from absorbing the strikes into the sword. It seemed to be getting weaker by the minute.

"How noble in reason!" *CLANG!*

"How infinite in faculty!" *CLANG!*

"In form and moving how express and admirable!" *CLANG!*

At last, she managed to hit my left arm with the whip. I cried out, dropping the sword. Wearing a nightmarish grin, she kicked me in the chest, sprawling me on the grass. I clutched the wounded spot, struggling to rise to my feet, but she tossed her whip aside and grabbed me around the neck. She slammed my head against the ground. Pain crackled through my skull.

I weakly tried to say, "Strike," but she wrapped those cold fingers around my throat and squeezed.

"In action how like an angel," Mulciber purred as she choked the life out of me bit by bit. "In apprehension how like a god; the beauty of the world, the paragon of animals."

I clawed at her arms, her face, getting blood and skin beneath my fingernails. My legs thrashed beneath me, trying to shove me upward, but I couldn't get out of her grip.

"Goodbye, sweet Jordan."

Darkness ate my vision and the last thing I heard was the sound of Michael calling my name.

CHAPTER TWENTY-FIVE

I stood in a field of pure white that seemed to have no end, with nothing inhabiting it except for me and the two people standing in front of me. To the right, there was a tall man with black hair and azure eyes that met my gaze with a strange sort of serenity. My eyes followed the pattern of several faded scars that marred the right side of his neck and one that bisected his right eyebrow.

The woman beside him was much more familiar — about 5'8", skin the color of coffee with cream, shoulder-length black hair that fell in curly waves about her oval face and chocolate eyes.

My mouth went dry. "It's you."

Catalina Amador and Andrew Bethsaida smiled at me then, speaking at the same time.

"Hello, *mi hija*."

"Hey, kid."

I felt as if someone had punched me in the gut—I couldn't seem to breathe or form words. Every part of me had wanted to see them again. There were so many nights when I thought of what I would say if I ever saw my mother or Andrew again. The only problem was that the words piled up in my tightened throat, jumbling like cars in a wreck on the highway. I swallowed hard and pushed past the lump in my throat.

"There are...so many things I've wanted to tell you..." I began, but my mother shook her head, a soft smile gracing her lips.

"We know what you're thinking, *mi hija*. We know you've missed us."

"More than you can imagine," I mumbled.

She reached out and wrapped her arms around me, solid, warm, comforting. Tears burned in my eyes and spilled down my cheeks in rivulets as I hugged her back, breathing in her scent, afraid that she'd disappear again.

After a moment, she drew away. I turned my attention to the Seer by her side.

"Andrew, I—"

He shook his head when he saw the wounded expression on my face, removing his hands from the pockets of his black slacks.

"It's alright. I'm not angry with you."

My voice came out a near whisper. "I'm so sorry."

He sighed, giving me a look as if I were hopeless. "It wasn't your fault. You were young, and in danger."

"But—"

Andrew laid a gentle hand on my head, stroking my hair. "I forgave you a long time ago, Jordan. It's about time you did the same."

His words somehow jolted me back to realize our strange surroundings. "Oh, *God*. Am I dead…again?"

Andrew chuckled before answering me. "No, you're not dead."

A great exhale escaped my lungs. "Where are we, then?"

My mother answered instead. "Think of it as a world between worlds—a space suspended from time.". We thought you could use some help, so we brought you here."

They started walking and I followed, wondering where we were going. The ground felt solid beneath me, but it didn't have a texture. It was like being inside a snow globe.

Just as I opened my mouth to ask her what she meant, they stopped. I nearly tripped when I realized we'd reached a cliff of some kind, where the ground gave way to an enormous gorge. I could only stare in awe.

There were millions of spirits, wispy and grey, floating through the chasm below us. The stream of ghosts stretched from as far as I could see in both directions. Some were holding hands, others gliding past alone with expressions of wonderment. No one seemed to be in a hurry; they all crossed my vision leisurely. No soul traffic. Good to know.

"What is this place?"

"This is where the dead cross over to Heaven for final judgment. Think the River Styx, but a little more pleasant," Andrew said.

I nodded, trying to wrap my head around the concept. "Why did you bring me here?"

They both turned to face me with mirrored serious expressions, so exact that they seemed as if they were one with each other. "There are quite a few people down there that you've helped," my mother said. "You're far more important than you think, Jordan. Seers are rare, and that makes you a very valuable woman."

"So there aren't others like me?"

"There are some, but they don't surface until their abilities have matured."

"Like you?" I asked.

"Yes. I had the same ability as you, though you were probably too small to remember."

"I thought so. Look, all of this is a relief to know, but shouldn't I be getting back? There's a war going on and we're not doing so well."

Andrew glanced at my mother and she nodded slightly in response. He squared his shoulders, the pleasant smile evaporating. I immediately missed it.

"Before we get to that, there's something we need to tell you. We wanted to wait until you were strong enough to handle it."

I swallowed, heart fluttering in my chest. "About what?"

My mother spoke in a gentle voice. "How I died."

I wrapped my arms around myself and averted my eyes to control the wave of loss that rolled up my body. No. I could handle it. This was the goal of my journey — to find out the truth. I needed to know what she had gone through for me, for herself, for the security of the world. I needed to know what they had sacrificed in the fight against evil because soon I would have to do the same.

Finally, I took a deep, shaky breath.

"Tell me."

Time had run out.

He knew how insane his plan sounded, but he had no other options. Tonight or never. With this in mind, he squared his shoulders and turned to face the door. Showtime.

The closet door opened and he walked into the long, white hallway of the psychiatric hospital. He'd never liked this place. It felt like being trapped inside a doctor's pocket; oddly appropriate imagery in itself. Straightening his grey duster, he made sure there weren't any spectators before walking over to the Fire Alarm on the wall, slipping on a rubber glove from one of his pockets. He yanked it hard and a bright blue ink sprayed onto his gloved palm, which would have identified him as the culprit had he not known it would happen. Immediately, a near deafening ringing sound filled the air. He tossed the glove in a nearby wastebasket and slipped back inside the closet seconds before the hospital personnel began pouring out of the patients' rooms. He had started a fire downstairs, hoping to set the alarm off earlier, but the building was old. He had little time and needed the place evacuated as soon as possible.

Soon, the hallway was filled with employees questioning one another about the nature of the alarm and heading towards the supervisor's office to find out what was going on.

"Are all the patients accounted for on this floor?" One male doctor asked the nurse by his side.

"I'll do a head count." She disappeared down the hallway. A couple of the other employees who had gone to Dr. Vulcan's office came back with news.

"She says there's a fire in the kitchen downstairs. The Fire department is on its way. We're going to have to evacuate."

The male doctor heaved a sigh. "Great. It'll be Pandemonium. Let's go."

The hospital personnel dispersed, giving him a chance to slip out of the closet.

"Hey, what are you doing here? I thought you were off today," one of the nurses said as he approached.

He flashed her a sheepish smile. "Had some last minute files to complete. What's with all the noise?"

She knocked on the reinforced metal door to Room P82, alerting the security inside to her presence, shaking her head and raking a hand through her curly brown hair. "There's a bit of a fire downstairs so we're gonna have to evacuate until the fire marshal shows up. I'm just glad this didn't happen during visiting hours."

"Yeah. Bad luck, I guess. Need any help?"

She paused. "Well, sure. You know Ms. Amador better than anyone here. Guess it wouldn't hurt for you to be the voice of reason while we get everyone out."

The door to the room opened and a tall blond man in white stepped out, light eyebrows lifted in question as the ringing alarm reached his ears.

"I thought I heard some racket out here. What's going on?"

"We gotta get everyone out of the building. Escort Ms. Amador outside. He'll accompany you."

The guard sighed, going back into the room for a moment. "Roger that."

His breath caught as Catalina Amador walked out into the harsh luminescent lighting of the hallway, highlighting her midnight hair and coffee skin. Even with tousled hair and bags under her eyes, she radiated pride and loveliness. Those entrancing brown eyes locked with his and widened in surprise. He managed a somewhat genuine smile in return.

"Hey, Cat."

"What are you doing here?" She asked, surprise evident even beneath her warm Spanish accent. The guard didn't allow him to reply; instead he nudged her forward with a large, pale hand. "Walk and talk, please."

She bristled and reluctantly complied, following the shuffling masses towards the short flight of stairs leading outside.

Andrew placed a gentle hand on the small of her back, leaning in slightly. "When we get outside, follow my lead."

Catalina's spine stiffened. "You can't do this. It's not going to work. It's too late for me."

His jaw clenched. "Don't say that. This isn't over yet."

They fell silent as the sound of feet on metal reverberated through the staircase. His pulse quickened as they reached the door and stepped into the cool night breeze. For a fleeting second, he almost forgot about the plan as he felt the New Jersey air closing in around them like a comforting blanket. This city always seemed more alive at night, at least in his eyes. Still, he steeled himself and reached down, strong fingers wrapping around Catalina's slender wrist.

In an instant, they were gone.

His hand on hers was rough and callused, squeezing to almost the breaking point as he pulled her after him. She nearly stumbled and fell on the damp grass, but kept running. They had only moments before the guards would notice their disappearance, and the security cameras would already be notified on the disturbance. At last they reached the wall that encompassed the entire facility, pressing their backs to it as they caught their breath.

Andrew reached into his duster and withdrew a folded up tarp, shaking it open and tossing it over the barbwire on top. He cupped his hands and she stepped into them, grabbing onto the top of the wall as he lifted her. She crawled on top and offered him her hands in return, straining as she hauled him up with her. She spotted the guard who had been monitoring her running towards them in the darkness with his taser raised.

"Freeze!"

Andrew grabbed her hand, shouting, "Jump!"

They leapt from the wall just as he fired, missing them by mere inches. They hit the ground and rolled down the grassy hill that led to a single street where an unmarked car was already parked, the engine running.

Andrew helped Catalina to her feet, ushering her inside the car before climbing in himself. The driver slammed on the gas the second their door closed, gunning it down the narrow passageway to the gate of the psychiatric hospital, where the guards had already been knocked out and the divider lifted.

"Where's Gabriel?" Andrew asked, turning around in his seat to look out the back windshield.

"He's waiting for us two blocks down the way at the helicopter pad."

"Fantastic," the Seer said with biting sarcasm, withdrawing the gun holstered on his waist and taking the safety off.

"That gives us roughly five minutes to get the hell outta dodge before the demons bring down the hammer."

A long howl cut through the air, raising the hairs on their arms with its chilling sound. The car screeched to a stop, throwing both passengers against their seats. Catalina struggled upright first, looking out to see what had stopped them. There, at the bottom of the street leading onto the city block, was a throng of hellhounds — each of them over six feet long and four feet tall, with steam pouring off their shaggy, matted fur.

The driver glanced back at Andrew with an apprehensive expression. "You were saying?"

"Well, no one ever said this was gonna be easy," he replied, counting the number of hellhounds and calculating how many shots he had in his magazine.

The driver nodded to the spot beside him. "Lift up the seat."

Andrew handed Catalina his gun and tore off the removable leather interior on the right side of the backseat, pleased to find two automatic shotguns and a box of shells in a secret compartment. He took them both out, handing one to Catalina and opening the box of ammo.

"You know how to use one of these?"

"I'm acquainted with handguns, not shotguns, but I'm a fast learner," she said, holding her hand out for the shells.

He smiled, though it was grim at the edges, and handed them to her. "Aim for their heads. Don't hesitate. Shoot straight, Cat."

She nodded. "I shall."

"Ready?" The driver asked.

Andrew readied his first shot, nodding to him with a determined smirk.

"Let's get some."

The car lurched forward at maddening speed. Both passengers rolled down their windows, taking careful aim. The hellhounds raced towards them, mouths open, fangs glistening, their roars slicing through the air. When they were only feet from the car, the Seers opened fire, immediately taking out the closest two beasts. The blessed bullets ripped through their furry hides. The beasts exploded into black ash.

One jumped up on the hood and the driver swerved, making the creature slide off and hit the pavement. Andrew whirled and shot at the ones closing in from behind, taking out another three. Catalina focused on the ones ahead of them, wounding two and killing another. Both seers took aim at the final two blocking the street as the car barreled closer. Just as they fired, the car hit a pothole, making them miss. Only one hellhound went down. The other dove for the front tires, puncturing one before the car ran it over.

"Shit!" The driver made a hard right onto the street. The entire car began to shake violently from the ruined tire.

"We can't make it there like this. I can probably get you one more block, but that's not a promise."

"I've got a back-up car waiting not far from here. Think you can get us there?"

The driver nodded, weaving in between cars. "Or die trying."

"Perfect choice of words there, Mr. Sunshine," the Seer said, reloading his shotgun as best as he could in the wildly swerving vehicle. Already he could hear the distant wail of sirens. He prayed that they were sending human policemen and not one of the fallen angels. He was armed for bear, not demon.

"Stop right up here, we can cut through the alleyway to the other car." Andrew pointed to an empty space just outside of a barbershop.

The driver raced through another intersection and screeched to a halt. Catalina opened her door and got out while Andrew paused to give further instructions.

"Now unless you want to be Alpo, I suggest you arm yourself and get the hell out of here. Thanks for your help," Andrew said.

"No problem."

The Seer slung the shotgun across his back and climbed out. Once again, he took Catalina's hand and lead her into the alley, which swallowed them in darkness.

"How far to the helicopter from here?"

"Not far. Gabe's got friends in high places, no pun intended," he answered in between breathless pants.

"Why couldn't he land the helicopter outside of the psychiatric hospital?"

Andrew shook his head. "Not enough space to land."

"What about my daughter?"

"Once we're at the next safe point, we'll send someone in to bring her to you." He tossed a grin over his shoulder at her. "Didn't think I'd leave the munchkin hanging, did you?"

They both stopped at the end of the alley, waiting to cross the street to the next one.

"I don't recall you being very fond of children," Catalina said.

He chuckled, watching for cars. "Maybe so, but if she's anything like you, I suppose I could take a liking to her."

The comment made her pause, realizing the gravity of what he had done for her. "Andrew, I — "

He shook his head. "Don't get soft on me now, Cat. We're not outta this yet."

"I know, but — "

"Hey," he whispered, cupping one side of her face in his large hand and meeting her dark eyes with a determined look. "You don't have to thank me for this, ever. I've spent my whole life fighting for people who will never know I even exist. You're the only thing I have left to believe in — you and that little angel waiting for us. Okay?"

She nodded once. "Okay."

She pulled him closer by the lapel of his grey duster and kissed him with abandon, allowing herself to be lost in him, if only temporarily. He kissed her back with equal passion, only *pulling away when he was sure that she knew exactly how he felt about her. Then he grabbed her hand and led her across the street to the next alley.*

They ran faster as the sirens got closer, filling the alley with a shrill shrieking that sounded almost as demonic as their pursuers. At last, they came up on the last turn that would spill them into a side street where the car and its driver were waiting.

"C'mon, it's just around the corner!" He went around it first, but stopped dead in his tracks, making her stumble as she ran into his back. At the end of the alley stood a tall blond man, holding their driver above his head by the throat. He turned his head slowly, looking at the pair with lifeless blue eyes.

"If you value this man's life, you will throw your weapons over to me. Now."

Andrew surveyed the man, noting the long, thin blade held in his right hand. It glinted dangerously in the dim light spilling in from the open end of the alley. Behind them was a dead end. The police were closing in. They were trapped.

He turned his head slightly to look at Catalina, warning her with his eyes not to move or say anything, but to be ready. Something was off about this man – not demonic energy, but something. "Let him go, first."

"You are not in the position to give me orders," the man said, digging his thumb into the back up driver's pulse point and making him cry out.

Andrew took the shotgun off of his back, making sure to seem as harmless as possible. The nameless man nodded towards the dumpster beside him.

"Throw it in there. Make any attempts to harm me and I will kill this man, and then you."

"Charming fellow, ain't he?" Andrew muttered, walking over to the dumpster and tossing the gun in.

The man gestured to Catalina next. "Yours as well."

She threw in her gun, her dark eyes glittering with hatred. "How much are they paying you to help them damn this world?"

The man allowed a small smirk to touch his lips. "Enough."

With that, he let go of the man, who stumbled and fell. "Get in the car and drive away. If you attempt to come back and save them, I will slit your throat and feed you to the hellhounds."

The driver's eyes darted to Andrew, who shook his head. "Go. We'll figure something out. I can't have your death on my hands."

"I'm sorry," the driver muttered hoarsely, picking himself up and limping over to the car. He got in and drove away, leaving the alley dark with the absence of the headlights. In the few seconds of dark that they had, Catalina slipped Andrew's handgun to him from the small of her back. She edged over to the dumpster in case she would get the chance to retrieve the shotgun.

The man tracked her movements with his eyes, lifting the blade to point at her.

"Walk over here. The police will be here shortly to arrest your lover and you will return to the facility unharmed. If you resist, that will not be the case."

She narrowed her eyes at him. "Come and get me."

The man cocked his head. "Do you doubt my intentions?"

"That's pretty apparent," Andrew snapped. The moment his eyes left Catalina, Andrew raised the handgun and fired at him. The man dodged his shots with unbelievable speed, darting over to Catalina and grabbing her by the neck. He pressed the tip of the blade to her heart, pinning her against his body.

"Fire one more shot and I'll kill her."

"Let her go," Andrew snarled, aiming at his head.

"Drop the gun."

"Don't you understand? They don't need her! Let them take me instead — I'm a Seer!"

The man shook his head. "You are not pure enough. The woman is what they want. Drop the gun."

"Don't," Catalina whispered. "They'll kill you."

Andrew shook his head wildly, gripping the gun tighter. " I won't let them take you, Cat."

"And I won't let you die because of me." The tone of her voice, the quiet serenity in it, and the calm look on her face told *him all he needed to know. Everything seemed to happen in slow motion.*

Her hand gripped the hilt of the blade and shoved it through her chest. It sliced through her body and plunged into the man's heart, killing him instantly. He dropped to the ground behind her and she fell to her knees, blood soaking her blue hospital shirt and turning it black.

"Cat!" He dropped the gun and ran to her, catching her before she could hit the pavement. He couldn't breathe. There was blood everywhere, even on her beautiful face. Her breaths were shallow and trembling and he knew she only had moments left.

"C'mon, stay with me, Cat! I can heal this, I know I can," he whispered, raising his hand above the knife. He poured every last bit of his energy inside her that he could, but the bleeding didn't stop. The wound was too severe. He didn't have enough power to save her and it killed him.

She smiled softly, watching him through half-lidded eyes as she lowered his arm.

"Mentiroso."

He almost choked on a sob, brushing the hair away from her forehead. "Why, Cat? I could have come up with another plan, I could have saved you — "

"You did save me, amor. I knew from the beginning that this would be the end of my life. It is ending on my terms, not theirs."

His head snapped upward as he heard car doors slamming in the distance. The cops had arrived.

She touched his cheek, making him look at her. "Go. You cannot let them catch you."

"Cat — "

"Go, amor. I will see you again. I promise."

He closed his eyes, ignoring the hot trails of tears streaming from them, and kissed her one last time, cradling her soft body in his arms. He pressed his forehead to hers, his voice so low that she almost didn't hear it.

"I'll hold you to it."

"Whatever happens...take care of Jordan any way you can."

"I will."

"I love you."

"I love you more."

Gently, he lowered her to the ground and folded her hands over her stomach, saying a quiet prayer for the passing of her soul, and then fled into the night.

When Andrew finished speaking, I didn't know what to say. In the end, I wiped my eyes, glancing at my mother.

"I guess we have more in common than I thought."

"Perhaps. I never intended for you to suffer the same fate as me, Jordan," she said, her brows wrinkled with worry. "I always wanted you to be happy and live free of the persecution we escaped."

I touched her arm, feeling a little stronger. "But I did. For the past few months, I have been happy. Between Lauren and the archangels...I have a family. It's not the one I always thought I wanted, but it's still exactly what I need."

A beautiful smile touched her lips just before she pressed them to my forehead. "Then my worries are at rest."

"Now," Andrew said, though he hesitated before breaking up the moment. "I hate to be Buzz Killington, but we've got a war on our hands, and one that you guys aren't exactly winning."

"I know. There's just got to be a way to defeat the false angel. Tell me you guys can help."

My mother shook her head. "Our souls have crossed over. We can never return to Earth. We can, however, offer advice."

"You can tell me how to kill it?"

"Yes and no. Think about it. What did it take to create the false angel?" Andrew asked.

I paused, remembering. "The sliver of the True Cross, my blood, and Belial's."

"So that, in essence, is a trinity of Christ, man, and angel, though fallen. Those are the greatest powers in all of existence. This tells us that violence alone will not destroy the false angel," my mother said.

"So you're saying we need to combat their trinity with our own kind of trinity?"

She nodded. I frowned. "But how? Gabriel said that we can't extend our defense powers to each other. We can only use them for our own protection."

"That's true, but there may be a way to bend the rules a little through you." Andrew stepped closer, touching my shoulder.

"When Belial stabbed you with the Spear of Longinus, Christ's blood was still on the tip. Do you understand where I'm going with this?"

I felt the blood draining out of my face. "You're saying that there is a small portion of the Son...in me?"

"Yes. It's very faint and it won't last forever, but it may be enough to allow you to join the archangel's powers together enough to form a trinity."

"What'll happen? Will we turn into some sort of Megazord?" I asked, growing anxious.

Andrew grinned, apparently getting the reference, but pushing past it anyway. "Not exactly. Your mother and I believe that you will become a conduit capable of connecting their powers together enough to destroy the false angel because each element represents a part of what created it. The attack comes from man, the defense comes from angel, and the healing comes from Christ. Use it well."

I hesitated, feeling the weight of their words, of my responsibility. "What if I fail?"

My mother met my eyes then. "What is it that Gabriel always tells you?"

"Have faith."

"That's all you need, *mi hija*. Go. We'll be watching over you always." She wrapped me in a hug one last time. I fought a fresh wave of tears when she let go. Andrew brushed a lock of hair behind my ear and kissed my forehead, sparing me another encouraging smile.

"Go get 'em, kid."

"Thanks. I love you," I whispered.

They began to fade from my vision, but I could still see them join hands and speak in unison. "We love you more."

CHAPTER TWENTY-SIX

Without warning, I crashed back into my own body—my poor, broken, aching body. I could still hear the sounds of dying and slaughter around me, but it took a minute for all my senses to return. When my eyes focused, I saw Michael hovering over me. His eyes darted between my face and my chest, checking to make sure I was alive. He sighed—a sharp sound—and brushed his thumb across my cheek.

"Welcome back."

I coughed hard, shaking and rubbing my bruised neck ruefully. "How did you…?"

Just as I pushed myself up to a sitting position, my hand brushed something cold and wet on the grass. I shrieked as I realized it was Mulciber's bloody, severed arm and scooted away.

"Oh. Well, that explains it then."

"You were unconscious. It was…the longest four minutes of my life," Michael admitted, helping me to my feet. Four minutes. It felt like I had been with Andrew and my mother for at least half an hour. Then again, they did say it was a place suspended from time.

Mulciber—minus her right arm—was on her knees with Ithuriel and Zephon holding blades against both sides of her neck. To my relief, it looked like they'd healed themselves.

She sneered at me. "I should have snapped your neck."

I punched her as hard as I could with my good hand, relishing the groan of pain that escaped her as a result.

"Yeah," I said slowly, my voice ice cold. "You should have."

"This isn't over, Seer."

Michael stared down at her with hard certainty in his eyes. "Yes, it is."

He made one quick motion to the angels with his hand and then ushered me away. The sickening slice of her head being removed from her shoulders still reached my ears. Good riddance. Bit by bit, I could feel my strength returning. The instructions from my mother and Andrew rang in my ears. Time to end this war.

"Come on, we have to get you out of here," Michael said.

"I know how to kill the false angel."

He stopped. "What?"

"When I was unconscious, my mother and Andrew Bethsaida came to me. They told me we need to form a trinity in order to destroy it."

He shook his head. "That's impossible, we can't form one without—"

"A conduit, I know. I am one. They told me there is a trace amount of Christ's blood in me. It might be enough to help combine our powers."

There was an unearthly roar in the distance and the ground trembled. Michael glanced in the direction of where Gabriel was fighting the false angel and then back at me. "I don't like this plan."

I couldn't help but smile. "It's all we've got right now."

He gave me a grim look, but nodded. "Alright. Just don't die. I'd hate to have to miss you."

"I wouldn't want to be such a bother."

Michael didn't smile this time, and I didn't blame him. He motioned for Ithuriel and Zephon, who had come up behind us after dispatching Mulciber.

"Follow me."

Michael picked me up and launched into the air, soaring over the heads of angels and demons alike until we reached the clearing where his brothers were fighting. Despite the dismal surroundings, the flight was breathtaking. His wings parted the sky with powerful movements. I wrapped my arms tighter around his neck, resisting the urge to touch one of his wings out of pure curiosity.

He landed us a good ways from the creature, calling for Gabriel's attention. The blond angel retreated quickly, commanding his soldiers to continue fighting in his stead. The false angel didn't seem to care. It attacked anything angelic within its reach like some sort of rabid animal.

"Am I to assume we have a plan?" Gabriel asked.

"Not the best plan, but it's better than nothing."

He stared at Michael then. "That's not very encouraging, brother."

"You don't know the half of it," he muttered, but pressed on anyway. "Jordan proposed using herself as a conduit to combine our powers and destroy the false angel."

Gabriel's eyes widened. "She can do that?"

"Here's the Cliffnotes version — I have a small trace of Christ's blood in me, and it should give us the power we need to kill the false angel," I said.

He frowned. "Should?"

I put one hand on my hip. "You got a better plan?"

He winced. "Point taken. How exactly are we going to pull this off?"

"I figure a three-pronged attack," I said. "Gabriel, you trap the false angel in the strongest shield you can conjure and keep it still enough for us to make a move. Michael will drive his sword into its chest to injure it. Raphael will use his healing powers. I think that should release the dead souls that give it its power. If I'm right, that'll cause all three elements to disengage."

"It might work," Gabriel said. "The only problem is that Raphael is fighting Belial, and I doubt he's going to let him just walk away."

"We'll take care of that," Ithuriel said, glancing at his partner. Zephon nodded. They stepped back and leapt into the air, flying over to the vicious fight between Belial and Raphael.

Michael touched my shoulder. "Do you know how to form this trinity?"

I hesitated. "More or less. I need to release my energy and meld it with each of yours to form a connection. It probably involves some form of physical contact to get it started, just like our healing powers."

I paused. "I always pictured my first foursome going a little differently."

Gabriel and Michael both sighed in unison, which made me grin. "Not now, Jordan."

"I'm here," Raphael's voice called out from behind us, making me turn. He was breathless and bleeding, but still in one piece. Michael scooped me up again and we launched into the air. The false angel was swatting angels aside like flies, covered in blood, dirt, and gore. The ground around him was littered with the dead and the dying.

After Michael set me down, I stood in the middle of the three angels, pressing one hand to Michael and Gabriel's armored chests while Raphael laid one hand on my back. I closed my eyes and reached down inside myself for the power that lay dormant, cajoling it to rise up between us. It felt like a warm, radiant light in my chest: comforting, soothing, and yet the most powerful thing I'd ever experienced.

The archangel's energy rushed in to meet with mine. They all mixed and blended and then hardened, as if three precious metals had been melted down and fortified into something unstoppable. At last, the connection solidified and our minds were on the same accord: *vanquish.*

The false angel spotted us and dove forward, reaching its monstrous hand for me, but Gabriel lifted his arm. An invisible force stopped it in mid-stride. The false angel let out a sickening roar of fury, struggling with all its might, but it couldn't move. Michael stepped away and unsheathed his sword, walking towards the false angel. White fire licked up the blade as he neared the creature. A spot in Gabriel's shield opened for him.

In the distance, Belial screamed "NO!" just as Michael plunged the sword into the false angel's chest. No blood came out, only a blinding white light, almost like the one that had been in Michael's body when Belial tried to overtake it.

Raphael stepped forward as Michael removed the sword, pressing his hand over the wound and closing his eyes in concentration. He murmured soft words in a Latin healing incantation. The false angel began to convulse in his invisible prison, its head flying back in a soundless scream. The light grew even brighter and shot into the sky like a beacon. All at once, the souls of the dead that the sliver had called to it flew from the wound in the false angel's chest. I felt it in my bones that they were now at peace and crossing over to the other side to see the Father. It was a beautiful sight.

When the very last soul left, the false angel evaporated into ash, nothing more than a black stain and burnt red feathers. Around us, all of the demons and angels had gathered to watch in wonderment, their battles forgotten as the light slowly faded from view, leaving us in the quiet embrace of night.

Belial rushed to the spot where the false angel had once stood, whispering "No" over and over again. He fell to his knees, his face anguished. I couldn't bear to see the look on Terrell's face. I took an unconscious step towards him, but Michael laid a hand on my shoulder.

"Jordan…I have to…" he struggled with the words.

I shook my head. "Please…there has to be another way."

"His soul left this world a long time ago," he whispered. "I have to put the body to rest."

I knew he was right. I knew it. But it still hurt.

Belial's voice was low and mournful as he spoke, and I could feel the tears welling up in my eyes as I recognized the words he recited. Ash Wednesday by T.S. Eliot. God help me.

Michael lifted his hand and pressed it over my eyes, closing them. Seconds later, I heard the sound of the sword slicing through the demon's chest and the quiet thump of his body falling over. When I opened them again, Terrell lay fallen by the ashes of the false angel, his face strangely peaceful. I knelt and kissed his forehead, my voice hoarse.

"Forgive me."

"So…what happens now?"

I sat on my own bed in my apartment with Raphael at my side, finishing up the final touches on my new set of bandages. He had healed my arm completely, mending the bones to their former strength, though he advised me not to do anything strenuous anytime soon.

After Belial's death, the demons had retreated back to hell and all the corpses disintegrated into ash as soon as they left. The angels went back to their various posts on Earth. Gabriel and Raphael escorted Terrell's body back to his home and arranged it to look as if he'd died of more natural causes. Michael took the sliver of the True Cross to Heaven and then came back to take me home.

"Fortunately, the tornado chased away all the innocent bystanders, and thus there were no witnesses to the event. However, we have people on standby monitoring major video sites for any possible footage. We also have people in the New Jersey police department to help cover up the sudden 'weather anomaly' that will be reported by said witnesses." Raphael stood and putting his First Aid kit back in his trademark leather bag.

Michael leaned against the doorframe with one hand pressed to his mouth, looking more solemn than I had ever seen before. Gabriel hovered by the bathroom door, his arms crossed over his chest as he listened.

"Good. I'd hate to have made up some sort of explanation for all this. A movie shoot. A LARP gone wrong."

Raphael sent a questioning look in my direction. "LARP?"

I smiled. "Never mind. What about the demons?"

Gabriel spoke up this time since it was a little more in his department. "It is too soon to tell, but I suspect their master won't be very happy with their failure. We won't hear from them in quite some time, until they come up with another scheme."

"And Terrell..." I let the sentence hang because it was too painful to finish.

Gabriel cast a sympathetic look on me, walking over and sitting to my right. "His family has already been notified. I assume they will contact you with information about the funeral."

I shook my head, my smile becoming bitter. "You don't know his family."

"Perhaps not, but...if it's any consolation, his soul is indeed in Heaven."

I looked up, shocked. "You...?"

"I checked for you."

A wave of gratitude rolled over me. "Thanks, Gabe."

"Of course." He kissed my forehead, standing up.

"Raphael and I need to get going. We will be in contact with you soon." He glanced at his brother and a look went between them that worried me. Neither of them bade the silent Michael goodbye. Something was going on. Something bad.

I waited until they disappeared out the front door before speaking. "What's going on?"

Michael looked at me then, seeming to be drawn out of deep thought. "What?"

"Don't pull that," I said, my voice confident and bold though I felt confused and scared on the inside. "I can tell when you're hiding something."

He sighed. "Jordan—"

"Michael, I nearly died today. I saw Andrew and my mother today. I saw someone I care about die because I was too late to save him. Don't keep anything else from me. Please," I added softly, walking over to him. He stared down at me for an instant and averted his gaze to the floor.

I touched the side of his face, like he had done so many times to mine, and made him look at me. "What's going on?"

"I've been reassigned."

My hand fell away like a dead weight and all the air in the room evaporated. "What?"

He pushed away from the doorframe and walked into the kitchen, pressing his hands flat against the counter until he was hunched over it, closing his eyes. "My Father has ordered me to do cases on my own, away from you, because it's too...dangerous."

"Dangerous how?"

He sighed again, his voice heavy. "You know how."

I touched my neck on reflex, getting a sudden sensory memory of his lips on my skin, traveling down my collarbone. Shit. He was right. I did know how. There was no doubt in my mind that if Gabriel hadn't interrupted us we would have ended up in bed.

"You can't contest this?"

"No, I can't. Orders are orders. To refuse them would cause Him to disavow me from my rank as an archangel."

My breathing started to hitch up, almost like I was having another panic attack. I wrapped my arms around my stomach to keep my hands from shaking. "So you're just gonna leave? No more protection, no more help with the ghosts?"

Michael shook his head. "Gabriel will be your new guardian. He'll look after you in my absence."

"Oh. Well, I guess that's fine then." My voice went cold on its own. I turned my back on him, storming in my bedroom.

"Jordan, don't do this, please."

I slammed the door, locking it and pressing my forehead against the wood as if it would push all of my memories out of my head. I'd been a fool. Had I really thought that I could cross those lines with him and not be punished? Did I really think I could have him to myself? The Prince of Heaven's Army wrapped around my pinky. Stupid, stupid little girl.

The doorknob jiggled and I heard him sigh. "Open the door."

"Go away, Michael. I can't do this right now." I tried not to sound as upset as I actually was. There was a thunking noise and a brief vibration that meant he'd either hit the door with his fist or his forehead. I couldn't really tell.

"I'm sorry. I am. I lost control. I should have been more careful of you."

I closed my eyes, steadying myself. "Just go."

Silence. Then, after a long moment, he spoke once more.

"Take care of yourself, Jordan."

His footsteps echoed on the hardwood floors until they were faint and then nonexistent. The front door opened and closed, swallowing me in silence. The second he was gone, I collapsed to the floor and buried my face in my knees, hiding my tears from no one but myself.

Stupid, stupid little girl.

I worked a six-hour shift the next day, getting home from the bus at around seven o'clock. I'd made lousy tips because, for the life of me, I couldn't muster a genuine smile. Good thing Lauren hadn't been there. She would have pulled me into the bathroom and grilled me with questions about what happened. Not that I could tell her anything. It was against The Rules.

My keys jingled as I took them out of my pocket. As I reached for the lock, my shoe hit something on the welcome mat. I glanced downward, surprised to see a medium-sized cardboard box with a UPS label. Confused, I picked it up, unlocking the door and carrying it all inside. I took the box to the kitchen table and sat down, reading the label on top.

To my absolute shock, the box was addressed to me from Aunt Carmen. What the hell could she possibly have to send me? Notes about how much she hates me? The souls of little orphan children? I tore off the masking tape and pulled the lid apart, going completely still when I saw what lay inside, cramming nearly every corner of the box.

Letters.

Dozens of them.

And all of them were addressed to me.

On the very top, there was a bright blue sticky note with one word on it in my aunt's handwriting.

Perdónome.

Forgive me.

My hands shook just the slightest bit as I set the note aside and dug into the piles and piles of letters with my name on them in an untidy script. I ripped the first one open and found it was a card for my 10th birthday. I sifted through all the envelopes, finding that each one came from a different address under the name Simon Patras, but they all were signed at the bottom of the cards with "A.B." It could only be one person.

Andrew Bethsaida.

She had been keeping them from me all these years, never letting me know that for over a decade this man had been sending his love and support.

My eyes felt hot. My hatred for her seemed to be at war with my gratitude. This was truly the only humane thing I had ever seen Carmensita Durante do, even if it had been years too late. Maybe Michael had put the fear of God in her after all.

It wasn't just letters, either. There were trinkets too: small stuffed animals with dusty fur, key chains with golden angels dangling from them, even a snow globe from Madrid. All at once, I understood. My mother had wanted him to take care of me in her absence, but since he couldn't do that due to being hunted by the demons, he sent me presents. He tried to reach me, to let me know that someone out there cared. God bless him.

I sat down and went through them all, putting the envelopes in one neat pile and the cards in another with the trinkets and stuffed animals in the middle. Maybe it was a good thing Michael wasn't around, because I couldn't seem to stop crying, though I was smiling through my tears. Even in writing, I could feel how much he cared about me — someone he had never even met.

The letters for my sixth through tenth birthdays were all simple and colorful, but the ones after that began to get serious. He didn't divulge his own whereabouts or the fact that he was a Seer. Most of them said that I need only know that he would look after me one day when I was ready.

"You may be asking yourself who I am or why I've been writing you, but just know that I want to make sure you are safe. That is what your mother would have wanted for you, and what I want for you as well. I know that right now things seem at their darkest, but there is an old saying: sometimes it's darkest just before dawn. There is a dawn for you, and me, and for us all. So hang a night light by your bed and wait for the sunrise, angel."

A.B.

A fresh wave of tears tumbled down my cheeks, but they weren't sad tears so I didn't mind. I wiped my eyes and took the letter to the fridge, clipping it on there with a magnet. I had fought in a war. I had nearly died three times in the past three months. I had been broken and beaten and bloodied. I had lost my mother, my lover, and the man who may have been my father figure if he had lived long enough. I had killed. I had suffered.

But for once in my life, I had love and no one could steal it from me.

CHAPTER TWENTY-SEVEN

During the first month without Michael, I felt like a quarter rolling around in an empty piggy bank. My apartment felt hollow and I rattled around it, lost, aimless, and uncomfortable. I hadn't realized how much time he occupied in my daily life. During the day, I'd go to work and when I got out, he was waiting for me. Ever since Belial abducted me, he never let me leave work to catch the bus by myself. I had tried and failed to convince him not to waste valuable money five days a week on the bus fare, but he never listened. On weekends, we went to movies and plays or walked in the park or perused the bookstores to collect literature I didn't have yet.

The silence killed me. I had my laptop open constantly to play music to combat the quiet. My weekends were spent sitting in the kitchen drinking coffee and reading. I deleted "Golden Brown" from my playlist and avoided every single sentimental love song I could just to stay sane.

My dinners went back to being simple: tuna salad, spaghetti, fajitas, and lasagna. I just didn't feel like trying new recipes yet.

Lauren immediately knew something was wrong. After a week of my unresponsive behavior, she dragged me into the bathroom at work and demanded to know what was going and where Michael went. I merely told her that we weren't seeing each other any more because his job took up too much time and he couldn't be with me. Part of it was true, after all. She believed me and offered her sympathy, promising to take me out to meet guys. I declined the offer. I wasn't ready yet.

The second month wasn't as bad as the first, though the urge to start drinking again got worse, so I started attending local AA meetings. Gabriel checked in on me every other week, sometimes by a phone call, other times in person. I never asked him how Michael was doing because I knew, to some degree. While flipping channels, I'd heard about some of his performances on the local entertainment news. The Throwaway Angels were making their way to the top. I didn't know how I felt about that.

The other problem was that my nightmares got progressively worse, and it wasn't just dreams about killing Andrew or Mulciber choking me to death. These dreams involved someone who knew my inner darkness and could bring it to life whenever I fell asleep.

I stood in a pure white field, much like the one Andrew and my mother had brought me to, but something was different. Wrong. In front of me stood a pane of glass that was a thousand feet high and a thousand feet across. On the other side, I could see the silhouette of a man walking towards it. I squinted, stepping closer to see. My breath caught as he came into focus.

Michael stood there, his beautiful silver wings flowing from his back, dressed in all black with the most mournful look on his face. He said nothing, merely lifted one hand and pressed it to the glass. I didn't understand why, but I did the same. I couldn't feel the warmth from his hand. The windowpane was too thick. God help us.

Then, slowly, the glass began to darken at the corners, spreading downward until it swallowed Michael's image in a rush of silver. It had turned into a mirror and behind me there was another man. A man in a suit with black hair on either side of his face and a serpentine smile.

I whirled around, a scream building in my throat, as Belial reached out and placed his gloved hands against the mirror, trapping me between them. He was so close that I could smell the metallic scent of blood on his breath.

"Poor, sweet Jordan," he whispered, his reptilian eyes swallowing my vision. "Without your angel, who will protect your heart?"

He let his gloved fingertips trail down the left side of my neck, resting the palm over the scar just above my breast. The demon leaned in, his lips brushing my ear and making me shiver.

"Will you give it to me or shall I take it?"

"You can chase me for a thousand years. You can hunt me wherever I go, threaten everyone I love, and take away everything I care about...but I will never...ever...give myself to you." My voice came out clear and harsh, almost brash, but it was the truth.

Belial inhaled sharply, dragging his hot tongue over my pulse. "I was hoping you'd say that."

His fangs pierced my skin and I screamed until I woke up.

As if the nightmares weren't stressful enough, Terrell's family had engaged in a legal battle about where and when to inter his body. Apparently, he hadn't specified in his will and his mother's side wanted to bury him with her grandparents, while his father's side wanted to bury him in their grandparents' graveyard. The only reason I knew about any of it was because of his sweet younger sister, Grace. Even after we broke up years ago, she never hated me like his mother did and so she called to tell me it would be a while before they got the issue settled. I tried to refuse the invitation, but she wouldn't take no for an answer, bless her heart.

When the third month rolled around, the depression slackened. I threw myself into work and put more energy towards solving cases. Ghosts poured in at a steady rate. I took extra care to carry my gun, rosary, and a couple vials of holy water with me in case one of the demons resurfaced, but there was no sign of them. Though I did develop an intense fear of cats. Every time I saw one, I hurried off in the opposite direction. Sad, but true.

I also started watching Food Network on a regular basis. I started simple with dinner entrees and then worked my way up to baking. By the end of the month, I could make cornbread, chocolate chip cookies, and banana bread from scratch. I let Gabriel and Raphael try some of them. After that, all of Gabriel's visits were in person just so he could try whatever new sweets I'd made that week.

By the fourth month, I still didn't feel busy enough, so I started looking into enrolling in Excelsior College for their Bachelor of Science program for restaurant management. After all, I couldn't be a waitress forever. Spending time at the restaurant made me realize how much I enjoyed cooking food and being around people while they ate. It would be a while before I'd be able to afford it, though. I made a folder for the pamphlets I found and wrote "Promises to Keep" on it.

It was the end of March before anything related to Michael cropped up. I sat in my kitchen, sharing half of a loaf of banana bread with Lauren after our shift at work. Lily was at the babysitter's, because Lauren needed to vent about her divorce over sweets. Our conversation had fallen silent for a few comfortable moments before she spoke.

"I need to tell you something, but first you have to promise not to get mad at me," she said after downing half her glass of milk.

I eyed her. "Go ahead."

"I bumped into Michael the other night."

The sudden mention of his name made my heart rate spike. "Oh."

She dropped her gaze to the table top, folding one corner of her napkin. "We went out for a drink."

The look on my face must have scared her, because she held up her hands in supplication. "No, no, not like *that*. He wanted to catch up, not go on a date."

I relaxed a little. Before he left, Lauren and Michael did get along pretty well so it made sense he'd want to talk to her.

She continued. "I asked him how things were going and he said he pretty much just writes songs, works at Guitar Center, and sleeps. Nothing in between. He's not seeing anybody, in case you were wondering."

"I wasn't," I said, and she rolled her eyes at me.

"He asked me how you were."

"What did you tell him?"

Lauren shrugged. "That you were good. Busy."

The silence mounted. She folded the napkin into a limp little goose. After a while, she sighed. "Jor, he looked awful. Like he hasn't been sleeping or taking good care of himself. Around other people, he can hold it together, but I could tell he was miserable."

She met my gaze, her voice soft. "He misses you."

I closed my eyes. "Lauren..."

"I don't run your life. I won't tell you what to do with it because it's not like I know anything, I mean, I'm getting a divorce. But he's not the same without you."

She dug into her purse and withdrew a CD in a plastic sleeve, placing it on the table. "He did a cover of Eels' 'Beautiful Freak' that I think you need to hear. I cried for a week after I heard it."

"Look, I appreciate that you're concerned about fixing things between us. I really do. But some things just aren't going to happen no matter how much we want them to." My throat started to tighten. Emotions were welling up beneath the surface of my mind, threatening to spill out if we kept talking about him.

"Okay. I just thought you should know." She stood up, brushing crumbs off the front of her skirt. "I've gotta get going. Call me tomorrow."

"I will. G'night." She waved and left the apartment. I sat in silence, staring at the CD at my fingertips for a long moment. My mind told me not to listen. It would only open old wounds and smear salt into them. But my hand reached out and placed the disc in the laptop.

It whirred for a few seconds, and then I heard the polite sound of applause. He had recorded this at the Devil's Paradise, probably, during a live performance. I folded my hands over my mouth and listened to the first few lines.

His voice was heavy and had a rough texture that made shivers roll down my spine. There were some artists that had a polished, pop sound to them. Michael wasn't one of them. When he sang, he meant every single word.

I couldn't get through the entire thing. I stopped the recording and pressed my hands over my face, inhaling deeply. No. I wouldn't backslide when I had come so far. He had his life and I had mine. We would be fine without each other.

No more, no less.

The next day after work, I walked into my apartment, shut the door, and turned around, only to freeze in place.

Michael was standing in my kitchen.

My throat closed up and my entire body seemed to go cold from head to toe as it tried to absorb the shock of seeing him after six months of no contact. No phone calls, no visits, nothing. Part of me wanted to race across the room and catapult into his arms, to bury my nose in his shirt and smell that familiar scent, to have him smile at me and erase any negative thoughts my mind could conjure. But that was just part of me. The rest was hollow.

"Hey, Jordan." His voice came out soft, meaningful, and hesitant. The words seemed to jolt me out of my paralysis. I realized I'd been standing there staring at him for nearly half a minute. Lauren hadn't been lying. There were dark smudges under his eyes and his skin had an unhealthy pallor.

I let my face go blank and slid out of the duster, walking towards the kitchen table and draping it over the back of a chair. "What are you doing here, Michael?"

It was hard to concentrate on anything in the room other than him, but I managed as I went to the refrigerator and searched for the food to get my dinner. Chicken salad. Nothing special.

I heard him take a deep breath. "I have something to tell you."

I sat the Tupperware container of food on the counter. "And you couldn't tell me over the phone because...?"

He sighed. "Jordan, don't do this."

I slammed the door shut, whirling on him. "*Don't.* Don't you tell me what to do. You can't just waltz in here and expect me not to be upset."

Michael shook his head. "No, that's not what I'm talking about. You know I wouldn't have come here if I didn't have something important to say."

"What makes you think I even want to hear it?"

His green eyes narrowed just barely. "Because if you didn't, you would have thrown me out already."

The truth of his words slapped me in the face, rendering me silent. I crossed my arms, leaning against the counter with a cold expression. "Two minutes."

The angel set his jaw, but nodded. He turned his back on me and ran a hand through his hair — a painfully familiar gesture — then rested his large hands on the counter opposite of me as he spoke.

"Yesterday, Father called me to His side for council."

Shock crackled through me. From what I'd heard, direct conversation with God was an extremely rare occurrence. His orders were often sent out through the Son, not the Man himself.

Michael paused to let this information absorb before continuing. "When I knelt before Him, He only asked me one thing."

I couldn't help myself. "What?"

"Do you love her?"

My heart rate tripled. I dug my fingers into my arms, trying to keep myself from having a panic attack. It was stupid, really. Of course He knew. He was God. But I had never in my life thought that the thing hanging between Michael and me would receive acknowledgment from on high.

Eventually, I managed to calm down enough to ask: "And...what did you say?"

His voice was a mere whisper. "Yes."

I closed my eyes. It was true. Over the past six months, I had convinced myself that Michael had merely been struggling with his lust for me, but love...it was too scary to even think about. How could someone so pure and just fall in love with me? Didn't he see the scars? Didn't he know how bitter and jaded my soul had become?

When I opened my eyes again, Michael had turned around, his handsome face strained as if he were in physical pain when he spoke. "I have no right to love you, Jordan. I want nothing more than to disappear and leave you in peace."

"Who says I want you to?" I murmured, staring at the floor and rubbing the goosebumps that had appeared on my arms.

"You don't know what it's been like since you left. The dreams...God, the dreams..."

Michael stepped towards me, but I held out my hand, stopping him. "The truth is that I don't know what to do with this information right now, okay? It's not like He gave you a ultimatum or something—"

"He did."

My eyes snapped to meet his. "What?"

It was Michael's turn to look away this time. "He told me...that under normal circumstances, a human and an archangel would never again be allowed to be together. However, because you are a Seer, you aren't completely human. You're one of the anointed. Therefore, you could be with me if and only if you agreed to enter the Marriage of the Souls."

"Marriage of the Souls?"

"We would be bound together for life, both on Earth and in Heaven. But...in exchange for this, we can never..." he faltered.

I touched his cheek, making him meet my gaze like he had so often done to me before.

"Never what?"

His lips just barely moved. "Have children."

Those two little words sunk into my skin like liquid poison: thick, sickening, and deep. I slumped against the counter, my head pounding as I tried to understand what he'd told me. "That's some ultimatum."

He offered me a weak smile. "You can imagine I didn't get much sleep after He told me."

"I'll bet."

"Jordan, I won't ask this of you. I came down here to tell you because you deserve to know and to make a decision for yourself. I don't want this life for you. I don't want you to have to wait up nights praying that some demon doesn't get lucky and finally succeed in killing me or capturing you. If you ask me to leave and never come back, I'll do it."

My voice was quiet. "Even though you love me."

He flinched. "Yes."

My breath came out in long sigh. "Michael, you can't expect me to know what to say to you right now."

He nodded. "I don't. I'll come back tomorrow for your answer. This is an important decision and I want you to truly think about what you want, whether or not it removes me from the picture."

His head dipped slightly, as if he were bowing, a gesture so formal that it bothered me. His speech, too, was as proper as it was when he'd gotten his memory back. It made me realize that he was speaking as the angel, not the man. The angel who loved me. *Me.*

I couldn't find it in myself to say anything as he brushed past me, wrapping my arms around my waist in an attempt to calm myself. The front door clicked shut, leaving me in a deafening silence. Twenty-four hours to make the biggest decision of my life. Where to start?

I wandered into my bedroom and plopped down on the mattress, staring blankly into space as I tried to figure out what to do. His words echoed in my head until I felt dizzy so I finally resolved to do something slightly childish. I grabbed a sheet of notebook paper from the shelf and a pen, folding my legs so that I sat Indian-style on the bed. Time to do what I did in fifth grade when I had a crush and couldn't decide if I should tell the boy the truth—make a list.

On one side of the paper, I wrote: *Reasons Why I Shouldn't Do It.* Not very elegant or insightful, but it was effective enough. I chewed on the pen cap as I started to fill in the reasons.

1. *He gets on my nerves*
2. *He's always right*
3. *He's too damn tall*

I paused, scanning the page. Okay, so these were superficial. I was avoiding the real issues, the ones that scared me, the ones that actually made me want to say no to the offer. Slowly, I lifted the pen again.

4. *He'll live forever and have to watch me grow old and die*
5. *I'll never get to be pregnant*
6. *I'll never get to have an ultrasound*
7. *I'll never have a baby shower*
8. *I'll never get to see my hair and Michael's eyes on our baby.*
9. *I'll never be alone again*

The pen lowered and I stared at the paper, feeling a heavy weight in the center of my chest. Truth be told, I had never really thought about having kids until now. Sure, I liked them, but I always thought that I'd figure it out when I met Mr. Right. Did I want children? Could I handle having children despite my crazy lifestyle? Moreover, would I even want children if Michael wasn't in the picture?

Now came the even harder part. Moving to the other side of the page, I wrote: *Reasons Why I Should Do It.* There were only two things under this category.

1. *Because I love him*
2. *I'll never be alone again*

They were two tiny sentences, and yet just looking at them made my heart race as fast as it had when I'd found Michael in my kitchen. Somehow, seeing the words "I love him" made me want to freak out. I had loved people before — my mother, Lauren, Andrew — but none of them romantically. Terrell had been the closest I'd ever encountered to The One. He had been handsome, smart, good-looking, and sweet, God rest his soul. No matter what I chose, I would always regret what happened to him because of me. Still, kind though he was, I never loved him.

Truthfully, loving Michael should have been more obvious to me. He made me laugh. He never seemed to grow tired of me. I didn't have to act perfect around him. He smelled wonderful. He cooked like a god. His music was amazing. His voice was soothing. When he smiled, I felt the world melting at the edges. Yeah. Pretty obvious.

I slumped back against the headboard, curling my fingers into my hair. *Well, now what?*

I debated on whether I should distract myself by reading or watching a movie. Another thought occurred to me, so I rolled over and grabbed my cell phone, searching through the numbers for one in particular. It rang about seven times and I almost hung up, but then the voice of an elderly woman with a New Orleans accent wheedled in my ear, making me smile.

"I was wondering when my monthly call was coming."

"Hi, Mrs. Lebeau."

"Oh, you stop that, child. Use my first name," she scolded.

I smiled wider, shaking my head. She never changed. I could still see her in my head even now — her perfectly-styled grey wig, her black-frame bifocals, and her cinnamon skin spotted with freckles across her weathered cheeks. Without her, I'd either still be in New Jersey or dead. I never forgot to call her, but I did forget how informal she liked things between us.

"Sorry, Mrs. Selina. Old habits die hard."

"Mm-hm. How've you been, cher?"

I cleared my throat, trying to keep my voice level. "Oh…y'know. The same. What about you?"

"Same as always," she chuckled. "Shop's doing well. Hired me some new blood. They cause as many problems as they solve."

"I'll bet." I hesitated. "Can I ask you something?"

"Anything."

"When your husband asked you to marry him…how did you know he was The One? The right one for you?"

"Hmm…that's a good question. It was so many years ago, but I recall the proposal like it was yesterday. Anthony and I had been together for a whole year before that night. We had just finished dinner and we were leaving the diner. It was raining. I'd forgotten my umbrella, so Tony lent me his jacket. We walked out into the rain. Halfway to the car, the heel of my shoe broke. Now, mind you, these were expensive shoes that he'd saved up a month's worth of paycheck to buy and the damn pavement ripped it right in half. I started to get upset, and he told me not to worry about it. I asked him why, why wasn't he upset since he had spent so much on them. He said that it didn't matter to him one bit, because he was prepared to spend the rest of his life with me and buy me any pair of shoes I could ever want. I'll never forget that moment. He knelt down, in the middle of a puddle, no less, and pulled out the ring."

"Weren't you scared?"

"Child, I was terrified!" She laughed, her voice soft around the edges. "I'd never thought in a million years that he wanted to spend his life with some little girl who owned a candy shop. He was a beat cop. I knew that if I married him, one day I'd lose him, and I did. But the thing is, my dear…his love was worth the risk of losing him. I knew he was the one because as frightened as I was…I still wanted to brave through the pain for him."

Her words set in, both affirming some things in my mind and stirring others. "Thanks. I needed to hear that."

"No problem, cher."

"I'll talk to you soon."

"I'll be here." I hung up, staring at the lit surface of my phone for a long moment just before dialing another number. She picked up on the second ring.

"Hey," Lauren said, sounding energetic despite the fact that she had also worked for eight hours. I envied her in that regard. She always seemed bursting with life.

"Didn't think you'd be awake. You worked a long shift today."

"Yeah, I'm pretty beat. Listen, I know you have tomorrow off too, and I was wondering if maybe we could hang out. Y'know, you, me, and Lily?"

"Sure. She hasn't seen you in a little while and I'd love the company."

"Good."

She hesitated. "Are you okay? Your voice sounds kind of…hollow."

"I'm fine. I'll meet you at IHOP around ten o'clock, okay?"

"Sounds great. See you then."

We hung up. I sat the phone on the nightstand, my thoughts churning in my head. Tomorrow morning sounded nice. I had no idea what to do about tonight. How could I get to sleep with something like this on my mind?

Before I even knew it, I was on all fours on my floor, reaching beneath the bed frame for the bottle of whiskey taped to the bottom. I was a faithful member of AA, but I was still human. And I could really use a drink right about now.

I unscrewed the cap, holding the cold glass up to my lips, when I just went still. I stared at the amber liquid, the intricate patterns of the bottle, and felt a wave of disgust rolling up through my chest. No. That was the coward's way out. I remembered my mother's words, the ones she'd written on those papers so many years ago, and they were strong and firm with resolve.

I walked into the bathroom and poured the whiskey down the drain. After the last drop fell, I tossed the bottle in the trash and looked at myself in the mirror.

"I will endure."

"Lily! Would you give the Frisbee back to the dog, please? Thank you!" Lauren watched her overexcited daughter toss the plastic disc back to the begging black lab at her feet. We had been in the park for nearly half an hour, and she had managed to interact with every single animal in the vicinity. The kid was equal parts adorable and exhausting. After breakfast, the three of us caught a matinee kids' film, went bowling, had lunch, and came here to watch the sunset.

"She's going to be a vet someday," I said. "She is way too good with animals, even at her age."

"Ha, forget that. She needs to pick a cheaper career. I can't pay for vet school." Lauren raked a hand through her bangs. We were seated comfortably on a bench nearby, keeping an eye on the munchkin. Silence fell between us until she spoke again.

"Alright, so what's this really about? I can tell you have something on your mind."

I fidgeted in my seat, avoiding her intense eye contact. It was against the rules to tell anyone the truth about ghosts, angels, and demons. It would only be allowed if they accidentally witnessed something they

322

weren't supposed to. Lauren hadn't. Therefore, I would have to tread lightly.

"I know you and He-Who-Shall-Not-Be-Named got the divorce finalized this year, but I wanted to ask you..."

"Yes?"

"...knowing what you do now about your ex, if you could do it all over again, would you?"

She paused, turning her head to stare out at the park, now illuminated by the fading gold and orange of sunset. "Damn, Jor. I was expecting you to say you were pregnant or something."

I let out a small laugh. "No, that would mean I had a life."

She smirked at the comment, and then sighed. "Well...truthfully...the best thing to come out of my screwed up marriage is Lily. She's beautiful. She's my life. Her father was just an unpleasant accessory, I suppose. Things got painful and I know I'll never recover after being married to him, but I guess I would do it all over again if only because I love her so much."

Lauren then shifted in her seat, her brown eyes narrowing. "Now tell me why you asked me that. What's going on with you?"

I licked my lips, choosing my words carefully. "I have...a decision to make. A big one. A *very* big one. I just want a point of reference. I want to make sure I'm not going to regret it for the rest of my life."

She opened her mouth and I held up a hand. "And I can't tell you what it is. Not yet, anyway."

Lauren scowled. "Fine. But I don't see why you won't trust your own judgment. Your first instinct is usually the right one. You may be a cranky, asocial hermit crab, but you're a smart girl. And if this decision involves who I think it involves, you had damn well better say yes or I'll disown you."

I tossed her a sarcastic look and she grinned at
me. Just then, Lily scampered over to me with a huge smile
on her round face.

"Auntie Jordan!"

"Yes, honey?"

She handed me a dandelion, bouncing up and
down. "Make a wish!"

I chuckled, accepting the flower. "This is all so
sudden! I don't know what to wish for! Can you help me?"

"Yes! I know what you should wish for!" Lily
exclaimed.

"And what's that?"

"The thing you want most! Mom says that if you are
a good girl and you love really hard, you get to wish for
the thing you want the most."

That made me wince a bit. "I don't know if I've been
that good a girl, munchkin."

She shook her head, making her pigtails wag back
and forth. "Auntie Jordan is good. I can tell. I can always
tell 'bout good people. Make a wish!"

Finally, I smiled at the girl and blew the tiny seeds
away, watching them float along the warm afternoon air.
Lily cheered and kissed my cheek, racing back into the field
to find more flowers.

Lauren shook her head, a fond smile on her lips.
"What'd you wish for?"

"Lily's wisdom."

An hour slipped by. Lauren took Lily home and
wished me luck, leaving me on the park bench to watch the
leaves from maple trees gently waft to the ground,
illuminated by the lampposts on either side of the bench. I
had one hour to go before Michael's return, exactly twenty-
four hours after he had, in a fashion, asked me to marry
him. To spend the rest of my life and the life after it with
him. Christ.

Footsteps approached from my right, crunching through the dirt and gravel, coming to a stop next to me. The polished Armani dress shoes were a dead giveaway.

"Hiya, Gabe."

The archangel sat next to me. "Good evening, Jordan."

He paused, watching me curiously. "You seem...well. Not quite what I expected."

I glanced at him, lifting an eyebrow in question. "What were you expecting?"

He shrugged one shoulder. "Nervousness. Fidgeting. Any of the normal human reactions when faced with an important decision."

"Well, I'm not completely human, after all."

He smiled wider. "You're human enough."

I rolled my eyes. "Is this you offering advice? Because you kind of suck at it."

Gabriel chuckled, leaning his arms over on his long legs. The evening air was cool so he was wearing a dark brown sweater and black slacks. I never could get him to stay in casual clothing. He had told me it just didn't feel right to him.

"What would you like to ask me?"

I brushed a lock of hair behind my ear, fixing my gaze on the ground. "Has any other angel ever entered the Marriage of the Souls?"

He took a deep breath and sighed. "Yes."

"Tell me."

He interlocked his fingers, his voice losing all the charm and humor it had once held. "Centuries ago, there was an angel who fell in love with a Seer. It was in the early ages of man, back when certain events of the Bible were still happening. At this time, there had only been young angels mating with humans and creating nephilim. There hadn't been any cases where angels fell in love with Seers as there were so few, but this particular angel did. He came before the Father and asked him if there was anything that could be done to allow them to be together. Father considered his proposal with great wisdom and consideration. The angels are God's servants. He knew that man would need woman to be his companion, but He never considered that we would ever require the same kind of nurturing. He realized that it would make things easier for those angels working on Earth to have someone to love, and so He granted the angel's wish."

Once more, Gabriel paused and I didn't know why. I frowned, looking at him.

"What happened after that?"

He licked his lips, seeming to choose his words. "The Seer that he fell in love with...betrayed him."

"What?"

"It turns out that she had actually been corrupted by the archdemon Belial. He instructed her to seduce an angel, so that he would have a sort of 'double agent' on the inside. He would be able to know of our plans before we deployed them, giving the demons an edge. However, the Seer didn't know that having her soul married to the angel would allow him to track her no matter where she was and one night he found her meeting with the demon in secret."

I shook my head. "I can't imagine how he must have felt."

"Me neither," Gabriel admitted.

"What did they do?"

"It was very complicated. You see, her soul had been promised to enter the gates of Heaven after her death, but her sin was one so great that it made her too impure to enter. In her state, if she died, she could not go to Hell because she shared a bond with an angel, but she could not enter Heaven because of her pact with the demon. They ended up having to banish her to Purgatory."

"What happened to the angel?"

"He played no part in her wrongdoing, but he was too heartbroken to continue his work on Earth among mankind. God granted him the responsibility of guiding souls from Earth to Heaven."

My jaw dropped. "You mean that angel was—"

"Uriel." Gabriel nodded. "Afterwards, God forbade the union of angels and Seers. He did not want any other angels to suffer the same fate as Uriel. He will never be whole because his beloved resides in Purgatory until Judgment Day."

He looked at me then. "Until now."

I ran my fingers through my hair, trying to grasp what he'd told me. "But why? What about me is so important that He would reinstate the Marriage of the Souls?"

"Jordan, you have to understand that there is a hierarchy among the angels. We are all equal in spirit, but the truth is that Michael is one of the most important archangels in existence. Like all of us, he is brave, diligent, and obedient, but he is also the most vulnerable of the angels because of the little time he spent on Earth. Michael needs love and guidance, more than what my brother and I or even our Father can supply. He needs someone like you to help him reach his potential."

I swallowed hard, feeling the weight of his words. "Well...if it's not too personal to ask...why haven't you or Raphael ever considered the Marriage of Souls?"

He paused, seeming as if he hadn't expected the question. "I suppose it's because of how he and I view humans. To me, you are more like children—not that you are immature or incapable, but I tend to feel more fatherly love than romantic love for mankind. Raphael sees you like brothers and sisters, and so he too does not love you in the romantic sense. I think that because Michael believed he was human for such a long amount of time that he was able to care for you as a lover. There are literally millions of angels serving alongside the human race, but none of them have his heart and, if you don't mind me saying so, none of them have ever met you."

He smiled a bit when I blushed. I cleared my throat, trying to dispel the sudden bout of shyness. "So…do you think I can handle this kind of responsibility?"

"That, I am afraid, I cannot answer. Only you can."

I took a deep, slow breath. After a moment, he reached over and held my hand, making me meet his kind eyes one more time.

"Jordan, I have known you for years. You are kind and strong and impressively resilient. You don't need to doubt yourself. Whatever you feel you should do in this situation, do it. No matter what happens, I have faith in you."

He leaned over and kissed me on the forehead, in the same spot as always, and squeezed my hand before standing and saying goodbye. I watched him go as the wind caressed my face, my hair, my shoulders, and I felt just a little bit taller.

I had been in the kitchen for around ten minutes, about to make myself a chicken salad sandwich in order to keep busy, when the doorbell finally rang. My stomach plummeted into my feet. I took a deep breath and set the food aside, walking over to the door. My heart drummed a frantic rhythm inside me as I went.

Michael stood on my welcome mat with his hands in his pockets. His hesitance bubbled around him as he cleared his throat. "May I come in?"

"Sure," I said, standing aside. He walked in and I shut the door, going back to the kitchen. He trailed behind me, a silent but tense presence. I couldn't imagine what sorts of things were going through his head right now.

"I…understand if you need more time to think about this," the archangel began, sounding regretful. It was so unlike him. "It isn't an easy decision."

I shook my head. "No, it's fine. I talked to Gabriel. He told me what happened to Uriel."

His green eyes went wide, but I couldn't tell if it was fear or surprise.

"Oh. Well, at least you're making an informed decision," Michael replied, a weak smile tugging at the edge of his lips.

I nodded. "I am."

He inhaled slowly. "And…what decision is that?"

This was it—the moment that decided everything. There were so many feelings flowing through my body all at once, nearly making me dizzy. Then, I took a deep breath and spoke from the heart.

"Michael…you're smug, self-righteous, overprotective, and hardheaded. You make me feel as if everything I've learned over the course of my life is fleeting. You snore. You drink out of the carton when you think I'm not looking. You're way too fond of those band groupies and you're constantly telling me what to do."

I took another slow breath and smiled at him. "And if that's all I can come up with for reasons not to be with you, then I think we'll be alright."

He went completely still. "Jordan, what are you saying?"

"What do you think I'm saying, idiot? I'm in love with you." I grabbed a handful of his shirt and jerked him down to my height, stealing a kiss that made warmth crawl down my spine and envelope my entire body. It wasn't his lust or mine—it was the culmination of our very spirits, our energy, his and mine, somehow separate, somehow together, somehow whole.

He wrapped those strong arms around my back and held me steady as the kiss deepened, until we were both breathless and shaking. I broke from his lips, opening my eyes to look up into that gorgeous face.

"That reminds me. Should you be kissing me before our souls get hitched?"

"Point taken. Well, there are two important things you should know about the marriage."

I arched an eyebrow. "And those are?"

"One, with your soul bound to mine, no demon will ever be able to touch your skin without being burned. It's a side effect of becoming part of me."

A flood of relief went through me. "And two?"

"Two," he said, dropping his voice to a sultry tone. "The marriage is only effective after we've...*consummated* it."

A great thrill traveled up my spine, but I hid it with a nonchalant shrug. "How ever will I survive?"

His smile was decidedly wicked. "That's a legitimate question."

Before I could say anything else, he scooped me up in his arms and carried me to the bedroom, kicking the door shut. Just after he laid me down on the mattress, I remembered something.

"Wait, I forgot to put the chicken salad away."

He leaned over me with a smirk that gave me heart palpitations.

"It'll be there next week."

Hours later, I awoke to fingers gliding over my bare shoulder: slow, lazy, much like how I felt at the moment. Michael's chest was a wall of solid heat behind me, melded against my back, a comforting weight. He leaned over and kissed the nape of my neck, his voice quiet.

"Oh, good. You're not dead."

I choked on a laugh, rolling my head backwards to look at him. "Well, that was a romantic thing to wake up to."

He chuckled. "Sorry. It's just that you were pretty out of it for a while there. I was starting to think I accidentally killed you."

"That would have been one hell of a way to go," I admitted, stretching my back. A few things popped in response, further relaxing me.

Michael nuzzled his nose against the right side of my neck, sighing. "I think I owe you and the entire human race an apology."

I glanced at him again. "For what?"

"Well…" he said slowly, his face solemn. "Having experienced love-making for the first time, I am amazed that you don't simply do it all the time, seven days a week, twenty-four hours a day."

I couldn't help it. I erupted into laughter, so hard that my entire upper body shook beneath the sheets. Michael had enough sense to look sheepish after his statement, waiting patiently for me to regain composure.

I wiped my eyes, kissing him on the nose. "Congratulations. You are officially a human being. A human male, I might add."

I watched with wonderment as his face turned a fantastic shade of pink, my grin stretching. "Are you blushing?"

He scowled, looking away. "No."

"You are too cute for words."

He groaned, burying his face in the pillow behind me. "Don't say that. I hate it."

I shook my head, lying down as well. "Sorry, but you really are sometimes."

The archangel grunted in annoyance before scooting a bit closer so that our bodies were aligned, his right hand stroking the line of my side from my ribcage to my hipbone. He seemed oddly fixated on that part of my body rather than the more salacious bits, but I didn't mind since it was soothing. We lay there in silence for a long while, enjoying the simple comfort of being able to touch one another, until eventually his fingertips wandered to my back and began tracing the scars.

"I could heal them, you know," Michael murmured, his thumb caressing one scar that peeked around the small of my back and spilled onto the side of my thigh.

"I know. Raphael offered the same thing, but I turned him down."

"Why?"

"They're reminders of my past, of things I can't forget. Things that made me the way I am. Making them disappear won't change anything. I'll carry them like I carry everything else."

Michael pushed up on one hand above me and kissed my lips once, softly. "May I never become something you have to carry."

I smiled, brushing the dark hair out of his eyes. "You won't."

EPILOGUE

> *"I made him just and right*
> *Sufficient to have stood, though free to fall.*
> *Such I created all th' Ethreal Powers*
> *And spirits, both them who stood and them who fail'd*
> *Freely they stood who stood, and fell who fell.*
> *Not free, what proof could they have given sincere*
> *Of true alliance, Faith or Love*
> *Where onely what they needs must do, appeard,*
> *Not what they would?"*

The pastor's voice rose and fell with a distinctive cadence, accenting John Milton's powerful words about mankind's free will. Funny. Often, his poetry inspired me and filled me with a sense of purpose, but now it only served to squeeze a few more hot tears from the corners of my eyes.

I stood behind the seats of Terrell's immediate family, not good enough for a chair in their eyes, but I didn't expect them to treat me any differently now that he was gone. His mother dabbed at her eyes with a handkerchief that probably cost more than my dress, and his father had one arm around her shoulders, rubbing her arm. They met no one's gaze, only staring forlornly at their son's coffin, which overflowed with white roses and lilies.

Michael stood to my left, holding my hand, his thumb tracing a slow, comforting pattern across the back of it. I had tried and failed to convince him not to come with me. He knew this would be hard for me and he also felt the need to pay his respects since he had delivered the final blow.

The sun had begun to set. Orange light spilled in from the trees surrounding the cemetery as the pastor closed out the reading. Each family member was given the chance to select a flower before they interred the coffin into the grave. He would be resting next to his father's parents, who had died a couple years ago. He loved them dearly and so it was only right he remained with them in death.

One by one, his immediate family plucked roses from the decorations. The pastor glanced towards me. It was common knowledge that I was the only long-term relationship Terrell had ever been in. It led some people to believe I was sort of family. I shook my head, not feeling worthy of such an honor, but Terrell's younger sister Grace nudged my arm to encourage me. Her mother opened her mouth to object. Grace sent her a glare that would melt a glacier and she pressed her lips together in silent consent.

I let go of Michael's hand and selected a lily, my fingertips brushing the polished surface of the coffin. No one was close enough to hear me whisper, "Thank you for everything."

I went back to my spot and the pastor finished the ceremony with a powerful prayer. Shortly afterward, the crowd dispersed to get ready for the reception, which I wouldn't be attending because I didn't feel very welcome. It had only been at Grace's urging that I was allowed to come at all.

I gave her a firm hug, holding her hands before I pulled away. "I'm so sorry, Gracie. I really am."

She shook her head, attempting to smile. "It's alright. I'm glad you came. He'd want things to be right between our families."

I returned the tentative smile. "Good luck with that."

She giggled, but the sound didn't drown out her mother's cold voice as she walked over, her frown lines deepening with anger.

"I can't believe you, Grace. Inviting that trollop here like she's one of us, and with a white man, no less. Huh. Probably wants to know if she got something in the will." The old woman sneered, glaring between Michael and me.

I didn't know what came over me at that moment. Maybe I felt vulnerable or maybe that sneer reminded me of my Aunt Carmen, but either way words spilled out of my lips before I could stop them.

"*Don't*," I snapped. "Don't you stand here on your son's grave and soil his memory with your selfishness. I don't care if you don't like me. I don't care if you think you're better than me. Terrell was a great man and I will not let you stand here and act like you don't have any home training. I am here to pay my respects and I have paid them so you don't have to worry about me darkening your doorstep again. All he ever wanted was for the people he loved to be happy and you will never honor his wishes as long as you keep stepping on the people you think are beneath you."

She said nothing, only glancing away with a mixture of shame and anger. I exhaled and turned back to Grace. "If you ever need anything, you've got my number. Take care of yourself, okay?"

She nodded. "You too."

With that, Michael and I started towards the car. He reached for my hand again and I took it, glad as his warm fingers wrapped around mine. His voice was quiet when he spoke.

"Are you going to be alright?"

I sighed. "Maybe. Someday I'll wake up and this won't hurt as much. But that day isn't today."

He opened the car door for me, meeting my eyes as I climbed in. "Until then, I'll be around to remind you that you have saved more lives than you have taken."

For the first time that day, a genuine smile touched my lips. "That's sweet of you."

Michael leaned down and kissed me, whispering, "It's also completely true. I have faith in that day as I have faith in you."

"I couldn't ask for anything else."

Then he shut the door and drove me home.

******

Terminat hora diem; terminal Author opus.
The hour ends the day; the author ends his work.

Acknowledgments

To my parents, who had the grace not to murder me when I told them I wanted to be a novelist instead of a veterinarian. Mom, you're the best editor, advisor for weird medical injury questions, and personal cheerleader on the planet. Dad, your constant badgering forced me to take my work seriously and grow up in one fell swoop. You both rock.

To Sharon: no one else has understood the stuff I smash onto the pages better than you. You've made me realize things about this novel that I never would have seen on my own. You deserve all the credit for helping edit this monstrosity and helping me make these characters better than they would have been without you.

To Bryan: you had the patience to brave the twisted labyrinth that is my work and for that I am eternally grateful.

To Andy Rattinger: you are the writing sensei I pray that every young writer can stumble across someday. Your advice is invaluable (literally, because I can't pay you yet). I have no idea how you put up with my incessant questions and lack of self-confidence, but you did and I will never forget it. (Nor will I forget all the nagging. Just wait until I get famous. I'm going to get you back, you son of a bitch.)

To my family: your support is worth more than all the diamonds in the world and ten times more precious. You could have smashed my dreams into pieces, but you stood by me through all my awkwardness and self-doubt and helped me become stronger. Thank you from the bottom of my heart.

To my nakama: I'd be nothing without your support. You are my bones. I'd have no legs to stand on without you. Thanks for hanging in there with my spastic ass.

To Jennifer Troemner: You have the eyes of a hawk. I could not have asked for a better editor. Thank you, madam.

To Gunjan Kumar: the cover of this novel is breathtaking, striking, and exhilarating. You brought everything to it that I could have ever hoped for. Thank you.

To my readers: you picked up this silly novel and read it and if it were possible, I'd shake your hand and buy you coffee and ask you about your life. I value you more than I could ever explain because you took a chance on some skinny, weird, self-deprecating, Chandler Bing-esque nerd with a story she thought no one could ever care about. I truly hope you enjoyed what you read and were able to take something away from it, no matter how small.

-Kyoko

Author's Note

The most common question circulating in the writing world is, 'Why do you write?'

The short answer is because I've always dreamt of having a career that involves lying pantsless in bed fooling around on my laptop all day. Also, sarcasm and pretty men.

The long answer is because I bleed words. I ooze them from every pore. I can't shut up, no matter what I try. Writing is like breathing. I do it constantly, without thought, without regard for who notices, without limitations or permission. I have done it since I was a kid, which my parents will attest to thanks to the mile-high piles of boxes stuffed with faded notebook paper currently rotting away in storage somewhere in Atlanta, Georgia. I was a weird kid. Most girls wanted to grow up to be ballerinas or doctors or lawyers.

I wanted to be Catwoman.

And in many ways, I still do. But since Anne Hathaway beat me to the punch, I'll just have to stick with being an author slash novelist slash aspiring amalgamation of Richard Castle, Chuck Wendig, and Liz Lemon. Which, come to think of it, ain't too bad.

Er, I had a point somewhere, hold on, let me go find it.

Ah, there we are. Writing is hard. And painful. Not like stubbing your toe kind of painful — like cut open your shirt and shove a red-hot katana through your spinal column hard. It's a daily grind. It's insanity bottled up inside your brain meats. There are so many better writers out there and it's terrifying to think you can ever compete with any of the greats, from novels to screenplays to television scripts to comic books — King, Koontz, Patterson, Cannell, Marlowe, O'Neill, Straczynski, Moore, Dini, Timm, McDuffie, Nolan, Butcher — but you still have to grit your teeth, strap on your creativity cap, and smash the keyboard until it cries for mercy. I admit it is far less painful if you have a support system of some sort. Blood-related or nakama, being a writer isn't a solo mission. You need back up. You need a crew to your Malcolm Reynolds-ing. Find it. Do it. Now. Get to the choppah!

Ahem, sorry, I'm done with the references, I swear. Point being, I write because real life is not enough to satisfy me. I write the things that keep me up at night — sex, murder, ghosts, the afterlife, faith, redemption, loneliness, hatred, and tears. I write the things I love and despise. The things I want and the things I need but don't get. And I think that's the way it should be. Some people paint. Some people dance. Some people glue together thousands of Popsicle sticks and make beautiful lamps like my grandfather used to.

Me? I write.

And I hope that's enough to keep me going.

…y'know, until Nathan Fillion meets me and realizes I am his soulmate.

Just kidding.

Mostly.

Thank you for reading. You are the stars in the night sky that I reach for every time I open a Word document, or jot down an idea on a sheet of paper, or scribble on cheap copy paper. Never forget the power of words. They can save you.

After all, they saved me.

Love always,

Kyoko

Read on for a special preview of

She Who Fights Monsters

Book Two of *The Black Parade* series
By Kyoko M, coming in 2014.

There was a stranger in my house.

I knew it wasn't Trent and Marie. They had taken a father-daughter trip to the beach. My duties as a kindergarten teacher didn't allow me the luxury of a three-day vacation, nor did the ridiculous cold I'd caught, and so I had stayed home by myself.

Normally, I would just shake it off as house-settling noise but there was one slat in the kitchen's hardwood floor near the stove that made an unmistakable creak if you stepped on it. No way in hell I could shake that off, not when I was home alone.

I slipped from beneath the comforter and knelt beside the bed, my fingers finding the cool metal of my trusty baseball bat. My daughter was only seven years old and I wouldn't let Trent bring a gun into my home so we agreed to this as our form of protection. Ears straining, I opened the bedroom door, praying the hinges remained silent, and tiptoed to the stairs. Silence. A normal person would go back to their room and sleep, but there was a cold feeling in my chest that whispered something was wrong.

The carpet was soft under my bare feet as I crept down the steps one by one. The staircase spilled into the foyer and the front door was still locked. No broken glass or muddy footprints. I turned to the left and peeked around the corner to see into the living room. Every shadow looked like an intruder. I knew it was just my paranoid brain going into overdrive so I ignored it and carefully maneuvered past the den to the dining room. Nothing here either. That left the kitchen.

I pressed my back against the wall, closing my eyes and saying a quick prayer that I was just a hyper vigilant crazy lady before darting around the corner.

The kitchen was empty.

I licked my dry lips and snuck over to the double doors that spilled out onto the patio and the backyard. I pushed the curtain aside. Darkness greeted me. Nothing more. False alarm. I was indeed a hyper vigilant crazy lady.

I started to lower the bat and turn around but then I felt something cold and wet on the bottom of my foot, between my bare toes. Confused, I knelt and touched it with my fingertips but as soon as I was close, the smell hit me even through my stuffy nose.

Gasoline.

Then the floorboard creaked again.

I whirled around. A man stood there swathed in shadows and black clothing, but that isn't what caught my attention.

He was holding a gigantic scythe.

I screamed as he swung it at me and threw myself into a front roll. The enormous blade crashed through the window in the back door, sending glittering shards all over the floor. I scrambled backwards on my hands and knees until my back hit the legs of the table and then got up, hefting the bat at the intruder.

"Who are you? What are you doing in my house?"

His voice was so soft I almost didn't hear it. "I am sorry, but your death is necessary for the safety of mankind. Please forgive me."

"I'll forgive you when you get the hell out of my house!" I yelled, swinging at his head. He blocked the blow with the staff—a smooth, effortless move—and I stumbled backwards, my eyes darting around to look for the closest route of escape. He had already knocked the back door partially open but he stood a few inches to the left of it, barring any chances of me reaching outside. I could make a break for the front door, but it would leave my back vulnerable. Shit!

I kept swinging, hoping to corral him away from the door, but he merely blocked the blows and stood his ground, never turning into the light so I could see his face. All I could see was a fedora, a black leather jacket, and gloves on his hands. Desperation began to set in and with it came the blind hope that I could talk him out of his homicidal intentions.

"Why do you want to kill me? What did I ever do to you?"

"Nothing," the man said, adjusting his hold on the weapon. "It is what you may do to the world someday. Human beings have such a poor perception of time and fate. Your death is for the greater good — to prevent the Apocalypse itself."

I shook my head, hating the hot tears pouring down my cheeks. "You're crazy."

"No. I am prepared."

"Get away from me!" I kicked the table over and shoved it towards him, making him jump back. I raced for the front door, my feet pounding against the hardwood floor as I ran, and grabbed the doorknob. I yanked on it as hard as I could, but it wouldn't budge. He had somehow jammed it from the other side, trapping me in like a mouse in a snake pit. No more options. I would have to face him and look my death straight in the eye.

Only he didn't give me the chance.

The blade tore through my spinal column as if it had been made of paper. The tip burst out of my rib cage. My world dissolved into pain for a few seconds, but then a blessed numb cascaded over me. My brain faintly realized the shock blocked out what should have been an excruciating death.

He stepped backward and I slid off his blade, collapsing on my back. Blood bubbled out of me in crimson rivulets, tainting my husband's t-shirt. How unfair. He'd have to see my corpse wearing it when he came home.

The stranger reached into his pocket and withdrew a lighter, flicking his thumb to awaken a single orange flame. I watched him light the gasoline that had been poured at the base of every wall in my beautiful home, watched the paintings and furniture become engulfed in fire, watched the fire slowly creep closer to my dying body. The stranger pressed one cold, gloved finger to my forehead and made a cross, his voice constantly murmuring the same words over and over again. The cadence of his voice made the chanting stay with me until the last spark of life snuffed out and everything dissolved into darkness.

Marlowe, Christopher. *Doctor Faustus*. 1604.

Milton, John. *Paradise Lost*. 1667.

Shakespeare, William. *Hamlet. The Life and Death of King Richard III*. 1591. 1600-02.

Sophocles. *Antigone. Oedipus Rex*. 429 BCE. 441 BC.

Yeats, W.B. "A Cradle Song". 1899.

Made in the USA
Lexington, KY
27 December 2017